MW00415022

THE FIRST FACE OF JANUS

Also by Phil Valentine

THE GOD PLAYERS

For your reading enjoyment, we have included a pronunciation guide in the back of this book.

THE FIRST FACE OF JANUS

a novel by

Phil Valentine

Oxley Durchville Publishing

This book is a work of fiction. Any references to historical events, real people, or real places are used fictitiously. Other names, characters, places, and events are products of the author's imagination, and any resemblance to actual events or places or persons, living or dead, is entirely coincidental.

Book Cover and Interior Design by Red Raven Book Design

Oxley Durchville Publishing
118 16th Avenue South
Suite 4-387
Nashville, TN 37203

OxleyDurchville.com

For information about special discounts for bulk purchases, please contact Oxley Durchville Special Sales at business@oxleydurchville.com.

For foreign and subsidiary rights, contact rights@oxleydurchville.com.

The Library of Congress Cataloging-in-Publication Data is available upon request.

Library of Congress Control Number: 2017909524
ISBN 978-0-9968752-3-3 (hardcover)
ISBN 978-0-9968752-2-6 (ebook)

Printed in the United States of America
10 9 8 7 6 5 4 3 2

Indeed, the hereditary gift of prophecy
will go to the grave with me.
~ Nostradamus

Prologue

July 1, 1566

Salon-de-Provence, France

Death approached the two-story row house in the center of town like the distant clapping of hooves on the cobblestones. The courier passed through the north gate not yet grasping that this would be the most important night of his young life. The scents of the village hit his nostrils, the sweet smell of baked bread being prepared for morning market mixed with the hay and manure of a nearby stable. Light glistened from the moonlit rain puddles on the dark street. He came as quickly as was humanly possible after receiving the urgent cryptic message. His horse was prompted up the slight incline and guided left down the narrow side street. He dismounted and secured the leather reins to the wooden post, hoping beyond hope that he was not too late. With an empty saddle bag draped over his shoulder, he shifted from one foot to the other. He waited for an answer at the door and glanced up at the dim light that shone weakly from a second story window. It burned like the dying embers of a once-blazing fire whose gray ashes were the sole reminder of its former glory. A shadowy figure appeared in the doorway and scanned either direction up and down the street. The courier disappeared inside.

The two men scaled the well-worn spiral stone staircase without a word passing between them. Jean de Chavigny, the bedridden man's loyal secretary, opened the door to the room with the reverence of a temple guard. He took the saddle bag and showed the young man in then closed the door behind him. A single candle on the table cast a yellowish hue across the face of a bedridden old man. It brought to life the vibrant colors of his blanket that danced in the light oblivious to the dire condition of the man they covered. The sweet scent of colchicine used to treat his gout hung in the air. He struggled to remain lucid enough to convey his instructions to the courier who had been summoned to his bedside.

The younger man approached the bed like one would an open coffin. The candlelight illuminated the rugged lines of the wise old face that clung to life among the linens. The wide-planked wooden floor creaked beneath the student's feet. The slits of his master's eyes glistened like two hot coals in a snow bank. His lips hid among the whiskers of his silvery beard dry and cracked with age.

"Devin," the apprentice almost whispered. The title was respectfully reserved for only the most renown soothsayer. "You asked to see me?"

The elderly gentleman tilted his head toward the sound of the voice and motioned with one decrepit finger with what appeared to be his last ounce of energy, pointing for the young man to take a seat at his bedside. The apprentice did as he was commanded and drew his ear close to the dying man's mouth.

"You have been tasked with a monumentally important assignment," the old man began. "Although we have tried nobly to veil the nature of your journey, there are already sinister forces that are mounting against you."

"I am not afraid," the young man assured him.

The old man managed a slight smile. "I know you are brave, my son." He coughed and his face once again assumed the seriousness of the message. "Monsieur de Chavigny has a special parcel for you. Place it in your satchel and ride until you reach the destination which I divulged to you on your last visit. Ensure that you are not followed. Be ever mindful of your surroundings. There are those who wish as much for your failure as I do for your success."

"I understand."

"These forces cannot allow you to reach your destination, but listen to me carefully. You must complete your journey. Do you understand? The very future of humanity itself depends upon your success."

The young man's jaw tightened. His nostrils flared with resolve. He righted himself in his seat. "I will not fail you."

The old man reached for his hand and squeezed it for a brief moment then eased his grip.

"Go now, and may God's providence protect you."

The young man rose and headed out the door. On the other side, Jean de Chavigny fretted, "You are sure of your destination?" He handed him back his saddle bag and wiped the edges of his beard with a trembling hand.

"I am," the young man answered confidently.

Chavigny held the boy's eyes in his. "He has told me I will not find him alive at sunrise."

The young man turned his head slightly, absorbing the pain. "He has lived a long and fruitful life." He looked back up at Chavigny. "His great wisdom will not die tonight. I understand my role in preserving his legacy, and I am honored to grant him this last request."

Chavigny smiled through his tears then turned to walk down a hallway. The young man followed. Chavigny pushed a panel on the wall and it opened to reveal a hiding place. He reached inside and produced a thick leather-bound book secured by a wide leather strap. He handed the book to the young courier. The man stuffed it into his bag and slung the bag over his shoulder.

Chavigny smiled and clasped the man's hand in his. "Godspeed."

The courier looked with caution at his surroundings then secured the saddlebag to his saddle. He paused to look once more up and down the empty street before mounting his horse. The hooves clicked off the sides of the buildings. He stopped for a second to get his bearings. That's when he heard a different set of hooves on the cobblestones some ways behind him. They came to a stop a few beats after his own. He paused for a moment, frozen in fear. He steeled his resolve and dug his boots into the sides of his steed. His horse whinnied and bolted forward. The other horses were in pursuit. Within seconds he exited the gates of the city and directed his horse out onto the moist dirt of the countryside road. He swallowed hard to keep his heart from his throat.

The sound of hooves grew louder. The two horsemen were closing fast. The courier peeked over his shoulder. Sweat dripped from his forehead. He popped the reins on his mount to draw more speed from him. He knew it was only a matter of time before they overtook him. What to do with his parcel? He could not let it fall into the hands of these marauders. He had made a solemn promise. The words echoed in his head, *The very future of humanity itself depends on your success.*

The two men galloped ever closer. The young courier was too terrified to look back. He squeezed every extra inch of speed he could from his horse. His whip flailed the poor creature on one shoulder then the other. His boots dug into its sides. He didn't have to turn around. The thundering hooves were in his ears.

He rounded a bend as quickly as he dared. Two men on horseback positioned on either side of the road startled him so much that he instinctively pulled the reins back hard. He thought he caught a glimpse of one of their faces in the momentary flash from their wheel locks. Burning gunpowder from both guns simultaneously lit the night sky. Lead balls flew from each barrel. His horse reared up and spilled him onto the hard dirt of the well-traveled road. In that moment, he was sure he had met death. Suspended in time, he made his peace with it, but his heart grieved over the failure of his mission. And so soon after it had begun. *The very future of humanity itself depends on your success.* He feared failure worse than death itself.

The two balls ripped through the heavy night air above his head and exploded in the chests of their targets. The courier whipped his head around in time to see his pursuers torn from their saddles. They lay instantly dead in contorted heaps beneath the full moon. The assailants, cloaked in partial darkness and black capes, remained only long enough to be certain their task had been completed. Without a word, they galloped off in opposite directions one from the other.

The young courier gathered his wits about him. He calmed his horse, checked to make sure the contents of his saddlebag were still intact, then remounted. In a fleeting moment, he considered checking on the two men who had so feverishly chased him but thought better of it. He whipped the reins around. His horse pranced in the moonlight. He looked once more over his shoulder at the still remains on the ground then dashed off into the night to make his pre-appointed rendezvous with history.

Chapter One

Present Day

New York City

The crosswalk light turned from red to white and the mass of humanity moved in unison like cattle to slaughter. Listless eyes focused on the space in front of them never meeting the faces of any of the oncoming sweaty horde. A wild-eyed man with matted hair, tattered jeans, and soiled t-shirt talked full voice to himself and inexplicably sniffed the seats of parked bicycles. Bellicose taxi drivers rested their palms on their horns like gunslingers with itchy trigger fingers unable to resist the temptation to draw for more than a few seconds at a time. Hucksters with counterfeit watches twist-tied to sheets of stiff cardboard hawked their wares to naive tourists. A police siren a few blocks away segued into the squeaky brakes of a city bus which, in turn, gave way to the obnoxious whine of a motorcycle weaving its way through traffic. The smell of burnt pretzels from the street vendors blended with hot trash, sulfur-laden steam from a manhole, and day-old urine to give New York City its own unique odor. Hundreds of thousands of ravenous workers at a time poured from its skyscrapers onto the streets during lunch hour like pulling the drain plug from an ice chest on this hot July day.

Publishing snobs, the kinds who lived on the Upper East Side and vacationed at Nantucket or 'The Vineyard,' truly believed the twenty-five blocks between Central Park and 34th Street were the center of the universe. At least of the cultured and civilized world. Benson Crow thought otherwise. He'd rather be flogged than visit this godforsaken town. He walked like a man in search of an exit through the maze of cubicles at Dolos Publishing Company, one of twelve imprints in the Worldwide Press stable that called this corner of New York City home. Crow loathed the very thought of having to fight the teeming throng to make the planning meetings. He suffered the pretentious prigs of publishing about as well as he endured the block-long cab line on a frigid, sleet-soaked day in front of Madison Square Garden. He couldn't imagine living in this manmade hell hole. He only came because he was contractually bound to do so. As soon as the meeting was over, he was making his way out as quickly as he came in. Thomas Browning, a man elevated to a position beyond what Benson Crow deemed appropriate, followed on his heels pleading his case.

"It's a big convention, Benson. It's great exposure."

Crow kept walking. "Read the contract, Tom. I'm obligated to a *reasonable* promotional tour. I don't think a weekend in Montreal is reasonable. Did you know they actually charge you to *leave* Canada? You can't go home until you pay their ransom. It's ridiculous."

"That's where the North American Futurists Convention is being held this year. I didn't pick the location. You're already on the schedule. They're expecting you. You're a futurist. You need to be there."

"Futurologist," he corrected, "and I know the types that are going to line up for the signed books. Conspiracy kooks, alien abductees, Bigfoot sighters."

"Benson, that's your audience."

Crow stopped abruptly and turned to face him. "I don't want that audience, Tom. They're nuts. I'm not. I'm a serious writer. These are the same folks who just got off the bus from the Star Trek convention. I want to talk about subjects that matter. I want to *write* about subjects that matter, but all this company wants is cyberpunk and space goth."

"That's what sells." Tom noticed several employees listening too closely. He stepped past Benson and held open the door to an empty conference room. "Let's take this conversation private."

"Look, I have a train to catch," Crow said.

"This'll only take a minute."

Benson walked past him through the doorway and Tom followed closing the door behind them.

"I didn't want to say this in front of the staff in the meeting, so let me get straight to the point," Tom said. "You've read your royalty statement. Your sales are lagging. You barely covered the advance on your last book. As your publisher, I'm wide open to any subject within the futuristic genre. That's what we do at Dolos, but this next book has to deliver or..."

Crow tried to pull Tom's downcast eyes up to meet his own. "Or what?"

Browning hesitated for a moment. "Or we won't be renewing your contract."

"Aw, come on, Tom. Are you serious? You're gonna drop me? Just like that? After six books? All of them bestsellers, I might add."

"Bestsellers, yeah, but your advance is so large we hardly cover the nut. We can't operate on those margins."

Crow cast a disgusted look toward the floor.

"You're a fine writer, Benson, but this is a business. I know you enjoy a lavish lifestyle. I get that, but we can't keep paying these massive advances without results. You're running on fumes, my man. You have to deliver this time."

“The last book was your idea,” Crow snapped.

“Yeah, because we were up against deadline and you didn’t have any ideas of your own. We need something compelling. Something that’ll sell books. This industry is struggling. You know that.”

“And Montreal is supposed to help?”

“These conventions move inventory, Benson. They’re gold for your type of writing. Listen, I know how you hate this city. It’s a rat race. Get out of the country. Relax. Enjoy yourself. Clear your head. Maybe it’ll spark an idea. They speak French up there. Maybe a little French-speaking groupie?” He smiled a conciliatory smile. “Come on, what do you say?”

“Montreal,” Crow said it with a little less disdain in his voice as if he were trying on a new suit coat.

“Yes, Montreal,” Tom said. “We’ve got you a suite at the Hotel Le St-James in Old Montreal, right around the corner from the convention. A relaxing weekend. You’ll love it. One signing in the afternoon. That’s it.”

“Just one?”

“Just one. I promise. You’re in, you’re out. Limo, staff handling your every need. You sell a ton of books. You recharge your batteries, and you’re ready to start writing that next big novel.”

“One signing.”

“You have my word.”

UNLESS ONE HAS known the joy of free-flowing ideas, it’s hard to imagine the frustration when creative thoughts simply stop coming. It’s like a river of imagination being dammed up. When the creative process is at its zenith, lucid inspiration falls in sheets from the sky. Clever lines puddle on the roadway of one's mind leading the writer to believe the fresh flood of ideas will never end. Then the clouds burn away, and the scorching sun of dullness and vapidity sets in for a long drought. Such periods last for days, sometimes weeks, even months. When months turn into years, confidence is sapped, oftentimes to the point of no return. Brilliant writers are no longer regarded as such and are unceremoniously cast aside, their usefulness drained by publishing houses like wringing water from a wet washcloth. Benson Crow was living on borrowed time and that reality served to quash any inventiveness he might have left. He had strong doubts that Montreal was going to change his condition.

"Seat backs in their upright position, please," the flight attendant instructed.

Crow adjusted his seat and pulled up the shade in the first class cabin in time to catch the jet's final approach to Montréal–Trudeau International. The city was an enchanting balance of old and new. The skyscrapers respectfully sprouted among the historic sites, unlike New York where builders competed to see who could shoe-horn the tallest building into the smallest space. The St. Lawrence River lazily snaked through the city allowing wide expanses of waterfront green space as if to say no one was in a hurry.

From his comfortable seat, Crow noticed that the city was actually an island in the middle of the St. Lawrence. A factoid in the airline magazine in his seat back told him Montreal was named after the triple-peaked hill at its center, Mt. Royal. After initially feeling indifferent, perhaps even resentful, Crow found himself excited to explore this new gem he had discovered.

He emerged on the other side of customs a tad earlier than anticipated and waited for his limousine at the curb just outside baggage claim. He had but one carry-on bag slung over his shoulder.

He stood beneath a curved canopy of metal and glass that kept departing guests from the elements. Out of habit, he checked his e-mail on his phone.

He was lost inside a message when he got the uncomfortable feeling he was being watched. He looked up to see a disheveled man with a white beard and long white hair pulled back in a ponytail staring at him across the several lanes of taxi and civilian traffic. From the look of his clothing, Crow figured him to be homeless. Being stared at was nothing unusual—Crow was a fairly well-known author—but this guy, for some reason, gave him goosebumps. The man was the type who didn't divert his eyes even after he'd been caught staring. His stare was the kind of uncomfortable gaze that made one shift one's stance and look the other way, but Crow couldn't. It was an entrancing fixation that Crow only imagined the Manson Family had experienced once upon a time. Just as he was getting a good look at the guy, his limo arrived.

Once the solid door of the car slammed shut, Crow was alone in the muffled luxury of the limousine. Cool air hissed from the chrome vents. Limos were standard fare for him, but somehow the homeless man made him embarrassingly mindful of its opulence. It was so unlike Crow to give a damn, and he cursed himself for it. He conjured up a defiant glare even though the old guy would never see him through the smoked glass, but when he looked back to the place where the tousled soul had stood, he had vanished.

Chapter Two

The limousine pulled away from the curb at the airport and Crow simmered in his unaccustomed feeling of guilt. He knew that a man's circumstances were not happenstance. Where we find ourselves at any particular juncture in life is due to a sequence of choices. Sure, some are born into an advantage of wealth, but being born so does not guarantee success nor does *not* being born so guarantee failure. Crow took pride in knowing that he was born to no advantage whatsoever. Fate could have put him in place of the man back at the airport had he not decided he wanted something better for his life. If wealth was about making smart choices, then poverty was about making poor ones. It was that simple.

He remembered specific crossroads in his life when he had to make those choices. He chose to find a quiet place to write, while many of his friends opted to find alcohol and drink until they couldn't see straight. Both were ways of coping with the hopeless surroundings of their drab little town. Crow's fantasies took him far away from his tortured home life to any place his mind could imagine. It was a defense mechanism. Anywhere was better than where he was. The future and even a fabricated past were always more pleasant than the present. His stories helped him bind up the wounds of neglect and abuse. The little attention he got at home was filled with booze-induced rage from his father on the rare occasions he was even around. His mother's downfall was that she was wholly unsuited for motherhood. She hadn't a nurturing bone in her body. She was merely holding on to life, trying not to get bucked off.

If anyone had an excuse for failure, it was Benson Crow, but he refused to succumb to it. He had been told more than once that he could never rise above his circumstances. Over time, it was the negativity—even the doubt—that made him dig in. He had a vivid imagination that could see a better life, and he kept plodding toward it, never looking back until he was far, far away from the agony that, ironically, would be the fuel for the rocket ship that launched his meteoric career.

Crow gazed out the window at the river that seemed to race the highway into the city. It flowed into a swift current of memories that melded into the chilly waters that ran through the mill town of his youth.

"Make sure you come straight home from school," the woman at the red-topped Formica kitchen table said, taking a puff from her cigarette.

"Mom, I've been sixteen for six months. I need a car. It's humiliating showing up at high school on a bike."

Her eyes turned angry. "Where do you think we're going to get the money for a car? We can hardly afford the one I have, and your dad's truck has over 300,000 miles on it."

"Where is he anyway?"

"At a new construction project in Lewisburg. Should take about six months."

"Lewisburg? That's two hours away."

"Gotta go where the work is, Benson. It ain't gonna come to you."

Benson flung his backpack over his shoulder and heard the screen door slam behind him. His sneakers hit the gravel and he pulled the handlebars from the dirt, mounting the bike in mid-stride. The pedaling became easier once his tires reached the asphalt. The day was gorgeous. Too gorgeous to be cooped up in some dreary classroom listening to the teacher drone on about nothing. The ticking of the ten-speed's spokes slowed. He balanced on one side of the bike until he could disembark. He let the bicycle fall then slid down a slight embankment where he could hear the rushing water. He used a large rock as a back rest and pulled a notepad from his backpack. He fished down toward the bottom for a pen then flipped the pages to where he'd left off. The pad rested on his knees and his pen tapped against his teeth as he thought. An idea swirled around in his head like the churning currents of the river and he grabbed it, massaged it, and shaped it just so, then wrote it down on his pad.

The door opened and shattered his thoughts. "Your hotel, sir," the driver said.

Crow emerged from the automobile. He reached inside the breast pocket of his jacket, pulled out a couple of large bills from his wallet, and placed them in the driver's palm. Montreal felt a world away from New York City. The air was a bit cleaner, the atmosphere markedly cheerier. It possessed the bustle without the hostility. The Quebec sovereignty movement was very much alive. All the signage was in French. The shop clerks spoke French, and English only if they had to. Had he been blindfolded, he would have no trouble at all believing the Eiffel Tower was just a cab ride away.

Crow stood on the sidewalk on Rue Saint-Jacques and a doorman opened up a luxurious world in front of him. Walking past the ivy walls through the front door into the small but elegant lobby of Hotel Le St-James one got the feeling that money was no object. He walked beneath an arched canopy ceiling reminiscent of a cathedral, but in miniature, across the inlaid marble floor up to the front desk. The building was originally a merchant bank established in 1844 that was transformed into one of Canada's most elegant hotels.

A smiling clerk greeted him, ready to check him into his suite. He took the moment while she checked his reservation to drink in his surroundings. The wood-paneled walls and the elegant dining room with its grand staircase leading up to a cozy sitting room exuded grace and refinement. The clerk gave him his room key and a quick synopsis of the hotel's amenities. He located the elevator, the doors of which were handpicked from five different continents, and showed himself to his accommodations. The Heritage was a sizable one-bedroom suite with 1,000 square feet of living space. It featured a separate living room, exquisite nineteenth-century oak wood flooring, and mahogany wood paneling. The centerpiece of the bedroom was a king-sized four-poster bed with Bruno Richard linens. *Thomas Browning might not be much of a publisher, Crow thought, but he sure knows how to book a hotel.*

A walking tour of Old Montreal was recommended by a studious-looking lady sitting next to him in first class on the plane. She was the type of woman who watched public television and read the arts section of the paper before the front page, if she read any other section at all. She looked at him over the white-framed reading glasses she used to work the crossword puzzle. He allowed as to how he was staying at the Hotel Le St-James and she noted with glee that he was already staying in Old Montreal. She gave him a list of 'you simply musts' that Crow jotted down in the notebook he kept handy for random ideas.

At the top of her list was Notre-Dame Basilica, a church in Old Montreal dating back to 1642. The church was only a three-block stroll from his hotel. He was just before entering the church when he happened to notice something across the street on a pedestrian walkway. There, by a bench under a tree that grew out of a metal grate among the street pavers, stood the unkempt man from the airport staring at him. At least he thought it was him. A delivery truck passed between them for a brief moment. When it was gone, so was he.

New York architect James O'Donnell designed the basilica. Crow learned he was born a Protestant but converted to Catholicism just before his death in 1830. Some say he was inspired to do so by his own design. It intrigued Crow that a man's own creation could bring him closer to God. The painted wood of the sanctuary struck Crow as something you were more likely to see at Disney World rather than a church. The rich hues of blue were accented by lights which created a sky effect above an altar that bore a striking resemblance to Cinderella Castle.

Crow soaked in the history, eavesdropping on a tour group from the United Kingdom. When the tour group was on the move, Crow ducked out a side door which spilled onto a narrow street to the left side of the front entrance. He descended the wrought iron staircase and turned left back toward the front of the church. He spotted the old man once again across the street on the pedestrian walkway near the bench where he'd been before. He stared intently at the entrance of the church as if he were expecting someone to emerge.

Crow waited for cars to pass then headed across the street. The man noticed him with a start and turned to head down the cobblestones of Place d'Armes. Crow didn't want to look like he was chasing the man in broad daylight, but he didn't want to lose him either. Why was this odd man following him? What the hell did he want? Crow picked up his pace to a faster clip to keep up with him.

The stranger crossed Rue Saint-Jacques without looking. A car skidded to a stop just inches from crushing his legs. The smell of burnt rubber hung in the air. The old man scampered up the steps of the old Bank of Montreal building. He disappeared through one of two heavy, ornate wooden front doors. Crow looked both ways before sprinting across the street. He scaled the steps of the historic bank building two at a time. He grabbed the knob and pushed the door on the move, fully expecting it to open. It didn't. His left shoulder acted as a shock absorber. He rattled the doors for a moment then backed up looking to see if he was mistaken about where the old man went in. He wasn't. It was the only entrance.

"They are closed," a courteous lady with a French accent passing to his right offered.

Crow looked up. "Did you see a man just go inside?"

She laughed slightly. "Non. It is closed."

"On the weekends?"

"Non, monsieur. Permanently."

Chapter Three

Crow soaked in the tub sipping Hors d'Âge cognac and thinking about the old man. He was obviously being stalked. But why? A deranged fan? The most disturbing part was he seemed to know where Crow would be even before he did. He was sure he saw the stranger enter the bank building in Old Montreal, yet the door was locked.

He lay awake in the four-poster bed until his thoughts turned from the old man to his own destiny and where he might be when he reached the same age. For so long—too long—he had been in control of his future. Complacency crept into his camp like the enemy. Time was its sword. It gashed his genius until its creative juices drained onto the floor. He forced himself to sleep, less out of a need to rest his body than a yearning to escape the notion that all he knew, all he enjoyed in life, might well be coming to an untimely end.

The luxuriousness of the night's sleep helped soften the blow of his reality and Benson Crow awakened surprisingly refreshed. His brain had all but erased the odd encounters with the old man. He pulled out his computer tablet and stared at a blank screen for an interminable time. The ache returned. He powered down and flipped through a magazine. Bored, he ventured out of his room and down to the elegant dining room with its gorgeous chandeliers casting shards of light upon fine works of art on its walls. He enjoyed a light lunch of fruit, yogurt, and crêpes.

After a lazy nap on the sofa in the living room, he dressed himself for the event. A two-button dark green and navy windowpane-checked sport coat from Sartorio of wool, silk, and linen hung from his broad shoulders atop an all-cotton band-collar shirt in white dressed down by an old pair of jeans—no belt—and sockless blue boat shoes. The doorman anticipated his exit from outside and pressed a button to open the heavy glass doors of the Hotel Le St-James. Crow all but ignored him and descended the steps onto the sidewalk and into the warm summer afternoon. A slight breeze blew through the ivy on the facade of the building. Crow turned left at the corner and down the street for the one-block walk to the Palais des Congrès—Congress Palace—a rather odd-looking convention center with windows each of a different color of red, yellow, orange, green, blue, and purple. It looked like a faddish relic of the '60s, one that had gone out of style with white belts and Nehru jackets. Crow wondered if the designer had been dropping acid all the way to its inauguration in 1983 only to learn that the psychedelic facade was added much later, which he found inexcusable in a town with as much style as Montreal.

A rep from Congress Palace waited at the front door to escort him. Jennifer or Jessica or something like that. She bubbled as she pointed out Lipstick Forest, a collection of 52 pink concrete tree trunks, which was the focal point of the main floor. Crow couldn't fathom how it and the elegant architecture of the Hotel Le St-James could co-exist on the same planet, much less a city block from one another, but he held his tongue.

They took the escalator and arrived just outside a large conference room. Crow was delighted by the size of the crowd. A new futuristic film had just screened inside to a packed audience. He wasn't sure if the movie crowd was sticking around to see him or if his fans decided to take in the movie, and he didn't much care which. They were lined up down the hallway to buy his book, so it meant a trip well worth making.

Two organizers from the convention greeted him with wide smiles and walked him over to a long table with a white tablecloth set up in the large hallway in front of the conference room. His books were stacked as if on display in a bookstore, and he sat down to the enthusiastic applause of his fans. A huge backdrop banner featuring his almost-smiling face and the cover of his latest book stretched the length of the table behind him. His "people" handled the coordination of sales and made sure the line was orderly. A couple of stern-faced security guards in dark suits with corkscrew wires leading to their ears stood as sentinels at either side of the table, a touch insisted upon by Thomas Browning. Although they'd never discussed it, Crow assumed his publisher arranged it more to evoke an air of importance rather than any real threat, perceived or otherwise.

Crow often pondered the paradoxical relationship he had with his readers. He stopped just short of loathing them, but he wanted as little to do with them as possible. Yet they were the very reason for his existence. One astute old mentor once counseled him, *Don't feed the fans.* What he meant was don't get involved with people who hold you in such unrealistic regard that getting to know you can only lead to bitter disappointment. Much like his books, Benson Crow, the man, was a mere fantasy.

Crow signed books and posed for selfies for the better part of two hours. He was signing one of the last books when he happened to look up and see him, just off to the side, away from the crowd, observing. The old man from the airport. Crow had completely dismissed all thoughts of the man from his mind. This time he was closer, and Crow could make out the piercing blue eyes that seemed to betray a man younger than his haggard look suggested. Crow broke out in a cold sweat. Another fan asked to pose for a picture. Crow smiled for the camera. When the blinding flash subsided, he looked back at the old man. He was gone. His uneasiness grew. His sentinels stood unaffected, either not concerned about the old man or never seeing him at all.

He finished signing the books and thanked the staff who had helped him, posing for a picture with the convention director and the several people who worked the event. His security team asked if he needed an escort back to his hotel and he declined the offer. The afternoon was late and he was trying to decide what to do with himself for the rest of the day. He stopped by the men's room before heading back to his hotel and sat in a bathroom stall exploring his options. Too late to do any more sightseeing. He thought about an early dinner at Bouillon Bilk. He heard the foie gras served with bananas, smoked apples, and sour cream was delicious. Perhaps Casino de Montreal for a little gambling afterward. A relaxing hour or two at the blackjack table might do him good. The idea sounded more appealing the more he thought about it. He exited the stall and washed his hands, thinking through the sequence of events. He wrung the water from his hands, reached for a paper towel, and looked in the mirror. That's when he saw him. His heart raced. There, in the shadows of the restroom behind him, stood the old man with the blue eyes. Crow whipped around.

"Who the hell are you? What do you want?"

"Excusez-moi, monsieur," the man pleaded. "I mean you no harm. I have something for you," his words dipped in French.

Crow took a step back.

"I know how you love books, monsieur," the man continued. "I have a very special one for you." He started to reach inside his dusty old coat.

"Easy," Crow warned.

The old man slowed his reach and, with a gentle tug of his forefinger and thumb, produced a red velvet sleeve. "It is a very special book. Do not look at it here. You can examine it later."

Crow just stared at the old man.

"Take it," he said. It was less a command than an invitation.

Crow tossed the towel in the trash and cautiously took the book by his own forefinger and thumb, only because he didn't want to get any residual water from his hands on it. He slipped the velvet sleeve into the inside pocket of his sport coat.

"Go now," the man said. "You do not have much time. Before the sun rises on Sunday it will be done."

"*What* will be done?"

"There is precious little time. You must hurry."

"What the hell are you talkin'—"

"Shhh," the old man scolded.

The restroom door opened. The old man moved quickly in front of a urinal and unzipped his pants. The leather soles of the entering footsteps echoed off the tile. Crow reached for another paper towel and finished drying his hands. A blonde-headed man in a dark blue suit stood before the mirror beside Crow and combed his hair. After a short moment, the old man zipped his pants and headed out the door. The suited man stopped his preening and made for the door behind him. Crow threw the paper towel in the trash and strode to the door. Looking out, he saw the suited man trotting up beside the drifter. Another man in a dark suit quickened his pace to join them. They escorted the old man out a bank of glass doors onto Rue Saint-Antoine. Crow ran across the convention center hallway to the same side door, reaching it just in time to see. The old man waved his arms wildly arguing with the two men before being shoved violently into the back seat of a black SUV and driven away.

Chapter Four

"I don't bloody care how much it costs," the woman in the smart business suit snapped at the telephone in her refined British accent. Her auburn hair was neatly tucked away on the back of her head. "I simply need to know we can get it through customs." Her furrowed brow eased. The corners of her mouth relaxed and even seemed to resemble the early stages of a smile. "Splendid." Then her face went serious again. "Not a word of this. Do you understand?"

"Señorita," the man with the gold tooth on the other end of the line assured her, "discretion is our specialty."

"See that it is," she said. "You'll be paid properly when the package is delivered. Are we clear?"

"Sí, señorita." He sucked his teeth. "Very clear."

"If my employer is exposed in the papers, we'll know exactly where the leak came from and the consequences will be swift and severe."

"There will be no leaks, this I can assure you."

"Very well. We will rendezvous on Thursday."

"It will be my pleasure, señorita."

CROW STOOD IN stunned silence. The SUV with the odd stranger inside melted into the afternoon traffic and out of sight. He gave a brief thought to alerting someone about what he'd just witnessed, but what would he tell them? He didn't know the man nor did he know the men who took him away. Perhaps they were from the local mental institution. Maybe they were the police. Whatever trouble the man was in was not his concern.

He exited through the same door they had escorted the stranger and turned right up Rue Saint-Antoine. On the short walk back to his hotel he started to pull the red velvet sleeve from his coat but decided to keep it safe within his breast pocket.

He took the elevator to his room and made sure the door was double-locked. He didn't give a second thought to his inexplicable desire for security. It seemed to be the natural course of action. The book burned in his pocket like a secret waiting to be whispered. He sat at the table in the living area of his suite and produced the red velvet sleeve from his jacket. With great care he pulled the small old book from its resting place inside the sleeve. He examined the cover. It was French. Not unusual, since he was in French-speaking Montreal. Crow didn't speak French, but he didn't have to in order to understand what he held in his hand. *Les Propheties*, the cover read, *de M. Michel Nostradamus*. The Prophecies of Michel Nostradamus, the famous sixteenth-century prophet. He wasn't able to translate the Roman numerals MDCXXXIV by sight. He pulled out his computer tablet and searched the Internet for an online converter. 1634. This particular edition was printed about 70 years after Nostradamus' death.

He turned the pages with care until he came upon a folded sheet of paper that was not of the same age as the book. It was the size of a page of stationery, the kind used to write a short correspondence. In blue ink was written what appeared to be a poem.

Dans le siècle de quatre

Son âge est de soixante et onze

Sa première face voit

Quand l'horloge sonne douze

Ajouter la note de C deux fois

Et enlever le score

Compter sur de bonnes actions

Riche en grâce

He called up a language translator on his tablet and typed in the words. He got his answer and wrote it down in his notation pad.

In the century of four

His age is seventy-one

His first face sees

When the clock strikes twelve

What could it mean? It seemed to point to someone in the fourth century, someone who was seventy-one years old. His first face sees? That didn't make sense. The last line was more straightforward. When the clock strikes twelve. He noticed it wasn't in the past tense, so it indicated something was going to happen in the future, which was confusing given the reference to the fourth century.

The second stanza was just as confounding.

Add the note of C twice
And take away the score
Count on good stock
Rich in grace

Add the note of C twice? A musical clue, but what did it mean? Add it to what? And what kind of score was he to take away? A musical score? A sports score? If sports, it depended on the game. Given it was French, he figured it must be referring to soccer. Take away one? From what? The last two lines were a little easier to decipher, or so he thought. Good stock was most often in reference to a good family. Rich in grace could denote elegance or a philanthropic family.

There was no way he was going to be able to decipher this on his own. He did a search of people dealing in old books, Nostradamus in particular. It appeared as though the closest to him was Rothschild's in Boston. They had handled a few of the early editions of Nostradamus. It was a reputable auction house according to all he read about them. He searched their website for the resident expert on books and manuscripts and came up with the name Dr. Sidney Rosenfeld. Maybe he could send Dr. Rosenfeld an e-mail, ask him what he thought about the strange verses. But then again, Rosenfeld could very well think he was crazy. Besides, did it really matter? Crow was curious but not to the point of looking like a fool. He closed the tablet and placed the book back in its sleeve laying it on the bedside table with the odd verses folded on top.

He flipped on the television and readied himself for bed. The news anchor was droning on about the autumn meeting of the board of governors of the World Bank meeting in Montreal in a few months. The only thing that made the boring meeting even the least bit interesting was the squabble over who would be its next president. Crow pulled back the covers and climbed between the sheets. The Chancellor of the Exchequer in the UK appeared to be the skunk at the garden party, almost singularly opposed to the consensus pick. He vowed to "take a stand in Montreal," as he put it, and derail the establishment's choice. The anchor returned after the sound bite to tease a sports story coming up after the break. Crow turned the volume down and looked over at the red sleeve. He picked up his note pad and read the translated verses. Very strange. He thought about them for a few moments then reached for the tablet. He opened it and found it still on the Rothschild's page. Crow clicked on Dr. Rosenfeld's name, which brought up an e-mail form. He chose his words with care then began to type.

He informed Dr. Rosenfeld that he was in possession of an early edition of *The Prophecies* by Nostradamus. He was cautious not to reveal too much. Perhaps when he was back in the States he could bring the book up for Dr. Rosenfeld to examine.He left his phone number and powered down the tablet. He lay there in bed forgetting all about a night at the casino, thinking of nothing but the book—and the odd verses—until he drifted off to sleep.

The ding on his phone woke him from a deep sleep. He looked at the clock on the bedside table. 6:14AM. It was Monday morning. The text was from Rothschild's in Boston. Dr. Sidney Rosenfeld was interested in taking a look at the book. Crow looked up to gather his thoughts for a reply. That's when the image on the television, that he didn't realize he had left running all night, grabbed him. Crow had goosebumps on his arm. He scooted to the foot of the bed to get a better look and turned up the volume. The police fished a man out of the St. Lawrence River.

"The yet unidentified man is believed to have been bludgeoned to death then thrown into the river," the reporter on the scene said. "At this point, they don't have a motive or a suspect."

The cameraman was careful not to zoom in too closely out of respect for the viewers' sensitivities, but it was unmistakable. Crow's mouth went dry. His breathing became shallow. Terror gripped his very soul. Even in the man's wet, lifeless state—the hair, the clothes, the shoes—there was no doubt. Crow could see him clearly in his mind. The dead man on Crow's television screen was the mysterious blue-eyed stranger.

Chapter Five

They killed him, Crow thought. But why? It clearly had something to do with the book. The old man was all too eager to pass it along to him. Even obsessed to do so. That had to be why he'd been stalking him since he landed. The killers were after the book, that was certain, but what was it about that book that drove men to murder? Panic set in. Now he had what they wanted. If they pieced everything together, they would come for him. He was sure of it. How sophisticated were they? Did they have access to video footage at the convention center? They wouldn't need it. The blonde man in the bathroom had gotten a good look at him. A couple of questions and they would certainly figure out he was Benson Crow. He had to get out immediately. They had probably already interrogated the convention people. Everyone associated with that convention knew where Crow was staying. They could be coming for him right now.

After seeing the awful images on the screen, Crow texted back a serious reply to Dr. Rosenfeld, trying hard to mask his hysteria. Rosenfeld immediately responded to his urgent request for a meeting. If he were in the city, Rosenfeld could see him this morning. Crow then grabbed his tablet and called up the airport website. He booked the next direct Air Canada flight to Boston. One first-class one-way ticket. He dressed, grabbed his overnight bag, and headed for the door.

Everything about Benson Crow screamed 'unapproachable.' He

was distant, antisocial, naturally disinterested in those around him. Fame exacerbated those qualities. He had become all but totally detached. Some might call him a recluse. His first inclination was to avoid contact with anyone unless it became absolutely necessary, eye contact in particular. His customary gaze was at the floor or his phone, avoiding any body language that would invite interaction. The events of the last several hours altered his behavior. He was now hypersensitive to each face he passed. Even paranoid. It was as if the handful of people he saw in the lobby of the hotel were staring at him. He studied every face, analyzed every reaction. Some, perhaps, recognized him from the inside back flap of a book or from the signing event the prior day, or maybe they were just being pleasant. That look of recognition could also mean they were one of 'them.' If they were willing to murder a man with nothing on him, he could only imagine what they'd do to him. Trying to convince them that he had just come into possession of the book by happenstance would be futile. Did the old man steal the book from them? Is that all they wanted, the book back? Surely if the old man only wanted to save his own skin, he would've ratted Crow out. But that wasn't the man's intent. He wanted desperately for Crow to have the book. But why? Why him?

Crow went straight to the front desk to settle his bill. He laid his room key on the counter and canvassed the lobby.

"How was your stay?" the clerk asked.

"Fine," Crow said. "It was fine." He continued to survey the room.

"Monsieur Crow, there was a man here asking for you."

"What?" Crow snapped his head in her direction. "What man? When?"

"Just about 30 minutes ago. He wanted to know if you had checked out."

"What did you tell him?"

The clerk smiled. "We don't divulge any information about our guests. I told him as much."

"What did he look like?" Crow asked.

"A man in a suit." She looked Crow over. "Probably a couple of inches taller than you. Well-built fellow. Very business-like."

"What color hair?"

"Blonde. Short."

The man from the bathroom. "Where'd he go?"

"He left."

Crow tucked the final bill into his coat pocket and cautiously walked past the concierge's desk to the front door. He stopped abruptly. Directly across the street, wearing dark glasses and the same blue suit from the day before, stood the blonde man. Crow could see him in his mind stuffing the homeless guy into the SUV. He hurried back to the front desk.

"Is there another way out of the hotel other than the front door?"

"Oui," the clerk answered. "Through that door," she pointed behind him, "down one flight of stairs."

He hurried through the dark wooden door and down the steps. Beside the hotel spa, he spotted the exit that spilled out onto Rue Saint-Pierre. The double doors were coated with tinting that allowed one to see out, but those looking in only saw a reflection. Standing across the street was the blonde man's accomplice from Congress Palace. A hotel worker was coming out of the spa.

"Is there another way out of the hotel other than here and the front door?" Crow asked.

"Oui, monsieur," the demure woman said. "Just down this hall. It leads to the alley."

"And what's beyond the alley?"

"The World Trade Center."

"What's that?"

"Restaurants, boutiques, and the like to your left. Straight through is the InterContinental Hotel."

"Perfect. Do you mind," he said, half-pulling her along by the arm, "taking a look out the door and see if you see anyone who seems to be just standing around?"

She looked at him curiously.

"Apparently, I've made an enemy with a jealous husband. I'd rather not run into him, if you know what I mean."

She smiled. Easing the door open, she peeked out and looked both ways. Then she motioned to Crow that the coast was clear. He stuck his head past hers to see for himself.

"Merci," he said before disappearing through the door, across the alley, and into the rear of the InterContinental.

He saw no one and continued down the large hallway and around the escalator that led up to the main lobby. A man stepped off the down escalator and Crow froze. He passed with a casual glance and a polite nod. Crow stood and contemplated his next move.

"Could I help you find something?" the voice behind him said.

Crow whipped around coming face-to-face with a hotel employee in a gray suit with a name tag.

"I, uh, I seemed to be turned around," he said. "Where's the front entrance?"

"No problem. Through there and to your left," he pointed.

Crow moved again past the concierge and through the automatic glass doors that led to the street. He found himself catty-corner to Congress Palace on the same street where the old man with the Nostradamus book was abruptly whisked away. The image played again in his mind. He shuddered. Crow was afraid to glance around the corner to see if his sentinel still guarded the side door. Instead he hailed a cab on the street in front of the hotel, cutting his eyes to the side as the car pulled away from the curb. He caught a glimpse of the man still standing on the side street and instinctively slunk down in his seat. If they hurried, he could just make the 8:10 flight, accounting for customs and security. He eyed the driver with suspicion in the rearview mirror. He had no intention of ending up in the St. Lawrence River. His only concern at the moment was getting out of the country and getting to Boston and Dr. Rosenfeld. Maybe Rosenfeld could help him make sense of the strange verses and tell him why on earth someone would be willing to kill for them.

They came to a stop at Pierre Trudeau. Crow handed the cabbie some bills and exited the taxi.

"Did you pack your own bag?" the ticket agent behind the counter asked.

"Yes."

"Is Boston your final destination?"

"Yes."

He thought he caught the man in the next line looking at him. Did he recognize him? Was he one of the killers?

"According to your passport, you're not from Boston," the agent said.

"I'm visiting a sick sister. I don't know how long I'll be there. She's pretty bad off. The doctor says she may have months, but most likely it's weeks."

The agent laid his passport back down on the counter. "I'm so sorry to hear that."

"Thanks," he said.

Every answer he gave was guarded. He wasn't comfortable telling anyone the truth about his movements. He wouldn't feel safe until he was on the plane, and even then he craned his neck around the edge of his headrest to see who might be watching. He had never experienced anything like this before. A man with whom he'd just had a brief encounter was murdered. Could he have saved the man had he alerted the authorities? Why were they after the book? It must be worth a fortune if they were willing to kill for it. Did they connect the dots and realize the man had handed it off to him? They were staking out his hotel. They knew who he was. That much was certain. Whoever these people were, they were killers, and the killers were now after him.

He felt a touch on his shoulder. He jumped.

"Oh, I'm sorry," the flight attendant said. "I didn't mean to startle you. Would you like something to drink?"

"No, thanks," Crow answered. She started to ask the next passenger in front of him. "On second thought, yes. A bourbon, please. No ice."

Should he call the police? He thought better of it. There would be interviews, interrogations, police reports, news reports. Too risky. His best bet was to slip out of the country. Try to find out why someone would kill for the book then decide on a course of action. For that, he needed the help of an expert.

The taxi dropped Crow at his destination right in the heart of Boston just past eleven o'clock in the morning. He paid the cabbie, looked around, and entered the building where 'Rothschild's' was engraved in stone above the entrance. The solemnity of the interior was a stark contrast to the bustling street just outside its doors much like walking into a library. Cooler. Quieter. He felt safe and calm in an odd sort of way. The soft scent of books met his nostrils. He loved that smell. That smell was one of the reasons he chose to be a writer. His steps reflected across the marble entrance to the receptionist's desk.

"I'm here to see Dr. Sidney Rosenfeld," he announced.

"And your name?" the receptionist asked.

"Benson Crow. I have an appointment."

The receptionist reached for the phone. "Please have a seat.

Someone will be with you in a moment."

Crow sank into the overstuffed sofa and examined his surroundings. The tall pilasters leading to the interior of the business beyond the receptionist were in keeping with the federal style of early Boston. They looked old, but he couldn't determine how old. Large tapestries hung on the walls to either side of the ornate center doorway that had been modernized over the years for security purposes. He was examining the intricate woodwork on the door itself when it opened. Through it stepped a striking woman with skin as smooth as silk, the color of caramel with a hint of cream. She looked across the room and spotted him.

"Mr. Crow?"

He rose from his seat. "Yes. I'm Benson Crow."

"This way, please."

She turned and walked back to the door. Her business suit told him she was more than Dr. Rosenfeld's secretary. She moved with too much confidence and grace. Research assistant maybe? Lover? If the man should be so lucky. She held her keycard to the sensor and the door buzzed. Crow followed her down a long hallway. He observed a meeting full of people going on in a conference room. The other offices along the hallway were occupied with workers, some of whom had not tidied those offices in years. Papers were stacked high on desks. Books were arranged on shelves in peculiar order. Some were piled on floors. Most were of the thick variety about art and history. There was a quiet reverence to the place. They reached an office on the left at the end of the hallway. She opened the door and held it for him before closing it behind them. Only then did she extend a hand. Crow held it in his for a brief moment. It was soft, delicate.

"I'm Sidney Rosenfeld. It's nice to meet you."

Crow was stunned. "*You're* Dr. Rosenfeld?"

Chapter Six

"Is there a problem?" Dr. Rosenfeld asked.

"I'm sorry, but you're not quite what I expected," Crow said.

She walked around her desk and took her place. "What were you expecting, Mr. Crow?"

"I was expecting someone a little more—"

"Male?"

"Well, I was going to say Jewish."

"Jewish," she repeated.

"And older."

"Well, you're full of preconceived notions, aren't you?"

"It's just that, well, let's face it. You don't look Jewish," he joked.

"That's because I'm not," she said, "but neither is Whoopi Goldberg. And you don't look Indian."

Crow smiled. "Crow is Irish, actually."

"You know, it's dangerous to jump to conclusions. Things aren't always as they appear. We've had to learn that the hard way in this business."

"I do apologize, Dr. Rosenfeld."

"It's not a problem. You said in your e-mail you'd found an early printing of *The Prophecies* by Nostradamus. May I see it?"

"Sure." Crow produced the velvet-covered book from his coat pocket.

Dr. Rosenfeld took the sleeve from him and set it atop a cloth pedestal on the desk. She then reached in a top drawer and pulled out two white gloves. She approached the task with the seriousness of a doctor suiting up for surgery. After sliding her slender hands into the gloves, she removed the book from its velvet sleeve. She pulled a swiveled magnifying glass between her and the book and examined its front cover. She then turned it over to examine the back. Crow looked around her office. There were leather-bound books stacked on a shelf behind her. Blue reference books occupied the entire row below them. A small white bust of George Washington held up one small cluster of books and a glass award with her name on it served as a bookend on the other side. An impressionist painting rested on an easel in the corner. In another corner was a wooden coat rack on which hung an umbrella, a plaid scarf, and a white lab coat. The gentle ticking of an antique clock on one of the shelves was the only sound in the room. She laid the book back down on the soft cloth and opened it. Using the magnifying glass, she scanned the page in silence then turned to another, then another. Satisfied, she pushed the glass aside and closed the book.

"What many people don't realize is this is how the book was first printed," she explained. "They hear about the works of Nostradamus and they expect a large leather-bound book. *The Prophecies* were meant for the common man. They were printed as little books that could fit in your pocket so you could easily pull them out while you were traveling."

"Much like paperbacks today," Crow said.

"Exactly. There were many editions of this book that were printed in the late sixteenth and early seventeenth centuries. Part of the problem in interpreting Nostradamus is the fact that so many different shops printed his books, and mistakes were made in typesetting for different words. This particular edition is from 1634. It's in remarkably good shape. I would think it would fetch around $20,000. Of course, that's just a ballpark estimate. We would need to do more research to get a more accurate asking price."

"Twenty-thousand dollars," Crow said.

"Give or take a few thousand. That's minus the fifteen percent seller's fee, of course. Would you like us to list it for you?"

Crow looked down at the book then back up at Sidney Rosenfeld. "I don't know. I mean, that does sound very tempting. Is that enough to kill for?"

"Sorry?" Rosenfeld said.

"There's a bit more to this particular copy. You got a minute?"

Rosenfeld leaned back in her chair and steepled her fingers over her stomach like someone who relished a good conversation. "Sure."

Crow proceeded to tell her the whole tale. The creepy drifter who stalked him in Montreal. The encounter in the men's room. Watching the two men force the old guy into the back of the car. The story on the news of the alleged murder. He left nothing out. Rosenfeld was intrigued.

"Very interesting, Mr. Crow. Sounds like a great idea for a novel to me."

It took a second for her meaning to sink in. "Oh, now wait a minute. Are you suggesting I'm making all this up?"

"I'm familiar with your work, Mr. Crow." She leaned forward. "It's not unusual for clients to, let's say, embellish stories surrounding items we sell. You know, to drive up the price?"

"Hold on a second. You can check with the Montreal police."

"And I'm sure I'll find a homeless man was found dead in the river this morning. Of course, it could be that someone stole the book from the homeless guy and dumped him in the river. That would be an interesting twist for your novel. Don't you think?"

Crow stood up and held his hand out for the book. "I see I came to the wrong place."

"Mr. Crow, I'm not accusing you of anything, but you have to see things from my side of the desk. I don't know you from Adam's house cat. You schedule a hurried meeting, then you tell me a man gave his life for this book."

"I know it all sounds rather fantastic, but it's absolutely true."

"It's not me you'll have to convince. I'm just telling you what to expect if you list this book. This is the kind of interrogation you'll go through from my higher-ups. Do you know how many people walk through our door wanting to fence stolen goods?"

Crow eased back down to his seat. "Dr. Rosenfeld, I can assure you my motivation is not money. Certainly not twenty grand."

"As if twenty thousand dollars is something to sneeze at."

"Let's just say I have bad allergies."

She smiled slightly. "A man who will exaggerate the size of his bank account, Mr. Crow, will exaggerate the size of other things, too."

Crow didn't flinch. "I can assure you, it's no exaggeration."

"Which one?"

"Take your pick."

She studied him for a moment then fixed her lower jaw forward tilting her head back. "What *is* your motivation?"

"Well, for starters," Crow said, "I want to know why someone would kill for this book."

"That's not hard to figure out. Twenty thousand dollars is a lot of money. It may not be to you, but it's a lot of money to most people."

"Not to these people," Crow said.

"I thought you didn't know who killed him."

"I don't, but these were hired goons. I can't imagine that someone who has that kind of muscle on retainer needs a measly twenty grand.

I'm more interested in finding out why that man gave me this book. I mean, I'm the least likely person to know what to do with it."

"I have no way of knowing," Rosenfeld said.

"Well, there's more than just the book."

Rosenfeld gave him a curious look.

He pulled from his pocket the sheet of paper he found in the pages of the book. "This is what I'm intrigued by." He handed her the paper. "I found it inside the book."

Rosenfeld looked it over. "It's written in quatrains like Nostradamus wrote," she said, "but these are not his."

"Quatrains?"

"Yes," she looked up, "four-line stanzas. It's how Nostradamus wrote his predictions. Heavily coded, most believe, so the Church wouldn't directly accuse him of witchcraft or sorcery."

"Any idea what any of this means? I have the translation." He reached for his notation pad.

She ignored his offer and read the French verses to herself. "I'd only be guessing. Ordinarily, century of four would refer to the fourth century, but that would be before Nostradamus' time. That really wouldn't make any sense. It probably refers to Nostradamus' centuries."

"Nostradamus' centuries?"

"Yes, he divided his quatrains into centuries, usually with one hundred quatrains per century." She opened the book and held it up so he could see. "For example, in this book each chapter is called a century. Century of four probably means century four or chapter four. The age most likely refers to the quatrain. Seventy-one. That's what that could mean but, like I said, I'd only be guessing."

Crow finished writing in his note pad. "Any ideas on what the rest of it means?"

"I don't."

"Do you know anyone who might?"

She put the book back in its sleeve and hesitated before handing it back to him. "Mr. Crow, I'm not sure you're ready for what you may have gotten yourself into."

Crow took the book and looked at her with concern. "Well, you *have* to tell me now."

"I don't think I should."

"Why?" He slid the velvet sleeve back into his coat pocket.

"Because this isn't some game. I'm sure it sounds rather exciting to a novelist. A mysterious man gives you a mysterious book with a mysterious cryptic message. Like some childhood scavenger hunt."

"I, uh—"

"This isn't some riddle to be solved by a bored writer," she continued. "The study of Nostradamus and his writings is very serious. The people who study him are very serious. Some have spent their entire lives trying to unravel the quatrains, trying to make sense of the odd references. They've dedicated their professions to understanding the man and his so-called prophecies. I would never want to insult them by subjecting them to an amateur sleuth who thinks he's in some Hardy Boys mystery."

"Dr. Rosenfeld, I can assure you that I take my profession very seriously as well. Yes, I'm a writer, but I'm a writer because of my insatiable curiosity. Do I love a good challenge? You bet I do, but I don't go around accepting them just to give me something to do. This man in Montreal went out of his way to give me this book, to give me those…those quatrains, as you call them. I don't know why he chose me, but he lost his life in the process. I owe him the courtesy of at least being curious enough to ask why."

She stared at him until the sincerity of his words penetrated her skepticism. "OK," she said, pulling off her white gloves. She jotted something down on the back of her business card then handed it to him along with the odd verses on the paper. "That's the foremost Nostradamus expert in this country." She pointed to the card.

"Dr. Benedict Grumbling," he read aloud.

"He lives on an old plantation in Virginia not too far from D.C. You can't call him. He doesn't have a phone. You'll just have to show up. That's his address on the back of the card. On the front is my direct line. If you have any questions or any problem finding Dr. Grumbling, give me a call."

"I appreciate that." Crow took one of her business cards from the desk and wrote his phone number on the back. "If you think of anything that might help me, please give *me* a call."

She took the card then extended her hand. Crow shook it.

"Good luck, Mr. Crow. Sorry if I offended you."

"No problem," Crow replied. "Just doing your job."

Rosenfeld smiled. "Just doing my job."

Chapter Seven

Crow took the noon non-stop to Reagan National. By half-past-two he was pulling up to an old plantation house, the tires of his rental crunching on the pea gravel drive. The stately old home looked as though it had been neglected for years. The smell of old hay cut through the humid summer afternoon. The yard was a mess. The rusticated exterior was beveled at the edges when first constructed and sand was thrown on the wet paint to make the yellow pine siding appear as stone. Now the paint peeled. The porch creaked.

He knocked on the large wooden door with the weathered brass knocker. He was about to knock again when the door opened and a woman appeared. She was slight of stature and dressed in a monochrome skirt and blouse of gunmetal grey. Crow took her for a servant, not a wife. Certainly not a lover.

"I'm here to see Dr. Benedict Grumbling," he said. "I, uh, couldn't call because…" His voice trailed off as the door opened wide.

The woman said nothing. She turned and walked. Crow followed. He glanced around the huge foyer. If she was the housekeeper she was a damn sorry one. Dust was everywhere. The windows were caked with dirt. No pleasant smell came from the kitchen. No sweet scent of potpourri. Just mustiness.

He was shown to a large library just off the foyer where he found an elderly man with a pipe hunched over an antique desk staring with great intent into a magnifying glass. Wisps of white and gray hair streaked his balding skull and became thicker at his temples. He sported a close-cropped salt-and-pepper vandyke. Smoke seeped from the corners of his mouth. He was studying a book that was taken from one of the tall shelves of the library that must have reached fourteen feet high.

"Dr. Grumbling?"

"Mr. Crow," he answered without looking up. "I've been expecting you."

Expecting me? How?

Grumbling anticipated the question before it was asked. "Word gets around, Mr. Crow," he said looking up. "Especially when someone begins gnawing at their pant legs. Don't look so surprised. When you paid a visit to Dr. Rosenfeld it was inevitable you'd end up here." Crow still looked uneasy by his prescience. He couldn't quite place the accent. British maybe, but somewhat watered down. Definitely European. "What?" Grumbling feigned offense. "I *do* have friends who live in the twenty-first century, you know." He rose from the desk and motioned to a sofa then grabbed a bottle of whisky from the bar. "Can I offer you a refreshment?"

"No, thank you." Crow took a seat on the sofa.

Dr. Grumbling poured a drink as he puffed on his pipe then returned the bottle to its resting place. "In order for me to be of any assistance, I first need to know where you are in your journey."

"My journey?"

"How much do you know about Michel de Nostredame?" Grumbling settle into the leather chair beside the sofa.

"I know just enough to be dangerous."

"The only thing more dangerous than too little knowledge is

a man who *thinks* he knows everything but knows nothing atall." Grumbling took a sip of his whisky.

"I've never actually taken him seriously, but I know a little about his prophecies," Crow said. "He supposedly predicted all sorts of world events including World War II. Even Hitler himself, although he called him 'Hister,'" Crow stated authoritatively.

Grumbling toked on his pipe and chuckled. "Dangerous, indeed. Too many late night documentaries, my boy." He adjusted himself in his chair. "Hister is not a misspelling of Hitler. It refers to the lower Danube River. It's Latin. Michel de Nostredame, or Nostradamus as most people know him, rarely mentioned people by name. He was a prophet, but he didn't have a crystal ball. The quatrains do speak of 'a captain of Great Germany' who 'will come to deliver through false help' and 'his revolt will cause a great flow of blood.' That would indicate he was talking about Hitler, but there was no specific reference. Anything else you know about the man?"

"I'm afraid not. I mean, I know he wrote in a sort of cryptic language. What do you make of this?" Crow handed him the strange verses he'd found inside the book.

" In the century of four," Crow began translating from his notation pad.

"No need, my boy. I speak five languages and French is my favorite."

Crow looked down and cleared his throat.

Grumbling read over the verses, chuckled slightly to himself, then handed the paper back to Crow. "Very clever."

"What does it mean?"

"Well, that's just it. It could mean a number of things. It's without question the work of the society."

"The society?"

Grumbling looked a bit perturbed as he puffed his pipe. "Yes, of course. Are you not familiar with the secret society of Nostradamus?"

"I'm sorry. I'm not a Nostradamus expert."

"You don't say."

"I was just given this book and the paper yesterday." He held up the red velvet sleeve. "Dr. Rosenfeld tells me it's from 1634. It's an early French edition."

"I can tell you the book is inconsequential," Grumbling stated emphatically. "It's the verses they wrote that are important."

"They?"

"Yes, *they*."

"This secret society?"

"Yes, of course." He took another swallow of his drink. "The First Face of Janus."

"The First Face of Janus?"

"It's been around since the time of Nostradamus and few people know of its existence."

Crow wrote the name down on his pad.

"It started as a handful of his students," Grumbling continued, "but it's grown to something much bigger. They make sure the master's predictions come to fruition."

"Wait a minute. You want me to believe there's some secret society running around out there that does nothing but make Nostradamus look good?"

"It's not a matter of belief, my boy. The First Face of Janus is very real. They've had a hand in every Nostradamus prediction that's come true thus far."

"Did they purposely go find a guy named Hitler and groom him to wage war on the world?"

"Of course not. What they did was take note of someone who

appeared to be fulfilling the prophecies, and they simply helped him along."

Crow looked puzzled. "When you say 'helped him along,' what do you mean?"

"I mean they provided him with the necessary tools—money, intelligence, personnel—to be successful."

"Then why didn't he triumph?" Crow asked with a tinge of dubiety in his voice. "Why was he defeated by the Allies?"

Grumbling smiled. "Because it was in the quatrains, my boy. Hitler recognized the power of Nostradamus. He even tasked Goebbels with making propaganda out of the prophecies. Had he only taken them seriously, he would've realized his own demise. You see, Nostradamus made mention of the Suevi. The Suevi were Germanic people who once lived in an area called Gaul. Have you any idea where Gaul is?"

Crow gave him a blank stare.

"Of course not," Grumbling said. "Gaul is modern-day France. Nostradamus wrote, 'Through the Suevi and neighboring places / They will be at war over the clouds,'" he said dramatically. "That's an obvious reference to France and surrounding areas and airplanes fighting in the skies, you see. He goes on to write, 'Swarm of marine locusts and gnats / The faults of Geneva will be laid quite bare.' The 'marine locusts' passage clearly refers to the D-Day invasion at Normandy. 'The faults of Geneva' undoubtedly means the Geneva Conventions begun in 1864 which established the humanitarian standards of international law in a time of war. Hitler mocked the prophecies by trying to exploit them for political gain, but they were ultimately his undoing."

Crow looked skeptical. "So they just help things along, this society you're talking about."

Dr. Grumbling took a taste of his drink. "You're sure you won't join me?"

Crow waved a polite but dismissive hand.

"It really depends on how much the prophecies need helping," Grumbling explained. "You see, it's much like a jigsaw puzzle. A couple of pieces become an eye, then two eyes begin a face, and pretty soon you've got the whole picture. Once the First Face of Janus understands what has to be done, they'll stop at nothing to see that the prophecy is fulfilled." He took another nip from his drink then continued. "Remember when Lee Harvey Oswald called himself a patsy?"

"Of course."

"That's because he was. Once Kennedy came into office, it became clear that he was the one Nostradamus said must be killed and killed he was. 'And from the roof evil ruin will fall on the great man,' the quatrain says. 'They will accuse an innocent, being dead, of the deed.' Oswald, obviously. 'The guilty one is hidden in the misty copse.'"

"Copse?" Crow asked.

"It's a thicket of bushes."

"The grassy knoll," Crow said to himself, writing on his pad.

Grumbling looked at him and toked on a dry pipe. He relit it with a match and puffed.

"Was Oswald a member of this First Face of Janus group?" Crow asked.

"Hmm?" Grumbling shook the match in the air until nothing but smoke trailed from its head, puffed, then removed the pipe from his teeth. "Oh, no. Heavens no. That's strictly forbidden. A First Facer cannot take it upon him or herself to make the prophecy come true. They can only arrange things so the prophecy happens without interference."

Crow looked up from his writing. "I'm sorry, but that's just too incredible to believe. You're saying that in order to fulfill the prophecy they had to find just the right place, just the right time, the perfect scenario that would bring all the elements together? I mean, they had to arrange Oswald, Dallas, the school book depository, everything. Sounds like pajama party gossip to me."

"Pajama party gossip indeed," Grumbling said with an edge of agitation. "I'm saying a trip to Dallas presents itself. There are those who want Kennedy dead. There's a man, Oswald, who's not too keen on the country. These men need a lightning rod. Oswald is only too willing to play the part because of his hatred of America. All he's got to do is stick a rifle out of a warehouse window and fire. They promise him he'll never go to prison for the deed. Jack Ruby is already in Dallas. He already knows he's dying of cancer. There are people in Dallas who need Oswald disposed of after the fact. The First Facers merely facilitate a meeting and Ruby's tapped for the job. They simply help align the players and the prophecy is fulfilled. And Ruby keeps the promise. Oswald never serves a day in prison."

"Not sure that's what he had in mind."

"Well, a promise is a promise," Grumbling said with a playful grin.

"This sounds too fantastic," Crow insisted. "All that's impossible."

"Nothing is impossible for them, my boy. They have unlimited resources. Nearly unlimited manpower. They do it because it must be done and they cannot fail. The very future of humanity itself depends on their success."

"Ah, but you said they couldn't make the prediction come true. How about Jack Ruby?"

"They didn't *force* Ruby to kill Oswald. They only made him available. Ruby had his own motivation. He was a Kennedy fan. He was acting chivalrously on behalf of JFK's grieving widow, saving her from the spectacle of a long drawn-out trial."

"Okay, well, let's assume this *is* all possible. How do we know which event is going to be manipulated by these people?"

"*We* have no way of knowing," Grumbling said, "not without le Manuscrit Non Rédigé, the Unriddled Manuscript. *They* don't even know until the prophecies reveal themselves."

Crow jotted the name down on his pad. "What's this Unriddled Manuscript?"

"It's the prophecies of Nostradamus decoded."

"Where did it come from?"

"From Nostradamus himself," Grumbling said. "He worked several years to compile the prophecies in plain language so his closest associates could better understand what was to transpire. This way they could make sure nothing or no one stood in the way of his predictions."

Crow rubbed the back of his neck. "I don't get it. How does this society make sure the prophecies come true?"

"Look at it this way. The prophecies of the Old Testament said Jesus would be born to a virgin in Bethlehem. They said he would be of the lineage of David. These are all things that are impossible to arrange. However once Jesus was born and began his ministry, it became obvious to those who had been waiting for the messiah that he was it. Now then, the prophet said the messiah would enter Jerusalem riding on a donkey. This is something Jesus had full control over. Once you've found the messiah, then knowing the prophecies makes that prediction considerably easier. Do you see? Much like many Shia Muslims believe in the coming of the Twelfth Imam riding on a white horse. There are several things that need to happen before his return—chaos, a world filled with violence, and such things—and there are many who are feverishly trying to make that prophecy a reality. This is how the Shia Muslims plan to hasten the coming of the Twelfth Imam."

"This current prophecy they—the First Face of Janus—seem to want to see fulfilled. How do we find out what it is?"

"Careful, my boy. It's not the prophecy they choose to fulfill. It's the prophecy that reveals itself to them. They don't go searching the quatrains for prophecies. They wait until circumstances reveal themselves so that consulting the writings of Nostradamus seems obvious. In the immediate aftermath of 9/11 the single most searched name was not bin Laden or Bush. It was Nostradamus. The difference is the First Facers see the prophecy taking shape long before it happens. Of course, they're at a distinct advantage having the Unriddled Manuscript. Only they know how much it reveals. The quatrains on that sheet of paper certainly appear to be consistent with the First Facers."

"Why are they called that, by the way?"

"The First Face of Janus? One can only assume it was formed by Nostradamus' secretary, Jean de Chavigny. There was a book written by an author calling himself Jean-*Aimé* de Chavigny. Aimé means adored, so he could have added that himself. Same person? Well, there's some dispute about that. What's not in dispute is that the book was published in 1594, almost 30 years after Nostradamus' death, and it interpreted his prophecies. It was titled *The First Face of the French Janus*. Janus was the ancient Roman god of beginnings and transitions and was depicted as having two faces, the second face looking into the past, the first face of Janus looking into the future."

"Interesting." Crow continued to take notes. "Seems his secretary used symbolism like his boss."

"Yes, Nostradamus and the people he surrounded himself with were rich with imagery and coded meaning," Grumbling continued.

"Many say it was to hide their true meaning from the Church. The Inquisition was a nasty piece of business and seers like Nostradamus were thought to be of the devil. Although the days of executing heretics had all but passed, the Congregation of the Holy Office of the Inquisition established by Pope Paul III in 1542 meant that people like Michel de Nostradamus could be completely stripped of their worldly possessions, which would put an end to his writing. He was wise enough to ingratiate himself with the royal family of France and thus insulate himself, but he was ever cognizant of the fact that they could turn on him at any moment. Therefore, he shrouded his public predictions in language he hoped would be deciphered centuries later. Of course, his disciples are no safer now than they were at the time of his death."

"What do you mean?"

"What I mean is the Church. Since the days of Nostradamus, the Custos Verbi has tried to stop the prophecies. Custos Verbi is Latin for 'Keeper of the Word.' A secret well-armed force that has disposed of people like Nostradamus and any other perceived threats to the Church for centuries."

"Custos Verbi, you said?"

"Yes."

"Spell that."

Grumbling spelled it out for him as he wrote.

"When you say they've 'disposed of people like Nostradamus,' are you suggesting they killed him?"

"Most certainly."

"I thought he died of old age."

"Edema was the official cause of death, but many believe he was poisoned."

"But he was sixty-two when he died. That's pretty old for the sixteenth century."

"Ordinarily, yes, but Nostradamus was quite hardy. He had survived the plague that killed his entire family. It was not unusual for his contemporaries in the upper class to live long lives into their 80s. Edema is the accumulation of fluid beneath the skin and in the cavities of the body. It was not that common in his day. It's interesting that arsenic can cause edema. Many believe he was murdered by the Church. They had been suspicious of Nostradamus for a long time, but he was under the protection of the crown. However, word leaked that Nostradamus had been compiling the Unriddled Manuscript. The Church took his predictions very seriously. Legend has it they sent out two agents to intercept the Unriddled Manuscript the night Nostradamus died. They were ambushed by two members of the First Face of Janus, and they've been trying to get their hands on that book ever since."

Crow pointed to the paper he'd been given. "Any idea what these verses mean?" Crow asked.

Grumbling read them over again. "Well, they seem to point to the seventy-first quatrain in the fourth century." He pulled himself from the chair and fetched a newer English-language version of Nostradamus' prophecies from the tall book shelf. He licked a finger and thumbed through the pages until he found the quatrain he was looking for. "That quatrain says, 'In place of the bride the daughters slaughtered / Murder with great error no survivor be / Within the well vestals inundated / The bride extinguished by a drink of Aconite.'"

Crow wrote then looked up from his pad. "These girls are going to be murdered."

"One would surmise from the quatrain," Grumbling said.

"But where?"

Grumbling shrugged.

"A wedding, maybe?" Crow said. "It mentions a bride twice."

Grumbling returned the book to the shelf, took a puff from his pipe, and sat back down in the chair. "Perhaps, but remember, Nostradamus often wrote in allegorical terms. He did, however, speak directly as well. The quatrains written on that paper mention the clock striking twelve. We would presume it's noon if we're talking about a wedding. Not many people get married at midnight," he chuckled. "You can rest assured that the verses point to some prediction in the prophecies. It's a matter of finding an event that fits and, unfortunately, that usually happens after the deed is done."

"Well, we know that whatever it is, it's happening soon."

"And how do we know this?" Grumbling asked.

"That's what the man in Montreal told me. I won't insult you by assuming you don't know about him."

"The man on the bridge, you mean," Grumbling said.

"How does he fit in?"

"You want my opinion? Because that's all I have to offer."

"I do," Crow said.

"I suspect he was Custos Verbi. He found out what the First Facer's next prophecy was and tried to blow the whistle on them. It got him killed."

"Why would he choose me?"

"I haven't a clue."

"You're sure he wasn't part of this First Face of Janus?" Crow asked.

"Why would they need to tell *you* about their next prophecy?"

"I see what you mean." Crow contemplated the situation for a moment. "This guy was trying to warn me so I could stop the murders of these daughters. I have to find out what that next prophecy is, and I have to do it fast. The old man in Montreal said whatever is going to happen will happen before the sun rises on Sunday."

"Well, you can drive yourself mad by trying to figure out the unknowable, or you can just go home and forget the whole affair," Grumbling said.

"Are you kidding me? I can't just forget about it. I'm a writer. I've been waiting for something like this all my life."

"Oh, I see." Grumbling's tone turned disappointed, almost as if he'd been wasting his time. "This is that next big book, is it? So, you write a book about it and you have no proof. You're labeled a kook. No one will ever take you seriously again. Is that what you want?"

"These people need to be stopped."

"Listen to me and listen to me good. *These people* are everywhere, in places you can't even imagine." He leaned forward in his seat and lowered his voice to a reverent tone. "They permeate all levels of nearly every society on earth. Don't give a thought to involving the authorities. You have no idea who might be one of them. Your only choice is to stand aside. The fact that the quatrains have been passed to you means the next prophecy is in motion. Walk away from this now. Once the killing starts, it will not stop until the prophecy is fulfilled."

"Then somebody has to stop the prophecy," Crow said.

Grumbling's eyes narrowed. "Listen to me, my boy. These prophecies have been coming true for centuries and there's absolutely nothing anyone can do about it."

"If it means they're going to murder innocent children, I can stop it," Crow insisted.

Grumbling let out a huge laugh. "You? With your vestigial knowledge of the subject? Don't be ridiculous. You could no more stop the next prophecy than you could stop the sun from rising on Sunday morning."

The shattering of the window made no more than a hiss. It was the thud of the bullet entering Dr. Grumbling's back that lodged itself in Crow's memory. And the guttural moan as the last breath of air left his lungs. Crow plastered himself to the back of the sofa before his senses had a chance to process what was happening. Grumbling's eyes looked at him for a scant second, but Crow could see there was no awareness in them. The pipe fell from his mouth. His drink dropped to his side and spilled with an awkward splash on the floor. Gravity took over and Grumbling's lifeless form slumped forward. His knees hit first, then the rest of him tumbled face down. Crow sat petrified at the image of the still-smoldering hole in the chair. He cast his eyes down on the horrific scene of the ever-expanding stain of blood on Grumbling's back, and a wave of terror swept over him.

Chapter Eight

It was as if Benson Crow was fastened to the sofa. He wanted to move. He just couldn't. Not until the lamp beside him shattered into a million pieces. Reflexes kicked in and he sprinted for the door. He opened it and almost tripped over the corpse of the housekeeper. He gasped. She lay face down with a bullet wound in the back. Crow desperately looked around the foyer. Whoever killed these two was now inside. He bolted past the staircase toward the rear of the house. He jiggled the knob one more time than was necessary to realize it was locked. Back around the staircase to the other door leading to the back. Locked. He stopped. That's when he heard it. A high-pitched hum. It was coming from outside. In front of the house. He listened intently to the hum and squinted his eyes to bring what he was looking at into clearer focus. A gleam of sunlight was piercing through the dimness of the foyer. It passed through a small hole in the dirty window by the front door. The lint and dust that hung in the air created a perfect line of sight for the now lifeless body of the housekeeper by the library door.

He rushed to the window and rubbed clean a fist-sized clearing just in time to see the source of the hum. A drone. A small flying contraption just large enough to carry a gun turret like one might see on the belly of a B-17 Flying Fortress, but in miniature. It was rising away from the house. He cracked open the front door and watched through the slit as the drone shrunk smaller in the afternoon sky.

Why didn't it stick around to kill him? Did it not see him? When it shot the lamp next to him, did it assume it had a hit? Or were real humans on their way to finish the job? He wasn't about to stick around to find out. After scanning the sky to make sure he wasn't being lured out into the open, he darted across the porch and through the gravel to his rental car, started it up, and sped away. Crow strained through the windshield then out the driver's window to detect even a speck in the sky as he drove.

"Yes, I'm sure," he insisted. "Two dead. Dr. Benedict Grumbling and his housekeeper. I dropped a pin and sent it to your phone. Contact the police. Give them that address."

"Who would want them dead?" Thomas Browning asked.

"I'm not sure. There are two groups, and one is as suspect as the other."

"Two groups? What two groups?"

"It's rather involved and it's a little hard to believe, so I need you to reserve judgment until after I've told you the whole story. Understand?"

"I understand," his publisher said.

Crow craned his head again to make sure no drone was following him. "I did the book signing in Montreal and this odd character gave me this really old book written by Nostradamus. Next thing I know, they're fishing him out of the river. I saw who killed him."

"You saw the man killed?" Browning asked in disbelief.

"No, I saw them stuff him into a car while he was alive. Next thing I know, I'm watching the police pull him from the river on the news. I got on the Internet to find an expert on old books and I found a lady out of Boston." Then it dawned on him. "Crap! Tom, I'm gonna have to call you back."

Crow terminated the conversation then fished feverishly in his pants pocket until he produced the business card. He dialed Dr. Rosenfeld's direct line. As it rang he scanned the sky.

"Dr. Sidney Rosenfeld," the voice answered on the other end.

"Dr. Rosenfeld! It's me, Benson Crow. I think your life may be in danger."

"What? What are you talking about?"

"Dr. Grumbling's been murdered."

"Oh my God! What happened? Who killed him?"

"I'm not sure. It was a sophisticated hit. They used an armed drone."

"A drone? Why would anybody want to kill him?"

"Probably the same reason someone killed the man in Montreal. Listen to me. I was apparently followed from Montreal all the way to Virginia, which means they know I talked with you. You've got to get out of there. If they killed Grumbling just for talking to me, you're bound to be a target."

"You're scaring me."

"You need to be scared. Get out of there now. Go someplace secure."

"I'm coming to you," she said.

"No! It's not safe to be around me."

"Look, Crow. I'm not going to sit around here waiting for them to track me down. I know quite a bit about this. I can help you."

"I can't risk it," he insisted. "It's too dangerous."

"Have you called the police?" she asked.

"My publisher is doing that right now, but I've got to hide. It's complicated. There's a group of people involved. It's hard to explain, but I can't go to the police myself. Grumbling told me these people are everywhere."

"The First Face of Janus?"

Crow held the phone down to his leg for a second in exasperated frustration then lifted it back to his ear. "Why the hell didn't you tell me about them when I was in your office?"

"Because I had no idea who you were. You could've been one of *them* for all I know. Knowledge can be a deadly thing."

Crow's phone beeped. He held it out and looked. "That's my caretaker on the other line. I'll be right back."

"Caretaker?"

"Hold on just a second. Don't hang up. I'll be right back." He hit the button on his phone. "Gordy?"

"Mr. Crow, you all right?" his caretaker said on the other end. The weathered man stood by a tractor dressed in overalls. The bill of his hat cast a shadow from the afternoon sun on his concerned tanned face.

"I've been better. Why?"

"There were two men just here at the farm asking about you."

"What kind of men? What did they look like?"

"Very serious. Suits. Well-built fellows. One white and one black."

"What did they say?"

"They asked if I knew when you would be back," Gordy said. "They seemed to already know you weren't here."

"What did you tell them?"

"I told them you were out of the country and I didn't know when you'd be back. Is everything OK?"

"I'm not sure. Look, I need for you to get out of there for a few days. Go visit your sister. Tell Maria up at the house to take some time off, too. Lock everything up and get out as soon as you can. Hey, Gordy, don't talk to anybody about this. Understand? Not even your sister. As soon as I know what's going on I'll let you know."

"You gonna be all right, Mr. Crow?"

"Sure. I'll be fine. Just take a few days off. I'll call you when it's safe to come back."

"Well, OK, if you insist."

"I do. Gotta go." He hit a button on his phone. "Dr. Rosenfeld."

"Yes, I'm here," she said, stuffing items into her purse.

"They've been to my house."

"Look, Crow, you're going to need my help. It sounds like the prophecy has already begun. If they think you're standing in the way of that prophecy, they won't stop until you're dead."

"Crap," Crow said under his breath. "That's what Grumbling said." He looked around frantically in search of a solution. "OK, here's what I want you to do. I want you to leave there right now. Don't take your car. Take another way out of the building other than the way you normally come in. Make sure no one is following you. Grab some things from home you'd need for a few days' travel but no big bags. Just a shoulder bag. And grab your passport."

"My passport?"

"Do you have one?" Crow asked.

"What kind of rube do you take me for? Why do I need my passport?"

"To give us options. Obviously, they're watching my place. We can't go there. We may have to leave the country."

"And go where?"

"I don't know where," he almost shouted. "Do you still have the card with my number?"

"Yes."

"Call me when you're away from the building and you're sure no one's following you. Got it?"

"I got it."

"Listen to me," Crow said. "Whatever you do, do not let these people find you."

Chapter Nine

"Have you finished the book I loaned you?" one of the gentlemen seated at a booth in the rear of the cafe asked of his dining companion in Spanish.

The heavyset, mustachioed man behind the counter worked a toothpick from one side of his mouth to the other and looked at nothing in particular out the front window of his cafe. His attention was focused on what was coming from the earbuds in his ears. They connected to a phone in his pocket that was set to record.

"I do not understand," the second man said.

The man behind the counter pressed a finger to tighten the left earbud. The two gentlemen had come to his cafe several times before. The mustachioed man seated them this time at a special table, the one with a tiny microphone inside the plastic flower that sat in the waterless vase.

"Did you finish Don Quixote?" the first man asked.

"Oh, yes, I did finish it," the other diner replied. "Excellent read."

"He was the fallen angel."

"Yes, he was."

"Honey is sweeter than blood," the first diner said.

The proprietor's mustache twitched. He pulled the toothpick from his mouth and eyed the men over his shoulder.

"Is that so?" the second man said.

"Yes, my cousin Montserrat told me that. He heard it from a couple near the fortress."

"Near the fortress?"

"Yes," the first man said, "there is a knight at the tower."

"A real knight?" the second asked.

"No, do not be silly. Not a real knight. I think he was called the Knight of Death. Sort of the enigma of Hitler."

"A terrible man."

"He was a monster. They say the apparition of monsters presages the outbreak of war," the first man said.

"Yes, I suppose it does."

A frown passed over the cafe proprietor's face.

SIDNEY ROSENFELD GRABBED her scarf from the coat rack and slid out the side entrance of Rothschild's showing no intention of following Crow's advice. She was determined to take her own car. It was the fastest and safest way to her place and away from Boston. Her car was across the street from the front entrance in a parking lot. She approached the sidewalk and froze in her tracks. A man was watching the front entrance of Rothschild's. Her pulse quickened. She backtracked and took an alleyway between two buildings which dumped her out on the street a block away. She hid among the crowd at the crosswalk, watching the man in the distance. The crowd moved across the street and she moved with it ever watchful of the man on the street a block away. Once on the other side, she used the cover of the other cars in the parking lot to make her way to her own vehicle.

After grabbing some personal items from home, as much as she could cram into a shoulder bag, she headed out. Once she was back on the road she dialed up Crow.

"Where are you now?" he asked.

"I'm driving south on I-95."

"You're driving? I told you not to take your car."

"Yeah, well, I'm a big girl, Crow. I can make my own decisions. What's your plan?"

"I'm still working on that. Ditch the car and meet me in Washington. You can take the 4:15 out of South Station and be here just after eleven tonight. I'll meet you at Union Station."

"South Station?"

"Yes."

"I'm nowhere near that. I just passed Newton."

"Hold on a second." He consulted a map on his phone then put it back to his ear. "OK, then hit Westwood Station. It's about fifteen minutes later."

"Fine. I'll see you then."

"Make sure you're not followed."

"I'm not an idiot, Crow."

Westwood Station saw just under a half-million passengers per year, a quiet station compared to the 11 million who hustled through Boston's South Station in the same period. Easier to get lost in the crowd at South Station but much easier to spot someone following you at Westwood. Rosenfeld loitered around the terminal eying the waiting passengers. She bought a paperback at a newsstand then waited until the last possible moment to board the train, taking care to make sure no one boarded after her. She made herself comfortable for the six-and-a-half-hour trip to Washington.

Before she settled in, she examined with suspicion each person who walked down the aisle until she was satisfied no one in her car was a threat. After the conductor came to collect her ticket, she read a few chapters of her book. By New Haven, Connecticut, she was gazing out the window at the daylight that still lingered among the pink ribbons of clouds. The gentle sway of the train carried her off to a deep, if fitful, sleep. She awoke with a start just after the New York stop to see a man sitting next to her.

"Sorry if I scared you," he said softly.

"No, that's OK," Rosenfeld said, still woolly-headed. She sat up in her seat. It was dark outside. "Where are we?"

He looked past her out the window. "Just left New York. Where ya headed?"

"Washington," she said.

"Business or pleasure?"

"Uh, pleasure. I'm meeting a friend."

"Hmm. I envy you. I'd love to go to Washington just once and not have to go to a meeting." He paused a moment. "I'm Marcus, by the way."

He extended a hand. She shook it.

"Sidney."

"And what do you do, Sidney?"

She hesitated, not feeling comfortable revealing anything about herself to a complete stranger. "I'm an antiquarian."

He laughed. "A what?"

"An antiquarian. I study old things. Mainly old books and manuscripts."

"Sounds a lot more interesting than what I do." He waited for her to ask the logical question. She didn't. "I'm a lawyer, by the way," he volunteered after an awkward pause. "I have to meet with our elected officials from time to time. That's a different breed. Now, some of them are good people, but too many of them get down there and get Potomac Fever and never want to leave."

Rosenfeld forced a smile. The Acela Express glided down the rails at 150mph. The lights of the small towns whizzed past the window. Passengers used overhead lights to read newspapers and books. Some worked on their computers.

"But here's another thing about congressmen. They expect rose petals at their feet," Marcus said. Rosenfeld tried to keep her sanity. He hadn't stopped talking since New York. "And they expect *me* to pay. That's the gall of these guys. Hell, I'm paying already. You're paying, we're all paying. Our tax dollars are paying their salaries. I mean, we're their bosses, and their handlers make sure we call *them* 'Congressman.' The congressman likes this, the congressman wants that. You know what they call me? They don't call me 'Mister.' They call me Marcus. That is, when they can remember my name. You know why? You know why they call me Marcus? Did you ever see *It's a Wonderful Life*? Remember when George Bailey goes to talk to Mr. Potter about a job? He sits down in that chair and it's so much lower than Mr. Potter's? That's why they do it. It's so they can look down on you. That's why these congressmen want to be called 'Congressman,' and they call you by your first name. Doesn't that just infuriate you?"

She felt as if she were being ear-raped. She pulled out her paperback and opened it to a dog-eared page. Marcus started to speak again but picked up on the not-so-subtle hint. He looked down at her book and smiled to himself then pulled out his newspaper.

They rolled along down the Northeast Corridor in silence. The only sound was Marcus rattling his paper as he turned pages and the muted hum of the steel wheels on the track. The Acela floated along with hypnotic grace.

The conductor made his way through the car as the train left Philadelphia's 30th Street Station. Rosenfeld continued to read. Her new travel mate was fast asleep with his newspaper folded across his chest. Just after Baltimore's Penn Station, Rosenfeld drifted off to sleep again with the book in her lap. She shook gently with the motion of the train. Her lips were turned up in a slight pout that made the now-awake Marcus wonder what she must be dreaming.

He gave her a gentle nudge and she was brought back to reality out of a deep sleep. "We're pulling into Union Station," he said.

She rubbed her eyes. "What? Oh, thanks."

She peered out the window at the drab interior of the platform. Marcus grabbed her overnight bag from the luggage rack for her, and she thanked him politely, not locking eyes with him for fear it would start him talking again. The groggy column of passengers heading for the terminal resembled the walking dead. They trudged toward Union Station, most heading for the front of the station and the cab stand. Rosenfeld hurried past the sluggish herd and saw Crow standing to the side waiting just inside the station. A second or two later, Marcus passed by.

"See ya, Sidney. Have a nice visit."

"Thanks," she answered.

"Who was that?" Crow sounded like a jealous husband.

"Some guy I sat next to on the train."

"You don't need to be talking to anybody. We don't know who to trust."

"Look, Crow, I've lived a long time without your help. I don't need you telling me what to do."

They began walking to the right then turned left toward the front of the train station.

"I'm just concerned about your safety, that's all."

"Well, that's very sweet of you, but I can handle myself."

Crow looked around and lowered his voice. "I don't think you understand who we're dealing with."

"I know exactly who we're dealing with, and if you want my insight, I'll be happy to give it to you."

They walked out through the automatic doors of the train station. The warm air hit them in the face. Even at eleven at night it was still muggy. Just a block from the train station was the Phoenix Park Hotel.

"Did you eat on the train?"

It hit Sidney that she was starving. "No."

They entered the front lobby of the hotel and headed for the elevators. Crow pressed the call button. He pointed to a door. "Right through there is The Dubliner. Get us a table. Here, let me have your bag. I'll put it in our room and meet you there. It'll be crowded and loud enough so we can talk without anyone else hearing us."

"Hold up a second, did you say *our* room?" Rosenfeld asked.

"Yes, *our* room," Crow said. "Two double beds. I roped you into all this. I can't let you out of my sight."

She raised an eyebrow.

"I don't bite, Rosenfeld."

"It's not your teeth I'm worried about."

An expression of recognition passed across the face of the black man in the suit who walked in unnoticed through the glass door entrance of the hotel.

"My own room, Crow," she said.

"OK, OK. I'll handle it."

Rosenfeld disappeared through the restaurant door and Crow watched the lights above the elevator. He got the uncomfortable feeling that someone was watching him. He looked sharply to his left and saw him. It wasn't just a casual glance or a curious gawk. The man was unmistakably looking at him. Not only that, he was walking his way.

Chapter Ten

The man they called Otto sat in his study in a high-back leather chair reading *The Life of Charlemagne* by Einhard with just a single reading lamp to light its pages. His senses told him something was imminent. He had an instinct for such things. Even so, he wasn't quite prepared. He never was. In those moments of doubt, he sought inspiration. He heard the distant footsteps growing closer.

Any successful organization needs hierarchy. Hierarchy breeds respect. Respect demands loyalty. Loyalty provides discipline. Discipline promotes fear. Otto didn't rise to the top position in the organization without a healthy dose of all, especially fear. He was known simply as Otto. No last name. No date of birth. No one dared inquire. He was referred to formerly as 'His Excellency.' He was born into the organization and rose through its ranks, but there was no such thing as tenure. He earned every promotion along his climb to the top. His word was final, his decision supreme. The only entity approaching his dominance was the council that placed him in this lofty position. No single person wielded as much power.

Otto was an imposing figure. His head, with its balding dome and large size, resembled that of a bull. His jowls gave him the distinction of a middle-aged executive. His gaze was penetrating and intimidating. He had a disconcertingly kind smile that turned into a terrifying scowl without warning. His temper was short. His decisions were quick. His retribution was lethal. He tolerated neither weakness nor incompetence, yet he expected no more from his subordinates than he did from himself. The operation was paramount. No one would deter him from its completion. No one.

"Your Excellency," the messenger said softly from the doorway. He had been dispatched from the nerve center of the complex. Otto placed the leather bookmark in the page of his book and turned his large face toward the young man. The messenger waited until Otto's attention was fully his before he spoke again. "It has begun." He waited for some sort of body language cue before he felt comfortable enough to leave. Otto smiled slightly then turned his head forward again. Satisfied the man had heard him, the messenger disappeared back down the hallway. Otto rose with some reluctance from his warm chair and placed the closed volume on the table. He stood there a moment in silent reflection then closed his eyes. He opened them again with a renewed sense of resolve and went back to work.

THE MAN WAS only a few feet away in the hotel lobby and was closing fast. Crow did a double take. He turned to engage him, but the man pushed Crow's outstretched hand aside and wrapped both arms around his neck. Crow was thrown off balance. The man squeezed hard. "Benson Crow," he howled. "I *will* be damned."

"Terrance Warner. Great to see you again. I was hoping I'd see you here. You working tonight?"

"Just came on." Terrance took a couple of steps backward. "Come talk to me." He walked behind the small check-in desk. "What brings you to Washington?"

Crow followed him over. "I'm doing some research for a book. I had reservations for just one room, but I need another. Next to each other, if possible. Sorry for the confusion."

"Yeah, I saw her when you two came in," Terrance said. "She's a looker. Overplayed your hand, did ya?"

It took Crow a second to catch his meaning. He smiled, "Oh, it's nothing like that. I'm just in charge of her safety. She's a bit on the stubborn side."

Terrance straightened himself. "Ain't nothin' gonna happen to her here. I can promise you that. Not on my watch. We have a hotel detective. You want me to have him keep an eye on your floor tonight?"

"That would be great. I really appreciate it." Crow signed the paper before him acknowledging the rate.

"What kind of trouble you expecting, Benson?"

"That's the problem. I don't exactly know. But I do know this." He looked up at Terrance. "It's trouble I have never seen before."

Crow found Rosenfeld at a two-top in the corner of the crowded restaurant. The long wooden bar was lined with after-work civil servants, congressional aides, and lobbyists. Crow took a seat at the table beside the small stage that held an Irish quartet on Friday and Saturday nights. The kitchen closed at 10:30pm, but Crow arranged to have a meal prepared for Rosenfeld. He ordered a Guinness.

"I didn't know if you were one of those vegan types," Crow said. "I took a chance with the Capitol Hill Burger."

"It's fine," she said, dipping a thick french fry in ketchup. The smile drained from her face. "I still can't believe Dr. Grumbling is dead."

"Well, we have two prime suspects. It was either the First Face of Janus or the Custos Verbi."

"I thought a lot about this on the train ride down here," she said. "I would guess the latter."

"So you know about them, too?"

"I do."

"How do you know so much about all this?"

"Dr. Grumbling. He was sort of like my mentor. There's no one who knew more about old manuscripts and books than he did. When I showed a special interest in Nostradamus editions, he finally let me into his confidence. He told me all about the First Facers and the CV and how historical events had been shaped by both of them."

"I'm sorry." Crow looked down. "I didn't know you and he were so close."

"It was a professional relationship, but I did adore the man."

"And you believe all this? This hocus-pocus about secret societies?"

"I do."

"Why?"

"It's a matter of logic. When you look at how closely Nostradamus' predictions line up with real events, it's amazing how accurate he is."

"But so many of these predictions miss the mark."

"For example?" she asked.

"Well, I did some research while I was waiting for you. For example, Nostradamus predicted somewhere in his writings that something big would happen in 1999. He even mentioned the month specifically. Nothing happened."

"You're referring to Century 10, Quatrain 72. 'The year 1999, seventh month / From the sky will come a great King of Terror / To bring back to life the great King of the Mongols / Before and after Mars to reign by good luck.'"

"Damn, girl. You are hardcore."

Rosenfeld laughed, "The life of an antiquarian nerd."

"But in July of 1999 there was supposed to be some king of terror who came back. It didn't happen."

"You think it didn't happen because you're looking in the wrong direction. When people hear 'King of the Mongols,' they think Genghis Khan. When they hear Genghis Khan, they think Chinese. The truth is, the Mongol Empire covered modern-day northern China, yes, but it was primarily modern-day Russia and four former republics of the Soviet Union. 'From the sky' was a colloquialism of Nostradamus' time. It meant roughly 'out of the blue' or 'suddenly and unexpectedly.' On August 9, 1999, Russian President Boris Yeltsin appointed a virtual unknown that nobody saw coming as acting prime minister. The announcement was made public in August. That decision was actually made in July, the seventh month. You know who that was?"

Crow looked at her with anticipation.

"His name was Vladimir Putin."

"The hair just stood up on the back of my neck right now," Crow said.

"And guess what he did."

Crow finished, "Putin set about annexing neighboring countries trying to put the old Soviet Union back together."

"Or what used to be known as the Mongol Empire. And then he cozied up to China to build an alliance there. Still think there's nothing to it?"

"How did everybody miss that one?" he asked.

"They're not in tune with the prophecies."

"And did the First Facers facilitate Putin's rise?"

"It's hard to tell," she said. "There's no doubt they helped bring about the end of the Soviet Union. Whether they played a direct role in Putin's ascent is unknown."

"So they do some good things, these people. Like defeating the Soviet Union."

"I guess you could say that," Rosenfeld said. "They don't really look at it as good or bad. It's just what has to be done to follow the blueprint laid out by Nostradamus."

"And the Custos Verbi?"

Her face soured as the server brought Crow's beer.

"I'm assuming you're not a fan," he said.

"I guess you could say that. It's just the motivation behind them."

"Aren't they stopping the First Facers from allowing some of the most horrible things in history to happen? I mean, Nostradamus doesn't seem like Mr. Sunshine. Most of his prophecies are rather depressing."

"If that were their only motivation I might agree."

"What do you mean?"

"The Church is all about control," she said. "They control what people know, and what they don't. They were the ones who decided what books of the Bible would be included and, more importantly, which books would be thrown out. They've always seen Nostradamus as a threat. Anyone who can predict the future—and predict it with such accuracy—can run rings around any religion that relies on a hierarchy to tell people what to think and how to behave. In other words, each time Nostradamus is proven right it undermines their grip on their followers. They have to prevent the prophecies from coming true, and they'll stop at nothing to do it."

"That's what tells me they weren't the ones behind the Grumbling murder," Crow said. "I'm trying to do the same thing. I'm trying to stop the next prophecy."

"But they have no way of knowing that. All they know is you were given the quatrains. They assume you're a First Facer yourself.

And they will kill you if they can find you. Believe me, if you think the Church is powerful, you ain't seen nothin' like the Custos Verbi. They have agents all over the world. And these folks are die-hard zealots. They are absolutely relentless." She took a bite of her burger.

"That's just it," Crow said. "They could've killed me today, but the drone just flew away."

Sidney finished chewing. "Maybe they thought they got you."

"Maybe. I don't know, I just found that part odd." Crow took a long drink from his glass. "You don't buy Grumbling's theory that the old man in Montreal was Custos Verbi?"

"Dr. Grumbling was a brilliant man, but I have to disagree with him on this. I think the guy was a First Facer."

"What's he doing with the quatrains?" Crow asked.

"Helping to fulfill the prophecy, naturally."

"They just carry things like that around, quatrains from the Unriddled Manuscript?"

"Who said they came from the Unriddled Manuscript?" Rosenfeld said.

"Where else would they come from?"

"They could be his own notes shrouded in mystery just like Nostradamus but meaningful to him or whoever else is helping see to it that the prophecy comes true."

"Why would he give me the quatrains?"

"For safekeeping maybe," she said. "If he knew the CV was closing in on him, then maybe he passed them off to you hoping to come back later and get them."

"Which he never did because they killed him," Crow added.

"They killed him because he no longer had the quatrains on him," she said, "and once the Custos Verbi realized he no longer had the quatrains on him, they figured out he handed them to you in that restroom and they tracked you to Grumbling."

"OK, let's go with that theory. It's clear they know who I am. They didn't just pick Grumbling's place at random. They picked it because I was there, because they were following me from Montreal. Even if they think they got me, I can't go back home. They're apparently watching my place. Gordy, my caretaker, told me two men came looking for me."

"Let me explain something," Rosenfeld said. "If they sent people looking for you, going home is definitely out. Even if they get the quatrains from you, they're still going to have to kill you. You know too much."

"Then I have to make contact with them."

She snickered, "Are you serious?"

Crow stared back at her.

"You *are* serious," she said. "What do you mean, *make contact with them*? If you're on their radar, and evidently you are, the only contact they'll have with you is a bullet in the brain."

"Yeah, but what if I tell them I'm on their side?"

"You won't have a chance to tell them," Rosenfeld said. "It's not like you walk into the home office and announce yourself."

"Really? Why not?"

"Come on, Crow. You're talking nonsense now."

"Listen to me. We have to show them that we're trying to stop the prophecy. You know, like holding our hands out to show them we're not armed. But we have to make sure they see that. They're bound to have a base of operations. I know it's not like walking into some corporate headquarters, but they have to work from somewhere. The Vatican maybe?"

"Well, I can tell you it's not the Vatican," she said.

"How do you know?"

"For starters, the Vatican is too obvious. The pope also needs plausible deniability. I think they're headquartered far away from Rome."

"Where then?"

Rosenfeld shrugged.

Crow tapped his index finger on his glass then looked up. "I have an old friend I think we need to visit in the morning. He works at the National Archives. I've used him as a source for a couple of my books. He's into all this secret society stuff. Maybe he can help us."

"In finding the CV?"

"That and decoding those quatrains. I have to prove to these people that we're not part of the conspiracy to fulfill Nostradamus' prophecy. We have to do something to demonstrate to the Custos Verbi that we're on their side. Otherwise, we'll spend the rest of our lives running." He took another drink of beer. "If we're going to stay alive, we only have one play. We *have* to stop that prophecy."

Chapter Eleven

Kyle O'Hara was not what one would expect a deputy archivist at the National Archives and Records Administration to be. Deputy archivists are usually businesslike and buttoned down. They take themselves and their jobs extremely seriously and demand a respectful reverence around the items they study. O'Hara was none of that. He wore a rather unorthodox sport coat with no socks and no tie. He was a tad on the plus side with hair over his ears. Hard to tell if he was trying to grow a beard or just hadn't bothered to shave for a couple of days. He was examining a document under a binocular microscope when Crow and Rosenberg came calling at his office at 700 Pennsylvania Avenue, NW. It was Tuesday morning.

"Kyle, this is Dr. Sidney Rosenfeld. She's an antiquarian at Rothschild's in Boston."

"Nice to meet you," Kyle shook her offered hand.

Crow said, "I wanted to get your opinion on this quatrain."

"Yeah, I'll take a look. First, check out this signature, dude."

He led Crow over to the microscope. Crow put his eyes to the glass.

"Wow. Abraham Lincoln."

"Is it?" O'Hara asked.

"Looks like it to me. Of course, I'm no expert."

"Let me see," Rosenfeld said, leaning down to the eyepiece. She stood upright. "It's a fake."

"And how do you know?" O'Hara asked.

"The upstroke on the last 'n' in Lincoln."

"And what's wrong with it?"

"Lincoln had more of a hook. This one's not quite tall enough."

O'Hara looked at Crow. "I think I'm in love." He turned to Rosenfeld. "What are you doing later? Could we possibly get married this afternoon?"

Rosenfeld giggled.

"You're exactly right," O'Hara said. "Brava, Dr. Rosenfeld. Some clown wanted us to fork over seventeen grand for that." He turned to Crow. "She doesn't *look* Jewish." He turned back to Rosenfeld. "You don't *look* Jewish."

"Kyle, we're sort of in a hurry. Can you take a look at this?" He produced the red velvet sleeve from his coat pocket.

O'Hara donned his white gloves. He pulled the book out and laid it on the table. "Nice. Nice. Did you steal this?"

"No, I didn't *steal* it. It was given to me. Some old guy gave it to me at a book signing in Montreal."

"He *gave* it to you?" O'Hara turned the pages with care. "He must be some fan." He turned another page then looked up. "Twenty grand."

"That's what I told him," Rosenfeld said.

Kyle's smiling eyes lingered on her.

"I'm not interested in selling it," Crow said. "This is what I really need your help with." He showed him the paper with the quatrains. "This came with the book."

Kyle studied it for a moment. "Yeah, like, it's in French."

"Oh," Crow said. "I thought you might..."

"Speak French?" Kyle said. "I took a few years in high school and college. I can order wine in Paris, but that's as urbane as I get."

Crow handed him his pad with the translated verses.

"That's more like it." Kyle read the eight lines. "Definitely not Nostradamus but certainly someone who's intimately familiar with him."

"Like, maybe, the First Face of Janus?" Crow asked.

O'Hara looked up slowly from the pad. "How do you know about them?"

"Apparently you do, too," Crow said. "It looks like I'm the only one who didn't."

"Is that who gave you this?" Kyle asked.

"We don't know. The man who passed this along to me was killed shortly after."

"Jeez, man." He glanced suspiciously around the room as if someone were watching. "Why couldn't you stick to writing cyberpunk or whatever it is you write? This is major league stuff, bro."

"Any guesses on what the quatrains mean?"

"Well, I would say they refer to Century 4, Quatrain 71."

"That's what I told him," Rosenfeld said.

O'Hara gave her a flirty glance and a wink. "This part," he said to both of them, "'His first face sees' certainly means the First Face of Janus. 'When the clock strikes twelve.' Hmmm." He opened a drawer and scrambled around for his book of quatrains then opened to the one in question. He read the four lines to himself. "I'd say a wedding, maybe. That would be my guess. 'Add the note of C twice / And take away the score,'" he said, referring back to the notepad. "Sounds like something musical. Maybe the score is a musical score. I don't know. I'm gonna have to pass on that part. 'Count on good stock / Rich in grace.' Probably something to do with a fine family? All this is maybe."

"Any chance this is from the Unriddled Manuscript?" Crow asked.

Kyle looked at Rosenfeld then at Crow. "How do you know about that?"

"I just know. Is it from the Unriddled Manuscript?"

"Doubtful."

"Why?"

"Because it's still riddled, dude. My guess is it's meant for internal use."

Rosenfeld cleared her throat.

"What?" Kyle said.

"That was her theory, too," Crow said. "How do we figure out what it means?"

"If you're in the clique, you probably understand all this gobbledygook," Kyle said. "Of course, you're obviously not in the clique."

"The Custos Verbi is trying to stop him," Rosenfeld said.

"We think," Crow added. "We're not exactly sure what's going on."

"Jeez, you've got the CV on your ass, too? What did you do to piss these people off?"

"Nothing. I was minding my own business. This thing drops in my lap. I go see a guy named Dr. Grumbling in Virginia."

"An old professor friend of mine," Rosenfeld said.

"He tells me all about the First Facers and the CV," Crow said, "and they shoot him dead right in front of me."

"Holy crap!" O'Hara covered his mouth then lowered his hand to his chin. "The CV killed him?"

"And his housekeeper," Rosenfeld said.

"We *think* it's the CV," Crow said.

"They used a drone," Rosenfeld added.

Kyle's eyes darted back and forth between them.

"And we *think* they killed the man in Montreal," Crow said. "The man who gave me the book and the quatrains."

"Look, man," Kyle said, "I don't know how far into this thing you are, but extricate yourself, like, right now. You've fallen right into the middle of a prophecy war."

Crow's look told him he was not dissuaded.

"I'm serious," O'Hara said. "That's what they call these things. They've been going on for centuries. These people play for keeps, man. For real. Get out while you still can. Go back to your Bingabobians and other space creatures you've created and forget you ever saw those quatrains."

"Somebody's got to stop this," Crow said.

"Are you frickin' kidding me? What are you, Superman? Benson, listen to me. You *cannot* stop this. Whatever happens happens. Comprender, amigo?" He turned to Rosenfeld. "I speak a little Spanish, too."

"I get it," Crow said, "but I can't help but think there's a book in here somewhere."

"A book?" He looked at Sidney with helpless exasperation then back at Crow with disbelief. "A book? Is that what this is all about? A book?"

"No, that's not what it's *all* about. Somebody's gotten me involved in this for a reason."

"Yeah, because you're stupid. Get out of it."

"The curiosity is killing me."

"Yeah, dude, it just might."

"I've got to chase this rabbit a little further. I've got to find the Custos Verbi and show them I'm on their side."

O'Hara gave him an astonished look then turned to Rosenfeld. "Is he serious?" He turned back to Crow. "Are you serious? You're playing with nitroglycerin."

"Listen to me, Kyle. I'm in too deep now. I'm a marked man. I can't go home. I can't go to my publishing company in New York. I can't surface until I convince these people that I'm not a First Facer. I'm like a fugitive." He looked at Rosenfeld. "We both are."

"How about all three of us," O'Hara said.

"I wouldn't do that to you," Crow said. "I made damn sure we weren't followed here. They wouldn't have any quarrel with you."

"Yeah," Kyle smirked, "like that old dude in Virginia?"

"Grumbling was up to his neck in this thing. He knew everything about the CV and the First Facers and they knew it. You don't know that much, do you?"

O'Hara said nothing.

"Do you?" Crow asked again.

"No. I'm not like some expert on this. I hear things, OK? I'm curious but not too curious. Know what I mean? Let me put it this way. I know enough to know that I don't get involved with anybody who's fallen into a prophecy war."

"But if we walk out of here empty-handed, I don't know where in the hell we can go, Kyle. We have to find them before they find us."

Kyle O'Hara looked at him for a moment. "OK, look, if you're determined to stay in this thing—"

"I don't have any choice."

"I get it. If you're in for the duration, then you need to go see somebody who eats and sleeps this stuff. He might be able to lead you to the CV."

"Who's that?" Crow asked.

"You didn't hear it from me."

"I promise."

"His name is Jean-Claude Delacroix. He's like the Nostradamus guru, man. He's the resident scholar at La Maison de Nostradamus in Salon-de-Provence."

"France?"

"Yeah, France. And if he doesn't know what these quatrains mean, surely somebody over there will. Nostradamus is like a cottage industry in those parts."

"What about the book itself?"

"This thing?" O'Hara put it back in its sleeve and handed it to Crow. "It means nothing."

"Then, why did he give it to me?"

O'Hara pulled the white gloves from his hands. "Let me ask you something. If some guy showed up at a book signing and gave you a sheet of paper, what would you do with it?"

"I'd toss it."

"Exactly. Even if he put it inside a contemporary book it would hit the circular file, or even if you kept it you'd never look inside. He gave you a valuable ancient book to get your attention and guess what, bro? He got it."

"But why me? I know so little about Nostradamus."

"I don't know, man. Maybe because you're gullible enough to get involved, but this is shadow government stuff like you've never seen. I'm tellin' you, it is bad news."

"Could be, but I've got to follow this thing until I clear myself. I do that by proving to the Custos Verbi that I'm on their side. I do that by stopping this prophecy."

"And you think stopping the prophecy will prove to them you're not a First Facer?"

"Yes," Crow said.

"Yeah, well, good luck with all that. Look, I'll give you Delacroix's info, but that's as far as I go, man. Keep me the hell out of all this."

They left with Delacroix's contact information and descended the steps of the Archives building. Rosenfeld caught a familiar face out of the corner of her eye.

"It's Marcus," she said under her breath.

"Who?" Crow asked.

"The guy from the train," she said through clenched teeth. "This guy'll talk your ear off." She flashed a look his way. "Oh, crap. He's coming toward us."

When Marcus was about five steps away he called for her. "Sidney?"

She turned around trying to act surprised. "Marcus? What are you doing here?"

"I thought that was you. I was going to ask you the same thing. Doing some sightseeing?"

"Yes. Yes, we were. Oh, Marcus, this is my friend Benson Crow. Benson, this is Marcus…"

"Foster," Marcus finished for her. "Nice to meet you."

They shook hands.

"Nice to meet you," Crow returned. "So, Marcus, what brings *you* here?"

"Oh, me? I have a meeting inside."

"I see. Who with?" Crow interrogated.

"Benson," Rosenfeld scolded.

"No, that's OK," Foster said. "I'm, uh, I'm meeting with the deputy archivist."

"Is that so?" Crow exchanged a quick look with Rosenfeld. "What about," he pressed, "if you don't mind my asking."

"Not at all. I have a client. He has a letter written by Abe Lincoln. We're trying to make a deal with the National Archives."

Crow backed down. That was a little too specific to be made up. That or this was the luckiest guy on the planet. "Lincoln, huh?" Crow said.

"Yeah, the guy's grandfather died and he found this letter in his papers. Pretty cool stuff," Foster said.

"Yeah," Crow said. "Pretty cool."

"Well, good luck. It was nice to see you again," Rosenfeld said.

"Likewise. You folks enjoy your visit."

She and Crow turned and continued down the sidewalk. Crow's cellphone rang.

"Tom?"

"OK, so it took me a day to figure this out," Tom Browning said.

"You found a wedding that fit the quatrains?"

Browning laughed, "You're getting me back for making you go to Montreal."

"What are you talking about?"

"This whole story," Browning said. "You had me sucked in."

"This is no joke, Tom. The guy in Montreal gave me Nostradamus' book of prophecies and the quatrains."

"Yeah, I got all that," Browning said, "and the next prophecy has something to do with a wedding."

"That's what we believe," Crow said.

"We?"

"Dr. Rosenfeld and me."

"Dr. Rosenfeld?"

"She's with Rothschild's in Boston."

"She?"

"Yes. She's an expert on Nostradamus. She's here with me."

"Let me guess. Some gray-haired little old lady with a beaded eyeglasses chain attached to her horn rims?"

"Not exactly."

"Uh-huh. That's what I thought. Hot chick with that librarian thing going on?"

"Stop it, Tom!"

"You stop it, Benson. You send me on a wild goose chase looking for some wedding. I did a search on the Internet. There's nothing about the First Face of Janus. There's nothing about the Custos Verbi. Explain that."

"I can't explain it, but everything I've told you is true. I swear it. The First Face of Janus and the Custos Verbi are very real."

"Yeah, like Dr. Grumbling and his housekeeper?"

"Yes, like Grumbling and his housekeeper."

"There was no murder, Benson."

"What?"

"The police checked it out. Nothing but an old plantation house. No Grumbling. No housekeeper. No murder."

"That's impossible."

"They found the owner. He's very much alive, and he's not some old guy named Grumbling. It's a guy named Stevenson. Fortyish. He and his family live in Georgetown. The plantation has been in his family for generations."

"So he rented it to Dr. Grumbling, right?"

"No, Benson. You're not listening to me. The place has been empty for twenty years. There *is* no Dr. Grumbling."

Chapter Twelve

"Alejandro, they were here again," the mustachioed man said softly into the phone in Spanish.

"Did you record them this time?" The small man's hand was barely large enough to grasp the smartphone.

"I did."

"And?"

"And it was more of the same. Small talk. Nothing."

"Nothing?"

"Just two men talking about books."

"What kind of books?"

"Don Quixote."

"What else?" the little man asked.

"Something about a cousin and a fortress. I fear my suspicions may have been misplaced."

"Carlos, I trust your instincts. We are in this together. You think that it is them, then it is them."

"And if I am wrong?"

"Then we have surreptitiously recorded the conversation of two old men discussing their favorite books. No harm done."

"And what about the prophecy?" Carlos asked.

"Sh-h-h," Alejandro scolded, "never ever speak of it on the telephone. Is that understood?"

The mustachioed man dropped his eyes. "I am sorry. Never again. I promise."

"I'M JUST ASKING you to trust me, Tom. As long as we've been together you owe me that much."

Sidney Rosenfeld eyed Crow with concern. "What's wrong?" she whispered.

He held up a finger. "I can't relax, dammit! Somebody's trying to kill me! Would you relax if somebody was trying to kill you?" Rosenfeld frowned. "Please, Tom, just do me this favor, OK? Keep checking on those weddings and call me when you have something. I promise you, this is not a hoax. Great. Thanks." Crow ended the phone call. "That's impossible," he almost screamed back at the phone. "I saw Grumbling die!"

"What did he say?" Rosenfeld asked.

"Tom says the cops were there at Grumbling's place within twenty minutes of my call. He says there was nothing there. No bodies, no blood, no furniture, no nothing."

"Are you sure they had the right house?"

"It was the right house. Same address. I dropped a pin. He says Grumbling didn't even own the house. Some guy in Georgetown does."

"I know that's not right," she said. "I've been there myself. So, he thinks you made it all up?"

"Yeah, basically. He thinks I'm playing a joke on him." They walked a few steps before Crow asked, "If Tom's right and there was no murder scene, who could pull off something like that?"

"What do you mean?"

"I mean it's clear Grumbling and his housekeeper were murdered. Who could possibly come in, clean it up, and make it look like it never happened?"

"It would make sense that it was the people who killed him," she said. "You have to look at motive plus the resources to be able to make a double murder disappear that quickly. There's only one organization that fits. The Custos Verbi."

The flying time from Dulles to Paris was seven-and-a-half hours. Tedious if spent in coach. Delightful in first class for even the most jaded traveler. Stainless steel cutlery, prime cuts of beef, champagne, sumptuous desserts. It's how successful authors traveled, or those who fancied themselves so. Rosenfeld took in her opulent surroundings while the first class flight attendant removed her dinner plate.

"I could get used to this," she said. "I wish Rothschild's treated us this good."

Crow smiled and took a sip from his cocktail.

"Why are you doing this?" she asked.

"Flying first class?"

"No. Why are you chasing this story?"

"Well, seeing as how somebody's trying to kill me and I can't go home, I don't have much choice, now do I? I can either sit around my house and wait for the bullet, or I can try to get out in front of this."

"Is that really the reason?"

He pulled his bag from underneath the seat. "Isn't that enough?"

"Come on, you're an author. This is a juicy story. Aren't you the least bit curious as to how it ends?"

He pawed through his bag. "Sure, I guess. I'm more curious as to how I get my life back. Why are you with me?"

"You really have to ask? You dragged me into this, remember? I was perfectly content with my work before you crashed into my life."

Crow dug down deeper into the bag. "Yeah, well, I'm sorry about that."

Rosenfeld smiled. "Don't be. Actually, I've had a fascination with this whole story for years. I never would've pursued this on my own. It's not my nature. I'm just not very adventurous. I've always lived vicariously through the books I've read. Now I have a chance to actually get close to a subject I'm really enthralled by."

Crow checked the side pockets of his bag.

"What are you looking for?" she asked.

"My phone charger. I think I left it in the first class lounge."

"You can use mine."

"Let me see your phone."

She held it up.

"Thanks, but it's not compatible with mine."

"You can always buy another one."

"No, I'll tell the airline where I left it. They'll hold it for me."

"If you can afford two first class tickets, you can probably swing for a phone charger."

"It's no big deal. I charged up before we got on the plane. I'll just turn it on when I need to use it. Those damn international fees will eat you alive anyway."

Rosenfeld scrunched her eyebrows. "You ever heard the term penny wise and pound foolish?"

Crow turned to her. "Let me explain something. I don't mind spending money on things that are worth it. Like first class tickets, for example. What I *do* mind is wasting money. Takes money away from things I like to spend my money on. Like first class tickets." He smiled at the logic.

"Whatever. It's your money." Rosenfeld closed her eyes and sunk back luxuriously in her seat. "I've never been able to sleep on a plane.

Then again, I've never flown first class to Europe. Pardon me while I give it a shot."

Crow reclined his own seat and reflected on the reality of their predicament. He'd researched a lot of books but never one where his own life hung in the balance. What had he gotten himself into? Everyone kept telling him to leave it alone, to suspend the chase. His better judgment told him so, but he couldn't. More than not being able to go home, it was a burning curiosity. The story had everything his imagination could have ever conjured up. He had to see it through. He stared out into the nothingness that lay outside his window until he could no longer keep his eyes open.

School would be letting out any moment. It was his mother's day off at the diner. She told him to come straight home after school. Benson Crow gathered up his backpack and hurried up the river embankment. The afternoon sun beat down on his head. He could feel the burn in his calves, still he pumped the pedals faster.

Upon rounding the corner onto his street, he noticed something different right away. A strange car sat in his driveway. An ugly green one that looked vaguely familiar, but he couldn't quite place it. He dropped the bike in the dirt and opened the screen door to the kitchen. He wondered who was visiting. It dawned on him where he'd seen that green car about the time he saw the gentleman who sat in the easy chair in the den beside his mother on the sofa.

"You know Vice Principal Rotch, I'm sure," his mother said.

Benson said nothing.

"You didn't show up for school again today," Mr. Rotch said. "We became concerned."

"Where have you been, Benson?"

"I've been down by the river."

"What were you doing at the river?" Rotch asked.

"That's where he goes to write," his mother said.

Vice Principal Rotch laughed. "Is that so? You skip school and all the writing assignments so you can write?"

"Benson does have a vivid imagination," she said.

"I should say so. That's quite an imaginative excuse."

"I know my son, Mr. Rotch. He's no liar."

"You'll excuse me, Mrs. Crow, but I tend not to trust truants."

"He's not a truant."

"In the eyes of the law he is, and he's putting you in jeopardy, too. I can have him arrested right now. If he's found guilty, a judge can fine you or sentence you to community service for having a truant child."

"Me?"

"That's right."

"But he's 16," she said.

"Compulsory school age in this state is until age 17. He's in violation of the law, which means *you* have to pay the price."

"*I* have to pay?"

"That's the law."

She looked at Benson for a long moment while she spoke to the vice principal. "Are you going to have him arrested?"

Rotch rose from his seat. "No, not this time."

"Are you going to suspend me?" Crow asked.

Rotch smirked, "That's exactly what you'd want me to do." He walked past Crow. A bit too close for Crow's taste. "We'll expect you at school in the morning, Mr. Crow. I won't be so lenient next time. And I won't give you the satisfaction of a suspension, but I *will* bet you don't want to see your mother writing the judge a check."

When she heard the screen door slam, she let him have it. "What the hell do you think you're doing?" She lit a cigarette and threw the lighter on the coffee table.

"I don't know. School's boring. I had some ideas I wanted to work on."

"You think you're the first kid that hated school? The rest of 'em just suck it up and go. What makes you think you're so special?"

Benson lowered his head. He'd heard this speech before.

"No, really," she said. "What makes you think you're so damn special? You think you're better than everybody else in this town?"

He shook his head.

"I mean it. You've always acted like that. Like this little piece of shit town ain't got enough going on for you. Like you somehow deserve better. Well, I got news for you, sweetie. You ain't no better than the rest of us. You ain't no different and you ain't no better. You're grounded, you hear me? You come home every day right after you're done at the feed store. I mean it. Don't you walk away from me when I'm talking to you!"

Crow hiked his backpack further up on his shoulder and walked down the hall to his room. He didn't know how to tell her he lost the job at the feed store two days ago.

"Benson Crow, you come back here! Benson!"

"Benson," Rosenfeld said again, tugging on his arm.

His senses came to life.

"You're having a nightmare."

"What?" He rubbed his eyes. "Sorry." He pulled himself up in his seat.

"What on earth were you dreaming?"

"Hmm? Oh, nothing. I don't remember."

"Anything you want to talk about?"

He stretched his locked hands out in front of him and cracked his knuckles. "What are you, my shrink now?" he yawned.

"I'm just trying to be helpful. Maybe talking about it would—"

"Well, I appreciate that, but there's nothing I need to talk about."

Rosenfeld's expression betrayed her skepticism.

"Why do people always want to take me in like a stray dog?" Crow asked.

"Maybe they can tell behind that nasty bark there's a lost puppy."

"I don't want to be anybody's pet."

Rosenfeld glanced over at him. "Bottling things up isn't healthy. You know that, don't you?"

Crow looked back at her. "Trust me, you don't want to pop the cork on this bottle."

Chapter Thirteen

The plane touched down at Charles de Gaulle just before eight-thirty Wednesday morning. Crow and Rosenfeld waited through customs. His eyes darted from face to face trying to catch someone staring.

"Anything to declare, monsieur?"

Crow seemed startled.

"Anything to declare?" the customs agent repeated.

"Declare? No, nothing to declare."

"Are you here for business or pleasure?" she asked.

"Uh, business. No, pleasure."

The agent looked at him curiously. "Which one is it, monsieur?"

"What damn difference does it make?" he asked. "Every time I come to this country you ask me that. Do you keep some kind of tally or do you do that just to annoy the foreigners?"

Rosenfeld sidled up next to him. "Honey," she smiled at the agent. "The lady's just doing her job. Pleasure. He's here for pleasure."

"I asked *him*," the humorless agent said.

Crow managed a smile. "It's pleasure. Just seeing the sights."

The agent kept an eye on him while she stamped his passport. He moved forward and Rosenfeld pushed over her passport.

"Sorry about that," she said. "He had a rough flight. Nothing to declare for me. Here for pleasure."

The agent returned a sour look and stamped her passport. A supervisor observed sternly from a few feet behind the agent. He watched them walk away and picked up the phone.

"For somebody who hasn't done anything, you sure look guilty as hell," Rosenfeld said, catching up to Crow.

"I can't stand these frickin' power people."

"Attention: s'il vous plaît, restez avec vos bagages en tout temps. Tous les bagages sans surveillance seront détruits," the sultry female voice announced over the airport loudspeakers.

Rosenfeld giggled.

"What?" Crow asked.

Then the announcer translated her message into English. "Attention: please stay with your baggage at all times. Any unattended baggage will be blown up."

"It sounds so sexy when they say it in French," Rosenfeld said.

A group of six French soldiers wearing battle dress uniforms, flack jackets, and maroon berets ambled past making small talk with one another. Side arms were affixed to their belts and, most conspicuously, their arms rested on automatic weapons slung from their necks. Rosenfeld stared at them.

"My God," she said. "I feel like I'm in some sort of military dictatorship."

"Would you rather take your chances with the terrorists?" Crow asked.

"If this is the way these people have to live, it looks like the terrorists have already won."

"Paris has been an international battleground for decades," Crow said. "I'm sure the people here are used to it by now."

"Yeah, and that's a shame." She tried to keep pace. "Where are we going?"

"TGV station."

"TGV?" she asked.

"It stands for Train à Grande Vitesse," he explained.

"High-speed train," she said.

The train station, connected to the airport, was a superstructure of white metal and glass and a great expanse of marble floor. Crow booked them two tickets on the 9:58am train then led Rosenfeld down an escalator. They waited for their train to arrive. Crow inspected the faces of the others who stood around reading their newspapers and checking their phones.

"I think we lost them," Rosenfeld's voice dripped with sarcasm.

He shot her a disapproving look.

"Crow, we're almost 4,000 miles from home."

He looked over at her then back out at the crowd. "If these folks kill with drones, then nothing is out of the question."

"See anybody suspicious?" she asked.

"Not yet, but I don't really know who I'm looking for."

"Then why are you looking?"

"Just to see if someone is looking at us."

"Well, don't freak out and jump one of your fans. That would be embarrassing."

He turned to her. "You think this is funny, don't you?"

"No, I don't think this is funny. Well, your Nervous Ned routine is rather humorous. Actually, it's kind of irritating. You're making me jumpy."

"You need to take this more seriously."

"Relax, Crow. We're in Paris."

Crow turned angry but tried not to raise his voice. "I just saw a man gunned down right in front of me, and I almost tripped over another dead body. I'll be damned if I'm going to relax. We're into something extremely dangerous."

"Don't you think I know that?"

"No, I don't think you know that. I'm just being cautious."

"A little overly cautious, if you ask me."

"When somebody's trying to kill you, there's no such thing as overly cautious."

Their attention was diverted to the train arriving. The breeze blew the ladies' skirts as it slid into the station. The high whine faded and the brakes whispered until the locomotive came to a full stop. Passengers disembarked. Crow and Rosenfeld boarded and stowed their belongings overhead. The train glided away from the station.

"I didn't mean to make you mad," she said.

He gazed out the window. "I don't think you understand the gravity of our situation."

"I do," she said. "I really do. It's just that I don't get out much. You probably figured that out already. The sudden trip to France. Flying first class. I just got caught up in the excitement. I haven't really let myself stop and think beyond today. We *are* in a bit of a mess, aren't we?"

"Yes, we are. It's funny though. I've often daydreamed about disappearing somewhere in the world. Now that we're having to do it, it's not nearly as easy as I thought."

"Nor as much fun," Rosenfeld said.

After the graffiti and the decay of Paris passed from their window, it was replaced by fields of green and amber broken up by quaint villages and the occasional medieval structure. Every now and then a church spire passed in the distance. They chatted until Rosenfeld decided to curl up against the window. Crow warned her not to sleep.

"But I'm exhausted," she complained.

"We'll sleep tonight," he said. "Your body will never acclimate to the new time if you give into it the first day."

"A seasoned traveler, I see."

"I've learned the hard way."

"Do you have to travel a lot?"

"I don't *have* to. I love it, actually."

"Research for your books?"

Crow chuckled. "I write sci-fi. No amount of traveling is going to prepare you for that. I just enjoy getting away. Being someplace else."

"You travel alone?"

He looked out the window. "I'm not married, if that's what you were asking."

"I wasn't."

"I just enjoy traveling by myself."

"Thanks," she said.

He hadn't given a thought to how his comment sounded. "I don't mean now. I just mean in general. I come over here and ride the rails for days."

"All alone?"

"All alone."

"What do you do with yourself?"

"I write. I sleep. I read. I get off whenever the fancy strikes me. I explore new towns and cities. Go to museums. Sample the local food."

"You didn't say anything about the people."

He smiled. "I'm not much of a people person."

"Really."

He ignored the sarcasm. "I don't hate them. Traveling around like this wouldn't be much fun without other people, but I prefer to keep them at a distance."

"I see. Is that pretty much your life story? Keeping people at a distance?"

He thought about the question. "Let's just say I prefer to keep to myself."

A train passing the other way screamed past their window then was gone.

"So, it's just you and your novels."

"I guess you could say that."

"No time for anything or any*one* else?"

He looked at her with a quizzical look. "You psychoanalyzing me again?"

"Just curious," she said. "I like to see what makes people tick."

"I'm really not that complicated."

But he knew that was a lie. He tended to repaint the ordinary world into a more interesting place than it really was. The romanticized European train ride was an adventure to Crow. It was simply a means of transportation to the average European commuter. A relatively inexpensive way to get from Point A to Point B. Boring, in fact, were it not for the music coming from their earbuds or the print from their newspapers or tablets. To Crow, it was *Murder on the Orient Express*. He loved everything about it. The platform. The sounds. The smells. The cozy confines of first class. The claustrophobia of a sleeper car. He purposely waited to eat until he could enjoy the dining car. He mourned when the train schedules converted from the flap displays of the Solari boards to digital. He was old-fashioned that way.

"You're more interested in your books than you are in real people."

Crow smiled. "I find fantasy to be much more interesting than reality."

"Maybe you should give reality a chance," she said.

"Believe me, I have."

The closer to Avignon they drew the hillier the terrain became.

Small castles, or what was left of them, dotted the high ground here and there. A white glider turned lazily and followed their path before the speeding train made it just a memory. Amorphous clouds hovered over the landscape, some dark with rain. The sun fought its way to the ground between the clumps of white and gray. The hillsides grew to mountains and the dark clouds overtook the puffy ones.

An ocean away, Terrance Warner staggered to his parked car in front of his apartment in Washington, D.C. The blood was still fresh on his face. The gun was still warm in his hand. He fumbled for the key fob and unlocked the door. Throwing himself into the driver's seat, he slammed the door and locked it. He dabbed the cut on his lip with the back of his free hand then reached down and returned the pistol to the holster attached to his thigh. He pulled the mirror down to assess the damage to his eye. It was bruised but nothing a little ice wouldn't take care of. The sun was just starting to rise. He reached in his pocket for his phone, hit the contact, and held it to his ear. He winced looking in the mirror as the phone rang.

Crow frowned and answered, "Terrance?"

"When you said this was trouble you'd never seen before, you won't shittin'."

"What?"

"Two thugs. One white dude, one black. Caught me coming home from my shift. Damn, I need to pay better attention. Just locked the car and was heading up the steps to my apartment when they jumped me. White guy held me while the black dude interrogated me. Wanted to know where you were. I told him I had no idea. The dude did a number on my face. I didn't know anything. Wouldn't have told him if I did."

"Oh, my God. I had no idea they'd come for you."

"Ain't no problem, my friend. Those two dudes wished they'd never screwed with Terrance Warner."

"What happened?"

"I managed to bust loose long enough to reach my piece. White dude grabbed my arm. Got off a shot and I just did miss blowing the brother's head off. Knocked me back down and the gun went flyin'. With all the commotion I guess they knew the neighbors would be coming out to see what was happening, so they bolted. Picked up my gun and aimed, but they were already around the corner."

"Man, I am so sorry."

Terrance dabbed the bloody corner of his mouth. "Don't be. That's what friends are for."

Crow sank in his seat.

"Besides," Terrance said, "as far as my story goes, I just fended off two carjackers." He laughed, "I'm gonna be the neighborhood badass."

"Terrance, I don't know what to say."

"Ain't nothin' *to* say. Just wanted to let you know they're on your trail. Watch your back." He looked up to see a police cruiser pulling in front of his car and neighbors standing on their stoops in their bathrobes. "Hey, gotta run. The cops are here. Time to go be a hero."

The line went dead.

"Terrance from the hotel," Crow said to Rosenfeld. "Sounds like the same guys who came looking for me at the farm found him. They beat him up looking for us."

Concern was etched on her face. She turned her head toward the window with tears in her eyes.

Crow stared at her. "Still think this is a vacation?"

They pulled into Avignon TGV Station just past one in the afternoon. Crow gazed up at the modern 1,115-foot glazed roof of silver and white and thought how much it looked like a futuristic cathedral in one of his books. From the outside, it appeared to be an immense quonset hut. The entrance of the station resembled a bunker with grass-covered berms to either side, a place where one might seek refuge from a nuclear blast. They rented a small but luxurious Mercedes-Benz for the forty-minute drive to Salon-de-Provence from the rental agency across the parking lot on the north side of the station. The rental agent was extremely helpful showing them how to enter the address of their destination into the car's GPS. She waved them goodbye from the parking lot with a smile then retrieved her phone from her pocket.

Crow checked his rearview mirror every few seconds for signs they were being tailed. He also tilted his side mirror from time to time to scan the skies.

"You really believe you can stop them, don't you?" Rosenfeld said.

Crow checked his paranoia. "If I can get just one step behind them, yes. I don't believe in this fatalistic crap. Nothing's etched in stone."

She smiled at him then looked out the windshield at the road. "Maybe Dr. Grumbling and Kyle were right. Maybe you can't stop them. They've been doing this for nearly 500 years."

"Is that why you're here? To give me moral support?" he asked with a little bite in his tone.

"No, in fact, I'm here to give you intellectual support and expert advice."

"Are you ready to give up?"

She paused. "No, actually, I'm not. At least not until after we've seen what Delacroix has to say. At some point, though, you may have to determine that the code is uncrackable. I mean, think about the history here. They've apparently been able to watch Nostradamus' predictions come true for half a millennium. That's a long time to be right. They're very good at this. They've faced people like you before."

"I was chosen for a reason," Crow said.

She looked over at him. "This isn't *Lord of the Rings*, for God's sake. You're not somehow special because some homeless guy gave you a book."

"Then you explain why he went to so much trouble to give it to *me*."

"I don't know. Maybe he read *Destiny Raider* and thought you're some oracle."

Crow smiled. "I'm flattered. You're familiar with one of my books?"

"I actually read it."

Crow almost choked on his laugh. "You *read* one of my books."

"Long train ride from Boston to Washington. I saw the paperback at the newsstand at the train station before I left and couldn't resist."

"I'm humbled."

"You've never been humble in your life," Rosenfeld joked.

"OK, let's say I'm honored. How's that?"

"Much more honest."

"Your theory is the old man in Montreal was a fan and this is all just some elaborate joke concocted by a deranged reader?"

"Now, I didn't say that."

"Then what are you saying?" Crow asked. "Look, I know I attract a lot of nuts—that's part of the gig—but you and Grumbling, and now Kyle, all seem to be in agreement that the First Face of Janus is very real. If not, I wouldn't be here. If you didn't believe it, *you* wouldn't be here. So for some reason I've been given the quatrains. I'm not suggesting I'm 'the chosen one,' but maybe they knew I wouldn't be dismissive of them."

"Unlike me," Rosenfeld said.

"Are you saying you would just ignore something like this?"

She thought for a moment. “Not necessarily ignore. I would be curious, I guess. Just not sure I’d be as curious as you.”

“You mean, not curious enough to come all the way to Europe chasing a clue.”

“Well, yeah,” she said.

“But you’re here.”

“I am.”

“Why?”

“Somebody offers to fly me first class to France to see where Nostradamus lived in Salon, I’m down for a good road trip.”

“But you don’t expect to find anything?”

“Let me put it this way,” she said, “I’ve studied the First Facers and the CV for a long time. They’re not going to be found unless they want to be found.”

“And you don’t think I can find them?”

“If you do, you’ll be the first to find them in 500 years,” she said. “Chew on that, Mr. Chosen One.”

Chapter Fourteen

Crow and Rosenfeld rolled into Salon-de-Provence around 2:30 in the afternoon. The life of the most famous sage in the world was almost in the background of this bustling little village. The centerpiece was not Nostradamus at all but the Château de l'Empéri, a ninth-century castle that was home to the Holy Roman emperors.

They parked on the street across from the entrance of Old Salon and walked through the gateway of the Tour de l'Horloge, the Clock Tower, built in the seventeenth century. The narrow street looked like something out of a storybook. Quaint shops and outdoor cafes lined the tiny lane paved with bricks. Tourists relaxed at small outdoor tables enjoying beverages and conversation and the enjoyable summer weather. A bald man with an eye patch over his left eye sat alone. He watched intently with his good eye as the two strolled by.

Jean-Claude Delacroix had agreed to meet them at La Maison de Nostradamus, the House of Nostradamus. The museum was the site of Nostradamus' home where he lived from 1547 until his death in 1566. It was damaged in the earthquake of 1909 but restored and opened as a museum in 1992.

The second street up they took a left on Rue Nostradamus and there it was. They approached the entrance to the ancient home and Rosenfeld stopped.

"I'm sorry." She was surprised by her own reaction.

"You crying?" Crow asked.

"No. Well, maybe a little." She wiped a tear from the corner of her eye. "It's just that I've studied Nostradamus for so long. Yesterday we were standing in Washington, D.C., and here we are getting ready to enter a place where so much history was made. So much amazing writing was done over a twenty-year span. It's just a little overwhelming to think that I'm actually here."

"Take your time," Crow said.

"Makes me wonder why I never did it before." She dabbed another corner of her eye and laughed. "God, I am *such* a history geek. I'm so sorry."

"Don't be. I completely understand." She stood there trying to regain her composure. "You OK?" he asked.

Rosenfeld blushed a bit and waved a hand in front of her face. "Yeah, I'm fine. Let's go see Monsieur Delacroix."

Crow opened the glass door that replaced the wooden one from Nostradamus' day. He allowed Rosenfeld to enter first. Jean-Claude Delacroix was a slender man with a thin but prominent nose jutting from his angular face. He had a noticeable diastema which didn't seem to inhibit his contagious smile. Shoulder blades were never more appropriately named than the boney ones that extended below Delacroix's skinny neck, more closely resembling a coat hanger that had been slightly bent to a slope with a black jacket hanging on it. His receding hairline exposed nearly three-quarters of his skull which gave the illusion of a larger than normal brain. He stepped from behind the counter and greeted them warmly.

"Monsieur Crow?"

"Monsieur Delacroix." Crow shook his hand. "Thank you for meeting with us. Allow me to introduce Dr. Sidney Rosenfeld. She's an expert on ancient books and manuscripts from Rothschild's in Boston and a bit of a Nostradamus aficionado."

She held out her hand. "Delighted to meet you, Monsieur Delacroix."

Delacroix took it and gave it a gentle kiss. "Pleasure. Madame?"

"Mademoiselle," she said.

He addressed them both. "Would you like a private tour of the museum?"

Rosenfeld opened her mouth to answer.

"That's a very gracious offer, Monsieur Delacroix," Crow said, "but we're sort of on a tight schedule. Maybe some other time. Is there somewhere we can talk in private?"

"Yes, of course. Follow me, please."

He led them up a flight of stairs to an office where they all made themselves comfortable. Delacroix sat behind his desk, Crow and Rosenfeld in the barrel back chairs in front of it.

"Now, then," Delacroix began, "how can I be of assistance?"

Crow unfolded the paper he kept in his coat pocket and handed it to him. Delacroix reached in his own coat pocket for his reading glasses. He read over the quatrains in silence for a few moments then looked up.

"Where did you get this?"

Rosenfeld and Crow exchanged glances. "It's a rather long story," Crow said.

"I think you may be in for more than you bargained for," Delacroix said.

"Are you referring to the First Face of Janus?" Crow asked.

Delacroix leaned back in his chair. "So you know about them."

"Not by choice, I can assure you. I was thrust into this."

"Most unfortunate."

"That's why we've come all this way," Crow said.

"You can still walk away."

"I know that, but I won't. I would very much like your interpretation of the quatrains."

Delacroix tapped a pen to his thin lip and looked them over once again. "I think it is obvious they are referring to Century 4, Quatrain 71. I would have to consult *The Prophecies* to tell you exactly what that is."

"In place of the bride the daughters slaughtered," Crow read from his pad. "Murder with great error no survivor to be / Within the well vestals inundated / The bride extinguished by a drink of Aconite."

"I see you are well ahead of me." Delacroix held his bottom lip with his index finger and thumb and mulled over the words in the verses. "I would think it is referring to a wedding, naturally. It sounds as though the bride is the target of a murder, but her daughters are killed instead. Notice it says, 'Murder with great error.' Sounds like it is a mistake."

"And the next line? Within the well vestals inundated?" Crow asked.

"I suppose it depends on where you put the emphasis."

"Meaning?"

"Meaning if it were meant to be read 'within' pause 'the well vestals inundated,' then one could presume the word 'well' was meant to modify 'vestals.' In other words, 'good' vestals. I would take that to mean 'inside, the good vestals are inundated.' Vestals can refer to virgins, but it can also mean unmarried women."

"But there is no comma after 'within,'" Rosenfeld pointed out.

"There aren't any commas in the entire line," Crow said.

"This is true," said Delacroix. "One would think Nostradamus would have placed one there if that were his meaning."

"But it could be a typographical error," Rosenfeld said. "I explained to Mr. Crow that many publishing houses printed these prophecies, and several made mistakes in the typesetting."

"You are correct," Delacroix said. He reached behind him for a large volume and began thumbing through it until he landed on the page he was looking for. "Just as I thought. There was no comma in the original text."

"OK, so hold on a second," Crow said, "if we read that verse without a pause, it reads 'within the well.' Like a drinking well?"

Delacroix shrugged. "There is really no way of knowing for sure."

Crow frowned and rubbed the back of his head. "'Within the well vestals inundated.' What do you think 'inundated' means in this context?"

"'Inundated' means overwhelmed," Delacroix said.

"But 'vestals inundated.' The word 'vestals' is plural," Crow said, "meaning there are more than one."

"Yes, we can assume the vestals in question are the bridesmaids," Delacroix pointed out. "And, if you believe Nostradamus' prediction, it's more than just the bridesmaids. He said, 'no survivor be,'" Delacroix observed.

Crow's face turned grim. "So, it's not just the bridesmaids. Everybody at that wedding dies?"

"It would appear so. Except the bride, of course. At least, not right away."

"'The bride extinguished by a drink of Aconite,'" Crow said.

"Aconite is a poison," Delacroix said, "but I suspect it is used here as a euphemism for suicide. I would guess that the bride is so distraught over the death of her daughters—and if we're correct, everyone at the wedding—that she takes her own life."

"Yes, that's pretty much what we had guessed," Rosenfeld said, "that the bride takes her own life."

"And it is just that, mademoiselle. A guess."

"But it's a plausible guess," Crow said.

"I am sorry you came all this way for me to tell you something you already know."

"Don't apologize," Crow said. "You've been tremendously helpful, but there's more." He pointed down at the paper.

Delacroix read the second quatrain. "'Add the note of C twice / And take away the score / Count on good stock / Rich in grace.'"

Crow looked at him and cocked his head slightly.

"My guess is 'the note of C' and 'the score' are both musical references," Delacroix said. "What they mean, I do not know. The part about 'good stock' and 'rich in grace' I would think refers to a well-to-do family."

"Yes," Crow said, "that's what we figured, too."

"Again, I tell you something you already know," Delacroix said regretfully. "It is possible whoever wrote these quatrains may be employing the same Green Language that Nostradamus used."

"Green Language?" Crow asked.

"Also referred to as the language of the birds," Rosenfeld said.

"I don't get it." Crow looked at the two of them as if he were the only one who wasn't in on the joke.

She said, "Nostradamus used little techniques like anagrams, homonyms, and metathesis."

"Metathesis?" Crow said.

"That is the interchanging of consonant sounds," Delacroix said. "Dionysius used this technique in Greece in the first century before Christ. You exchange one consonant for another. For example, the word 'broom' becomes 'broon.' Dionysius did it to make texts flow more naturally. Nostradamus did it to mask his true meaning."

"So, we don't know if this is really a wedding or a webbing?"

Delacroix chuckled, "It doesn't appear Nostradamus used metathesis in the quatrains in question."

"But he could've used other deceptions," Crow said.

"And it is likely that he did. The trick, of course, is figuring out the puzzle."

"Well, we're going to assume it's a wedding."

"I believe that would be a safe assumption," Delacroix said.

"The big question is which bride? Which wedding? That's actually what we were hoping you could help us with."

"That is the proverbial needle in the haystack," Delacroix said, rubbing his sharp chin. "However, keep in mind that Nostradamus only predicts events of large consequence. I do not mean to sound elitist, but this is not going to be just any ordinary wedding. 'Rich in grace, good stock.' It will involve people of breeding and importance. People of fame or power or both."

"So we could be talking about some kind of society wedding?" Rosenfeld asked with a flavor of contempt in her voice. "Those affairs are meaningless exercises in excess."

"Perhaps, mademoiselle, but Nostradamus predicted events that would change the course of history. This would be a wedding of monumental importance. However, keep this in mind, the importance may not be readily apparent. Michel de Nostredame has a way of revealing things in his own time."

"I guess the first place to look is the social pages, but it could be any country on earth." Crow said.

"Any country, yes, that is correct. But do not be surprised if the wedding is not listed at all."

"What do you mean?" Crow asked.

"What I mean is this apparently is not going to be a wedding on the order of, say, Prince Charles and Lady Diana. If it were, then everyone would already know about it. No, I suspect this wedding is being kept under wraps."

"Then how do we find it?" Rosenfeld asked.

Delacroix said, "I would suggest you concentrate your efforts on venues."

"Venues?" Crow asked.

"Yes, venues. It is doubtful royal weddings are going to take place in a barn. Read the prophecies and your new quatrains. Find the venue and you find the wedding."

"So, you think it's a royal wedding?" Rosenfeld asked.

"I would suspect so," Delacroix said.

"Why?" Crow asked.

"Count on good stock," he said quoting the new quatrains. "I've studied the First Facers long enough to pick up on word play. It may sound odd, but they have a wicked sense of humor sometimes. I believe 'count' refers to a title of nobility."

"Very interesting," Crow said. "You have been a tremendous help, Monsieur Delacroix."

"Please, call me Jean-Claude. And it has been my pleasure."

"By the way," Crow said, "I tried to research the First Face of Janus on the Internet, and I didn't find one word about them."

"And you will not," Delacroix said. "They have the capability to whitewash the Internet, to strip it of any mention of themselves whatsoever. Authors have written about them on the Internet only to find their pieces mysteriously gone the next day. With that kind of power, writers do not dare post them again. And no one writes books about them. If they know what is good for them."

"Scary stuff," Crow said.

"It is, indeed. And I would be remiss if I did not warn you of something else. Beware of the Custos Verbi."

"Yes, I think we've been introduced."

"I see," Delacroix said. "That is most unfortunate. You do not want to be on their radar."

"I'm afraid that's too late," Rosenfeld said.

Crow could see the worry on Delacroix's face. "I know we weren't followed here. I made sure of it."

"I am not concerned about that," Delacroix said. "They know

very well who I am. I have studied them for decades. They are like a tiger. You can enjoy their awesome power from afar, but do not get too close."

"So, you're an expert on the Custos Verbi?" Rosenfeld asked.

"I would not say that. It is hard to be an expert on something you cannot see. I know they have tried to stop the prophecies since Nostradamus' death."

"Have they ever been successful?" Crow asked.

"To my knowledge, not really, but we do not know what has not come true. Only what has."

"What you're saying is the First Face of Janus only brags about their victories," Crow said.

"They do not brag, monsieur. They do their job and they do it quietly. It is the Nostradamus enthusiasts who do the bragging."

"The enthusiasts?"

"Yes, the fellows with the blogs and the books and the videos. They are not real students of the man. They are profiteers. The more sensational Nostradamus is portrayed, the better."

"Certainly doesn't hurt your business here," Crow noted.

"We do fine. The money from the tourists helps fund our research."

"Research into Nostradamus or the First Face of Janus?"

Delacroix hesitated. "Both, monsieur. Both. Of course, I do not make my research on the First Facers public."

"Why, then?" Crow asked. "Why do you research them if you're not going to share that research?"

"Maybe there will come a time when I can make my research known," Delacroix said. "Much like Nostradamus in his time, what I write must remain coded or secret, but someone needs to be watching the First Face of Janus. For history's sake."

"I want to know more about the Custos Verbi," Crow said.

"What would you like to know?"

"Who are they?"

Delacroix laughed. "If I knew that..." his voice trailed off. "I would say this. They are as secretive as the First Facers."

"And as cold-blooded?" Crow asked.

A corner of Delacroix's thin mouth twitched. "Yes."

"Do you know anyone who can tell us more about the Custos Verbi?" Crow asked.

"I do, but I cannot give you their name until I first check with them. They are not too willing to talk, but given the fact that you possess the quatrains, I may be able to persuade them. Where can I find you?"

"I've been giving that some thought," Crow said. "They may not have followed us here, but they might very well start snooping around if they think we'd come here looking for answers. I don't think it's safe to stay in a hotel here. I was thinking we'd go back to Avignon. I know a great little hotel there."

"That would not be wise," Delacroix said.

"Why's that?" Crow asked.

"You said the Custos Verbi didn't follow you here?"

"Right."

"They are already here. In Avignon."

"Well, that's just great," Rosenfeld said. "We travel 4,000 miles trying to get away from these people and we end up on their doorstep."

"In Avignon? What do you mean?" Crow asked.

"Palais des Papes. The Palace of the Popes."

"Yes, I'm familiar with it," Crow said. "Vaguely. I've been to Avignon. As I recall, a pope used to reside there."

"Several, in fact. I believe the Custos Verbi is also based there," Delacroix said. "It was the seat of the Catholic Church during much of the fourteenth century. They actually held six papal conclaves there, the last being the election of Antipope Benedict XIII in 1394."

"Antipope?" Crow asked.

"Yes, it led to what's known as the Western Schism. Benedict's predecessor, Gregory XI, had returned the seat of the papacy to Rome. There was a split between those who thought the Church should remain in Rome and those who favored Avignon. In 1377, the move back to Rome became absolute, Benedict's election to the contrary. Thus the schism. Benedict is referred to by the Catholic Church as Antipope Benedict XIII."

"Then the palace no longer belonged to the Roman Catholics," Rosenfeld said.

"For a time. The Council of Constance ended the schism in 1418, which returned possession of the palace to Rome. The Church maintained the palace as an outpost of sorts. They remained very powerful in this region. It is said that when Nostradamus became a problem, the Custos Verbi was headquartered out of the Palace of the Popes because it gave the Vatican plausible deniability, and because it was so close to Nostradamus himself, they could more readily keep an eye on him. Some say the CV still secretly conducts its business from the palace."

"And you believe that?" Rosenfeld asked.

"I do, but I am no expert on the CV. I know a priest in Avignon. Father Pierre Simonin." Crow wrote on his pad. "He has spent his life studying the palace," Delacroix said. "He would know better than I. Personally, I believe they still reside there. Whether you believe it or not, it is better you did not tempt fate. I would not recommend staying anywhere near the Palace of the Popes."

"Where then?" Crow asked.

"I have a friend. He has a farm just outside of town. He and his family are on holiday. He has asked me to look in on the place while he is gone. You can stay there for a few days."

"Are you sure he won't mind?" Rosenfeld asked.

"I am positive. I need to check on the place today. You can follow me out there."

Crow and Rosenfeld strolled past the modern bronze statue of Nostradamus by François Bouché just steps from the museum's front door while Delacroix gave them a brief history of the historic town and the great prognosticator's time there. The bald man with the eye patch watched with his beady good eye from his seat in the statue's shadow as they turned right down Rue de l'Horloge then passed under the great clock tower. He dialed the number on his phone and held it to his ear.

"Yes," the baritone voice with the German accent said.

"He is here. In Salon."

"You are sure it is him?"

"Yes."

"And you are sure he is the one?"

"He met with the curator at the museum."

"Interesting. Then it is confirmed," Otto said. "Do you know where we can find him?"

"No," the bald man said. "Would you like for me to talk with the curator and find out?"

"That is not your area of expertise. We have people who specialize in that. Stay on your task. We will find him."

"He is traveling with a companion," the bald man said. "A woman."

"A woman," Otto repeated. "I see. How unfortunate for her."

Chapter Fifteen

Crow positioned himself in the driver's seat of the Mercedes and followed Jean-Claude Delacroix out of Salon and into the French countryside past the flowing fields of vineyards that seamlessly melted into a rural lane lined with plane trees. The nimble automobile felt good in his hands as passing traffic became sparse and the road grew more twisting and narrow. They turned up a winding gravel driveway that disappeared over a hill. The drive led to a two-story country farmhouse of stone and mortar with ivy growing up the walls. The casement windows with their gentle arches appeared to be original to the house. A faded green doorway was contrasted with a deep red front door. The old place looked as though it belonged in a period movie. Time had tried its best to ravage the house but had only left it more enchanting. The walkway leading up to the front steps was of small, individual stones harvested from the property with moss growing between them. The roof was weathered tile of gray and brown and Tuscan red.

"I adore it!" Rosenfeld almost leapt from the car.

Crow ambled behind carrying their shoulder bags. Delacroix unlocked the front door which opened up to a slate floor foyer. The stairs leading to the second floor were about fifteen feet from the front door. The sun cast a shadow across the treads and banister from the bank of windows above the door.

"This is so charming, Jean-Claude," Rosenfeld gushed, twirling in the foyer.

"I am glad you like it. I thought you would. Eighteenth-century farmhouse. Almost all original."

Rosenfeld's wide eyes took it all in.

Crow looked the place over then turned to Delacroix and extended a hand. "We really appreciate it. We have to pay you for this."

"Nonsense." Delacroix shook his hand. "When I tell the owners Mr. Benson Crow, famous American author, slept here they will be delighted. You are my guests."

"Well, at least let us buy you dinner tonight," Crow said.

"I would love to take you up on your offer, but I am afraid I cannot. I have an important engagement tonight that I must prepare for."

"No worries," Rosenfeld said. "I'd love to prepare dinner here if you think the owners won't mind. We'll be sure to clean up after ourselves."

"Perfectly fine," Delacroix said. "Make yourselves at home. I will call you when I know something about your contact."

Delacroix excused himself and headed back to town. Sidney Rosenfeld walked around like they'd just bought the place.

"Isn't this fabulous?"

"Don't get used to it." Crow set their bags on the long farm table in the kitchen. "We have work to do. We probably won't be staying here long."

"Come on, Crow. This is like something out of a magazine. We're in a charming farmhouse in the south of France and…" She noticed Crow was in no mood to play along. "What's wrong?"

"What's wrong? You're joking, right? The clock is ticking and we're really no closer to stopping the prophecy than we were when we left the States."

"The man in Montreal," she said. "Have you ever stopped to think his finding you there was just a coincidence?"

"There's no such thing as coincidence," Crow said. "Everything happens for a reason. You just have to figure out what that reason is."

"I see. Synchronicity." Rosenfeld took a seat at the wooden farm table.

Crow looked at her. "Carl Jung."

"Yes," she said. "So, you're familiar with him."

"I am." He pulled up a chair.

"I'm guessing you must be familiar with his theory of unus mundus."

"One world? Yes," Crow said. "With the physicist Wolfgang Pauli. Not sure I completely buy their theory. They believed everything is inter-related, including people. Of course, shrinks and scientists love their unknowns wrapped up in little packages of logic. It's not that easy."

"But you said you don't believe in coincidences," she said.

"Yes, that's true, but I'm not convinced that one man's stone causes a ripple in everyone else's lives. I think of life more like a sock drawer."

"A sock drawer?" She rested her elbow on the table and her chin in her palm.

"Yes. If I happen to find two socks that match, then I understand those two items go together. I put them on and I wear them. That's the purpose. I don't, however, believe they have anything to do with the other socks in the drawer."

"What about that orphan sock," Rosenfeld asked, "that stray sock you can't seem to find the mate to?"

"You just have to wait until the other sock shows up."

"*If* it shows up," Rosenfeld added.

"It always shows up if you're patient and you wait long enough. I was sent to Montreal and that book signing for a reason. I was supposed to be there."

"To get the Nostradamus book?"

"Yes."

"And then what?"

"I guess I'm still waiting for the other sock."

"Jung once said, 'You are a slave of what you need in your soul.' What do you need in your soul, Crow? Are you trying to scratch an itch or exorcise demons?"

"Both maybe. I don't know. All I know is when something as odd as this drops in my lap I can't simply cast it aside like it doesn't matter. I know it matters. The question is *why* does it matter?"

"Then you would agree that there has to be some logic to it."

"Of course."

"Well, then let's go over what we know," Rosenfeld said. "We know the old man in Montreal gave you the book and the quatrains and lost his life in the process. We know you visited Dr. Grumbling and he and his housekeeper lost *their* lives. Will it be just a coincidence if we're next to die? Or will it be because we just didn't grasp the logic and couldn't leave well enough alone? Are we masters of our own destiny, or are we victims of it?"

"I thought you were all about solving this puzzle. That's why you're here, isn't it?"

"I'm here because you dragged me into this," she said with a tinge of resentment. "I'm here because it's safer than going home and waiting for them to show up—whoever 'they' are—now that your thirst for coincidence has made me a target."

"Just a second, on the plane you were excited about this trip."

"I was excited about visiting the home of Nostradamus. We've done that. I'm not too excited about dying."

He pointed to the front door. "You're welcome to head home right now. You can turn yourself over to the police for protection."

"And what am I suppose to tell them? That I'm afraid the same people who killed Dr. Grumbling—whose body they can't find—are the same people after me?"

"Look, I'm sorry I got you into all this, but I don't think my meeting you is a coincidence either. I think you're here for a reason, too."

Rosenfeld looked uneasy. Crow's cellphone rang.

"Yes." He paused for moment. "I can't thank you enough." Another pause. "Yes, I can find it." He glanced at his watch. "We'll be there. Thank you so much." He hung up. "That was Delacroix. He called the Custos Verbi guy from his car. He's agreed to meet with us."

"How far are you going to chase this?"

"To the end."

"What does that mean?" she asked. "To *its* end or to ours?"

"We've been given an opportunity maybe nobody else has been given. Somebody's trying to tell us something. They're trying to tell us what the next prophecy will be. You heard Delacroix. We find the venue of this wedding and we can stop those people from being slaughtered."

"If that's really the prophecy," she said.

"It has to be. Think about it. That old man in Montreal was one of two things. Either he was Custos Verbi and he was trying to tip us off to stop the prophecy, or he was a First Facer."

"Why did he choose you?"

"I don't know," Crow said. "Maybe because he knew his days were numbered, and he knew with me he wouldn't die in vain."

"This battle's been going on for centuries," she said. "You aren't the first one to try and stop the prophecy. Maybe that man in Montreal did die in vain." She paused. "And maybe we're next."

Chapter Sixteen

The St-Michel Chapel was in the historic center of Salon-de-Provence, just around the corner from the House of Nostradamus. It faced what was the central square of the city in olden times. The wooden doors were accented with a modest semi-circle tympanum above the Agnus Dei relief and the relief of a lamb and a cross. They looked rather primitive even for a thirteenth-century structure. The unremarkable facade was almost lost as just another entrance in the tangle of narrow streets in Salon. Crow opened the door and held it for Rosenfeld.

"Oh, I think I'll do some shopping," she said.

"You don't want to hear what this guy has to say?"

"I'll wait for your recap."

"Oh, come on," he said.

"No, really. I'm good. You go ahead. I'm going to grab some things for dinner."

"You're sure?"

"I'm sure," she said.

"OK," Crow shrugged. "I'll meet you back at the car."

She walked a few streets over to an open-air market at Place Morgan where local farmers brought their fresh fruits, vegetables, and meats.

Crow entered the simple but impressive nave. No ambulatory or side-aisle, just a basic center aisle that led to a gold altar with candles and a beautiful old painting as the centerpiece. It felt cooler than the outside like walking into a cave. The slightest sound echoed. Crow looked above him. The intersecting ribs of the vaults were painted white to form a dome and, along with the gilded apse, combined for one of the earliest examples of the Gothic style in Provence.

He surveyed the room. A lone soul sat on the second row of wooden pews in hooded monk's attire gazing up at a painting by Belgian artist Jean Daret depicting two scenes of importance in the Catholic Church. At the top of the painting was the Annunciation, the announcement by the angel Gabriel to the Virgin Mary that she had been chosen to give birth to the Son of God. The lower part of the painting characterized St. Ursula in submission to St. Augustine symbolizing an order of nuns called the Company of St. Ursula being placed under the Rule of St. Augustine by Pope Gregory XIII in 1572.

Crow took his time walking toward the front of the church, each step reverberating against the stone walls. Without looking back, the monk pointed with a thumb to the row behind him. Crow took a seat. After a moment, the man knelt down and prayed. He crossed himself then sat back in his seat, continuing to look up at the painting.

"Come with me," he whispered at last in a thick, guttural French accent.

The man rose from his seat. Crow followed him past the altar and out the back door into a courtyard with a garden. The man sat on a concrete bench facing one way, his face obscured by the hood. Crow sat next to him facing the other.

"I need your help," Crow began.

The man said nothing.

Crow tried again. "I need to get a message to the Custos Verbi. We're on the same side and I don't think they understand that."

"You have reason to believe they would do you harm?" the monk said.

"I was given an early copy of *The Prophecies* by a stranger in Montreal. In it was a piece of paper with two odd quatrains. He was killed for it. When I visited a Nostradamus expert in America he was murdered right in front of me."

"And you believe the Custos Verbi killed them?"

"Yes. I think they killed both men and now that I have the quatrains, they're trying to kill *me*."

"Why would they want you dead?" the man asked.

"I think the guy in Montreal was an agent of the First Face of Janus. He passed the quatrains to me."

"Why?"

"I don't know why. Maybe he knew the Custos Verbi were closing in on him and he gave them to me thinking he could come back later and get them."

"And you believe the Custos Verbi killed him once they discovered the quatrains were missing, then came after you?"

"Unless you have a better theory," Crow said.

"Perhaps he was a First Facer who grew a conscience."

"What do you mean?"

"What I mean is this man you met in Montreal was maybe trying to expose the organization. He knew what the next prophecy would be and was trying to stop it. When he realized his mission had failed, he charged you with completing it."

"But if that's true," Crow said, "why wouldn't he just come right out and tell me everything?"

"Did he tell you anything at all?"

"He said I didn't have much time. He said before the sun rises on Sunday it will be done. Whatever 'it' is."

"The prophecy, naturally."

"Then the CV shouldn't want me dead. I'm on their side."

"Precisely. The very reason it must be the First Face of Janus that is trying to kill you. You find yourself in the eternal struggle between good and evil, monsieur. Between right and wrong."

"And which one's which?"

"That should be easy to determine. The First Face of Janus is all about one thing. Total control through the predictions of a third-rate con man. The First Face of Janus hides behind Nostradamus when their true aim is world domination. They merely twist the quatrains so they fit their agenda. They say there is more detail in the Unriddled Manuscript."

"And you don't believe that."

"Monsieur, I am not so sure the Unriddled Manuscript even exists."

"But the Custos Verbi, they kill people just like the First Facers do."

"Only when absolutely necessary and only to stop the First Face of Janus."

"And they call themselves Christians?"

"You are not a religious man." It was more a statement than a question.

"To be honest, I'm not a huge fan of organized religion," Crow said.

"Meaning?"

"Killing in the name of God."

The monk shifted on the bench then said, "The Church was certainly overzealous in fulfilling the Great Commission during The Inquisitions, if that is what you mean. We have had popes who have turned out to be scoundrels." He thought for a second then added,

"And worse. The Church has certainly seen its dark moments. The molestation scandal was a travesty, a body of leaders simply in denial that something so wicked could have happened under their noses. But there are the countless millions who have been fed and provided with clean drinking water. One Mother Teresa counters a multitude of wicked priests. We have built villages, provided health care, alleviated suffering among the poor, joined with the secular world to bring down an evil empire. We have commissioned unfathomable works of art, contributed unimaginably to the world of architecture, financed exploration and scientific research, and, most humbly and most importantly, we have brought billions to know Jesus Christ. You are not a perfect man, Monsieur Crow. None of us is. There are probably things in your past that you do not wish anyone to know. Does that override your positive contributions to this world? The Church is no different. We are a body. A body that sins. A body that learns. A body that stumbles and falls and then gets back up and tries to do the right thing. And a body that is hopefully judged on the totality of its work rather than the negatives that detractors want to focus on."

"And the Custos Verbi?"

"They may just be our most important contribution of all. Their goal is noble."

"Noble? They're killers."

"Do you remember how World War II ended?" the monk asked.

"The atomic bombs dropped on Japan."

"And it was one of the most horrific acts ever committed by man. Why did the Americans do it?"

"To save lives and end the war," Crow said.

"Precisely. More lives were saved by the bomb than taken by it."

"The lesser of two evils?"

"Necessary steps, Monsieur Crow. The Custos Verbi takes the necessary steps to try and stop a society that has been manipulating death and destruction for half a millennium. The First Face of Janus gave us Hitler, 9/11, and countless other tragedies. When a life is taken by the Custos Verbi, it is taken with great deliberation and with great regret knowing that, in the end, it is necessary."

"So you understand the gravity of these prophecies."

"I do," the monk said, "but these matters are best left to those who understand them better than we do."

"I'm not sure how well they understand them. As far as I can tell, the First Facers are running rings around the Custos Verbi."

"If all you see are the prophecies that come true," the monk said.

"Meaning?"

"The attacks in America in 2001. They were foretold."

"But the Custos Verbi wasn't able to stop them."

"They tried. Two Custos Verbi went down on the plane that crashed in Pennsylvania. They saved its target but were unable to save the others. They have gotten better at figuring out when the First Facers are on the move. They just have not figured out how to stop them yet."

"I can help," Crow said. "I have the quatrains that point to the next prophecy. They need to know that."

"Perhaps they already do."

"Are you one of them?"

"Custos Verbi?"

"Yes," Crow said.

The man laughed. "If I were a member of the Custos Verbi, I would not be sitting here talking to you."

"Then who are you?"

"I have nothing more to offer."

The man started to rise.

"Wait a minute," Crow urged. "How do I find the Custos Verbi?"

The monk turned toward Crow, almost revealing his face, then turned his head forward again. "Monsieur, you do not find the Custos Verbi. The Custos Verbi finds you."

Chapter Seventeen

Crow waited until they arrived back at the farmhouse to unpack the details of his conversation with the monk. Rosenfeld wasn't buying the rogue First Facer theory.

"What did this man in the church look like?" she asked, chopping the ends off green beans.

"I never actually saw him. The hood kept his face covered."

"Mm-hmm. A monk in a church telling you the Church's secret police force had nothing to do with it?"

Crow's attention was drawn to the fluffy white clouds of the summer afternoon that were slowly being replaced with darker ones. The clouds hastened dusk. Lightning flashed on the horizon.

"Looks like we're in for a nasty one." He looked over at Rosenfeld busy in the kitchen. "What is it you're making?"

"Pork Chops au Poivre. It's an old French recipe."

"What can I do to be helpful?"

"You can get out of my kitchen," she playfully pointed with her knife.

"That's fine," he said. "I know when I'm not wanted."

Crow took the opportunity to explore the house. He was a snoop by nature, the kind of guy who'd look through your medicine cabinet while pretending to use your bathroom. He was never satisfied with taking things at face value. The house, he discovered, had four bedrooms—two up, two down. A hallway connected the large den with the two downstairs bedrooms. Two bedrooms on either side of the landing at the top of the stairs were large with sloped ceilings and exposed beams. On the landing were a couple of shelves and an armoire. He peeked inside.

"Dinner's ready," Rosenfeld yelled from the kitchen.

The chops dripped with a sour cream and brandy sauce and were served with roasted sweet potatoes and green beans. Crow poured the wine. The two sat at the large wooden table in the kitchen, Crow at the end and Rosenfeld just to his right. He cut into his first bite and marveled out loud at how delicious it tasted. Rosenfeld followed and, for a time, they concentrated on their meal.

"This monk you met with," she said, "did you ever consider he might be trying to throw you off the scent?"

"I know. I thought about that. He could be Custos Verbi himself." He stabbed a morsel of the pork chops with his fork. "But what he said made sense. What if the old man in Montreal was trying to expose the First Facers?" The piece disappeared into his mouth.

"Then why would he go to you? Why wouldn't he just go straight to a news network?"

Crow finished chewing and laid his fork down. "I don't know. That's the thing that keeps bugging me. If I were—"

A loud clap of thunder hit. The lights flickered then went out.

"I thought that might happen." Crow rose from his seat. He grabbed a candle and candlestick he'd found in a closet and set aside just in case. He lit the candle with a kitchen match and placed it between them.

"Did you plan this?" Rosenfeld asked with mischief in her voice.

"No, I swear to you," he chuckled. "I was a Boy Scout. I'm always prepared."

The thunder and lightning continued as the rain poured down.

"You were saying?"

Crow frowned. "I forget now."

"You said it keeps bugging you and if you were…" She took the last bite of her meal and moved her silverware to the center of her plate.

"Oh, yeah, if I were that guy in Montreal and I wanted to expose the First Face of Janus, would any reporter at a news network believe me? Probably not. Then you've got a guy like me who writes about bizarre things. I mean, my last novel was about a time-traveling cyborg from a thousand years in the future who comes back and assumes the identity of Neville Chamberlain to stop World War II from happening."

Sidney struggled to swallow her sip of wine as she laughed. "Oh, my God."

"Yeah, I know. For the record, that was my publisher's idea. I didn't want to do it, but after five books, I was out of ideas."

"I thought *Destiny Raider* was very good, actually," Rosenfeld said.

"That was the book before this last one. Yeah, I probably should've stopped while I was ahead. You really read it?"

"I told you. On the train down to Washington. I've read some sci-fi, but this was different. Very insightful."

"Really?"

"Yeah." She rested her chin on the palm of her hand and caressed the stem of her almost-empty glass of wine. Thunder roared again outside and lightning illuminated the kitchen like the flash from a camera. "I don't know if it's the candlelight or the wine or your stories of cyborgs, but this is rather romantic."

"Yeah, I'm sure." Crow cleared his throat. "Tell me about you."

"Not much to tell."

"Well, let's start with family. Siblings?"

"Four older brothers. I couldn't help but be a tomboy. They needed me to complete the basketball team."

"Center?" Crow teased. "Power forward?"

"Point guard. Killer with three-pointers. Why do you hate people so?"

Crow took an awkward sip of wine. "What makes you ask that?"

"Because you don't seem to have people in your life. I mean, you have necessary people like your publisher and your 'caretaker,'" she said with air quotes, "but I don't hear you speak of much else."

"Maybe I'm just a private person."

"Maybe you're hiding something."

"Hiding something?" Crow asked. "Like what?"

Sidney leaned back and held her wine glass with both hands. "You use people."

"Is that so?"

"I don't mean that in a sinister way," she said. "You don't like people because people have always let you down. You've obviously been hurt. Do you want to talk about it?"

"Do I look like I want to talk about it?"

"The irony is you need people. At arm's length, but you need people. You need people to buy your novels. You love to write, but you hate what you're hired to write. You hate New York because it's brimming with people, and you're not comfortable around people. People remind you that you haven't been true to yourself. They remind you that, in your mind, they're just consumers. You need people to buy your books to keep you in the lifestyle to which you've become accustomed."

"Is your doctorate in psychology?" Crow asked.

"History, but I minored in psychology. Comes in handy when I'm dealing with people wanting to part with so-called priceless artifacts."

"And you think you have me tied up in a nice little psychological profile."

"Not really," she confessed. "You're complicated."

"Am I now?" He placed his wine glass on the table.

"See? Like that. You try to act as though you're easy to read, but you're not. Can I take another stab at it?"

"Like I can stop you," Crow said.

"This subject, this Nostradamus thing, it fascinates you because you view it as important. Not like your cyborg novels, which make you cringe when you write them. This is the kind of subject you feel you were meant to write about, only you've been typecast. You're trapped and you're looking for a way out, and fate has led you to a way out, only your publisher is blocking the doorway. He's telling you to go back, that you made a wrong turn, and you know you haven't. You know you've finally found the right path. The path you've been looking for your entire life."

"Sounds a bit melodramatic, doesn't it?"

"Does it?"

Crow adjusted himself in his chair. "Delacroix," he said changing the subject. "There's something odd about him."

"He can't help his appearance."

"That's not what I mean," Crow said. "He seemed too eager to get back to town."

"He's a busy man," Rosenfeld said.

"Really? The guy does nothing but study a man who's been dead for nearly 500 years. Where's the urgency?"

"What are you saying?"

"I'm saying there seemed to be something pressing, something he had to do."

"He's probably got a life beyond Nostradamus. Maybe his wife wanted him home."

"He's not married."

"I know he's not the most attractive man in the world but—"

"No wedding ring," Crow said.

Rosenfeld smiled. "Usually it's the woman who notices that kind of thing."

"Only if she's interested."

"Good point."

"He said he couldn't meet us for dinner because he had an engagement later tonight."

"Maybe he has a date."

"No, he said he's preparing for something that happens later. Something at midnight."

"How would you know that?"

"The calendar blotter on his desk. He had the number 12 written on this date."

"That could mean anything," she said.

"Like what?"

"Like…" She couldn't think of anything.

Crow rose from his seat. "Well, I'm not going to just sit around here in the dark. I'm going back into town."

"At this hour? What in the world for?"

"Just to look around. See if Delacroix is still in his office. Maybe see what's happening at midnight. I'm curious about what seemed to be occupying his mind. Care to join me?"

"No, thanks. Not in this weather. I'll stay here and clean up."

"Suit yourself. There's another candle in the drawer," Crow said, grabbing the key fob off the table. "Don't get scared here all alone."

Rosenfeld frowned. She cleared the dishes from the table with just the light of the candle and set them down in the sink. "Wait."

Crow paused at the door and looked back at her.

Rosenfeld quickly ran her hands under the faucet then wiped them on a dish rag. "I'm coming with you."

Chapter Eighteen

The cobblestone streets of Old Salon were wet from the recent rain, casting a reflection of silver and black. The tourists were all gone. The shops were all closed. Crow and Rosenfeld stood on the corner opposite the modern bronze statue of Nostradamus with no light except the moon that shone between the remaining clouds. She tightened the plaid scarf around her head that protected her from the winds still blowing from the passing storm. They were gazing up at the only window illuminated on the dark street: Delacroix's office.

"What if he sees us lurking around?" Rosenfeld said.

"Relax. We're just out for a night stroll."

"Stroll? It's almost midnight. Nobody goes for a stroll at midnight."

The light in Delacroix's office went dark. A minute later, he was exiting the glass doors at La Maison de Nostradamus and turning the key in the lock. Rosenfeld and Crow flattened themselves against the stucco exterior of the fine watch shop on the corner at Rue de l'Horloge.

"Nobody goes for a stroll at midnight?" Crow whispered.

"He's probably going home."

"Let's find out."

"What if he comes this way?"

Crow ignored the question and peeked his head around the

corner. Delacroix set off in the opposite direction. Crow watched him reach the end of Rue Nostradamus then take a slight right. He continued up Rue Tronc de Codolet. Crow and Rosenfeld followed a safe distance behind. By the time Delacroix reached the next intersection at Cours Victor Hugo, Crow and Rosenfeld were a block behind. Delacroix stopped and turned to look behind him. Crow pulled the two of them back behind the corner and waited.

"This is nuts," Rosenfeld whispered.

When Crow felt it was safe to look again, Delacroix was gone.

They hurried down Rue Tronc de Codolet and stopped. Crow looked to the right down Cours Victor Hugo. Nothing. He looked left. Nothing.

"OK, we lost him," Rosenfeld said. "Can we go now?"

Crow looked across Cours Victor Hugo to what appeared to be almost an alleyway.

"Come on," he said and tiptoed across the street.

He just caught the image of Delacroix up in the distance making a right at the end of the block onto Rue du Grand Four. They raced to the end of the short, narrow street to see Delacroix making a left onto Rue Maréchal Joffre. Delacroix strolled up the street past brick planters overflowing with flowers in front of three-story stucco apartments with black iron knee-high railings that marked the border between the sidewalk and the street. The only sound was the slight breeze blowing between the buildings, trickling water falling into the storm drains, and the distant bark of a dog. The asphalt blended with brick pavers at a small plaza and fountain called Place Louis Blanc. Crow felt exposed along the long avenue and moved left among the trees and bushes to give them cover.

Delacroix's thin frame strained up the incline of Rue Maréchal Joffre and, after sufficient space between them, Crow and Rosenfeld resumed the stalk. At the end of the street, Delacroix turned right and ascended a set of stone steps. Crow and Rosenfeld quickened their pace to the intersection and Rosenfeld suddenly stopped.

"What is it?" Crow asked.

She nodded to the figure of Jean-Claude Delacroix disappearing behind massive wooden doors into a large building. "I know where we are," she said.

"Where?"

She pointed up at the imposing stone edifice in front of them. "Collégiale Saint-Laurent, the Collegiate Church of Saint-Laurent."

"Midnight mass?" Crow said.

"No." She took him by the shoulders. "It's time for a little history lesson."

"We don't have time for that now. We need to see where he's going."

"I know exactly where he's going."

"Then let's follow him."

"He'll keep. I need to give you the backstory."

"I'm listening."

"When Nostradamus died, his remains were laid to rest in what's now a restaurant," she said.

"Doesn't sound too glamorous for a man of his position."

"It was a Franciscan chapel at the time. It was the site of numerous pilgrimages. Both Louis XIII and Louis XIV came to Salon to pay tribute. During the French Revolution in 1792, some soldiers were passing through Salon and decided it would be a great idea to get drunk and visit the Nostradamus tomb. Things got out of hand and they ended up breaking into the tomb and scattering his bones. Some say Nostradamus predicted this. Century 9, Quatrain 7 says, 'He who will open the tomb found, / And will come to close it promptly. /

Evil will come to him, and one will be unable to prove.' Well, two days after the desecration of the tomb, the soldier who robbed it and scattered the bones was shot dead."

"Nice," Crow said.

"The entire month of July is commemorated by Nostradamus faithful because he died on July 2. His remains were moved for safekeeping after that incident. He now lies in rest inside this building in the Chapel of the Virgin."

Crow started walking again.

"Where are you going?" Rosenfeld said.

"Are you kidding? Delacroix's undoubtedly headed to the chapel. I want to see what's going on."

Rosenfeld grabbed his arm. "That wouldn't be wise."

"Why not?" He looked at her a moment. "Wait a minute. You're afraid of the Nostradamus curse."

"I am not."

Crow chuckled, "You are. Look, I know you study this guy, but you don't believe all this mumbo-jumbo, do you?"

"Crow."

"You're an educated woman. Please tell me you don't buy into all this superstition."

"It's just disrespectful. If he's meeting with other Nostradamus enthusiasts, let them have their time."

"OK, I'll tell you what," he said, "if that front door is locked, we turn around and go home. If not, we take a peek inside."

"Crow."

"Deal? It's midnight. There's no way that place is left open this late. Deal?"

Rosenfeld hesitated. "OK, but that's it. The door's locked, we go home. No more snooping around."

"I promise."

Jean-Claude Delacroix's steps echoed off the marble floor of the church narthex and he pulled the wooden door open to enter the large nave. There were eleven chapels inside the church. He walked straight ahead toward the Chapel of the Virgin.

Crow and Rosenfeld scaled the steps Delacroix had climbed just moments before and stopped in front of the large wooden doors of the Collegiate Church.

"Ready?" Crow said, looking around and rubbing his hands together.

Rosenfeld nodded slightly.

Crow eased his hand toward the knob. He grasped it and started to turn.

"Hold it a second," Rosenfeld said.

Crow pulled his hand back and rolled his eyes. "What?"

"What if Delacroix sees us? As kind as he's been to us, it would be humiliating."

"OK, let's say Delacroix does see us. We were just walking around town, you told me about the whole tomb story, and I insisted on seeing the tomb. I'm curious that way. I'll take the heat."

Rosenfeld bit her nails. "OK."

Crow reached for the knob again. "Ready?"

Rosenfeld nodded.

He clutched the large knob again and turned it. The massive door moved forward ever so slightly and creaked open.

Crow looked back at Rosenfeld and smiled. "Show time."

Chapter Nineteen

Delacroix entered the chapel directly across the great hall from the entrance to Collegiate Church of Saint-Laurent. It was one of eleven chapels inside the church which were more like alcoves honoring notable figures in Christendom like John the Baptist, Joseph, and Mary. The Chapel of the Virgin featured a limestone statue of Mother Mary holding an infant Jesus atop a round pedestal set inside the wall. She gazed down on a white vase filled with yellow daisies. A liturgical pool was carved into one wall. On the back wall was a marble grave plate marking the tomb of Michel de Nostredame with an epitaph chiseled on it. A thick wooden table was set before the tomb, and behind the table sat a gray-bearded man with the hood of his black robe covering the bulk of his face. A half-dozen men also dressed in black robes with large hoods and red sashes sat in silence in a semi-circle facing the table. Three bulky men in suits stood rigid watch over the others, one by the entrance to the chapel, the other two unobtrusively to either side of the bearded man at the table.

In front of the bearded man was a stone bowl filled with water. Beside the bowl was a crystal decanter with a dark liquid inside. Just to the side of the decanter was a wooden cup with a thick stem. On the other side of the bowl was a large wooden spoon. In front of the bowl lay an open book with a pen resting on a blank page. The room was illuminated by a series of votive candles that lined the floor in front of the tomb and several on each end of the wooden table.

The suited man by the chapel door held out Delacroix's robe. Delacroix turned his back to him and slid the robe over his clothing tying the robe with the red sash and pulling the hood over his head. He took his seat in the semi-circle with the others.

Crow pushed the front door open with caution. He allowed Rosenfeld in then held it to a quiet close. They looked around the narthex and listened to the voice in the distance. Crow crept up to the wooden door leading to the nave and ever so slightly cracked it open. Rosenfeld positioned an eye below Crow's head to get a look.

The old man at the table outstretched his arms and began a recitation in French. Rosenfeld translated the words in her head. "Here lie the bones of Michel Nostredame, whose almost divine pen was considered by all worthy of recounting and reporting coming events beyond Earth's sphere to men, according to the influence of the stars."

"What's he saying?" Crow whispered.

"Sh-h-h," she said. "I'll tell you in a minute."

"He departed this life in Salon-de-Craux in Provence," the old man continued, "in the year of grace 1566, on 2 July, aged sixty-two years six months and seventeen days. O posterity, do not take his ashes, and be not envious of his rest here."

"He was quoting the epitaph on Nostradamus' tomb," she whispered.

The old man took the decanter of black liquid and dramatically poured it into the bowl of water. He then took the cup, reached down inside with his fingers, and sprinkled some of the contents into the bowl. Setting the cup down, he stirred the concoction with the wooden spoon, swirling the contents round and round, his eyes getting bigger with each stir. He laid the spoon aside and pulled the hood of his robe down until his face disappeared. Then he leaned over covering the bowl with his hood. His back bowed as his lungs filled with air then exhaled. Again he breathed deep until he could draw no more air into his body and expelled the air from his lungs. The edges of his hood rippled under the force of his breath. He sucked air through his nostrils again and pushed the air out through his mouth.

He sat motionless for a time with his head still covering the bowl. He seemed not to breathe at all. The room was perfectly still, but the inside of the man's brain was a boiling cauldron. Disjointed images flashed in his head and began to bubble up from a smoky abyss until they were dizzily spinning in circles. Lightning struck. Hurricanes swirled. Great fires raged. These images spun in his mind like a huge tornado round and round and round. Gigantic waves formed in the ocean and pounded ashore swallowing everything in their path. Earthquakes toppled large buildings reducing them to rubble. Masses of humanity fled in terror. He closed his eyes tighter and braced himself with his hands on the table as if he had vertigo. His head slowly rotated in a circle while the horrid images compounded in his head, one disturbing scene replaced by another. The death and destruction climbed and climbed, the images churned out of control until the spinning torrent of horror reached a fever pitch. The images spun faster and faster. The noise inside his head grew louder and louder. He strained his mind's eye open wider to take it all in. The tornado of images spun even faster. He struggled to retain his sanity. Faster and faster the images passed in front of him as if he were watching them fly by on some out-of-control merry-go-round. He moaned and closed his eyes even tighter. The images spun in a torrent circle like a flood of water rushing down a massive drain, like a genie being sucked back into its lantern, until there was nothing but sudden darkness. He bolted upright. His eyes were wild and large. His robe snapped at the speed of his extended arm, and his boney finger pointed straight ahead across the great expanse of the cathedral to the door behind which Crow and Rosenfeld stood. "Les intrus!" he yelled.

"What the hell does that mean?" Crow said.

"Intruders," Rosenfeld translated.

"Shit!" He grabbed Rosenfeld by the hand and bolted out the front door of the church. The three bulky men sprang into action and headed for the door. Crow and Rosenfeld scrambled down the stone steps and Crow made a split-second decision. The road they had taken to the church had too long of a straightaway. They cut to the right then dashed down a narrow street to their left.

The three men sprinted down the stone steps and stopped at the bottom looking around in every direction. The lead man motioned with his pistol sending one to the left and one straight ahead. He took off to the right and just caught a glimpse of them at the bottom of the street as they were turning right. Crow took the next immediate left. The man rushed down the street in pursuit. He turned right at the bottom. They couldn't have reached the end of the Boulevard of the Kennedys without his seeing them. He took the left that Crow and Rosenfeld had just taken. He paused at the next intersection scanning the street to his right. He looked to his left. There they were entering General de Gaulle Park.

Crow pulled Rosenfeld by the hand. They dodged playground equipment and benches in the tree-lined park. At the other end of the block Crow looked over his shoulder. The suited man was scaling the waist-high park fence like a hurdle. They exited the park and scooted up Rue Théodore Jourdan.

"Hand me your scarf," Crow said.

"What? Why?"

"Don't argue. Just do it."

Rosenfeld untied the plaid scarf from her neck as they ran and handed it to him. Just a few yards up Rue Théodore Jourdan was a cobblestone pedestrian path to their left. A set of steep, narrow steps leading up to some apartments was on their right.

"Up there," Crow pointed.

Rosenfeld scampered up the steps. Crow darted a few feet into the pedestrian path, dropped the scarf, then raced back across the street and up the narrow steps. They huddled inside a doorway at the top. A few seconds later, they heard the hurried footsteps of the man. He spotted the scarf on the ground at the entrance to the pedestrian street and stopped. Snatching it up, he examined it in an instant then tossed it aside and dashed down the cobblestones and around the corner.

"Hurry," Crow said leading her back down the steps.

They shot back past the park and took a sharp left. Running full speed, they took a sudden right at Place Eugène Pelletan. Rosenfeld let out an involuntary scream and they both came to an abrupt halt, standing there panting in disbelief of their misfortune. Just as surprised was another of the suited men who came to a stop from a dead run in front of them. He stepped slowly, his eyes fixed on them. He reached inside his coat and pulled a gun from his holster.

Chapter Twenty

Crow and Rosenfeld stood there for a moment catching their breath. Their eyes were glued on the man with the gun. He edged toward them. They instinctively raised their hands. Crow felt to his right and pulled Rosenfeld behind him, putting himself between her and the gun. The man inched closer until he was just a few yards away then stopped. He frowned and tilted his head slightly, keeping his eyes locked on the two of them. Crow's heart was beating out of his chest. His mouth was dry. He took a big swallow then continued panting. His hands were raised shoulder high. Rosenfeld peered over his left shoulder at the man's face then down at his gun. The man seemed confused. He took a step back, still watching them. Then another step. He holstered his gun inside his suit coat, turned, and jogged off in the opposite direction.

"HOW MANY TIMES are you going to ask me that? I have no idea why he let us go." Crow tried the light switch just inside the front door of the farmhouse. "The power's still out."

"It makes no sense," Rosenfeld said, lighting the room with her phone. "One minute they're in hot pursuit, then the guy corners us and just lets us go?"

Crow threw the car key fob on the kitchen table and relit the candle. "What did you want me to do? Call after him and ask him if there'd been some mistake?"

She ignored the quip.

"All right," Crow said, "you told me when we got back here you'd explain what all that weird crap was about with the guy in the hood."

She sat down at the table. "You may want to take a seat. This'll take some time to unpack."

Crow sat down next to her.

"Nostradamus didn't just have these prophetic visions out of thin air," she said. "He had some help."

"Help?"

"Yes. You saw all those items on the table, right?"

"Yeah."

"The bowl in front of him was filled with water."

"What kind of water?" Crow asked.

"Ordinary tap water. The glass decanter was filled with ink."

"You mean ink like you find in a pen?"

"Exactly. Nostradamus would pour ink from his inkwell into a bowl of water. Then he would add nutmeg."

"That's what the guy was sprinkling from the cup?"

"Yes. Remember, Nostradamus was an apothecary, so he understood what mixing nutmeg, ink, and water would form."

"And that is?" Crow asked.

"Well, the Egyptians used nutmeg as a substitute for hashish, if that tells you anything. Nutmeg is also said to promote vivid daydreams. Nostradamus discovered that mixing it with water and ink created an elevated state of awareness. It stimulates the central nervous system."

"Like an amphetamine."

"Exactly. You saw the book on the table and the pen? Nostradamus would inhale the mixture of nutmeg and ink then wait for his visions to come and write them down. I suspect that's what this man was doing, too."

"And you buy all this?"

"I'm not saying I buy it. I'm just telling you what they were doing. It *is* rather spooky that after sniffing that stuff he suddenly was aware we were there."

"Yeah, I guess. These guys have to be First Facers."

"We can't be sure."

"Oh, come on. Delacroix is this Nostradamus fanatic and we see him with a group of grown men in hoods trying to conjure up Nostradamus' visions?"

"Or they could be just what you said, Nostradamus fanatics. I can't imagine if the First Face of Janus already has the Unriddled Manuscript that they'd need to resort to such tomfoolery. More like a bunch of kids playing with a Ouija Board."

"What about the muscle?"

"I don't know," she said. "Maybe they treasure their privacy."

"Look, I've done the Ouija Board thing. We didn't hire thugs to make sure our moms didn't find out."

"I don't mind telling you, that was freakin' me out," she said.

"Yeah, I know. I'm getting chills just thinking about it."

Rosenfeld shuddered. "I don't know if I'll be able to sleep tonight."

The distant sound of glass breaking at the other end of the house startled them both.

"What the hell was that?" Rosenfeld whispered.

"I don't know." Crow concentrated on the hallway leading to the bedrooms. "I'm going to find out. Stay here."

He grabbed the candlestick and started sneaking toward where he thought he'd heard the sound. Only after getting halfway there did he realized he was defenseless. He looked around the den and homed in on a poker hanging beside the limestone fireplace. Armed with the iron weapon, he continued his trek toward the source of the sound. He eased down the hallway. One of the wide planks creaked below his feet. He stopped. Lightning lit the hallway for a brief second and the thunder crashed a second later.

Rosenfeld jumped in her seat. She hugged herself rubbing her arms and looking warily around the room.

Crow could hear something coming from one of the rooms down the hall but it was hard to tell which one. He began creeping again, gripping the poker tighter. He felt a knot in his stomach. He approached the room on the right and could hear some kind of commotion, but it sounded muted or muffled like someone rummaging through a closet. He was at a disadvantage in opening the door, since he held the poker in one hand and the candlestick in the other.

A chill came over Sidney Rosenfeld and she shivered.

After some studying on the situation, Crow set the candlestick on the floor next to the doorway and eased up to grab the doorknob. He counted down from three in his mind to prepare himself for what lay beyond the door. Three. He clasped the poker tighter. Two. Sweat beaded above his upper lip. One. He threw open the door and burst inside. The candle shone up from the floor enough for his mind to piece together what he was seeing. A window was slightly ajar. His eyes shot down to what appeared to be shimmers from pieces of broken glass on the floor then back up to the window. The wind was pushing it in and, once the wind subsided, gravity was pulling it back shut. He retreated a step and knelt to reach the candlestick behind him.

He shone a light on the floor. The light revealed the broken drinking glass that the window had knocked to the floor when the wind first blew it open. Crow knelt to pick up the broken pieces. He set them back on the table and stood up relieved that he had only allowed his imagination to get the best of him.

And that's when he felt it. The hand on his arm was as terrifying as anything he had ever felt. Blood rushed to his head as if he were in some sort of nightmare. He was acting on pure adrenaline and reflex. It was like watching himself from afar no longer in control of his own muscles. He dropped the candlestick and the flame extinguished plunging the room into darkness. He spun around and away from the hand, grabbing the poker with both hands above his head like a medieval executioner's axe. His biceps tightened. In that tiny moment he knew he had only one shot at it. His mind channeled all of his strength and energy into that one singular action of bringing the iron weapon down on the head of his assailant.

Chapter Twenty-One

"It's me!" the voice rang out in the darkness.

The flood of built-up power drained from Crow's arms. They dropped and dangled limp by his side. "Damn, Sidney! You scared the hell out of me."

"I'm sorry. I didn't like sitting there in the dark all by myself."

Crow fumbled on the floor for the candlestick. About the time he had both the candlestick and candle in hand, the lights came back on down the hallway. Rosenfeld tripped the switch by the door and lit the room. Crow reached over and secured the window. They looked at one another and chuckled with relief.

"Are we freakin' out maybe a little too much?" she said.

"We can't be too careful."

"Yeah, well, we can't be killing each other either."

"You shouldn't be sneaking up on people."

"I wasn't sneaking. I was creeped out in there. You shouldn't leave a girl all alone like that."

"Oh, I should've sent you in here with the fireplace tool?"

"It's been a long day," she said. "We need to get some sleep."

Crow looked around. "I'll take this room. There's a master across the hall. You can have that one."

"See you in the morning," she said.

"Yeah," Crow said. "See ya in the morning."

THE CRATE WAS unloaded from the transport plane at the aduana—the Spanish word for customs office—along with dozens of other packages. The crate was a square box encased in wood. The ceiling fan barely made a dent in the heat. A clerk dressed in short sleeves with sweat stains under his armpits scanned the label to begin processing the package. He read over the paperwork. The sides and top were stamped 'FRAGILE' in both English and Spanish.

"I will handle this one, Miguel," said the man who seemed to appear out of nowhere. "It is your break time."

The clerk looked up. "I do not mind. I have already begun processing it."

"No, no, no," the first man said. "This is a large shipment. It could take some time. Go. Enjoy your break."

"Are you sure?" the clerk asked.

The man with the gold tooth smiled widely. "I insist."

THE HYPNOTIC SOUND of water rushing in the river below had lulled Crow into a deep sleep. He leaned against his favorite rock, pen in hand resting on his notepad. The horn blowing from the truck that had just been cut off in traffic on the road at the top of the embankment brought him back to reality. Eyes wide open, he looked at his watch and jumped up cramming his belongings into his backpack. He climbed the hill and hurried onto the seat of his bicycle.

He had planned to only miss one class then sneak into second period gym class unnoticed. Too late for that now. A friend had signed him in at homeroom, but the school had gotten wise. They now required roll to be called just after lunch. He could grab something to eat at home. His mother was at work, so she'd never know. After a quick sandwich, he could peddle up to the back of the school unnoticed and blend in with the other kids changing classes. Skipping a full day would raise the suspicion of that Nazi Rotch. As long as his homeroom teacher didn't do a head count, which she never did, he would be fine.

He peddled as quickly as he could and rounded the corner onto his street. His heart sank. In the driveway was the now-familiar ugly green car. So was his mom's car. Busted. They would be waiting for him in the den, Rotch with that pathetic smirk on his face. His mom would almost be in tears, chain-smoking, pacing. Crow slowed his roll. Why hasten the inevitable? He dropped his bike in the dirt and slowly opened the screen door to the kitchen. He was prepared to take his medicine.

He walked into the den. No one there. He thought he caught the scent of his mom's perfume, the one she put on only when she was going somewhere nice, which was almost never. He could see her in his mind in that white dress she always wore when she wanted to impress. The one that accentuated her leathery tan skin. He was just before calling her name when he heard it. Faint at first, but as he crept closer to her bedroom in the back of the house, the sound was unmistakable. The rhythmic tap of her bed's headboard lightly beating against the wall. As he approached the door, he could hear her soft sighs of ecstasy. Almost in unison was the unthinkable. The grotesque moans of Vice Principal Rotch. Crow was gripped with rage. His jaw tightened and his nostrils flared like a demented beast.

He wished he had access to a gun. He was sure he could kill them both. He stood there at the door, unable to move, listening, seething, crying. The tapping of the headboard and sounds of raw, animal sex began to be replaced by a low whine in his head that seemed to be in four parts. He frowned. The room blurred into an effulgent white almost blinding him. The four sounds would hit the same pitch momentarily then diverge only to intersect again. The whine seemed to get louder and louder.

He jolted awake and struggled to get his bearings. His head jerked to the left then to the right. He was in France, in a farmhouse. He willed himself wide awake and, once there, knew exactly what the sound was. He could see the shadow of it on the sheer curtains in the morning light. He hit the floor just as the first shot came through the window shattering the window pane. The bullets thudded in a row into the mattress shooting foam and fabric into the air. Several other shots were fired while he scrambled across the floor. Dressed only in his pajama pants, he was out the door. He ran into Rosenfeld in the hallway in a nightgown wondering what the hell was going on.

"Drone!" Crow shouted.

They huddled together outside her room.

"All we have to do is keep away from the windows, right?" she asked.

"I wish it was that simple. Some of these drones can launch grenades."

"How do you know that?"

"I write about stuff like this," he said.

"How do they know where we are in the house?"

"Heat signatures. That damn thing can see us anywhere in the house."

"What are we going to do?"

"I have an idea, but I need you to stay right here. You promise this time?"

Rosenfeld nodded.

"I'm going to draw its fire."

"But—"

Crow was gone. He dashed without fear down the hall and through the den. Glassware on the table shattered behind him as the bullets tore through the windows. He flattened himself against the wall. His heart was racing. He knew what he had to do, but getting there was the problem. He had spent the time Sidney was preparing dinner exploring the old two-story farmhouse and was now glad he did. He found something that might save them, but it was all the way upstairs, and there was a bank of windows over the front door that exposed the stairway. He wondered why the drone hadn't launched a grenade, but then it hit him. If they were tracking heat signatures, the resulting fire from a grenade would be a nightmare for the drone. Setting the house ablaze would not only make it harder to find them, it would surely attract the attention of the neighbors at the nearest farmhouse.

Crow had to get upstairs, but even running up those steps at full speed, he'd be easy pickings in front of that bank of windows. The drone would have to reposition to the other side of the house, but the distance from where he was to the front foyer might be just enough time to do that. He knew he couldn't make it to the top of the stairs without the drone getting off a clear shot. It hovered like a nervous bumble bee at eye level at the rear of the house.

"Sidney!" he called down the hallway. He had a line of sight to her.

"Yeah?"

"I need you to do something for me. Walk down the hallway slowly toward me. I need you to draw the attention of the drone."

"You want me to draw fire from that thing?"

"Yeah."

"Are you crazy?"

"Well, no, not really draw fire. Just fool it."

"How?"

"When you get to the edge of the hallway at the den I want you to stop then prone yourself like you're going to run through the den."

The drone operator's screen showed two heat signatures in the house. One up against the wall in the den and the other easing down the hallway. His finger hovered over the red button.

Sidney reached the end of the hallway and conformed her body to that of someone getting ready to sprint across the room. Crow could see her in position. She trembled in terror.

"Now, when I say 'go,' I want you to run one step into the den then turn immediately around and run back to where you are. Do you understand?"

She nodded.

"No more than one step, real quick, then back to where you are. You got it?"

She nodded again.

"OK. Three, two, one, go!"

Rosenfeld sprinted the one step out. Crow tore through the den and into the foyer then up the stairs. The drone fired two shots where it anticipated Rosenfeld to be, but by the time they hit, she was back in place. Crow opened the armoire in the hall upstairs as fast as he could. The camera on the drone scanned the downstairs. It only detected one heat signature. It tilted its camera toward the upstairs and saw the figure of Crow standing in the hall. It immediately shifted to reposition itself heading directly above its prior position toward the top floor. Crow unfastened the latch and threw open the windows.

The screen showed the side of the house as the drone ascended. Crow was fumbling with something when he came into view on the drone's screen. The infrared tracking device locked in on him and a green square lit up to frame him. The drone operator placed his thumb on the red firing button.

Crow pumped the Mossberg 500 All Purpose shotgun once and fired from the hip. The drone was no more than a few yards away. The shot was a direct hit. Sparks flew from its gaping hole. The propellers that remained intact spun the craft out of control. It gyrated about in midair until it lost power and the bulk of what was left of it dropped like a smoldering cinderblock to the ground.

"Throw some clothes on and grab your bag," Crow yelled, descending the stairs with the shotgun in one hand and a canvas duffel in the other. "I don't know if there's another one of those damn things nearby, and I'm not waiting around to find out."

They threw their bags in the back seat of the Benz. Crow put the pump action shotgun and the canvas duffel of shotgun shells under a blanket in the floor of the back seat. In less than three minutes, they were in the car and speeding down a backroad through the French countryside.

Delacroix's right hand was just a few inches from the cellphone that sat on the desk in his office, but his hand didn't even flinch when it rang. Crow heard the voicemail message in French. "Hello, this is Jean-Claude Delacroix. I am unable to take your phone call. Please leave a message."

Crow anxiously waited for the beep. "Jean-Claude, this is Benson Crow. We had visitors at the house. We're heading to Avignon. Call me back. You've got some explaining to do, my friend."

Delacroix was reclined in the chair at his desk. His right hand casually rested on the desk. His left hand was limp by his side.

The crimson semi-circle that reached from his left ear underneath his chin and over to his right ear still oozed with blood. His shirt was drenched in dark red. His eyes stared straight ahead never to witness another secret again. Whatever he harbored was now lost to the ages. Standing in front of the desk staring down at the lifeless figure was Marcus Foster.

Chapter Twenty-Two

It was Thursday morning. Just fifty-two hours until the wedding, if they had interpreted Nostradamus correctly. Crow and Rosenfeld drove north toward Avignon and, for a time, were too shocked to even speak. Had what just happened really happened? Crow had seen it before. The stealthy, sinister nature of a drone attack. He had described it to Rosenfeld, but his depiction didn't do the horror justice. The feeling was violent and terrifying. The disorientation of such a silent but brutal attack was psychologically violating and demoralizing. It shattered one's sense of security. It could appear anywhere any time without warning. Now she understood why Crow scanned the sky.

"Who the hell *was* that?" Rosenfeld finally asked, looking out the window.

"There's no way to be sure. It looks to be the same people who killed Grumbling and his housekeeper, whoever that is."

"It's the Custos Verbi," Rosenfeld said. "It has to be."

"That would be my guess."

"They want those quatrains."

"Which would explain why they didn't torch us." Crow took a deep breath. "We have to go to Avignon."

"Why?"

"Because that's where the Palace of the Popes is. Delacroix believes that's where the Custos Verbi is."

She pulled a tube of coral lipstick from her purse and pointed with it.

"OK, so explain something to me. Why are we now going looking for the Custos Verbi if they're trying to kill us?" She placed the lipstick to her full lips and looked into the mirror on her visor. The coral made her lips glisten.

"If the CV really are behind this, I need to tell them what's going on. Make sense?" Crow said.

Rosenfeld pushed the visor up, leaned forward, and gazed up at the sky through the windshield. "Not in the least." She turned back at Crow. "Can I ask you another question?"

"Sure."

She threw the lipstick back in her purse. "Have you lost your frickin' mind?"

"What are you talking about?"

"I'm talking about some guy who was just hunted by a drone who now wants to walk into the headquarters of the guys *with* the drone and say, 'Hey, fellas, this has all been some huge misunderstanding.' If they're trying to kill us—and it is *us* now—you won't get anywhere near them before they blow you away."

"Relax. I have a plan."

"Mm-hmm, yeah, I've seen your plans."

"Look, I'm not stupid. I'm not going to just walk into the lion's den."

"Then what are you going to do?"

"I'm going to work Delacroix's connection."

"The priest? In Avignon? And what if he's one of them?"

"If he were one of them, he wouldn't have been exchanging information with Delacriox."

"Unless it was Delacroix who gave away our location," she said.

Crow shrugged. "A valid point, but if Delacroix wanted us dead, why didn't he just kill us when he led us all the way out to the house? If he's CV, he would've taken us out when he had the perfect chance to. No, there's more to it than that."

"You just called him to cuss him out!" Rosenfeld said. "You think he ratted us out, don't you?"

"No, I don't think he ratted us out, but I think he may have inadvertently told someone. Someone he shouldn't have. He's just not being careful enough. He'll call me back. We'll sort this whole thing out."

"Somebody knows who we are."

"Obviously," Crow said.

"I mean the goon who let us walk last night," she said. "Delacroix could've decided to leave us alone until we saw them involved in that creepy ceremony. At that point he could've decided we were too much of a liability. That's when he sent the drone."

"Well, that's why I don't think he's involved. The guy last night could've killed us. Why let us go last night then drone us this morning? Plus, Delacroix has a key to the house. If he's CV, he'd just let them in."

Rosenfeld pondered the observation. "Maybe the leak was that monk you met with."

Crow thought about it for a moment. "Could be."

"And you told him everything."

"I didn't tell him *everything*," Crow insisted.

"You told him enough. Enough to get us killed."

"I didn't tell him where we were staying, if that's what you mean. And I know we weren't followed back from town. I made sure of that."

"We just got droned, Crow. The only thing you can be sure of is you can't be sure of anything."

They rolled into Avignon on the N100, crossed the Rhone River, and followed the signs for Centre Historique, the historical center of Avignon. Crow stopped alongside a call box at Rue Peyrollerie and pressed the intercom for his hotel. He was entering an area with roads so narrow only authorized vehicles and guests of the hotels were allowed to enter. He was cleared to proceed and Crow drove the Mercedes further into the ancient town center of Avignon. Old sycamores shaded cobblestone lanes and loomed over white umbrellas where locals and tourists gathered for breakfast in the shadow of history itself. The Mercedes barely cleared the centuries-old buildings on either side that lined a medieval maze of incommodious streets. Crow turned onto Place de l'Amirande and pulled up in front of their hotel, handing the key fob to the valet.

There was only one way up the narrow, one-lane cobblestone street to the hotel. Its entrance was blocked by two rising and falling bollards controlled by the front desk. Another single bollard blocked the only exit and one had to call the hotel on the intercom to have it lowered. Crow wasn't sure what he might encounter in Avignon and wasn't comfortable having to wait on his car from the valet if they had to leave in a hurry, but it was their only option. There were, of course, other hotels, but, for Crow, this location was exactly the signal he wanted to send.

Avignon sits on the edge of Provence, an area of France that derived its name from being the first Roman province beyond the Alps. They named it Provincia Romana in the second century BC, which evolved over time into simply Provence. Through the ages, it became world renown for the arts and synonymous with culture. Famous painters who either hailed from Provence or did their best work there included Cézanne, van Gogh, Renoir, and Picasso. F. Scott Fitzgerald wrote most of *The Great Gatsby* in Provence. Crow had actually drawn inspiration from drinking in the culture and history, especially at this particular hotel. Rosenfeld wondered why he went to so much trouble to stay there. It was more than just its location. Her question was answered the moment they walked through the front door.

La Mirande Hotel was a flashback to La Belle Époque, the Beautiful Era, a period of time between the end of the Franco-Prussian War in 1871 and the outbreak of the first World War in 1914. That period was known in the United States as the Gilded Age. The hotel appeared frozen in time. Menacing-looking stone-carved faces looked down on passersby from atop the arched windows outside. A single lantern hung over the modest entrance that belied the five-star accommodations inside.

The large wooden doors were flung wide during the daylight hours and two thick glass doors with large brass knobs kept the elements from the tasteful elegance inside. A single carriage lantern hung from the center of the entrance hall surrounded by light-brown intricately-cut carvings spaced every foot or so inside the gray dentil molding. To the right through a doorway was the front desk made of carved wood paneling painted gray to match the large cornice that framed the ceiling. An enormous tapestry hung on the wall behind.

Rosenfeld wandered toward the rear of the hotel into another room and gazed up in awe. A huge atrium lounge was the central room of the hotel, which more resembled an old French manor. Its walls were made of hewn stone and they stretched several stories high. One could imagine that it had been a central outdoor courtyard at one point in the structure's rich history. It doubled as a dining room and sitting area, depending on the time of day, with round tables and white tablecloths.

She peeked through an oversized doorway. Adjacent to the atrium lounge was another sitting room where guests passed the time reading or enjoying conversation. The walls were weathered green wainscoting from the waist down with bold stripes of red, gold, and green stretching from the wainscoting to the crown molding at the ceiling. Period portraits hung from the walls along with intricate tapestries and gold and crystal chandeliers. A gold-framed mirror hung above a French provincial fireplace adorned with painted vases and a glass-enclosed French porcelain figurine of a pale young lady fanning herself. Small round tables with white linen tablecloths were surrounded by comfortable club chairs upholstered in a rich gold and wine brocade below a Renaissance period wooden coffered ceiling. An antique table was covered with books on art. A large oriental rug pulled all the eclectic elements together.

Parts of the hotel dated to the fourteenth century, but the bulk of it was constructed in the seventeenth and eighteenth centuries. The entire hotel retained the feel of the fine country manor it once was. Its roots were that of a mansion to a cardinal once upon a time. The old palace was seized in 1410 and the mansion burned to the ground. Construction on the current structure began in 1653 and continued off and on for the next hundred years. The hotel epitomized what is known to the world as Provence.

They walked through another doorway and were back at the front desk.

"I feel like I'm in a dream," Rosenfeld said.

Crow smiled.

"Bonjour," the desk clerk greeted.

"Bonjour," Crow said. "Parlez-vous anglais?"

"Yes, I speak English," he said. "How can I help you?"

"I have a reservation," Crow said. "A suite. The name is Crow."

"Um," Rosenfeld said, looking to the clerk, "I have a question."

"Oui?"

"Does the suite have two beds?" she asked.

"The suites come with a queen bed."

"Wait a minute," Crow said gruffly. "They told me on the phone they could do two beds."

"If I may finish, monsieur. All of our suites come with queen beds, but our house service can remake the bed as two single beds."

"Two beds?" Rosenfeld asked.

"Yes," the clerk explained, "the bed comes apart as two singles, and we have one available already this morning if you would like."

"That's better." Crow signed the necessary papers and was handed a key to their room. "Send someone up immediately to do the two bed thing, will you?"

"Oui, monsieur."

He turned and headed for the elevator.

"I apologize," Rosenfeld said to the man behind the counter. "He's been up a long time." She hurried to catch up with Crow. "What is it with you and service people?"

"What do you mean?" he asked.

The clerk watched as the two walked through the atrium, past the grand staircase, and called the elevator. He reached for the phone and dialed, never even waiting for a 'hello.'

"They are here," said the clerk in a hushed tone.

The man at the outdoor cafe with the bald head and the black patch over his eye took a long drag from his cigarette and held it in his lungs before exhaling. He ended the call, blew smoke through his nose, and placed the phone on the table.

Chapter Twenty-Three

Crow and Rosenfeld took the small elevator to their floor and showed themselves to their spacious suite. An elegant crystal chandelier hung from the tall painted wood-paneled ceiling in the bedroom. The room was bright and airy. A floral love seat and two matching chairs created a sitting area at the foot of the bed. The walls were knee-high wainscoting and painted an off-white with thick molding above the doors and windows. Sheer curtains covered the windows in both rooms with beige silk-lined ceiling-to-floor draperies trimmed in wine and gold pulled to either side.

"You like living dangerously, don't you?" Rosenfeld said, dramatically pulling back the sheer curtains and gesturing like a game show model. Directly across the street, filling the entire set of windows, was the Palace of the Popes.

Crow pulled out his tablet and plopped down on the bed. "Why not? We don't want to sneak up on 'em. If they're there and they know we're here, they'll reach out to us."

"Yeah, that's what I'm afraid of."

There was a knock on the door. Crow and Rosenfeld looked at one another. Rosenfeld bit her nails. Crow rose cautiously from the bed and walked to the door.

"Who is it?"

A muffled response in a thick French accent came from the other side. "Guest service," she said.

Crow hesitated a second, looking back over his shoulder at his nervous companion. He opened the door. Two chambermaids stood in front of him in black dresses covered with full-length white aprons. One said something in French. Crow looked again over his shoulder to Rosenfeld.

"They want to arrange our bed." Then she spoke to the two ladies directly, "Entrez, s'il vous plaît."

They entered the room and went about removing the duvet.

"I'm going to take advantage of that buffet I saw when we came in while they're still serving," Crow said. "Care to join me?"

"I'm not very hungry. You go ahead."

Crow was eager to learn more about this Palace of the Popes. He needed to talk to someone who was an expert on the palace aside from those at the palace itself. On his way downstairs, he pulled out his phone and looked up the priest Delacroix mentioned he knew in Avignon, Father Pierre Simonin. He was a father at the Church of St. Agricol in Avignon and had given university lectures on the palace. Rosenfeld was right to be cautious. Simonin could very well be working with the CV. Crow had to be more careful this time. He made the call.

Marcus Foster sat at a table in his hotel room in a white tank top t-shirt cleaning the tool of his trade, a Beretta APX. Like a barber sharpening his razor, he regularly made sure it was in peak working order. The ceiling fan barely turned. The TV was tuned to a newscast in French. His room was nondescript like someone on a budget, or someone who just didn't give a damn where he slept. The room was hot, muggy, small, but it didn't matter. The job was what mattered. Completing the mission was paramount. His cell phone chirped three short beeps. Foster hit a button to engage the phone and turn on the speaker. He heard a phone number being dialed and then the number ringing.

"Eglise Saint Agricol," the woman said.

"Parlez vous anglais?" Crow asked.

"Yes."

"Great. I need to meet with Father Simonin for a few minutes this morning, if he's available. My name is Benson Crow. Please tell him I'm a friend of Jean-Claude Delacroix. He sent me."

"Hold please."

Foster placed the slide back over the barrel and pulled it toward him and into place then released it. He inserted the 15-round magazine into the grip and snapped it home with the heel of his palm.

"Monsieur Crow?"

"Yes?"

"Father Simonin can meet with you in about an hour if you wish."

"Perfect. I'll see him then."

Rosenfeld took a seat in one of the chairs at the foot of the bed to wait for the chambermaids to finish but quickly learned she had a ringside seat to a show. Like something from *Downton Abbey*, the two ladies folded the queen sized duvet and laid it to the side. They then pulled the bottom sheet and folded it with the precision of folding a flag at a military funeral. The queen bed was pulled apart into two separate twin beds. The ladies took new sheets and one ran her fingers along the bottom of the foot of the bed and neatly tucked the sheet underneath the mattress. In unison, on either side of the bed, they pulled each corner taut and formed perfect hospital corners simultaneously tucking each corner under the mattress. They did the same at the other end of the bed. They then took the single-sized duvet cover and, like magicians, lifted and turned it until the down-filled quilt disappeared inside of it. They repeated the process on the other bed. They added the final touch, what looked like an oversized placemat that floated to rest on the wood floor beside each bed so that the first thing guests felt in the morning was luxurious linen on their toasty feet. Rosenfeld smiled.

Crow entered the dining area downstairs to behold an elegant display of delicious breakfast items arranged on a short khaki linen tablecloth atop a floor-length white one. An assortment of juices and crystal glasses were at one end of the long table. Croissants and other fresh breads spilled out of a linen-lined basket at the other. In between were poached eggs, several varieties of meats and cheeses, fruits from the local farmers market, and various jams, jellies, and honey. Crow was shown to his table and brought a silver coffee pot which was poured into his fine china cup. He added a dash of cream from the silver cream dispenser and a lump of sugar. He stirred his coffee and waited for his appointed time to meet with Father Simonin.

Once the chambermaids were gone, Rosenfeld grabbed Crow's computer tablet and made herself comfortable on one of the freshly-made beds. She began researching the social pages for possible weddings that fit the quatrains. *Venue*, she told herself. Delacroix had said the key was the venue. She shook her head at the overwhelming possibilities.

Crow dabbed a napkin to the corner of his mouth after finishing his breakfast. He exited the hotel and took a left into the warm summer morning soaking in his surroundings. He walked past the impressive walls of the Palace of the Popes' east side wondering just what secrets they held behind them. An attractive brunette with white sunglasses, a white dress, black sandals, and a slight sunburn just above her cleavage sat outside the iron gates. She plucked an acoustic guitar and softly sang a mesmerizing song. The melody drifted up the wall of the hotel and into the open window where Rosenfeld, atop a plush duvet, fell into a deep sleep.

Crow followed the narrow cobblestone street around the corner and took a couple of side streets, looking back over his shoulder every few moments. Several blocks down, he passed through a large courtyard where restaurant workers were opening umbrellas on small metal tables preparing for the day's lunch crowd. Clock Square was named for the large clock tower that was separated from the city's main square by Avignon City Hall. The church was just two blocks beyond, and Crow ascended its ancient steps.

The church doors were large and imposing yet unpretentious and almost humble, much like the church's namesake, Agricol of Avignon. Agricol was a sixth-century monk famous for defending the sick and the poor from overbearing civil authorities. He was, oddly enough, made the patron saint of storks, something to do with a legend of preventing an invasion of storks with his blessing. Crow was reminded of the story when he saw the saint's emblem depicting him with the bird.

Crow entered through the paneled doors which were hung beneath the statuary of an angel on the left side and Mother Mary holding the baby Jesus on the right. He found an employee removing flowers from the altar. The smell of white roses and recently snuffed candles hung in the air. He informed her of his appointment with Father Pierre Simonin and was escorted out a side door into another part of the church. He sat in an outer office with a secretary while the father met with a parishioner behind closed doors. Crow could hear a faint conversation in French that he didn't understand.

The music outside her window went quiet and Rosenfeld awoke with a nervous start. She headed for the bath for a long shower making sure the door was locked. The bath had his and hers white pedestal sinks atop white Carrara marble floors with a luxurious tub and old-world fixtures. There was a separate shower and a water closet. She prepared to disrobe but hesitated. She went back to the bathroom door, unlocked it, peered out into the bedroom, then closed the door and locked it again.

Crow shifted in his seat. After what seemed an eternity, a stern but pleasant man wearing a black cassock with a black sash and white clerical collar emerged from his office. He offered a parting word of comfort to the elderly lady with whom he had been meeting then leaned down to hear the whisper of his secretary. The cassock hung much like a robe as he walked across the room to greet Crow.

"Thanks for agreeing to see me on such short notice, Father. I hope I'm not intruding," Crow said.

"Certainly not. I am never too busy for a friend of Jean-Claude Delacroix. I was just before making the long trek up the tower to do my weekly inspection of the belfry. Lots of upkeep on this old lady," he smiled. "I am in no hurry, believe me. How can I be of assistance?"

"Is there somewhere we can speak privately?"

"But of course," Father Simonin said. He led Crow into his office. The door squeaked to a close, and the priest took a seat behind his desk.

"I need to get a message to the Custos Verbi," Crow said.

Father Simonin tried to hide his shock. "I am, uh, I am not sure what you are talking about."

"Delacroix told me you're an expert on them. I need to let them know what's going on."

Father Simonin rose. "I am afraid you have come to the wrong place."

"No, I'm sure I'm at the right place, Father. Delacroix was very specific."

"Monsieur Delacroix was mistaken," Simonin said sternly.

"Would you be more open to listening if I were in the confessional?"

The father reflected on the question.

"Father, I'm begging you," Crow said. "I need your help. I'm afraid time is running out. In just two days the prophecy will be fulfilled unless somebody stops it."

"Monsieur Crow, you are putting us both in grave danger just by being here." He wiped his brow.

"I'm not the threat. I'm determined to stop the next prophecy, just as the Custos Verbi is trying to do, but I can't stop it if I'm dead. I need their help. I need their protection."

"Monsieur Crow, you must go now. I cannot help you."

The father moved from behind the desk toward the door. Crow rose and touched his arm. The father stopped and stared at him.

"All I need to know is if they're headquartered at the palace," Crow said.

Simonin's voice was low and grave. "You have no idea who you are involved with."

"Maybe not, but someone has to stand up for what's right."

"Someone *has* been. For almost 500 years. If you are smart, you will let them do their job without interference."

"Just like all the other times they've tried to stop them and failed? I've been placed in a unique position to do something, Father. I don't know why or by whom, but I have to see this through."

"You do not understand the bigger picture. No one ever sees the bigger picture until it is over."

"I can stop this," Crow said. "I just need to figure out where the prophecy is taking place. We're fighting the same fight, but I'm afraid they think I'm working against them. I have to let them know that—"

"I am not one of them," Father Simonin interrupted.

"But you know what I'm talking about."

The father walked to the door, cracked it open, then shut it again. Crow sat back down and Simonin resumed his position behind the desk.

With her hair in a towel, Rosenfeld exited the bath and checked the clock beside the bed. She took her hair from the towel and began to brush it, staring off in the distance. She was growing concerned that Crow wasn't back.

"I am a student of the Palais des Papes," Simonin told Crow. "I have studied it most of my life. I have spent a lot of time there. Many years ago I began to piece things together. I was warned not to ask too many questions, but my appetite for the truth was insatiable. I discovered the legends. I learned about the society of Nostradamus."

"The First Face of Janus," Crow said.

Simonin nodded. "And the Custos Verbi. How are you involved?"

Crow produced the quatrains from his breast pocket and handed the paper to Father Simonin. He read the verses.

"Where did you get this?" he asked.

"Long story. It was given to me in Montreal."

"By whom?"

"A man. I don't know who he was or why he gave it to me. He died for the cause. Now somebody's trying to kill me."

"Who?"

"I don't know. The CV, maybe. I was hoping you could help me figure that out."

"Me?"

"Yes. It's possible that Delacroix may have sold me out. If he did, I want to know to whom."

Simonin looked at him with disbelief. "Jean-Claude? That is preposterous."

"Why is that preposterous? If he's a First Facer or Custos Verbi then—"

"He is neither," Simonin insisted.

"How do you know?"

"I know. Jean-Claude and I are very close. We are curious outsiders. We study the prophecy wars. We are students, not activists."

"He was the only person who knew where we were staying and they came for us."

"Was he? There must be another explanation."

"That's why I'm here," Crow said.

"I cannot help you."

"I need to reach the Custos Verbi," Crow said. "Something big is happening. And soon. In just two days. This is urgent, Father. Innocent people will die. I need to figure out what the prophecy is and stop it. The Custos Verbi can help me. *You* can help me if you'll just tell me how I can contact them?"

The priest smiled. "You do not contact them. This is a centuries-old battle between good and evil. It is one thing to be a spectator. It is quite another to meddle."

"But I can be the difference this time. If I can join with the Custos Verbi, we can stop them. I'm already halfway there."

"Monsieur Delacroix is an intelligent man, but he is wrong about one thing. The Custos Verbi is not here," Simonin said.

"Where then?" Crow asked.

"I cannot say."

"You can't or you won't?"

Simonin said nothing.

"Do you believe in coincidence, Father?"

"I believe in providence," he answered.

"As do I. It's no coincidence that I was given the quatrains, and it's no coincidence that I sit here before you today."

The father gazed out the window.

"This whole affair started thousands of miles away," Crow continued. "I happened to be in Montreal at just the right moment. I had no connection to any of this, yet I was chosen. I have followed the trail, and it led me from Montreal to Boston to Washington to Salon and now here." He leaned forward trying to catch Simonin's gaze. "To you, Father. You've been praying for guidance. You've been praying for answers. Delacroix is your friend, but you're not like him. You're more than a student or a casual observer. His is a secular fascination. Yours is much more. You believe in the cause of the Custos Verbi. You've been praying for the First Face of Janus to be stopped, and now I come walking through your door? Coincidence, Father," Crow leaned back in his seat, "or providence?"

After a moment, Simonin pulled a small slip of paper from his desk not much larger than a fortune cookie paper. He used these slips to write Bible verses for the children to look up. He scribbled something on it, rolled it up tightly, and placed it in Crow's hand.

"Do not look at it now. When you are far from this place, please."

"Thank you, Father."

"I am only going to say this once, so remember it," Simonin said. "Understood?"

Crow nodded.

"Behold the cup and follow the choir. The straight path ends for the non-believer. Can you remember that?"

"Behold the cup and follow the choir. The straight path ends for the non-believer," Crow repeated.

Simonin said, "You must have faith. No man is an island. Find the defender of the rock by the sea and you will find your answer."

Chapter Twenty-Four

Rosenfeld wondered if this was what it felt like when a teenager was two hours past his curfew. She was frightened and angry all at once. If she could just know he was OK, she would stop worrying. She hated not knowing. What she really hated was not being in control. He was brand new to all this, a novice off on a lark. He had no idea who he was dealing with. She tried to tell him. Everyone tried to tell him. He was careless. Reckless. Case in point, booking a room directly across from the Palace of the Popes. A bold move that would surely evoke a response if they were there. Anything could go wrong, and she would be responsible if something happened to him. She remembered the name of the priest. Father Simonin. She did an Internet search on Crow's tablet and found it. Church of Saint-Agricol. She wondered if he'd think she was overreacting. Probably, but she always erred on the side of caution. In her line of work it was an asset. She reached for her phone and dialed Crow's number again. As before, it went straight to voicemail. He had turned it off again to save his battery.

Father Simonin began the long slog up the wooden steps of the bell tower. He'd made that particular trek hundreds of times and paced himself to save his breath. He allotted ample time for the task. Inspecting the belfry was one of the necessary tasks in the upkeep of a structure dating back to the fourteenth century. He could've hired someone to do it, but he took pride in it. The truth is he enjoyed it, and he appreciated the exercise. He wanted to think it kept him young, but who was he fooling? He tired a little more easily with each trip these days. He wondered when he might have to give it up for good.

Rosenfeld felt vulnerable leaving the hotel by herself. There were dozens of other people around in broad daylight, but she had no way of knowing if that even mattered. The Custos Verbi had killed in more brazen circumstances. She checked the map on her phone, stepped out into the warmth of the morning, and followed the blue line.

The father stopped for a brief moment and looked down to the bottom of the tower through one of the openings placed at intervals along the stairway to allow maintenance workers to make repairs to the inner wall of the tower. He peered up the shaft and figured himself to be halfway there. He continued the climb.

Rosenfeld glanced up at the towering walls of the palace to her right. She turned left and continued to weave among the tourists, holding her phone out in front of her. Her anxiety increased with each step. She looked over her shoulder every few seconds.

Father Simonin stopped at another opening and looked up at the floor of the belfry. He could see the rope extending through a hole in the floor and followed it all the way down to the bottom. Just a few more steps and he would reach a landing and a door that led to the belfry.

The church had appeared closer on the map. The tangle of small streets was confusing, but Rosenfeld plodded forward, relying entirely on the accuracy of the map. The crowd was getting thicker. She heard the bell and knew she was almost there.

The large church bell up close in the belfry was deafeningly loud. The wheel that was attached to the headstock from which the massive bell hung turned a quarter revolution. The clapper struck the inside of the bell and the sound reverberated out of the tower. Kinetic force turned the wheel in the opposite direction once the bell reached its peak and the clapper clanged loudly again. The rope was attached to the wheel, which then led down the assembly of the frame through an open trap door in the floor that, when closed, allowed the rope to pass through a hole. The trap door was opened on either side of the hole.

A slight breeze blew through the sycamore trees that cast shadows on the pastel sandstone buildings with their bottom-story cafes and their apartments and offices up above. Red canopies jutted out from the buildings with the names of the cafes and souvenir shops printed in white. Menus locked behind glass frames just outside cafes topped black chalkboards with yesterday's specials erased into a dusty-white memory behind the more vivid lettering of today's. On the arched third-story windows were weathered green shutters, some pulled shut, others left open, some with flower boxes, some with off-white wrought iron railings. In the large courtyard below, white umbrella canvases were pulled tight across teak ribs that shaded tourists who drank their drinks and nibbled at their sandwiches between conversations at bright blue metal tables with wood-framed wicker chairs. A Frenchman sat on the edge of a concrete fountain serenading the crowd with his acoustic guitar for tips. He turned his head in the direction of the ringing bell tower and frowned. Just feet away, the bald man with the black patch over his left eye sat at a shaded table sipping an espresso. He looked down at his watch. 11:17. He took a final sip of his coffee and rose from his seat.

The rope jerked from side to side in the opening of the trap door. Up and down it went to the sound of the bell. Down several yards of rope below the floor of the belfry hung a grisly sight. There, with the rope wrapped around his neck, swung Father Simonin, his head unnaturally turned to one side, his eyes ghoulishly open, his lifeless corpse bobbing up and down to the rhythm of the ringing bell. The black-robed figure twisted violently at the bottom of each cycle then rose like a rag doll as the bell's weight swung it in the opposite direction only to fall downward to snap and twist again. And again.

Crow emerged from the church and felt the unevenness of the small brick pavers underneath the soles of his shoes. A block or so away he pulled the phone from his pocket and brought up the two photos he had just taken. He had watched Father Simonin's secretary leave her office. He took the opportunity to ease back into the father's inner sanctum. Rummaging through his desk, he found a coin about the size of an American half dollar. The coin was silver with a unique double effigy, a conjoined obverse portrait of Nostradamus in the foreground and the Roman god Janus layered behind him. No inscription, just the two portraits. On the reverse was a coat of arms. On its upper left and lower right were wheels almost resembling a Ferris Wheel. At the upper right and lower left were identical birds with hooked beaks. Below the shield were the words 'Soli Deo.' He brought up Kyle O'Hara's number and typed 'Looks like Nostradamus and Janus on the front. Any idea what the shield and words on the back mean? BC.' He turned the corner into Clock Square.

Sidney Rosenfeld was just before calling out to Crow across the cobblestone plaza when two men in suits approached him from behind. Words were exchanged. Crow was grabbed by the arm and hustled to a waiting van. Another man opened the back. The first one pushed Crow in then followed. The man holding the door looked around and shut it behind them. He hurried to the driver's seat and drove away.

Panic paralyzed Sidney Rosenfeld. How had they found him so quickly? She and Crow had just arrived this morning. Crow's appointment with the priest was made at the last minute, yet they seemed to have been waiting for him. She scanned the crowd to see if anyone was looking at her. Suddenly it felt like *everyone* was looking at her. She tried not to be so obvious, vacillating between a quick walk and a run back to the hotel. But if they knew where Crow was, did they know where she was, too? Damned fool. Crow wanted to provoke them and he had. If the Custos Verbi were headquartered in Avignon, as Crow suspected, they surely saw them when they checked in right under their noses. Which meant they would have their hotel under surveillance. But she would have to take that chance. Everything she needed—passport, purse, travel bag—were all in that room.

Crow rumbled along in the back of the nondescript van, his wrists handcuffed together and the cuffs attached to a metal railing between his legs. The Frenchman opposite him refused to make eye contact. The driver kept his attention straight ahead on the road.

"Where are you taking me?" Crow asked.

It was as if his voice had no volume. Neither man gave even a hint that he had spoken. Crow ran through the options in his mind. They were limited. Escape was unlikely. Lying would be an option, but if they picked him up, they certainly knew who he was and where he'd been. Survival wasn't likely. He wasn't blindfolded, so they didn't seem to care if he saw their faces. Not a good sign.

Rosenfeld walked through the entry hall of the hotel as calmly as she was capable taking care to read each face she passed in the large atrium. Catching the elevator up, she reached her suite, made one more sweep of the hallway with her eyes, stepped inside, and locked herself in. She pulled all the curtains closed and fidgeted as she paced. She could run but where? She couldn't just leave Crow. She could look for him but had no idea where to start. After a moment, she pulled back one of the curtains ever so slightly to see if anything suspicious caught her eye on the street below.

The van came to a stop inside a parking garage. The driver opened the rear door. Crow's French companion unhitched him from the metal bar and gestured for him to go first. He exited the van and was escorted through a door and down a narrow hallway of tile flooring and gray walls.

Rosenfeld paced back and forth, chewing on her fingernails. She peeked out the window once more then sat on the edge of a chair in hopeless frustration. There was no one to call. There was nothing to do but wait. And hope.

Crow sat alone at a metal table inside a dark, sterile room. It smelled musty like the air inside was old. Every movement he made reverberated off the barren walls. He looked around. Right in front of him was a long glass mirror he assumed was for observation by those on the other side. He massaged his wrists to get the blood circulating where the cuffs had been. The door of the dark interrogation room opened and a man in a khaki suit strutted in followed by two plainclothes armed guards. The man's dark hair was graying at the temples. His jacket was unbuttoned. He didn't try to hide the fact that he had a shoulder holster and a gun.

"Monsieur Crow, I am Capitaine Legrand." He took the seat opposite Crow and added, "Of the Gendarmerie Nationale."

"The federal police? Am I being arrested, Captain?" Crow asked.

He ignored the question. "We want to ask you some questions. You called a man on the telephone this morning named Jean-Claude Delacroix. Why?"

"Why?" Crow was stalling for time. He tried to remember what he'd said in the message.

"You were angry with him, no?"

"Yeah, I was a little miffed."

"Why?"

"Because he had arranged a house for me to stay in. I wasn't happy."

"You told him you had visitors."

A light flickered in Crow's head. "Yes, that's right," he said. "Roaches."

"Roaches?"

"Cockroaches."

"And that is why you called him?"

"Yes. I can't stand the damn things."

The police captain leaned forward across the table. "What is your relationship with Delacroix?"

"He's helping me with some research for a book. I'm an author."

"I see," Legrand said. "And what services could Monsieur Delacroix provide for you?"

"Well, for starters, the book's about Nostradamus. Mr. Delacroix is an expert on the subject. I hope to learn a lot from him."

"When did you last see him?"

"Yesterday afternoon," he lied. "I followed him out to a farmhouse he was letting me use while I do my research. Now, do you mind telling me what this is all about?"

Legrand studied his face. "You really do not know?"

"Know what? How could I know? Your goons grabbed me and threw me in the back of a van and wouldn't even talk to me."

Legrand thought about it for a moment then said, "Monsieur Delacroix has been murdered." His voice was devoid of emotion. He was more interested in Crow's reaction than dispensing information.

Crow was stunned and everything about him showed it. "Oh, my God."

"We need to know your whereabouts this morning."

"I, uh, I left the house Mr. Delacroix had arranged for me and I drove here. To Avignon."

"Why?"

"Why?" Crow repeated.

"Why did you come to Avignon?"

"I had only planned to spend one night in Salon."

"My men picked you up leaving a church."

"I wanted to see the sights. That's a historic church. Look, let's not beat around the bush. You think I had something to do with Delacroix's murder. This is the first I've heard of it. I certainly had no reason to kill him."

Captain Legrand stared back at him.

"If I killed Jean-Claude Delacroix, why did I call a dead man and leave him an angry message? And tell him exactly where I was going? You're wasting your time with me. You should be out there looking for the real killer."

Marcus Foster glided past the clusters of tourists who gazed up at the sheer walls of the palace in wonderment. His plaid shirt and khakis acted as camouflage blending him into the fabric of the Avignon tourist scene. His eyes were not on the walls but on the bank of windows on the second floor across the street. The ones now darkened by closed curtains. He pulled the sunglasses from his head and lingered for a moment then stepped inside La Mirande Hotel. Rosenfeld pulled back the curtain and peered down into the street below. Seeing nothing, she sat back down on the chair at the foot of the bed. Marcus Foster paused at the foot of the grand stairway and looked up.

Legrand pulled a series of images from an envelope. "We have these photographs of pedestrian traffic caught on a surveillance camera a half-block away from La Maison de Nostradamus between the last time we're certain he was alive and the time his body was discovered." Crow had noted the camera during the time he and

Rosenfeld were waiting for Delacroix to emerge from the museum the night before. They had purposely walked on the other side of the street to avoid it. Legrand pushed a photo toward him. "We know from the surveillance camera that Delacroix returned to his office at 12:41 in the morning. We will not know a precise time of death until the coroner's report is completed. Do you recognize this person?"

Crow studied the photograph for a second. "No. What time was his body discovered?"

"Just after nine o'clock this morning. By a fellow employee."

"Did the person who killed him break in?" Crow asked.

"No sign of forced entry. Perhaps Monsieur Delacroix carelessly left the door open. We have no footage of the door itself. How about this one?" He pushed another photograph in front of him.

Crow looked down. "Nope."

"This one?"

"Look, I'm not from around here, Captain. I don't know anybody."

"The photograph, please, Monsieur Crow."

He glanced at it. "No."

"This one?"

Crow's eyes froze on the picture. He tried desperately to conceal his surprise. The whole scenario played out in an instant in his head. If he told them the truth, he would have to involve Sidney. Then they would surely not be allowed to leave the area as material witnesses in a murder case. Time was running out. He needed no more complications. Crow shook his head. "No," he said. But he was lying. He caught another glimpse before Captain Legrand pulled it away. There was no mistaking the man in that photograph.

Chapter Twenty-Five

Rosenfeld continued to pace the floor of the hotel suite. She knew she couldn't remain where she was. Staying in the room literally across the street from the Palace of the Popes made her a sitting duck. Then she heard it. The door mechanism engaged. Someone had a key to her room. Terror overwhelmed her. The latch retracted. The door opened, but the swinging guard caught the door and prevented it from moving more than a few inches. She looked around the room for another exit. No escape except for the windows, and the drop would probably kill her. She leapt to the bed and picked up the phone and began to dial the front desk. Then she heard the voice.

"Sidney. It's me."

Rosenfeld hung up the phone, rushed to the door, and unlatched the swinging guard.

"You scared the hell out of me. I thought you'd been taken by the Custos Verbi. Where have you been?"

Crow strode past her and sat down on the loveseat by the window. "Delacroix's dead."

She gasped.

"He was murdered."

"How do you know?" she asked.

"I was picked up by the French national police. They questioned me about my phone call to him this morning."

"That's who grabbed you after you left the church?"

"Yes," Crow said. "How'd you know I was grabbed?"

"I saw it. I was getting nervous about how long it was taking, so I went to find you. You met with the priest all that time?"

"No. Well, I did have to wait for him to meet with a parishioner, but our meeting didn't take that long. He had to go inspect the belfry. I knew he'd be occupied, so I snooped around."

"And?" Rosenfeld asked.

"Nothing."

"Did the police think you killed Delacroix?"

"Well, I thought so initially, but they really wanted to see if I could identify someone caught on surveillance near the Nostradamus museum."

"Could you?"

"I didn't tell them, but yeah."

"Who?"

"Your friend from the train."

"Marcus?"

"Yes."

"Why would he kill Delacroix?"

"Presumably to get to us. That would explain how that drone found us."

"Who is he with?"

"I don't know."

"I feel terrible," Rosenfeld said, grabbing her forehead. "It's our fault."

Crow banged the table beside the loveseat with his fist. Rosenfeld jumped.

"Son of a bitch!" he screamed. He composed himself. "Well, that tells me the monk was right. That man in Montreal was a rogue First

Facer. This guy, Marcus, is probably one of them and he's trying to kill me before I stop the next prophecy."

"Wait a minute. What makes you say that?"

"It's only logical."

"Only logical?" she said. "Marcus could very well be Custos Verbi."

"And following us—following *you*—all the way from America?"

"If he thinks you're a First Facer and I'm helping you, then yeah."

"Either way," Crow said, "I've got to somehow let the CV know I'm on their side."

"On their side? Are you kidding? You're trying to tell me the Custos Verbi are the good guys?"

"I don't think there *are* any good guys in all of this," Crow said. "What I mean is I need to let them know that we're working toward the same goal."

"That's kind of like trying to pet a cobra," Rosenfeld said. "And we checked in right across the street from the snake pit."

"They're not here," Crow said.

"How do you know?"

"That's what Father Simonin at the church told me."

"Where are they?"

"He wouldn't say. He only said no man is an island, and if I found the defender of the rock by the sea, I'd find my answer."

"John Donne," she said.

"What?"

"The English poet, John Donne. He's the one who said, 'No man is an island.' What did the priest mean by the defender of the rock by the sea?"

"I don't know." Crow remembered the rolled up piece of paper in his pocket. "Oh, and this." He pulled it out and unrolled it.

"What's that?" Rosenfeld asked.

"Father Simonin gave it to me." He read the words out loud. "Sánchez Muñoz." He looked up at Rosenfeld.

She shrugged her shoulders. "Who's that?"

The rolled paper struggled to stay flat on the table. Crow jotted the name down on the hotel's pad so he could search the name exactly as Simonin wrote it. "Let's find out."

He brought up a search engine and typed in the name. The first hit was the name of an associate professor at Cal State.

"Hers is hyphenated," Rosenfeld pointed out. "The one on your piece of paper isn't."

Crow kept looking. There was Miguel Angel Sánchez Muñoz, a former Spanish football player. His bio said he went by Michel. After that there were variations on the name, some with Carlos mixed in, others with Rafael or Juan, but nothing purely Sánchez Muñoz.

"We're getting nowhere." Crow powered down the tablet. "Come on." He balled up the note pad sheet and tossed it in the waste can.

"Where're we going?"

"To the palace."

They left their suite and took the elevator down to the lobby. The doors opened and they were startled to see a bald man with a black patch over his left eye standing there.

"Ah, excusez-moi," he said.

The man stepped aside and allowed them to exit then boarded the elevator. He watched them intently between the elevator doors as they closed, then he hit the button and the door opened again. He watched them rounding the corner into the front entrance hall. The bald man exited the elevator and paused a moment then walked through the corner of the central atrium that led to the front door. He followed Rosenfeld and Crow out onto the sidewalk. Watching from behind a newspaper in the atrium lounge was Marcus Foster.

Chapter Twenty-Six

Crow and Rosenfeld passed through a pedestrian walkway cut through the palace wall around to the front of the Palace of the Popes. Stone walls rising 164 feet into the summer air were accented by two matching towers with spires on either side of the main entrance doors. They walked up the side-set steps of the largest Gothic palace in the world. Crow paid for two tour tickets and they shuffled along with the rest of the tourists to get closer to the guide who spoke perfect English with a pleasant French accent. She began in the Grand Chapel by giving a quick history of the palace.

"The palace construction began in 1252. Pope Clement V moved the residence of the Popes from Rome to Avignon in 1309 to escape violence and chaos in Rome. What you will see on this tour is the result of several major renovations that took place over the decades the papacy resided here in Avignon. Pope Gregory XI was the last Avignon pope recognized by the Catholic Church. He moved the official residency back to the Vatican in 1377. After Gregory's death the following year, the cardinals elected Pope Urban VI and this is where it gets tricky. Follow me, please."

"If the CV aren't here, why are we?" Rosenfeld asked, walking along with the tour group toward the North Sacristy.

"Because Simonin said he'd studied this palace his entire life.

Whatever meaning Sánchez Muñoz has it's bound to be connected to this palace."

"So, what are we looking for?"

"I don't know. We're just looking. Hopefully, we'll know it when we see it."

The tourists gathered close to the guide who waited for the last of them to enter the room, then she resumed. "The French cardinals, some of the same who elected Pope Urban VI, became disillusioned with Urban and decided to elect another pope while Urban still reigned. They elected Clement VII in September of that same year and Clement reestablished a papal court back here in Avignon which led to what is known as the Western Schism."

"When it's not too conspicuous," Crow said softly, "we'll ditch this tour and do some exploring on our own."

The guide continued, "Clement VII is now officially recognized by the Church as an antipope, but he was succeeded here in Avignon by Benedict XIII. Benedict wanted to grow support for his papacy beyond France, Scotland, Portugal, and a few other countries. His eye was on Spain, so he sent his most trusted advisor as an envoy to the Bishop of Valencia to court his support for the Avignon papacy in Spain."

"They only let the public see about 20 rooms," Crow said. "Do you realize how massive this place is? 160,000 square feet."

"I'd hate to clean it," Rosenfeld muttered.

"Interestingly enough," the tour guide said, "that envoy would later succeed Benedict as Antipope Clement VIII. His given name was Gil Sánchez Muñoz y Carbón."

"I'm sorry, mademoiselle," Crow said, "did you say Sánchez Muñoz?"

"Yes."

"And who was he again?"

"He was Antipope Benedict XIII's envoy to the Bishop of Valencia who would later become Antipope Clement VIII."

"Thank you. Sorry to interrupt. Please, go on."

She smiled and continued, "The pontiff actually dressed here in the North Sacristy when he was hosting ceremonies at the palace. These plaster effigies are of prominent figures during the papal rule of..."

Crow and Rosenfeld peeled off from the rest of the group.

"Where are we going now?" Rosenfeld asked. She tried to keep pace with Crow heading toward the front of the palace.

"Back to the hotel. Now that we know who Sánchez Muñoz was, we need to do some research to see what that means."

"I don't mean to kill your Sherlock Holmes buzz, but I'm starving," Rosenfeld said.

"You can order something in the room."

They headed straight for their suite at La Mirande. Crow grabbed his tablet, opened the cover, and sat down at the table. The screen lit up. He brought up a search engine and began typing. He typed Sánchez Muñoz into the search engine. Rosenfeld picked up the phone to dial room service.

"Hold it a second," Crow said.

"What's wrong?"

"This tablet. I powered it down before we left. It's on." He slammed the cover shut and stood up from the desk looking anxiously around. "Somebody's been in here. Hang up the phone."

"What?"

"Hang up the phone. We gotta go."

They both grabbed their bags and began stuffing any loose belongings into them.

"Hurry," Crow said. "We gotta get out of here."

"Just a second. I have to get my things out of the bathroom."

Rosenfeld walked into the bathroom and threw items into her makeup bag. A few feet away, just behind the shower door, through a slight opening just above the smoked glass, eyes watched her reflection in the mirror.

The woman with the auburn hair pulled back in a bun deplaned the private jet into the hot summer sun. Shapely legs stretched below her navy business skirt and a gentleman in a tropical shirt extended his hand to help her down the last step onto the tarmac. She walked the short distance with purpose to the waiting limousine. The uniformed chauffeur closed the door and took his place behind the wheel. The man with the gold tooth sat waiting in the backseat beside her.

"Beatrix Cambridge," she said without offering her hand.

"I am Juan. We spoke on the telephone. I thought I would come personally to greet you."

"And collect your fee," she said dispassionately.

"That would be nice," he admitted.

"You will collect your money once I've inspected the package and I'm satisfied. Is that understood?"

"Sí, señorita."

Sidney Rosenfeld finished piling items into her makeup bag and turned toward the shower. The eyes behind the shower door narrowed. Rosenfeld stopped and turned to her right to examine the toilet in the water closet opposite the shower making sure she'd left nothing on it. She finished examining the water closet and closed the door, casually looking up at the mirror. She caught the reflection and let out an audible gasp. Marcus Foster's hand moved toward his gun. Rosenfeld whipped around to meet the image in the mirror face to face. Crow stared back at her from the doorway.

"What?" he said.

"You scared the crap out of me is what."

"Let's go." He headed back to the main door.

Rosenfeld followed, stuffing items into her shoulder bag, and got all the way to the door then snapped her fingers.

"Hold on," she said. "I left my shampoo in the shower."

Marcus Foster looked over to see the bottle of shampoo resting on the ledge beside him in the shower. Rosenfeld turned toward the bathroom. Foster raised the gun and pointed it at the shower door.

"I'll just be a second," she said.

Foster gripped the gun tighter.

She had taken two steps when Crow reached out and grabbed her by the arm. "Screw it," he said. "We gotta go. We'll buy more down the road."

The hotel door latched shut behind them. Complete silence filled the empty room. They bypassed the elevator and bound down the grand stone staircase. Crow instructed the desk clerk to have their car brought around and left their things to be placed in the trunk.

"Where're we going?" Rosenfeld asked.

"I need more to go on than just a name. I'm going to see if Father Simonin will tell us anything more now that we know who Sánchez Muñoz is."

Crow held Sidney's hand to ensure that she kept up. They wound through the narrow streets until they came to the open space of Clock Square. They hurried past the National Opera Theater and the carousel and City Hall and turned right down Rue Saint-Agricol. Approaching the church, they saw a crowd gathered at the bottom of the steps outside the entrance. Blue lights reflected off the side of the building just beyond the mob. Rosenfeld tapped a gentleman on his shoulder.

"What's going on?" she asked in French.

The man answered in French.

She looked back at Crow with shock in her eyes then asked the man something else.

Rosenfeld's blood ran cold. She turned to Crow.

"What is it?" he asked desperately.

"The priest," she said.

"Father Simonin? What about him?"

"There, inside the church," she pointed, "he just committed suicide."

Chapter Twenty-Seven

Crow grabbed Sidney's hand and jerked her in the opposite direction, running back toward the hotel. They dodged pedestrians and dogs on leashes. They bolted through Clock Square between the tourists and down the side street past a sign that read 'Palais des Papes' with a white arrow beside it. They dashed up the uneven cobblestones and rounded the corner on the street of their hotel. Crow came to a sudden stop and pulled Rosenfeld back as her momentum carried her past him. She looked up at him. He was pointing. Coming out the front doors of the hotel was Marcus Foster placing his sunglasses on his nose. Crow pulled them both back around the corner.

"Dammit! How the hell did he find us?" he asked.

"I don't know. Is our car out front?" Rosenfeld asked.

Crow closed his eyes then opened them and peeked around the corner for as long as he dared. He pulled himself back. "I don't see it."

The sound of the engine caused them to instinctively move to the side of the narrow passage, then they both realized it at once. Their car was coming up the cobblestone street. They ran down a few yards in front of the vehicle, waving until the attendant stopped.

"We'll take it here, if you don't mind," Crow said, plopping several bills in the startled man's hand.

They turned the corner in the Mercedes without being noticed. They were almost past the hotel when Rosenfeld looked back at

Marcus Foster who was intently canvassing the entire area. Their eyes met for a brief moment. He rushed to his car.

"He saw us!" Rosenfeld shouted.

Crow eyed his rearview mirror. "Yeah, I see him. We gotta hope we get to that damn bollard in time."

Directly across the street taking it all in beneath the towering walls of the Palace of the Popes stood the bald man with the black eye patch. Rosenfeld looked back and caught him staring.

Old Town Avignon is hazardous enough to navigate by automobile on the best of days, much less at the height of tourist season. Marcus Foster drove his little Fiat away from the curb and awkwardly through a group of sightseers coming up the cramped street in front of the hotel. He laid on the horn. Like stubborn geese, they were slow to move. Foster nudged them aside with his bumper. Some slapped his hood in rage as he passed.

Crow was already screaming down the precarious street as fast as he felt was possible in his larger Benz. Pedestrians scattered when he startled them around each bend of the road that arched ever slightly to the right. There was no sidewalk along most of the route, and tourists plastered themselves up against the massive palace wall to avoid being smashed. Within seconds, the bollard was right in front of them in the middle of the roadway designed to keep any and all vehicles from coming up the one-way street. Crow skidded to a halt in front of the call box and hit the button for the hotel on the intercom.

"La Mirande," the voice said.

"Benson Crow!" he shouted. "We need the bollard moved. We're in a hurry."

"Of course, Monsieur Crow."

Crow looked in his mirror. No sign of Marcus Foster yet, but he knew he couldn't be far behind. The bollard wasn't moving.

"Now!" Crow shouted.

Rosenfeld looked behind them. Foster was hitting the last bend, the headlights of his Fiat were flashing. "There he is! I think he wants us to stop," she said.

Crow didn't wait for the bollard to lower completely. As soon as he thought he could pass, he scooted over it and turned right. He hit the gas in mid-turn and his car straightened up.

Foster's car reached the intersection a few seconds later and the bollard had already begun to rise. It caught the Fiat at the very rear bouncing the little car up against the wall of the building in front of him while Foster tried to negotiate the right turn. He regained control almost hitting a blond-haired young man pulling a stack of cardboard in a metal-frame cart who waved angrily at him and shouted obscenities. A man who had begun to cross the street carrying a ladder jumped back out of the way, but the momentum of the ladder sent it crashing to the street just where the Fiat had passed.

Crow cursed the city officials who allowed parking on the right side of such a narrow street. More pedestrians leapt for their lives. If it were possible, the street became even more ridiculously narrow. He reached the stop sign at the corner of Rue de la Banasterie and Rue Petite Saunerie and promptly ignored it causing a cyclist to veer hard left into a boxed tree in front of a bakery and projectile on top of a table. Angry patrons enjoying a quiet espresso jumped from their chairs in anger.

"Shit! Sorry!" Crow called out even though no one could hear him.

Two seconds later, Foster was through the same intersection where Rue de la Banasterie becomes Place des Châtaignes.

Crow hit the gas on the short straightaway. Stunned cafe patrons with mouths agape watched pigeons scatter and Crow's Mercedes whiz by. At the next intersection, he started to turn right when

Rosenfeld shouted, "One way!" Cars slammed on brakes where the cobblestones became asphalt. Crow lurched left then fishtailed left again around a brick island in the middle of the five-point intersection. A black Peugeot coming the opposite direction from a one-way street hit the brakes to avoid hitting him head-on and a green electric 7-seater Baladine, an odd-looking vehicle that was something between a taxi and a small bus, rammed into the rear of the Peugeot throwing its passengers into each other. Crow shot up Rue Armand de Pontmartin.

Foster barely clipped a VW in the rear when he reached the intersection just over a second later, spinning the car around and out of his way. He made the sharp turn with tires squealing and streaked past the wrecked Peugeot and Baladine. He took the same street as Crow, which was still asphalt but extremely narrow. A white delivery truck hogged part of the street and Crow scraped two green rounded window grates on the right as he passed.

Foster's smaller Fiat passed with ease and he was now a mere second behind them.

"He's flashing the lights again," Rosenfeld said.

"Does he think I'm a fool? Like I'm gonna just pull over."

A car hit the brakes coming out of an alleyway. Crow adjusted quickly to the right then back straight and burst past. The driver was about to take his foot off the brake pedal when Foster flew by. The man screamed out his window.

The road curved sharply to the left and Crow grazed the side of the building with the right side of his front bumper. The scuff marks already on the building indicated he wasn't the first. Pedestrians scrambled for safety behind the permanent posts that marked the boundary between the threadlike street and the catwalk of a sidewalk. Foster made the curve with ease and was now on their tail.

The road came to a dead end and Crow squealed right onto

Rue Sainte-Catherine. Foster did the same but with more grace. Tourists fell all over one another getting out of the tiny street. On this straightaway the Mercedes had the advantage. Crow blew the horn and accelerated. A lady talking on her phone, oblivious to the rest of the world, was so startled she tossed her phone in the air and it bounced off Crow's windshield. Before she could retrieve it from the street, Foster's Fiat zoomed past and left it in pieces.

Crow began putting space between himself and Foster's glorified golf cart. Rosenfeld turned around to see the Fiat getting smaller. The lane curved to the right slightly, enough to put them out of sight for a brief moment.

"Take a left here," she shouted.

Crow was already in motion to take the hairpin left onto Rue Bertrand. "Way ahead of you," he said, fighting the steering wheel with all his might.

The tires screeched and skipped across the surface. The back end slid perfectly to head him back in almost the opposite direction up Rue Bertrand and he floored it. He had taken the turn just in time. His taillights vanished just as Foster straightened out of the curve and bore slightly to the right to follow the road he was on. Crow was nowhere in sight, but he immediately recognized the red sign with the horizontal white line dead ahead in front of him. Even if he didn't know what it meant, the blaring horns of the oncoming cars told him he was going the wrong way up a one-way street. Blue smoke rolled from the Fiat's back tires and Foster came to an abrupt stop. He banged the steering wheel with his fist. He reached in the pocket of his plaid shirt and unfolded the crumpled piece of paper again. Sánchez Muñoz.

Chapter Twenty-Eight

"We've gotta find a place to regroup." Benson Crow checked his mirrors obsessively. His mind struggled to process everything he'd just taken in.

"You really think the priest was murdered?" Rosenfeld asked. "The man at the church said he killed himself."

Crow shot her a sarcastic glance.

They turned right on Rue Banasterie past Chapelle des Pénitents Noirs, Chapel of the Black Penitents, whose congregants comforted criminals sentenced to death and even accompanied them to the gallows making sure the condemned had a decent Christian burial. They exited the ancient city walls at Porte Saint-Joseph and melded into the four-lane traffic of Boulevard Saint-Lazare. They followed the Rhone River and eventually crossed it at Pont de l'Europe. This was the same Rhone that passed through Arles and was made famous in van Gogh's *Starry Night*.

Just outside Avignon the landscape opened up to vineyards and horses and old stone structures on a two-lane highway with rolling hills in the distance. They hit a roundabout and Crow went around the entire circle before taking a spoke off toward the tiny village of Saze, just to make sure Marcus Foster hadn't managed to follow them. He didn't see anyone at all and felt safe enough to pull over for a bite to eat.

France looks quite different beyond the borders of Provence and the Rhone River. Saze looked like something out of a spaghetti western with stark, naked trees and tiled roofs. They stopped at a small pizza joint on the main square and sat down at one of the formica-covered booths. Crow put his computer tablet to the side and threw the car key fob on top of it. The smell of baked bread and tomato sauce became stronger each time the server passed through the metal swinging door to the kitchen. They ordered a pizza and a couple of soft drinks.

"What am I missing here?" Crow asked. "What does Sánchez Muñoz have to do with the Custos Verbi?"

"I don't know," Rosenfeld said. "Maybe Muñoz has something to do with Nostradamus."

"You studied this guy. Any connection to Spain that you can think of?"

"Not that I'm aware of."

"What about his parents?"

"No. They were French."

"And Catholic, I presume," Crow said.

"Yes. His father's father—Nostradamus' paternal grandfather—was actually Jewish but converted to Catholicism. Some say it was due, in part, to the Inquisition."

"The Spanish Inquisition?"

"Well, the Spanish Inquisition was a little later, but it's interesting you should say that. Nostradamus was falsely accused of heresy when he was about thirty-five. He made some off-handed remark about a religious statue or something. Agents of the Spanish Inquisition were after him for a time. He wandered through Italy for about six years."

"Hmm, interesting," Crow said. "Grumbling mentioned the Inquisition in our discussion. Said Nostradamus was afraid of the

Church, so he shrouded his predictions in verses. Is it possible the Custos Verbi sprang from those agents of the Spanish Inquisition?"

"Doubtful. His controversial writings didn't start for almost another twenty years, after he returned to Salon from Italy."

The pizza came and they each grabbed a slice. Crow took a bite, wiped his hands on a napkin, and opened his tablet. Using the restaurant's Internet connection, he called up a search engine and looked up 'Spanish Inquisition.'

"All right, it says here the Spanish Inquisition began in 1478. On February 6, 1481, they burned six people alive. Doesn't sound very Christian-like. These were mostly Jews who wouldn't convert."

"Yeah, they ended up burning quite a few people they didn't like," Rosenfeld said. "I'm sure that was always in the back of Nostradamus' mind when he was writing his quatrains."

"Let's see, in 1483 Pope Sixtus IV named an Inquisitor General. His name was Tomás de Torquemada. He was over Aragon, which is in Northeastern Spain." He mumbled as he read to himself, his fingers scanning across the face of the tablet. "OK, listen to this. It says here there were four tribunals in Aragon. They were in Zaragoza, Barcelona, Majorca, and Valencia." Crow looked up at Rosenfeld. "Remember what the tour guide said back at the Palace of the Popes? Sánchez Muñoz was an envoy to the Bishop of Valencia under Benedict XIII. The tribunal was in Valencia. Simonin said to find the defender of the rock by the sea and we'd find our answer. Valencia is on the Mediterranean Sea. Valencia's the common denominator."

"Quite a leap, isn't it?"

"It has to be Valencia," he said.

"And what about our tails," she asked.

"Tails?"

"Yeah, that creepy dude with the eyepatch was watching us as we left the hotel."

"The guy who was getting on the elevator when we were getting off?" Crow asked.

"Yep. I saw him outside when that Marcus guy started chasing us."

"We can't worry about either of them right now. They have no idea where we're going."

"*We* don't even know where we're going," she said.

"Look, Sánchez Muñoz is the clue, right? Other than Avignon, which Simonin told me was not where we'd find the Custos Verbi, Valencia is the only other place that pops up. Sánchez Muñoz was an envoy to the Bishop of Valencia. It's by the sea. I think Simonin was telling me we'll find the Custos Verbi in Valencia."

"Unless they find us first." Rosenfeld took a bite of the pizza.

"Yeah, well, we need to keep moving. I don't know how in the hell Marcus Foster keeps finding us, but it's harder to hit a moving target."

They buckled in and Sidney Rosenfeld entered Valencia into her phone's GPS. Seven hours away. Rosenfeld propped her bare feet up on the dash and stared out the window.

"It'd break your legs if we had a wreck," he said.

"What?"

"The air bag. With your feet up on the dash like that. Probably break your back, too."

"You love to tell me what to do, don't you?" She neither expected nor wanted an answer.

"Just trying to be helpful," he said.

"Is that what that is? 'Cause it sure sounds like a control freak to me." She folded her arms and looked out her window.

"A control freak? Is that what I am?"

"Yes."

"Fine. I'll stop trying to help."

Rosenfeld rolled her eyes. "Fine."

"Fine."

Crow drove in silence. It was supposed to be a relaxing getaway to Montreal. *Get out of the country*, Tom had said. *Relax*. Crow had most certainly gotten out of the country, but relax? He hadn't relaxed for one second since he met the mysterious man in Montreal. He wondered if he'd ever relax again. He almost wished he'd been kept in the dark. Almost. He knew himself too well. He loved a good story, usually the kind that was the invention of his own imagination. In his wildest fantasy he could not have imagined a tale as intriguing as the one he was living. This was the type of story he sat up late nights trying to conjure. The problem with this tale was he couldn't even *imagine* the ending. He'd never heard of anything like this before. The irony was the First Facers *did* know the ending. They could see the future, or so they believed. The truth was written in the Unriddled Manuscript. More accurately, what was written was the future Nostradamus envisioned, and they could control events leading up to it. That's how they worked with such precision. Crow couldn't even control the present. Each step left him more confounded, more confused, more frustrated.

But was their future real, or was their future what the First Facers made it? Crow couldn't bring himself to believe that Nostradamus could actually see the future. He had to be a lucky guesser. No, it was more layered than that. He wrote in riddles, Crow surmised, not to hide his prophecies from the Church, but to keep them ambiguous enough that any future event would fit. Like some cheap palm reader who throws out generalities until she hits a nerve then exploits that tenuous connection. But Crow had to admit that some of Nostradamus' predictions fit a little too snugly. Some were downright uncanny. It didn't matter if he believed. *They* believed. The First Face of Janus was obsessed with that belief like so many religious zealots who killed to confirm others to their beliefs. This was their very own Inquisition. People like Nostradamus had been hunted down in his day. Now the First Facers hunted down anyone who stood in the way of their religion. These fervent beliefs made these people extremely dangerous. He had to stop them, not just for the sake of the lives involved, but for the sake of humanity's future. If he could be the monkey wrench in the machinery, he could demonstrate to the First Facers that Nostradamus' word was not infallible. If he could do that, perhaps he could bring an end to a half-millennium of prophecy wars.

Crow's phone vibrated in his pocket. He looked over at a sleeping Sidney Rosenfeld then pulled it out. A message from Kyle O'Hara.

Last favor, dude. Yes, the obverse is obviously Nostradamus and Janus. Reverse is the Nostradamus family crest. Soli Deo means God Alone. The eight-rayed wheel is a reference to his Hebrew origins, symbolizes the wandering of the Jews. The bird is either an eagle or falcon. No clue what that means. P.S. Get out while you can. P.S.S. Lose my number.

THEY ROLLED UP to the Hotel Las Arenas Balneario Resort in Valencia well after dark. The hotel appeared oddly out of place in the neighborhood. The four-story facade of the resort looked like a movie set plopped down in the middle of a lower income mixed-use development. Apartments across the street could just as easily have been public housing. The shops were locked up tight for the night with their barred windows and doors. Rosenfeld felt a little uneasy as their car came to a stop, but she had learned not to question Crow's choice of accommodations.

"Bienvenido," the valet said to Crow.

Crow turned the Benz over to the him without a word and grabbed his bag out of the trunk.

"Gracias," Rosenfeld said uncomfortably. "El esta de mal humor." She explained that Crow was in a bad mood.

"You don't have to constantly apologize for me," he said to her as she caught up to him.

"You don't have to always be such an asshole to the help either."

"It goes with the territory of being a difficult author."

She smirked and shook her head.

Beyond the revolving doors was a luxurious oasis of white columns and stone floors with large brown resin chairs and comfortable cushions. Outside, past the lobby, was a beautiful blue rectangular reflecting pool with fountains. Palm trees lined it on either side illuminated at their bases with flood lights which gave them the appearance of almost being on fire. Beyond the grounds was the wide beach, and beyond that was the Mediterranean Sea.

The desk clerk, dressed in a summer-weight gray suit and white pocket square, was scribbling a note on a pad when Crow and Rosenfeld approached.

"Welcome to the Hotel Las Arenas," he greeted warmly.

"The name is Crow." He produced his passport and credit card.

The man typed a few words into his computer. "We have you for one night in the Suite Las Arenas."

"Let's keep that open, shall we?" Crow said. "Depending on how we like it here, we may stay longer."

"Very good, sir."

They showed themselves to the Suite Las Arenas with its two separate bedrooms and a spacious living room. The large terrace had a spectacular view of the Mediterranean Sea which shimmered under a waxing gibbous moon. The view was wasted on the both of them who felt the sand quickly draining from their hourglass. Crow paced between the white desk and the sitting area of the living room. Rosenfeld sat cross-legged on the white leather sofa scrolling through the society pages on the tablet.

"I'm getting nowhere on this," she said. "There are weddings all over the place. That's all these society people do is go to weddings."

"We've got to find one that fits," Crow insisted.

"How? We have virtually nothing to go on."

"Remember what Delacroix said? Concentrate on venues. We have to narrow it down," Crow said. "Let's go with what we know, or what we *think* we know. If we're supposed to take this literally, Nostradamus wouldn't be predicting just any wedding. It has to be someone prominent. And by prominent, it's got to be someone whose life affects others, not just some society couple. And remember, Delacroix was convinced it was a royal wedding."

"Do any of these people really matter to the rest of the world?" Rosenfeld asked.

"Don't be so cynical."

"Seriously? You know how these high-society weddings go. The Duke and Duchess of Whatever attend the wedding of Lady What's-her-name. Who are you wearing?" she mocked. "Oh, darling, you look fa-a-abulous. It's the social event of the year, darling. Blah, blah, blah. It's sickening."

"I'm not into this stuff either, but royal-watching is huge business, especially in the UK. In fact, I read the British royal family actually brings in far more money in tourism than it takes to keep them."

"Still, it's obscene. These people have done nothing to earn their privilege other than being born into the right family."

"That's the way it is the world over," Crow reminded her. "You think JFK would've ever been president had he been born to a working-class family? We can't worry about how superficial it might be. The quatrains are pointing to a high-profile wedding. We have to find which one or innocent people are going to die."

"What's one less royal family?" she said.

"I'll write that off to your lack of sleep. Besides, this goes way beyond saving lives. It's about stopping the prophecy."

Rosenfeld looked at Crow for a long moment. "Is that what this is really all about with you? Or is it about the story?"

Crow didn't say anything.

"I know your publisher has gotten in your head," she continued. "You're scared your days as a successful author are over."

"Here we go again with the psychoanalyzing."

"You're looking for that mid-career bump, that big book that puts you back in the game."

"You really think I'm sensationalizing this for the sake of the story?"

"You tell me. If you are, you're risking both our lives for your career."

Crow was silent for a moment. "You think that's what this is all about? My career?"

"I just want you to search your soul for your motivation. Are you trying to impress somebody? Your parents, maybe?"

"I don't have any," Crow said.

She looked down. "Oh, I didn't know. I'm sorry."

"Don't be. I haven't had any since I was sixteen."

"You want to talk about it?"

"Do I look like I want to talk about it?" He sat down in one of the overstuffed leather chairs next to the sofa and faced her. "It may be ugly to admit, but, yeah, I see real value in this story. If I said the plot hadn't been rolling around in my head I'd be lying. But you know what really motivates me? For nearly 500 years, a secretive group of people has been manipulating world events to fit the predictions of some guy who just very well may have been a crackpot. I've wrestled with religion all my life. I believe in God, but I'm not too keen on organized religion. In fact, it can be downright scary. They try to control people. Look at the Inquisition. They killed people who didn't convert to their way of thinking. The radical Muslims are doing that today. Why are people so obsessed with making people believe just like they believe?"

"What does this have to do with the First Face of Janus?" Rosenfeld asked.

"Because they're exactly the same. They fight the Church over these prophecies, but their sole existence is about manipulating events so that *their* religion is right. Their god just so happens to be Nostradamus. Am I motivated to stop them? You damn right I am. No one should have that much power. No one should be able to control world events with impunity. No one should be allowed to decide who has the power and who is left powerless. You're worried about privilege? No one should be allowed to decide who eats and who starves, who lives and who dies. Almost 3,000 people died on 9/11. Don't you think if I had a chance to save them I would? The First Face of Janus didn't help them. They let them die. For all we know, they *helped* them die. If that's the story that draws me to it, it's because that's the story that has to be told. For way too long they've wielded that power based on the writings of one man. One man! They've been stacking the deck based on their 'religion.' How are they any different from the Inquisition? Yeah, I may have gotten in over my head, but guess what, I have absolutely nothing to lose now. I can't go home because somebody's going to kill me. I can't sit still because I'm being chased. So I'm going to stop this prophecy with or without the help of the Custos Verbi. We stop this prophecy and we stop this cycle of insanity once and for all."

Rosenfeld leaned back slightly and nodded. "OK," she patted the tops of her legs, "good talk. Then we better get to work. It's gonna be an all-night cram. We'll need some joe."

She took the elevator down to the lobby past a scaled-down replica of the resort. She asked the clerk at the front desk if there were somewhere she could get a couple of cups of coffee at this hour.

"Sí, señorita. You should have called room service. They are open 24 hours and they would have brought it to your room."

"Ah, no problem. I needed to get out anyway."

He looked back over his shoulder at the large inlaid clock on the marble wall. It read 10:51. "The restaurant." He pointed straight ahead. "It is open for another few minutes."

"Gracias."

"De nada."

The gold Jaguar pulled off Carrer d'Eugènia Viñes onto the black pavers and up to the valet at the Hotel Las Arenas Balneario Resort in Valencia. The young attendant opened the driver's side door. The bald man with the black eye patch emerged elegantly from the automobile and took the stub the valet was offering. He inhaled the salty breeze blowing in from the Mediterranean Sea. The man strolled into the foyer of large boxed columns, tray ceilings, and modern low-back off-white sofas with the occasional palm tree as an accent. His sand-colored linen blazer was draped over his shoulders. He approached the man at the counter with the gray suit and white pocket square and checked his Cartier watch against the inlaid clock on the marble wall behind him. 10:55pm. He laid his passport and credit card on the counter and looked around surveying the area as if the clerk were just another fine fixture in the hotel. The desk clerk picked up the passport and greeted him with a smile.

"Good evening, Señor Babineaux. We have been expecting you."

Chapter Twenty-Nine

Chaos surrounded him. Broken glass, bits of steel, and other debris rained down around him. The myriad sounds were confusing and disorienting. Crow shielded his face with his arms and strained his eyes up at the unusually tall building in front of him. He couldn't make out the top for the smoke. Flames leapt from the highest story he could see. People screamed. Policemen shouted orders. Sirens blared. Hordes of people were running past him away from the burning building. And then he heard his name. Faintly at first, but it became louder and clearer. "Benson!" a woman's voice screamed. He looked up again. Through the heavy smoke he saw her, arms flailing wildly, screaming, tumbling closer to earth. "Benson!" He could now make out her face. Her terrified eyes locked with his. "Help me, Benson!" she screamed. Then the hideous thud as her body hit the concrete sidewalk and bounced. Crow turned away in horror. He couldn't comprehend what he'd just seen.

I actually watched her die!

Then he heard it again. His name. Being screamed. This time a man's voice. "Benson! Help!" He looked up between his protective arms into the smoky abyss. A man fell from the smoke and flames, terror on his face, screaming desperately. "Benson! Help!" Crow knew he was going to suffer the same fate as the woman before him. All he could do was stand by helplessly and watch. Crow cried out, "No!" He turned his head, hoping against hope he wouldn't hear that horrible thud of another life being snuffed out right before his eyes. The man's screams were deafening. Crow covered his ears. It was like the man was screaming right beside him. "Help, Benson! Ple-e-e-ease!"

Crow bolted upright in bed, drenched in sweat. His heart pounded. He fought to catch his breath as if he'd just run a marathon. The realization of where he was began to sink in. He calmed himself, but the image of the desperate people falling gnawed at him. He pulled back the covers and dressed himself. Instead of a shower, he grabbed a ball cap from his shoulder bag. He left Rosenfeld sleeping in her bed. The all-nighter proved fruitless and he wandered downstairs in search of fresh air and food about the time the restaurant opened at seven. He took his breakfast on the manicured grounds of the Hotel Las Arenas Balneario in sight of the distant sea. Out on the beaches of the Mediterranean, seagulls floated in place above the sand, steadying their wings against the morning wind, their sharp eyes looking for a morsel of food. They communicated with a cry that bordered on a laugh seemingly in rhythm and concert with the gentle roar of the small waves that broke on the shore. Servers dressed in black trousers and white mandarin-collar jackets ferried breakfast trays between the grass and the kitchen.

It was Friday morning. The sands of the hour glass poured relentlessly through his mind. He could see his chances slipping through his fingers. After ruminating over a quick bite, he planned to resume his research in the room but held out little hope that he'd find that snowball in the blizzard. Sánchez Muñoz. Valencia had to be the right place. Nothing else made sense, but the name had meant nothing to this town for centuries. Muñoz was born in Teruel, not Valencia. His tomb was in Palma, Spain. His only connection to Valencia was his brief stint as envoy to the Bishop of Valencia and that was well over 600 years ago. Crow fretted that he was in the wrong place. Maybe Teruel was where he was supposed to be, or Palma. But Teruel wasn't by the sea. Palma was, but it was actually an island off the coast of Spain. Simonin said, 'No man is an island.' The father had to know that Crow would consider the man's birthplace and burial site. Was that why he said that, or did he mean something else? Something to do with some English poet? He looked at his watch. Less than twenty-nine hours until the wedding. That was if he was even in the right time zone.

He took another sip of his coffee when the outline of a man with the sun over his shoulder appeared just a few feet away from the table. The sun glistened off his bald head and concealed his face in shadows. He reached for the back of the chair opposite Crow.

"Mind if I join you?" he asked in a refined French accent.

Crow thought it odd, with all the empty tables, that someone would feel it necessary to share his. Odd, that is, until the sun eclipsed behind his head and his face became clear.

"Who the hell are you?" Crow said.

"My name is Philippe Babineaux," the man with the eye patch said. His Façonnable navy linen blazer was accented with a sky-blue pocket square. The Breton blue and white stripe shirt and white pants made him look as though he'd just stepped off a yacht. He presumed he was welcomed and took a seat.

"I saw you in Avignon," Crow said. "You're following me. Why?"

"I want to help you, Monsieur Crow."

"Help me with what?"

"Help you in your quest."

"My quest?"

"You and I are very much alike," Babineaux said.

"Is that so?"

"Neither of us suffers fools. We also share the same tenacity. I believe we share the same goals."

Crow took another bite of his breakfast.

"You left Avignon in such a hurry," Babineaux said.

"I had business here in Valencia."

"Please, do not play coy with me. You want to stop the prophecy and you are quickly running out of time. I can help you."

"How do you know all this?"

"Father Simonin."

"You knew him?" Crow asked.

"Very well. He and I along with Jean-Claude Delacroix have been exchanging ideas for years. I urged Simonin not to meet with you. We knew a prophecy war was in progress. Very dangerous to get in the middle of one of those. He ignored my advice. When I heard the bell ring at the odd time, I knew they had killed him."

"They being…?"

The female server with long legs and a small face interrupted to take Babineaux's order.

"Eggs Florentine and a Bloody Mary."

"Coffee?" She gestured toward the silver pot.

"Yes."

She filled his cup.

Babineaux continued after the server was gone. "Who killed Father Simonin? Probably the same people who killed Delacroix."

"And who would that be?" Crow asked.

Babineaux reached for the cream and poured a healthy amount into his coffee. "If I were a betting man, I would say the First Face of Janus."

"Are you a betting man?"

He set the creamer down and stirred his cup. "That depends upon the odds."

"Did you just roll the dice that I would be in Valencia?" Crow asked.

Babineaux smiled. "I knew the good father would tell you."

"He didn't exactly tell me. He gave me the name Sánchez Muñoz."

Babineaux threw his head back and laughed. "Very clever. He did not want you caught with his explicit instructions on your person. He learned much in his studies over the years." His face turned solemn. "Too bad it got him killed."

"Unfortunately, I seem to have that effect on people. You don't appear to be too torn up over your friend's death."

"I never said he was a friend. I said I knew him well. We shared a similar interest in the prophecy wars. Just like Delacroix. They both knew death was a possibility, a hazard of the profession, Monsieur Crow. What else did Father Simonin tell you?"

"Nothing," Crow said too quickly.

"Nothing," Babineaux said with a sarcastic tinge to his voice. "You are sure?" He sipped his coffee.

"Nothing," Crow stated emphatically. "If there's something you're fishing for, just come right out and say it."

"Oh, no, no, no, monsieur. Just gathering information."

"If I'm such a death magnet, why are you brave enough to be seen with me?" Crow asked.

"Because if you are important enough to leave death in your wake, monsieur, you must be getting close to something."

"I see. And that something is worth dying for?"

"I should hope it would not come to that."

"And how'd you know I'd be at this particular hotel?"

"It is the only five-star hotel in Valencia recommended by the LHW. Where else would you be?"

"I'm that predictable?"

"You are Benson Crow, the famous author. How do you say? It is how you roll. And now you are on the trail of your latest novel. You are intrigued by the First Face of Janus. You can already imagine the story in the pages against the backdrop of France and Spain." His eyes became animated. "It has danger, conspiracy, secret societies. What is not to love, no? You are determined to find the Custos Verbi because you think together you can stop the next prophecy, and you think you will find them here in Valencia. Stop me if I have missed anything."

Crow didn't answer.

Babineaux took another drink of coffee and continued. "Father Simonin gave you the name Sánchez Muñoz for a reason. It was to lead you here to Valencia, but you do not yet know why. Are you not the least bit curious?"

Crow was dubious. "I'm listening."

"Did you know that most Christian historians from around the world agree that the chalice at Valencia Cathedral is the Holy Chalice, the authentic cup used at the Last Supper?"

The 'cup,' Crow thought, trying to conceal his excitement. *Behold the cup and follow the choir*, Simonin had said. "Wait a minute. Are you talking about the Holy Grail?"

"Bite your tongue, monsieur. The so-called Holy Grail is the product of fiction writers, most notably Robert de Boron who first dreamed up this mystical grail, and Chrétien de Troyes who forever linked the Holy Grail with King Arthur. The Chalice is, indeed, holy, but it is not magical. It does not bring its possessor special powers. It is simply the cup from which Jesus and his disciples drank during the Last Supper."

"And how does that fit in with the Custos Verbi?" Crow asked.

"Only that having the Chalice here attracts the most pious in the Christian faith. If it is, in fact, the cup from which Christ drank the night before his death, it is the only surviving holy artifact from the origins of the Christian religion. You can imagine that the most devout Christians have longed to be close to it for centuries. Perfect place to find volunteers to be the Keepers of the Word, no?"

"And you think they're still here," Crow said.

"I do. Whether you are likely to find any is another matter. Like the First Face of Janus, they are a highly secretive group. Very selective, very disciplined. Every move is calculated to accomplish the mission but not get caught in the process. Legend has it that the ceremony inducting them into the Custos Verbi is a communion using the Holy Chalice. If that is true, they are here."

"And what's your angle?"

Babineaux leaned away from the table as the server set his breakfast and his Bloody Mary before him. He waited until she was out of earshot before leaning forward again. "I am like Delacroix and Simonin. I am a historian. I want to continue their work so it will not be in vain. Like those gentlemen, I believe these two groups exist. However, it is only faith without proof. You are a rare gem, something we have been searching for for years. One of those groups has actually been in contact with you. You can help provide that proof."

"Which side are you on?" Crow asked.

"Me?" Babineaux smiled and cut into his eggs. "Neither. I am as impartial as a historian studying the Crimean War." He took a hefty bite.

"Since when do historians afford five-star hotels?"

Babineaux smiled a modest smile and dabbed the corner of his mouth with his napkin. "I also do some consulting work. France is full of museums that need advice. Plus, this is a business expense. It gets me next to you." He took another bite of his breakfast.

Crow seemed satisfied with the answer. "Why do you suppose the Custos Verbi has never really been able to stop the First Facers?"

Babineaux finished chewing and swallowed. "Because they are at a distinct disadvantage. They do not possess the Unriddled Manuscript." He pointed with his fork. "That is the key. Imagine being able to foretell the future. It holds immense power and wealth, a distinct advantage for the First Face of Janus."

"Tell me about this Unriddled Manuscript. Who gets to see it?"

"Only a select group is privy to the Unriddled Manuscript. The Premier Gnostique—The Prime Gnostic—and the Elite Council."

"The Prime Gnostic?" Crow asked.

"Yes. That's the top of the food chain in the First Face of Janus."

"So this Prime Gnostic and his council—"

"Or her."

"Or *her* council determine what predictions are taking shape and they dispatch their minions to make sure it happens," Crow said.

"Crudely put, but that is pretty much it."

Crow chewed on his breakfast as well as the information just laid before him.

Babineaux added between bites, "Oh, and in case you have not noticed, the First Face of Janus will kill you to keep you from interfering."

"You seem quite sure."

"That they will kill you?"

"About who's trying to kill me."

Babineaux laid down his fork. "It is obvious, no? You are trying to stop the prophecy and somebody is trying to stop you."

"There's more to it than that," Crow said.

"Like?"

"I've said too much already."

"Do not fool yourself, my friend. I already know everything. The man in Montreal. The killing of Dr. Grumbling and his housekeeper. Everything."

"How do you know so much?"

"I told you. Delacroix and I worked together."

"And you think it's the First Face of Janus," Crow said.

"Who else would it be?"

"Custos Verbi?"

Babineaux turned his head aside and cut the air with a sweep of his hand. "Please."

"What's so fantastic about that?"

"It makes no sense."

"They've been known to kill," Crow said.

"Sure, but why would they kill you if you are trying to stop the prophecy?"

"Maybe they think I'm an agent of Janus."

Babineaux laughed. "Unlikely."

"Why is that unlikely?"

"Because they have been doing this for nearly 500 years, my friend. They do not make mistakes like that. They kill when they need to, but they do not arbitrarily murder people they *think* may be agents of Janus."

"So you think it's the First Face of Janus."

"I do not think, my friend, I am sure of it. And you say you have no knowledge of the Prime Gnostic?" Babineaux asked.

"No. None. This is the first I've heard of all that."

"Interesting. Then you are flying blind." He cut into his breakfast then stopped. "And you actually intend to stop them? No one stops the First Face of Janus, monsieur. In their minds, their cause is noble and they must not fail."

"Look, if your theory is right, the First Facers killed Jean-Claude Delacroix. They killed Father Simonin. They killed my first contact in Montreal and my contact in America. And they tried to kill me. I don't give a damn how noble they think their cause is. I don't give a damn about some Prime Gnostic. They're common killers as far as I'm concerned. Do I intend to stop them? Hell, yeah, I'm going to stop them."

"How?"

"I'll worry about that."

"I see. Big-talking American. You are going to need my help."

Crow looked at him suspiciously.

"You do not trust me," Babineaux said.

"Should I?"

"I suppose you have no reason to at this point. I will have to earn that trust." Babineaux raised his Bloody Mary. "To stopping the next prophecy."

Crow reluctantly raised his coffee cup. Babineaux clinked the two together and took a healthy gulp.

Chapter Thirty

"Yes, *that* bald guy with the eye patch," Crow said as if Rosenfeld had several to choose from. "His name is Philippe Babineaux."

"What the hell is he doing here?" she asked.

"He's following us."

"And you're good with that?"

"No, I'm not *good* with that. What was I supposed to do? Call the police? He made no bones about the fact that he was following us. He says he wants to help us. In fact, he already has."

"Helped us?" Rosenfeld asked. "How?"

"Did you know the Holy Chalice is at Valencia Cathedral?"

"No. So?"

"So Babineaux says it attracts the most pious in the Christian faith. He says they actually use the chalice in the initiation ceremony for the Custos Verbi."

"And you believe him?"

"It's more than we had to go on this morning. And it fits. If the Custos Verbi is based at Valencia Cathedral then that's why Simonin sent us here."

"And what's in it for this Babineaux guy?"

"I don't quite know. He says he's interested from a historical standpoint, but he's not showing all his cards."

"You're not seriously thinking about hooking up with this character, are you?"

"We only have a little more than twenty-four hours to figure this out. He does know a lot about the First Face of Janus."

"Like what?" Rosenfeld asked.

"Like the Prime Gnostic."

"The what?"

"Exactly. I hadn't heard of it either. It's apparently the head honcho with the First Face of Janus. He or she is who deciphers the Unriddled Manuscript and decides how to aid in the prophecy."

"One person?"

"And the Elite Council," Crow added.

"Oh, come on, now." Rosenfeld held up her hands and shook her head. "This has hogwash written all over it. I've been studying these people for years and I've never heard of any of this."

"Let me get this straight," Crow said. "You're willing to believe there's a First Face of Janus. You're willing to buy into this secret police force from the Church called the Custos Verbi, but you can't swallow that there's a leader and some advisors who call the shots?"

"I'm along as your historical advisor," Rosenfeld said. "I'm saying I've never heard of such a thing. I'm also your bullshit detector, and it's going off right now."

"Look, I get the same feeling about Babineaux that you do, but he's all we've got right now. We're running out of options. Get dressed. We're meeting him for lunch at noon."

"We're having lunch with cyclops?" Rosenfeld protested.

"At the hotel restaurant. Afterwards, I want to poke around Valencia Cathedral."

Crow was a bit miffed that Rosenfeld insisted on dropping by the hotel's clothing shop before lunch. He waited impatiently while she disappeared interminably into the changing room. Then his heart almost stopped when she finally emerged. Dressed in a yellow sundress with white polka dots, Rosenfeld's dazzling white put-on smile glowed against her olive skin.

"Very nice, Rosenfeld," Crow smiled.

"Nothing like a shiny lure to catch a fish," she said.

They followed the maître d' through the restaurant. A few more steps and they were out on the portico with a sprinkling of four-top tables dressed in white linen and accented with small boxed clusters of pink geraniums. The palm trees gently swayed in the breeze. Water danced in the large rectangular fountain just a few yards away. Rosenfeld approached the lunch table first. Babineaux jumped to his feet.

"Mr. Babineaux, I'd like you to meet Dr. Sidney Rosenfeld," Crow introduced from behind. "Dr. Rosenfeld, this is Philippe Babineaux."

"Nice to meet you, Monsieur Babineaux," she said.

"The pleasure is mine, mademoiselle." He reached for her dangling hand and kissed it. "And I do hope it is mademoiselle."

Rosenfeld shuddered slightly but maintained her radiant smile. "Yes. Benson tells me you know quite a lot about the First Face of Janus."

Babineaux held her seat until she was settled in then took his own opposite her. "Apparently more than your friend here," he said lightheartedly to Crow who took a seat to his left. "And what is your interest, Dr. Rosenfeld?"

"I'm an antiquarian."

"Ah, as am I," Babineaux said.

"Really? Where did you study?"

"At Pantheon-Sorbonne University. I am a member of the Société des Antiquaires, the Society of Antiquaries of France."

Rosenfeld exchanged a glance with Crow. "At the Louvre?"

"Oui, mademoiselle."

"I'm impressed. Very prestigious."

"Well, thank you, but—"

"May I offer you something from the bar?" the waiter interrupted.

Babineaux deferred to Rosenfeld.

"Just water for me, thank you."

He looked to Crow. "Water."

"Señor?" he asked.

"I will have a whisky," Babineaux said. "Two ice cubes, gracias."

Once the server was gone, Babineaux continued. "I am afraid we are a dying breed, you and me," he said to Rosenfeld. "This new generation is more interested in technology. They would rather read a book on a tablet about history than actually hold history in their hands. To me, it is not really reading unless you can smell the scent of the paper, hear the crackling of the spine when you open the book."

"Benson tells me you do consulting work," Rosenfeld queried.

"Yes. Various museums across France hire me to authenticate manuscripts. That is my specialty."

"Mine too," Rosenfeld said.

"Is that your interest in this?" Babineaux asked.

"Well, my interest is two-fold. Manuscripts, yes, but I'm a bit of a Nostradamus nut."

"As in, you believe the prophecies, or you are fascinated with the man?"

"As in I'm fascinated with the man. It's intriguing, don't you think, that after close to 500 years an obscure physician from the south of France is one of the most studied and read authors of all time?"

"I am not sure who that says more about, us or him," Babineaux said.

Rosenfeld found his observation insightful. "Yes. I suppose that's true. One must wonder if all this fascination is over a brilliant writer or a gullible population."

"Gullible? Interesting choice of words."

"Maybe that wasn't the *right* choice of words," Rosenfeld admitted. "Maybe people are looking for answers. Maybe they find some comfort in Nostradamus."

"Is that why you study him?" Babineaux asked.

Rosenfeld hesitated. "I'm not sure. We see things in the quatrains that we want to see, I think."

"Like clouds," Babineaux said. "We see faces and shapes and animals in that odd assortment of water vapor. Or, at least, we think we do. And somehow we derive some pleasure from it."

"Yes," Rosenfeld said. "I suppose we do."

"Like a Rorschach test," Babineaux added.

"So, you're saying that what one sees in the quatrains is more a reflection of our deep-seated hopes and dreams than anything Nostradamus was trying to tell us."

"Or fears," Babineaux added.

"Or fears. Yes. You have an interesting way of looking at Nostradamus, Monsieur Babineaux."

"Philippe, please," he insisted. He turned to Crow. "Monsieur Crow, may I see the quatrains, please?"

Crow looked at Rosenfeld then back at Babineaux. "What quatrains?"

"You know very well what quatrains." Babineaux held out his hand.

"I don't know what you're talking about," Crow said.

"Please, Monsieur Crow, if I am to help you we must not play games."

Crow hesitated then pulled the paper from his coat pocket. Babineaux placed his reading glasses on his nose and looked over the verses. After a moment he grunted.

"Well?" Crow asked.

"I do not think there is any doubt," he said.

"Any doubt about what?" Rosenfeld asked.

He turned to her. "They are from the Unriddled Manuscript."

"But we were told that was doubtful," Crow said.

Babineaux looked at him quizzically. "By whom?"

"By someone—"

"By someone who has studied the subject more than I have?" Babineaux asked rhetorically.

"I withdraw the statement," Crow said.

Babineaux smiled.

"But what about the fact that the quatrains are still riddled?" Rosenfeld asked.

"Are they?" Babineaux asked. "To the untrained eye perhaps, but that is taking them out of context. We are only afforded these verses. Were we to see the others around them we would know exactly what they mean."

"Why do you think these are from the Unriddled Manuscript?" Crow asked.

"Because they are written in the unmistakable voice of Nostradamus."

"How do you know?"

Babineaux acted a bit irritated by the question. "How does a maestro know the difference between a Stradivarius and a fiddle? He just knows. I have studied Nostradamus my entire adult life, my friend. I know."

Babineaux's phone rang. He lingered on Rosenfeld's gaze longer than was comfortable then looked down at the phone and quickly scooped it off the table. "Please excuse me. I will just be a moment." He left the table.

"What in the hell are you doing?" Crow said firmly but quietly.

"What are you talking about?" she whispered.

"You're acting like a teenybopper at a rock concert."

"Oh, come on."

"What was that about your bullshit detector earlier?"

"I'm not blind. This guy's as slick as grease off a barbecue biscuit. What did you want me to do? Act like a bitch?"

"No. I just think you're coming on a little too strong. That's all. Did you just say grease off a barbecue biscuit?"

"You're jealous, aren't you?"

The waiter returned with their waters and Babineaux's whisky. Crow waited for him to leave.

"Don't flatter yourself, Rosenfeld. Besides, he's not the man he pretends to be."

"What do you mean?" she asked.

"Babineaux talks a big game," he said, "but did you see him when his phone rang? He looked like somebody's butler."

"Wish we knew who was calling."

"Somebody named Otto," Crow said casually.

"How do you know?"

"Because while he was ogling you, I was looking at his caller ID. He didn't notice with his bad eye. We need to find out who this Otto is."

"I have a friend in Paris at Bouchard's Auction House," Rosenfeld said. "If Babineaux is the high roller in the antiquities world he claims to be, my friend will know him. Maybe it'll lead us to Otto."

Babineaux looked back over his shoulder at the table where

Crow and Rosenfeld sat then spoke softly into the phone. "We just sat down to lunch."

"And?" the baritone voice with the German accent on the other end asked. "Does he know where it is?"

"I think he does."

"I do not pay you for conjecture," Otto said. "I pay you to know. Does he or does he not?"

"I will have a more definitive answer this afternoon. He has the quatrains. I will text those lines to you when we are finished here. They are from the Unriddled Manuscript."

"And what about the girl?"

"That is what lets me know he is here for the manuscript. She is an expert in ancient books from some auction house in Boston. He has brought her along to authenticate the Unriddled Manuscript."

"Interesting."

"Indeed it is," Babineaux said. "The only question that remains is if they already have the book in their possession."

"Time is dwindling. I will give it until morning. If he does not lead you to it, then you will have to become more persuasive."

"Understood," Babineaux said. "One more thing."

"What is it?" Otto said.

"If we are correct that he has brought along an expert to authenticate the Unriddled Manuscript, it would indicate that he is not one of them. If he were, why would he need an outside expert to authenticate it?"

"Interesting. Go on."

"I am convinced he is actually trying to stop the prophecy," Babineaux said.

"You are sure?"

"As you say, you do not pay me for conjecture."

"Does he know what the prophecy is?"

"Not yet," Babineaux said, "but he is getting closer. I am helping him put the pieces together."

"Excellent. I want that book, but do not let that keep him from his mission. If he can stop the prophecy, he saves us a great deal of trouble."

"Yes, Your Excellency."

Babineaux hung up then pulled the quatrains from his coat pocket. He took a quick photo with his phone and attached it to a text to Otto.

"You know he's trying to play you, right?" Crow said.

"Of course I know that," Rosenfeld said, "but we can play *him* to our advantage. Apparently, he knows a lot more about all this than he's letting on. Certainly a lot more than we know. We need him if you're serious about solving this quatrain. He's trying to divide us so he can pick my brain and see what we know."

"But you just said he knows more than we do," Crow said.

"He does, but he doesn't know that. If he came all the way from France, he thinks we're closer than we are. We have to find out why."

"Then let him divide us. I really need to check out that cathedral anyway. I'll find a way to excuse myself. Whatever I come up with, play along. I need to leave you here with—"

Rosenfeld cleared her throat. Crow looked up as Babineaux returned to the table.

"Office politics," Babineaux said with a smile. "Even here I cannot escape it. My apologies. Where were we? Oh, yes. The quatrains. Where did you get them?"

"The man in Montreal gave them to me?"

"Did you know this man?"

"I'd never seen him before."

Babineaux chuckled. "A complete stranger walks up to you and just gives you quatrains from the Unriddled Manuscript?"

Now Crow was perturbed. "What are you saying?"

Babineaux twirled the ice around in his glass and took a drink of whisky. "Probably what you are inferring."

"You're saying I'm lying?"

"I am saying you are not telling us everything." Babineaux looked at Rosenfeld then back at Crow. "We are both getting this story from you. We are having to take your word for it. Can you truly tell Mademoiselle Rosenfeld right now that you have told her everything?"

Crow looked at Rosenfeld who met his eyes with skepticism. "Now, wait a minute," he turned to Babineaux. "I don't know what you're up to, but I don't like it."

"Up to, Monsieur Crow? Are we sure it is *me* who is up to something?"

Crow stood up and threw his napkin on his plate. "I don't have to sit here and listen to this crap. Let's go," he said to Rosenfeld, pushing his chair back into place under the table.

Rosenfeld sat there in defiance.

"I said let's go," Crow said.

"Well, you know what?" Rosenfeld said. "I don't give a damn what you said. Take your machismo and cram it up your ass." She turned to Babineaux. "If you'll pardon my French."

Babineaux let out a hearty laugh. "I do not think that is French, but I certainly understand the translation."

Rosenfeld turned back to Crow. "I'm having lunch with Monsieur Babineaux."

"Philippe, s'il vous plaît," Babineaux said slyly then looked up at Crow.

"Philippe," Rosenfeld repeated with a smile.

Crow stood there holding out his hand.

"What?" Babineaux asked.

"You know damn well what," Crow shot back. "The quatrains."

Babineaux looked at Crow for a brief moment then reached in his coat pocket, pulled out the sheet of paper, and plopped it in his hand. Crow put the quatrains back in his own coat pocket and stormed off.

Chapter Thirty-One

Benson Crow parked his car a few blocks from Plaça de la Reina, Queen Square in the native Catalan. He weaved among the tourists toward Valencia Cathedral. Double-decker open-air buses collected sightseers at the curb for tours of the old city. Shops invited patrons in off the sidewalks with everything from chocolates to souvenirs. He cut through the pedestrian promenade with its benches and grassy areas and beautiful flower gardens dedicated to Queen Mercedes of Orleans. She became queen in 1878 after a scandalous marriage to her cousin, King Alfonso XII. She contracted tuberculosis after her honeymoon and lived to be queen only six months. She died at the tender age of 18, a fleeting opportunity, much like Crow's chances at solving the mystery of the prophecy.

He reached the main entrance of Valencia Cathedral built in the thirteenth century on the site of a Moorish mosque. He paid the admission fee and was handed an audio player with headphones. He grabbed a map of the cathedral and located the Holy Chalice Chapel.

The back wall of the chapel reached over 50 feet. The fifteenth-century canopies, openwork, and pinnacles framed two reliefs. The lower section depicted scenes from the Old Testament. At the top were scenes from the New Testament. Three staggered ogive arches framed the alabaster altarpiece that held the focal point of the room, in fact, of the entire cathedral. Crow could see it from far across the room. The Holy Chalice. A light that shone from above gave it a heavenly appearance. The room was surprisingly low key. A few tourists reverently observed the relic from the wooden pews, some taking pictures, but not the hordes one would see gathered around the Mona Lisa or Venus de Milo at the Louvre. He blended among the other tourists who came to catch a glimpse of either an incredibly holy relic and the only tangible link to Christ, or one of the biggest hoaxes of all time. Crow lingered while people came and went. He was sure he must be in the right place, but he was unsure what to do next.

Behold the cup and follow the choir, Crow remembered. *The straight path ends for the non-believer.* There were pews on either side of the altar. Crow assumed they were for the choir. That much he got, but follow them? Follow them where?

He stepped just outside the room and stopped an employee. "Habla Inglés?"

"Yes," the lady answered.

"Is this room used for anything now?" Crow asked.

"What do you mean?"

"I mean, do they have regular services here?"

"Oh, no," she said. "This is a very special room. It holds the Holy Chalice."

"Yes, I know," Crow said, "but they don't use it for church services or anything like that?"

"No. It houses the chalice only. OK?"

"But—"

"Use your audio," she said.

"My audio?"

She pointed to the headphones Crow forgot he had hanging

around his neck. He fumbled for the headphones and pulled them up on his ears.

"Number two," she said. "Press number two for the history of the room."

"Gracias."

He pulled the player up and pressed two on the keypad. He walked around the room and followed the British announcer's narration of the history of the chalice. The Holy Chalice was believed to have been left in a house belonging to the family of St. Mark the Evangelist where the Last Supper took place. This was the same Mark who was one of the "Seventy Disciples" Jesus sent out to spread the word. When Jesus claimed that his flesh was real food and his blood was real drink, many of the seventy left him including Mark. He later regained his faith and became Peter's interpreter and wrote the Gospel of Mark from first-hand accounts of Peter. While serving as Peter's interpreter, Mark is said to have brought the cup to Rome. It was used as a papal chalice until the third century when it was removed from Rome over fears of persecution. Spanish soldiers took it to Spain. During the Muslim occupation, the Church secretly passed it from place to place until the King of Spain took charge of it. The chalice was turned over to Valencia Cathedral in the fifteenth century where it has remained ever since except for briefly being removed for safekeeping during the Spanish Civil War of the 1930s.

The cup was made of agate stone and positively identified as originating in Palestine some time just before or just after the birth of Christ. The stones and pearls, as well as the gold work, were added somewhere between the tenth and fourteenth centuries. Then the narrator said something that made Crow's ears perk up. "The choir used to enter and exit the chapel from behind the altar. When the room was reconfigured, the choir door was moved. It's the door you now see on your right."

Behold the cup and follow the choir.

Crow looked around. There were maybe ten other people in the room. If he breached the velvet ropes and opened the door, someone would surely report him. He fretted for a moment then returned to the main counter by the entrance to the chapel. He turned in his headphones and player. He approached the chalice room again and just stared inside from the doorway.

You've got to act like you're supposed to be here, he told himself.

He clenched his teeth, took a deep breath, and strode back into the chalice room with purpose. He marched up to the velvet rope on the right, unhooked it from its brass stanchion, stepped through, and re-hooked it behind him. He didn't dare look back out at those assembled in the room. He walked smartly to the dark wooden door, opened it, and let himself inside. Getting through the door was the easy part. Now what?

The straight path ends for the non-believer.

The path wasn't straight at all. In fact, after about two steps into the alcove was a doorway to the left. There was a stone wall to the right and a stone wall straight ahead. Did Father Simonin mean take a left and then go straight? That's not what he said.

The straight path ends for the non-believer.

Crow studied on it. A crazy thought occurred to him. It was *too* crazy. He'd feel silly doing that. But then why not? *You must have faith*, Simonin had said. What if he was wrong? There was no one else around to make him feel embarrassed if he was. *Just go for it.* He closed his eyes and concentrated. *OK, what the hell. Here goes.* He took a slow step forward and stood for a moment. Then another step. He was even with the only way out, the stone archway to his left, but he didn't take it. He didn't even look in that direction. He took another step forward and then another until his chest bumped into the cold wall. *Now* he felt silly. He stood there for a couple of seconds thinking what an idiotic idea it was to think he could just walk through a wall. Even when he had mustered up all the faith he could, it was impossible. Then he thought his knees were buckling. The large stones below his feet began to lower. As they did, the wall in front of him parted ever so slightly. Crow smiled as a passageway opened up before him. He stepped inside and the stone wall closed behind him.

On the far side of the room were what looked like tombstones, solid slabs of sandstone with mid-reliefs of odd ornate designs. One was etched with what first appeared to be bows and arrows, but on closer examination were flowers capping an eight-sided design inside a circle inside a square. Another depicted men carrying crosses. The third seemed almost like a mason's square and compass design, but extending from what would have been the mason's square were what Crow interpreted as, perhaps, round palm leaves. The veins inside the palms formed what looked like scorpions with too many legs. This design was repeated at the bottom. All extended outside of a square which was positioned on one of its points. There was a clawed X at the top of the carving, the top right portion of it looking similar to the claw of a hammer. The fourth relief depicted warriors with swords and shields and a lead soldier with a horn as if trumpeting the others into war. Was this the defender of the rock?

Modern recessed lighting illuminated the room. Just beyond the grouping of four reliefs was a stone altar or pulpit. Between the four markers was a rectangular subterranean entrance with steps leading into the darkness. Someone had been there recently or was planning to return unless the lighting was left on permanently. He hesitated a moment then turned on the flashlight on his phone and began to sneak down the steps. The hallway was carved out of the stone. He touched the bottom step and stood for a moment shining his light 360 degrees. The mouth of the hallway where he stood was like the bulb of a plant with the corridor leading away like the stem. The walls narrowed as he moved forward. The ceiling became lower above him and he bent his neck to keep from scraping his head. From the slight burn in his calves, he could tell the tunnel elevation was dropping. The cave closed in around him and he became claustrophobic. Just as he was at his most uncomfortable a sound pierced his ears. The screech frightened him enough, but it was the claws on his shoulder and back that nearly scared him to death. He screamed an unmanly cry and banged the back of his head on the stone ceiling. He didn't even have to train his light. His senses pieced together what had just happened. A rat was spooked by his passing and leapt from a crack in the wall to his shoulder then down his back. He stopped for a moment to allow his heart to steady then proceeded.

After a few meters, the passageway began to widen a tad, yet the ceiling remained low. He could hear water dripping up in the distance. He shined his light further ahead but could make out nothing other than a widening in the rock. Were it not for his light, he wouldn't have been able to see his hand in front of his face. He plodded forward along the damp floor of the cave until he reached a rather sizable chamber which spanned about thirty feet wide. The ceiling opened up above him to roughly twenty feet. It looked more like a normal rock formation rather than anything cut by man. He surveyed the ceiling in front of him with his light. All he could see was rock. The cold, wet cave was completely silent except for the dripping of the water in the distance. Crow thought how if he had to endure that pure silence for a prolonged period of time, he would go insane. He felt extremely uncomfortable and vulnerable. His light showed him no way out. After following the passageway far from the entrance, he had hit a dead end. No telling how far below the church he was. Far enough where no one could hear him scream. Now he was starting to feel real uneasy. He was just before turning to leave when he was suddenly and violently grabbed by his head out of the darkness. He felt the weight on his neck of whatever had just jumped on him. It covered his eyes. He dropped his phone trying to free up another hand to fight it. The weight on his neck and shoulders felt like a bowling ball. He thought he sensed burlap draping down to his neck. Whatever had him tried desperately to wrench his head sideways as if attempting to snap his neck. Crow staggered. He tried to pry the creature from his face. Its grip was unusually strong. He threw himself backwards and smashed it against the stone wall of the cave. It wouldn't let go. He stumbled back out a few steps. It still clung to his head. He tried again, crushing it against the rock wall. This time the creature turned loose. For a brief second, he thought he heard the faint sigh of a man.

Chapter Thirty-Two

Crow dived to the floor for the light. He grabbed it and swept it up in one single movement and shined it toward where he thought he heard the creature fall, fearing it might already be upon him again. What caught his light was a little wisp of a man not barely three feet tall garbed in a brown monk's robe with hood, rubbing an aching back. One diminutive hand shot up to shield his eyes from the light. He spit out what almost certainly were Spanish obscenities.

"Stop!" Crow shouted.

The little man was moving toward a red lever on the wall.

"Alto," he repeated in Spanish.

The dwarf continued to reach for the lever.

"Father Simonin!"

The man stopped, his hand just reaching up and touching the red lever. "What about him?" he said in English.

"He sent me."

"Why would he send you here?"

"Then you knew him?"

"*Knew* him?" the little monk asked.

"You didn't know?" Crow said delicately. "He was murdered."

The dwarf hung his head. "Murdered? Like Jean-Claude."

"You heard about Delacroix?"

He reflected for a moment, then his sorrow turned to anger. "Who killed them?"

"I don't know."

"You?"

"No," Crow insisted. "Whoever killed them tried to kill me, too. At least twice."

"I thought you were Jean-Claude's killer. I thought you had come for me."

"I think Father Simonin also sensed the danger. He gave me some clues. He told me, 'Behold the cup and follow the choir. The straight path ends for the non-believer.' That's how I found this passageway. Where does it lead? What am I supposed to find here?"

"I do not know what you are looking for, señor. As for this passageway, I am afraid you have literally reached a dead end."

"Well, there's got to be something here."

"Simonin sent you to me?"

"No. He didn't mention you. He said—" Crow realized they hadn't been introduced. "I'm sorry, what's your name?"

The little man squinted. "Get that thing out of my eyes." He waddled over and hit a switch carved into the cave wall and illuminated the room. "My name is Alejandro de la Aiza."

"He didn't mention you or anyone else," Crow said. "He gave me the directions from the cup and told me to find…Wait a minute, did you say Alejandro de la Aiza?"

"I did."

"Alejandro. Alexander. Alexander means defender."

"That is correct."

"And Aiza means—"

"Rock, señor."

"Son of a bitch," Crow said almost to himself.

"How do I know Father Simonin sent you?"

Crow reached into his front pocket and produced a small piece of paper. "He gave me this." He handed the small paper to Alejandro.

The little man smiled. "Father Simonin's Bible verses." He unrolled it. "Sánchez Muñoz," Alejandro read out loud, recognizing the handwriting. "His way of sending you to Valencia. But why?"

"He told me to find the defender of the rock. That's you."

"And you are?"

"Crow." He extended his hand down and clasped the man's tiny hand in his.

"And you know the meaning of Basque words? Impressive."

"Words are sort of my business."

"And what is your business here?"

"I'm looking for the Custos Verbi."

Alejandro threw back his head and laughed. "Is that right?"

Crow was irritated. "That's funny?"

"Sí, señor. The Custos Verbi is a legend, a myth. Where did you get such wild ideas?"

"Let's stop the charade. We both know better than that."

"We do, do we?" Alejandro said.

"I have to find them. I can help them."

The little man stared at Crow for a time. "And what could I possibly have that you need?"

"Knowledge," Crow said. "Simonin said if I find you, I find the answer I'm looking for."

Alejandro smiled. "That depends on the question."

A perplexed look crossed Crow's face. He hadn't really thought what his question would be. He hadn't considered meeting someone who was the defender of the rock. He'd thought in much more esoteric and symbolic terms. "I'm trying to stop the next prophecy," Crow finally said.

Alejandro smiled. "And what prophecy is that?"

"I don't know exactly," Crow admitted. "I only have clues, guesses."

Alejandro walked over to the rock wall. He pushed two stones on the wall simultaneously and the rock parted to reveal a passageway. He hit a light switch just inside the opening and Crow followed him in. The rock closed behind them and they walked for maybe thirty feet until the corridor opened up into another chamber, what appeared to be the little man's living quarters. It was modestly appointed with just a small bed, a toilet, a sink, a bathtub, sparse furnishings, a bookshelf with a dozen or so books, and a dim lamp.

"Señor Crow, you said your name was?"

"Yes. Benson Crow."

The man turned to face him. "The author Benson Crow?"

"Yes."

"How odd," the man said. "Why you?"

"I've been asking myself that same question."

Alejandro took a seat at a small wooden table. "I do not know what it is that I can offer you."

Crow sat down beside him. "I want to know what the next prophecy will be."

Alejandro threw up his hands. "As do we all. Is that all you have? Just a desire to stop the prophecy? You are wasting your time and mine."

"No, I have more than just a hunch."

Alejandro leaned back in his chair and locked his tiny hands together across his chest. "I am listening."

Crow brought him up to speed. The odd quatrains, the trail that led him from Montreal to Valencia, the murders. He left nothing out.

"Then why did Simonin send you to me?"

"I have no idea," Crow said. "What was your connection with him?"

"We have been exchanging information for years, he along with Delacroix and several others." His eyes brightened. "You might call it our own little secret society."

"You each discovered pieces of the jigsaw puzzle," Crow said. "We have to put those pieces together. There's going to be a bloodbath. Most of a wedding party is going to be slaughtered. I'm looking for that wedding. I'm convinced that's part of the prophecy. But where? Who's getting married?"

"That's the trouble with these prophecies," Alejandro observed. "They make no sense until they happen, and then it is as if the clues were screaming at you the entire time."

"We *have* to change that. We *have* to see these clues before the event happens. This man Babineaux," Crow said, "is he part of your group with Simonin and Delacroix?"

Alejandro shook his head. "I have never heard of him."

"Interesting. He seems to be looking for the same thing we are."

"Yes, perhaps, but I was going to say that he seems a rather odd fixture in the story. Almost like he does not belong. How does he fit in?"

"I wish I knew," Crow said. "Surely I'm not the first to try and stop the prophecy."

"Yes, but this Babineaux does not strike me as them."

"Them?" Crow said. "So you *do* acknowledge the Custos Verbi exists."

"Who knows what is real and what is not?"

"What are you trying to hide?"

Alejandro looked at him intently for a moment then smiled. "Oh, you think I am Custos Verbi?" He let out a laugh.

"You're not?"

Alejandro said through his chuckles, "I hate to disappoint you, Señor Crow."

"But you admit they exist."

"If that is what you wish to believe."

"Stop playing games with me," Crow demanded. "Simonin said if I found you, I'd find my answer."

The little man lowered his defenses. "If there is such a thing, I am not a part of it."

"Then what are you?"

He held his arms out. "I am but a lowly caretaker. I am paid to roam these catacombs and check for leaks and rat infestation and," he gestured to Crow, "the odd lost visitor."

Crow pulled his phone from his pocket and brought up the photos. He turned the phone around and laid it on the table in front of Alejandro. The little man's eyes widened.

"Where did you get this?" He stared at the picture of the coin Crow found in Father Simonin's desk.

"Your boy, Simonin," Crow said.

"Señor, do you have any idea what this means?"

Crow leaned back in his chair. "Why don't you tell me?"

Chapter Thirty-Three

"It has been a delight getting to know you," Babineaux said. He motioned to the server for the check.

"Likewise," Sidney Rosenfeld said.

"There is still so much to discuss. One of the things I appreciate about the Spanish culture is the siesta. We have both traveled a long way and a relaxing nap would do us both good. I would love to continue our discussion over dinner."

"I'd like that," she lied.

"Splendid. I will have my automobile brought around at six. I know of a special place in town that features the local cuisine."

"I'll meet you at six."

ALEJANDRO STUDIED THE photograph of the odd coin on Crow's phone. "It is the calling card of the First Face of Janus."

"I'm confused. Simonin was a First Facer?"

"Not possible," Alejandro said.

"Then what was he doing with the coin?"

"He studied the First Facers for many years, señor. He must have come across the coin in his research. But that coin, if you *are* a First

Facer, opens many doors. I have heard about it. I thought it was legend, but there it is."

"Sounds like to me he was one of them," Crow said.

"He helped you in your quest to stop the prophecy. What kind of First Facer would do that?"

Crow had to admit he had a point. "You say Simonin is not one of them, how can you tell if someone *is* a member of the First Face of Janus?"

The little man laughed slightly. "That is a great question. The short answer is you cannot. They look like everyone else. They are in all sectors of society. Some are famous, most are ordinary people. That is how your 9/11 was allowed to happen."

"You're not gonna tell me President Bush was part of the conspiracy, are you?" Crow asked.

"In the conventional sense, as in, it was some kind of inside job and they blamed it on the terrorist like these people are saying—what do they call themselves?"

"9/11 Truthers?" Crow said.

"Yes, those people. No, but the First Facers were inside his administration."

"Really? Like who?"

"Before I answer that, you must understand how the First Face of Janus works. They do not fabricate events just to match up with Nostradamus' predictions. What they do is they either allow them to happen or aid in their happening. The terrorists had been plotting to topple the World Trade Center towers for years. The First Facers knew the towers must be destroyed based on their reading of something called the Unriddled Manuscript."

"Yes, I'm familiar with that," Crow said.

"Excellent," Alejandro said. "Then you will save me the time. As you have no doubt heard, that manuscript is in much more detail than the quatrains. Once they understood what had to happen, it was their job to make sure no one stopped it. Ask yourself this question. How did the hijackers get on those planes?"

"They bought tickets like everybody else."

"That is true, but had anyone simply run a background check on any number of them they would have learned of their terrorists connections. At the very least, they would have learned that some of their visas had expired, and they would not have been allowed to board the planes. One of the ticket agents said he saw the ringleader, Mohamed Atta, and knew in his heart that he was a terrorist but sold him a ticket anyway. There had to be a policy in place that would allow that to happen."

"You're right," Crow said. "There was a strict policy that there would be no profiling at airports. That ticket agent you're talking about was in Portland, Maine. He said he gave himself a 'mental slap' because they weren't allowed to profile. That no-profile policy came from the transportation secretary at the time, oh, what's his name?" Crow snapped his fingers.

"Norman Mineta," Alejandro reminded him.

"That's right. Norm Mineta. Are you telling me Mineta was a First Facer?"

"I am telling you it was either Mineta or someone in his close circle who influenced him to adopt the no-profile policy. Do you not find it odd that a lifelong Democrat would find himself in a Republican administration in the position to make such a decision at just the right time?"

"That's incredible," Crow said.

Alejandro lowered his eyes and his voice as if to draw him closer. "Several key members of the German government who paved the way for Hitler to come to power were First Facers. It is incredible, but it is quite common."

"The wedding," Crow said. "What wedding could it be?"

The little man shrugged. Crow turned his head in frustration and muttered something under his breath. Alejandro reached for a block of cheese protected by a rounded glass top and cut himself a piece. "Señor?" he offered, gesturing to the cheese.

Crow waved him off.

Alejandro took a bite then decided to speak. "I cannot imagine why Simonin would send you to me."

"It has to be you," Crow said. "Sánchez Muñoz obviously means Valencia. The directions from the chalice? Defender of the rock? Well, that's literally your name."

Alejandro turned the edges of his mouth down and tilted his head as if to agree.

"You may not even realize that what you know is important," Crow explained. "Think."

"Like pieces of a jigsaw puzzle, as you say," Alejandro said. He grimaced and scratched the back of his head as he searched the dark recesses of his mind.

"Anything you may have stumbled upon recently?" Crow asked. "It doesn't have to make sense to you. Any odd bit of information. Anything at all."

Alejandro slowly shook his head then stopped and tapped his lip with his index finger. "We have been monitoring a couple of gentlemen we believe to be First Facers."

"We?" Crow asked.

"A colleague of mine who runs a cafe."

"Go on." Crow pulled himself closer to the table.

"This is certainly an odd bit of information, as you put it. At least, it struck me that way. One of these men said, 'The apparition of monsters presages the outbreak of war.'"

"Interesting," Crow said.

"Given their dedication to Nostradamus, when they said 'presages' we took notice," Alejandro said. "But nothing else was that much out of the usual. They talked about a book."

"What book?"

"Don Quixote," Alejandro said, "and how one of the men thought he was a knight. Standard discussion about the book's meaning." Alejandro deliberated in silence for a moment. "Do you think the next prophecy will lead to war?"

"Wars have been started over far less. The assassination of an archduke started a world war. If this bride is someone of importance and the wedding party is murdered, there could be someone of note there. And you're sure there was nothing else they said?"

Alejandro shrugged.

"And you're *sure* these were First Facers?"

"Señor, can we be sure of anything these days?"

Crow knew no truer words had been spoken since he fell down this rabbit hole.

"The Custos Verbi," Crow said. "They're here?"

Alejandro frowned. "In Valencia?"

"Here at the cathedral."

"No, no, no," he insisted.

"But the Holy Chalice. I heard the Custos Verbi drink from that when they are inducted into the society."

"What?" the little man said. "No. Who filled your head with such nonsense?"

"But it all fits," Crow said. "If you're a devout Catholic, then this would be the holiest of holies."

"Señor, the Custos Verbi are not Catholic. Not as we know Catholics today."

"What do you mean?" Crow said. "Keeper of the Word? That's what Custos Verbi means."

"I know very well what it means," the man said impatiently, "but they would not be here in a Catholic church because they are not Catholic, at least not in the true sense that we know the Catholic Church." He cut another piece of cheese and plopped it in his small mouth. He smiled, "I can see that you are confused."

"You could say that."

"Well, then let me elucidate. You were on the right path with Sánchez Muñoz."

"He was a pope."

"He was an *antipope*," Alejandro corrected. "You are familiar with the Western Schism?"

Crow nodded. "When the papacy moved back to Rome from Avignon and the Avignon pope didn't want to give up his power. So there were two men claiming to be pope at the same time."

"Three, actually," Alejandro said. "There was Benedict XIII of Avignon. There was the real pope, Pope Gregory XII, in Rome. There was also a third man who claimed legitimate right to the papacy. His name was Peter Phillarges. He was the Archbishop of Milan. He was a proponent of reuniting the Church under one pope and advocated for the Council of Pisa. This is where he hoped to end the Western Schism. Representatives from both sides—Avignon and Rome—met in 1409 at the Cathedral of Pisa in Italy. You know, where the leaning tower is. The council did anything but reunite the Church. The council vacated the seat of the papacy and both Benedict and Gregory were told to step down. In their place, they elevated Peter Phillarges and he became Pope Alexander V."

"I see where this is going," Crow said.

"Sí, neither Gregory nor Benedict would step down. Furthermore, Rome declared the Council of Pisa illegitimate and there were then three men claiming to be pope. One of the cardinals of Roman obedience at the Council of Pisa was an unscrupulous scoundrel by the name of Baldassare Cossa. He changed allegiance to Pope Alexander V once Alexander claimed to be pope. Within a year, Antipope Alexander, while traveling with Baldassare Cossa in Bologna, suddenly fell ill and died. Some say he was poisoned by Cossa. Conveniently, Cossa was consecrated pope on 25 May 1410. He had been ordained a priest only one day before. He took the name John XXIII."

"And we still had Gregory and Benedict."

"Correct," Alejandro said. "John XXIII was very shrewd. A few years prior, in order to build his power base, he borrowed money from the Medici family, one of several Italian banker families in Florence trying to make a name for itself. Cossa did not forget the favor and upon becoming pope—or antipope as the Catholic Church now recognizes him—he made the Medici bank the official bank of his papacy."

"That must've been a huge boost to the Medicis."

"Indeed. This added considerably to the Medici family's wealth, not to mention their prestige, and was the catalyst that launched the Medicis into power in Florence that lasted for the better part of 300 years. It also made John XXIII extremely powerful. So powerful, in fact, that he took a gamble. He convened the Council of Constance ostensibly to reunite the Church, but it was all about consolidating his power. If he could eliminate the other two men claiming to be pope, then he would increase his power exponentially. And he got Gregory XII in Rome, the legitimate pope, to sanction the council."

"Gregory walked into this guy's trap?" Crow said.

Alejandro held up a finger. "But there is a twist. The council ruled that all three papal claimants should abdicate so they could name a new pope and settle the dispute. With John XXIII stripped of his title, his crimes were laid bare for everyone to see."

"What kind of crimes?" Crow asked.

"Murder, rape, sodomy, incest, piracy. Instead of facing his accusers, he disguised himself as a postman and ran like the coward he was, fleeing Constance with Frederick IV, Duke of Austria. The King of the Romans declared the two of them fugitives and they were pursued vigorously. The king's soldiers eventually caught up with them in Germany and Frederick was convinced that he had too much to lose harboring a fugitive. The duke agreed to surrender and to hand over the disgraced John XXIII. John was taken back to Constance where he stood trial. He was imprisoned but was freed in 1419 after a handsome ransom was paid by whom?"

Crow stared at him then said, "The Medici family?"

"Precisely. And that is when they made the pact. They would spend all the money it took, expend all the manpower that was necessary, spill all the blood they had to in order to exact revenge and overthrow the Roman Catholic Church. You see, the Keeper of the Word is not the keeper of the word of God. It is the keeper of the word between the Medici family and Baldassare Cossa. Not only Baldassare Cossa but all who were loyal to his papacy. These two factions intermingled for several decades until they became one, a group with two driving goals. First, to take their place as the rightful custodians of Catholicism and, second, to control all of the world's banks."

"So the Custos Verbi is an alliance between outcast Catholics and the Medici family?"

"Sí, but not just the Medici family bloodline, the Medici family as an organization."

"Like the Mafia."

Alejandro smiled and reached for another piece of cheese. "Now you understand."

"Did they ever take control of the Church?"

"Sí. Pope Leo X, who became pope in 1513, was a Medici, as was Pope Clement VII in 1523. Pope Pius IV was a distant Medici cousin and when he died in 1565 the Medicis lost control of the papacy."

Crow asked, "The last real Medici pope died in 1565? That was just a year before Nostradamus died. Is that the Custos Verbi connection with him?"

Alejandro smiled. "The author in you has a nose for this. When Nostradamus came along, the Medicis could see great power in predicting the future. Catherine de' Medici, the daughter of Lorenzo II of Florence, married King Henry II. Henry was king of France and Catherine became Queen consort. Very powerful woman. She summoned Nostradamus to Paris in 1556 after he predicted her husband would be struck in the eye and suffer a cruel death. She asked him to plot the horoscopes of her seven children. Nostradamus told her that all of her sons would become king during her lifetime. It was a test, of sorts, by the Medicis to see if Nostradamus really was the all-powerful prophet."

"Was he right?"

"He was right but for one son who died before he could become king. The other sons all became king and died on the throne while Catherine was alive."

"Still," Crow said, "that's pretty amazing. Six out of seven? What about the prediction of her husband being hit in the eye and dying?"

Alejandro nodded, "Three years after the prediction, the king was wounded in a jousting match. A splintered lance went through the visor in his helmet. It penetrated his eye. He suffered ten agonizing days before he died. Which only confirmed what the Medicis already believed, that Nostradamus possessed great powers of prophecy. Two years prior to Nostradamus' death, Catherine de' Medici paid a royal visit to his home in Salon. It is believed she made the trip specifically because she had heard about the Unriddled Manuscript and she wanted to verify its existence."

"Did he know she knew about the book?" Crow asked.

The little man shrugged. "Who knows? Probably not. He guarded that book with his life."

"He didn't suspect she was after it?"

"He trusted her. The queen had protected him from the Justices of Paris who were ready to accuse Nostradamus of engaging in magic. She bestowed upon him the title of Physician in Ordinary, which made him a personal physician to the queen and insulated him from prosecution."

"But he didn't trust her enough to show her the book."

"Nostradamus did not fully trust any Medici. As it was, his instincts were not misplaced. Six years after Nostradamus' passing, Catherine de' Medici instigated the infamous St. Bartholomew's Day massacre."

"I remember learning about that," Crow said. "The Catholics of Paris murdered thousands of French Protestants."

"Sí, the Huguenots. As many as 30,000. These were people who had split from the Catholic Church and the Medicis saw them as a threat to their power base."

"So, Catherine wasn't able to get her hands on the Unriddled Manuscript and—"

Alejandro finished, "The Custos Verbi, of which Catherine was a member, sent their agents to seize it on the night of Nostradamus' death. Their pope had died seven months prior. They were desperate to regain power by any means necessary."

"I'm guessing they weren't successful. Getting the book, I mean."

Alejandro shook his head. "But they have been trying to get their hands on it ever since. With each prophecy that comes true, their determination intensifies."

"Whatever happened to the Medici bank?"

Alejandro finished chewing on a piece of cheese then swallowed. "The rival Pazzi family took the papal business from them in 1478. By 1494, the bank had collapsed. But do not cry for the Medicis, señor. They drove their bank over a cliff on purpose."

"And the purpose being?"

"To take their finances underground. The Medici banks kept meticulous records. Too meticulous to continue to hide their financing of the Custos Verbi. The ineptness of the Medicis who controlled the bank in its final years was so laughable as to be unbelievable. No one could be that incompetent if they tried. By the end of the fifteenth century, their attention had shifted from the banking business to the royalty business. Catherine, Queen of France. Maria, Queen of France. Medici women were queens of Spain and England. There was one Medici whose brother-in-law was the Holy Roman Emperor. Who needs a bank when you have that kind of power?"

"They had power," Crow said. "Wasn't that enough?"

"Scattered power. A pope here. Queens, dukes, and archbishops there, but not enough. Once you taste power on the order of the Medicis, señor, there is only one type of power that will satisfy. And that is the power the Custos Verbi seeks to this very day. It is the power of religion and the power of money combined. The power of riches and the power of control over the people. It is like no other power the world has ever seen. My friend, what the Custos Verbi crave is absolute power."

Chapter Thirty-Four

"Bouchard's Paris," the man on the phone said.

"Hello, Romain, this is Sidney. How are you?"

Romain's eyes lit up on the other end. "Fabulous, mademoiselle," he answered in his theatrical French accent. "How have you been?"

"Just fine. Look, Romain, I'm in a bit of a hurry and I need a small favor. I'm trying to track down a client who does business with you. His name is Philippe Babineaux."

"Philippe Babineaux," he repeated. The painted nails of his fingers tapped his waist. "Why does that name ring a bell? Hmmm. Oh, I know. He's not a client. He's an agent. He's here from time to time representing different buyers. The man with the eye patch, no? Ew, flagorneur."

"Yes, he *is* a bit on the smarmy side. Do you know who he represents?"

"He represents several clients, I believe. Most of them less than reputable. Anyone in particular?"

"A guy named Otto. That's all I have."

"Otto, hmmm? It may take me a bit, but I will see what I can do."

"That would be great. I'm going to be in a meeting. Can you text me what you find?"

"Absolutely."

"You have my number?"

"I do."

"Oh, Romain, is there any chance Monsieur Babineaux is a member of the Société des Antiquaires?"

"At the Louvre?"

"Yes."

Romain chuckled. "Not a chance. Monsieur Babineaux is, how we say in French, mal élevé.

"Thanks so much for the information. Please let me know when you have anything on this Otto character."

"I sure will."

"You're a doll."

"Don't I know it," Romain snickered.

The line to Paris was only disconnected for a few seconds when Rosenfeld's phone rang. She placed it back to her ear. "Hello."

"Did it work?" Crow asked as he left the church.

"Like a charm," Rosenfeld said. "I'm on my way to meet him for dinner right now. We're going to 'join forces,' as he put it, and see what we have together."

"Have you called Paris yet?"

"Just got off the phone with them," Rosenfeld said. "Monsieur Babineaux has a less than stellar reputation. He's apparently lying about his credentials. They're trying to track down Otto for me. They'll let me know when they have something. How about you? How'd you make out?"

"A very strange encounter. I'll fill you in tonight," Crow said.

"Great. See you when I'm done."

"Oh, Rosenfeld."

"Yeah?"

"Be careful."

"I'm a big girl, Crow. I know how to take care of myself."

THE MAN THEY called Otto gazed out across the valley from his vantage point inside the greenhouse to the distant blue of the mountains, lost in thought. He caught himself and continued trimming the flowers he tended. It was his therapy. Although he could not possibly nurture all of the flora that rotated among the grounds of the great complex personally, he insisted on being involved despite his lofty position.

A suited man appeared in the doorway. "Your Excellency, I am sorry to disturb you."

"What is it?" Otto asked impatiently.

"A development from the field."

"What kind of development?"

"The little man in Valencia."

Otto pulled the garden gloves from his hands and headed for the main house.

ROSENFELD WAS GONE by the time Crow returned to the hotel suite. He used the time to renew his wedding search. Delacroix had said to concentrate on venues, so he included palaces in the search. He learned that even royal weddings of the past were not traditionally held in palaces. They were held in churches. Most of British royalty were married at Westminster Abbey. Charles and

Diana were an exception, being married at St. Paul's Cathedral. Some British royalty had been wed at the Chapel Royal at St. James' Palace, but the last was the Duke of Gloucester in 1935. Crow checked that venue to make sure no weddings were scheduled for the weekend. He found the tradition of royal church weddings to be the case in country after country.

He checked Almudena Cathedral in Madrid, the site of the wedding of Prince Felipe and Princess Letizia in 2004. Nothing. The Basilica of Our Lady in Trastevere in Rome where Prince Amedeo of Belgium was wed. No wedding this weekend. He checked the Cathedral of St. Michael and St. Gudula in Brussels, the Church of Our Lady in Copenhagen, St. Michael's Cathedral in Belgrade, Basilique de Sainte Marie-Madeleine in Provence-Alpes-Côte d'Azur in France. No royal weddings. No weddings of any kind.

He closed the tablet and stepped out on the balcony to think. The sea air caressed his face with a light breeze. What was left of the day glimmered atop the Mediterranean and storm clouds formed in the distance. Families lazily walked from the beach with their belongings bundled in their arms. Tanned tourists in their expensive clothes strolled along the wide promenade that separated the hotel from the beach beyond.

Crow's phone on his bed dinged and a message popped up on the screen. He stepped back inside and grabbed it up. It was from Rosenfeld.

Still meeting. Come join us.

She gave an address and nothing else. Maybe they had found something. He phoned the valet on the hotel phone to bring his car around.

Rosenfeld's shaking hand set the phone down on the table. A hand reached down to the table with a Cartier watch attached to its wrist, took the phone from the table, and placed it in his outer coat pocket. His other hand clutched the handle of a pistol that was aimed at Rosenfeld's head.

"Good girl," Philippe Babineaux said with a grin. "Good girl."

Chapter Thirty-Five

Night fell on Valencia. Sheet lightning lit the horizon in the distance. Crow didn't particularly care for the neighborhood he was driving into. He removed the sweat on his upper lip with his lower and turned where his phone's GPS instructed him to turn. The industrial part of town was desolate this time of night. From what he could tell, it was desolate any time of the day. Out his window it looked like a place time forgot. The moonlight peeked from behind clouds to shine on rusted pieces of equipment dotting the landscape around buildings that appeared abandoned long ago. There were no street lights. No sign of electrical power at all for that matter. He double-checked the GPS, parked, and stepped out of the car. The gold Jaguar looked out of place. He felt the energy of the impending storm.

He opened the creaky door of the warehouse and entered with trepidation. This was the address Rosenfeld gave him, odd as it was. He had tried to call her. She didn't pick up. Just enough natural light lit his way. Moonbeams sliced through a vent on the far wall. The floor smelled of dust and dirt, the musty smell that came from years of neglect, perhaps even decades.

"Rosenfeld?" he called almost in a whisper. He heard the distant rumble of thunder.

No answer. This just didn't feel right. Why would she ask him out here in the middle of the night then not be at the door to greet him? He lit a light on his cellphone and crept slowly under a balcony that used to house the office of the foreman when this warehouse was operational. Crow imagined the activity that might have gone on. The unloading of freight, the distribution of goods, the loading of trucks. The foreman could oversee it all either from his office or by pacing along the catwalk above him. Broken glass crunched under his feet.

"Sidney," he whispered.

The only light other than his own and the moon's was a pale light that emanated from the far end of the warehouse. He squinted and killed the light on his phone. As he drew closer he could barely make out two figures. One he took to be Babineaux. The other, seated beside him, he couldn't quite see, not at that distance. He figured it must be Rosenfeld. The outside sky lit momentarily and the scene came into clearer focus. The dire situation began to register in his mind. A bare lightbulb covered by a black metal shade hung above the two figures. It cast a light like a streetlamp down on Babineaux who was standing with his hands behind his back. Sitting next to him in a plain wooden chair with hands tied to the arms and duct tape across her mouth was Sidney Rosenfeld.

"It is a pity it had to come to this," Babineaux announced with feigned sorrow, his voice echoing off the barren walls.

"It's my fault, Sidney," Crow said. "I should've known."

"Yes, you should have," Babineaux said. "The Unriddled Manuscript. Where is it?"

Crow sneered. "Is that what this is all about? You're wasting your time, Babineaux. I have no idea where that book is."

Babineaux raised a gun to Rosenfeld's head. "I am not bluffing."

Crow's mood turned grave. "Listen to me. If I knew where the

Unriddled Manuscript was, do you think I'd be here? I'd already be stopping the next prophecy, wherever that is."

"Yes, of course. Unless stopping the prophecy is not really your objective."

"Ah, it's all coming back to me," Crow said. "At breakfast you said the Unriddled Manuscript holds immense power and wealth for whoever possesses it. *You* want to possess it."

Babineaux laughed. "I would not know what to do with the book. I simply represent clients. I make deals, Monsieur Crow. So here is the offer. You either tell me what I need to know or I kill the girl."

"You've got *me*, Babineaux. That's what you were after, isn't it? Keep her out of this."

He laughed again as a flash of lightning highlighted the right side of his face, the side with the good eye that seemed to smolder even after the light subsided. "I could not care less about you. I am after the manuscript."

"Clearly, she doesn't have it, so why don't you just let her go?"

The low roar of thunder accented his angst.

"Because she is more valuable than you. I can get information with her. You? You do not particularly care if you live or die."

Crow stared at him in silence. Rosenfeld's wide eyes jumped from one man to the other.

"You are a defective man, Monsieur Crow."

"Is that so?"

"Your life has been filled with one vagarious relationship after another. Hot and cold. Love and hate. You are a loner because of your persistently unstable self-image. You are reckless. You spend too much money. You take unnecessary risks. You go to extremes. Your life is chronically empty hoping the next book or the next purchase or the next adventure or," he glanced down at Rosenfeld, "the next girl will somehow fulfill you. A perfect recruit for whoever hired you."

Crow looked first at Rosenfeld then back at Babineaux. "You've lost your mind."

"Have I? I had my suspicions before, but once I saw the quatrains you carry, I knew. There was no man in Montreal, just as I suspected."

"Bullshit," Crow said.

"It was all a lie you made up to cover how you really came into the possession of the quatrains."

"He's playing you," Crow said to Rosenfeld.

"You do not know how long I have studied this man called Nostradamus," Babineaux continued. "As you well know, *The Prophecies* was not his only work. He wrote other manuscripts, including *Orus Apollo*. The only known copy, written in Nostradamus' own hand, is at Bibliothèque Nationale in Paris. I have read it myself many times. One of the defining traits of Nostradamus is he wrote almost completely devoid of punctuation. I know his voice as well as I know my own. The quatrains you carry are unmistakably Nostradamus. And they, too, are devoid of punctuation. They are directly from the Unriddled Manuscript and no one would possess them unless they got them from someone with privileged access to the book."

"Don't listen to this maniac," Crow said.

"Who are you working for?"

"I'm not working for anybody."

"You may be a troubled man, monsieur, but you are also a *determined* man. Whomever you work for knew this about you when they hired you. They knew because of your mania that once you got your hooks into something you would never let go. It is what has made you a success as a writer. It is what makes you a success as an agent." Babineaux looked back down at Rosenfeld. "He figured out the clues to Valencia a little too easily, did he not, mademoiselle? Poor Father Simonin unwittingly led him here. And then he conveniently met his demise."

"You're lying!"

Babineaux held Crow's eyes in his. "Am I? You have become the perfect liar. It is part of your psychosis."

"Go to hell, Babineaux."

"Ah, I see I have touched a nerve." He turned again to Rosenfeld. "Fantasy prone personality is what it is called, my dear. I am sure Monsieur Crow's psychiatrist has told him all about it. It is what makes him such a brilliant writer of science fiction, but it is also what has caused him to become completely detached from reality, which made him easily pliable by his employer."

"You have no idea what you're talking about," Crow said.

"Oh, but I do. You see, your whole life is a fantasy. You live in a paracosm, a detailed imaginary world you have created in your mind as a coping mechanism. This paracosm makes your relationships complicated. You see people for whom you deeply care as flawless." He gestured with the gun. "Mademoiselle Rosenfeld, for example. This was the mistake your employers did not anticipate." He lifted her hair with the barrel of his pistol and let it drop. "She *is* quite flawless. You have developed feelings for her, I can tell. Your life may be meaningless to you, but *her* life is extremely important. They say that people like you are selfish, but I disagree. Right now you care more about her than you do for your own life. That is why you are going to tell me where the book is because you do not want to see her brains splattered all over this warehouse. Where did you run off to this afternoon, Monsieur Crow? Hmm?"

"You know damn well where I was."

"You were at the cathedral, were you not? Searching for the Unriddled Manuscript. Did you have to kill anyone today?"

"Sidney, this guy is a lunatic! He's the one who told me about the cathedral. There's not a shred of truth to anything he's saying."

"Negotiations are over," Babineaux said. "It is time to close the deal." He pushed the muzzle up against Rosenfeld's head

"Wait," Crow said.

"The time for waiting is over. My client grows impatient. Now," he steadied his stance and tightened his grip on the pistol, "tell me where the book is."

Marcus Foster inspected Crow's car outside the warehouse, checked Babineaux's Jag, then looked briefly to the darkened skies. The muffled sound of voices drew his attention. He proceeded toward the door with caution, his gun drawn. Thunder rumbled. The door was already open. He slid just inside the doorway and could vaguely make out two people at the other end, maybe a third.

Rosenfeld's eyes cut to the side, wide with panic. She whimpered through her sealed mouth. Babineaux's .380 was pressed to her head, a caliber also known as a 9mm short, used in World War II by German officers in the form of the Walther PPK. Babineaux's choice was a Beretta Pico, the thinnest .380 on the market, a firearm with a relatively short range but one that would make an awful mess at this close proximity.

"Otto is not going to be very happy once you've killed off the only lead you have," Crow bluffed.

Babineaux looked mildly amused. "Very clever, Monsieur Crow. A name you have heard or seen. It means nothing. You *know* nothing."

"Can you be so sure?" Crow asked.

"I can. You see, I am so sure that I am going to count to three and then I am going to pull the trigger and kill your little girlfriend. That is, unless you tell me where I can find the book."

Another bolt of lightning was followed quickly by a clap of thunder. The storm was upon them. Crow's mind fled to where it normally retreated when his reality became too unbearable to face. He was sliding down the embankment and coming to rest on the flat rock by the tranquil sounds of rushing water. Wild imaginings of far-off places danced in his head, and he plucked them like apples and lay them in his basket.

"One."

Crow dragged himself back up the embankment and into the moment. "Look, I have no idea where it is."

"Two."

"Don't do this, Babineaux. It's not going to get you anywhere. I'm telling you, I don't know where the damn book is!"

"Three."

"No!"

The shot that rang out was almost completely silenced by the thunderbolt just outside. Both sounds bounced off the walls of the warehouse. Rosenfeld twisted in her seat with anguish. Crow's scream came from a primal place of horror deep down inside of him, a place he never knew existed. The pain would not have been more fierce had he been shot himself.

Chapter Thirty-Six

Marcus Foster made his quiet exit out the same door he came in and disappeared into the wet darkness. Crow looked at Rosenfeld with sheer panic. A handgun like Babineaux's makes a large hole. It also makes a helluva deafening racket at close range. Without ear protection, one's ears would be ringing for several minutes. Crow's hearing was perfectly clear. Babineaux collapsed backwards like a marionette with its strings severed. What Crow heard was not Babineaux's Beretta. It sounded more like a gun at some distance, but his mind was still trying to process exactly what just happened. Crow looked down. Babineaux had a hole between his good eye and his black patch. Blood wept from the small wound. His good eye was wide open. Crow stood there stunned for a moment, trying to regain his wits, then he whipped around to see where the shot had come from. All this within the span of mere seconds. He heard Rosenfeld's struggles through the fog and pulled the duct tape from her mouth.

"The shot came from back there," she said.

Crow untied her hands then her feet. "Yes, I know."

"I saw a shadow. They're gone."

"Looks like we had a guardian angel. Someone wanted Babineaux dead as bad as he wanted that manuscript. You OK?"

She nodded. "Who shot him?"

"I don't know, but we don't need to stick around to find out."

Crow retrieved Babineaux's cellphone from his coat pocket. He scrolled through the contacts. Dry cleaner, deli, grocer, nothing unusual. He scrolled down to the name 'Otto' and clicked on it.

"Otto's number's blocked."

"What are we going to do?" Rosenfeld asked.

"Well, we sure as hell can't go to the police." He began to wipe the phone with his shirt.

"What are you doing?"

"Getting rid of my prints." He slid the cellphone back into Babineaux's inside coat pocket. "I don't know if anyone heard that shot. If they did, we don't need to be here when they show up."

"We're just going to leave him?"

Crow looked at her with an almost sarcastic smile. "Can't take him with us."

They took a step for the door when Rosenfeld stopped. "My phone."

"Where is it?" Crow asked.

"In his outer coat pocket."

"Damn, girl." Crow reached inside the dead man's coat pocket and retrieved the phone. "We can't afford to be that careless." He handed the phone to Rosenfeld and they hurried to the door.

Crow looked around as they exited the building into the rain, making sure no one else was around. They felt safer once they were out of the elements with the doors locked and the car gliding away from the lifeless body of Phillippe Babineaux lying on the floor of the warehouse.

"You sure you're OK?" Crow asked.

She nodded.

"Son of a bitch!" he said. "That was *way* too close."

"What do we do now?"

Crow looked over at her. She was still trembling. "We're going back to the room and regroup." The rhythmic beat of the windshield wipers couldn't wipe away the awkwardness between them. "It was all lies, you know," Crow finally said.

He didn't have to explain what he was talking about. Rosenfeld nodded.

"I'm serious," he said. "Total nonsense. I mean, think about this. You've heard me talking to my publisher. He's the one who sent me to Montreal. I didn't even want to go. I was just minding my own business when—"

"It's OK," she said.

The silence returned.

She looked up at him. "Did you find anything at the cathedral?"

"Yeah. I found the defender of the rock."

"What is it?" Rosenfeld asked.

"It's not a 'what.' It's a 'who.'"

"A who?"

"Yeah, this little guy who lives underneath the cathedral. His name is Alejandro. He's been sharing information with Simonin and Delacroix and others. They apparently have this little network where they trade information about the First Facers and the Custos Verbi."

"And?"

"And he didn't have a lot to go on. He thinks he's been monitoring two First Facers at a local cafe, but I'm not sure it's anything more than his imagination. He said they used the word 'presages' in the context of war."

"Presages?" Rosenfeld asked. "Like Nostradamus?"

"Yeah. Alejandro is going to text me a transcript of the conversation." Crow felt the frustration of not adequately rebutting what Babineaux had just spouted off about. "I'm a frickin' novelist, for Chrissake. I'm not some secret agent."

"I know."

"Don't let that crazy asshole get inside your head."

"Crow," she turned to him, "I get it. Sounds like he's gotten into yours more than he did mine."

They arrived back at the Hotel Las Arenas and locked themselves in their suite. The trauma of Rosenfeld's abduction began to sink in. She sat cross-legged on her bed and wiped tears from the corners of her eyes. Crow sat down beside her and searched for the right words.

"Look, I'm sorry I got you into all this."

"It's not your fault," she said. "It was my bright idea to cozy up to that monster." She looked up and fought back more tears.

"Hey, come here," Crow said. He held her in his arms. "It was a good plan. Neither of us saw that coming. We just have to be more careful."

"Damn. I had such a vibe about him," she said. "Why didn't I go with it? I just thought I could use my charm and get anything we wanted out of him. Boy, was *I* wrong." She wiped her wet cheek with the back of her hand.

Crow gently moved away. "We're assuming he was working alone here in Valencia," Crow said, "but we *do* know he's working for Otto. If Otto can't locate Babineaux pretty soon, we also have to assume he'll send others." Crow's phone vibrated. He looked down. "It's Alejandro, the little guy from the cathedral."

"What's he say?" Rosenfeld asked.

"He sent a text of the conversation between the two supposed First Facers." Crow scrolled through the text on his phone. "I don't see anything here that's really unusual. Yeah, they say 'presages' and 'war' in the same quote, but that's about it."

"Let me see." Rosenfeld took the phone from Crow.

"They talk about knights and fortresses and the guy's cousin," he said. "They even mention Hitler, but nothing really stands out."

"Hitler?" she asked. "Seems a little odd."

"You're not going to tell me Nostradamus predicted Hitler, are you? Because 'Hister' in the quatrains refers to—"

"The lower Danube River. What do you take me for, some idiot?" Rosenfeld said. "What sticks out to me is this business about monsters presaging war."

"But it's true."

"No, I know that, but there's something familiar about that phrase. I just can't place it. Does Alejandro know who these people are?"

"No," Crow said. "Just two people his associate at the cafe thought were First Facers. You know, it might be absolutely nothing. And if that's the case, we're wasting valuable time."

"OK, well let's review what we're relatively sure of. A wedding. Probably tomorrow. A royal wedding of some sort, if Delacroix was right. The quatrains say people are going to die. Important people, we assume."

"While I was waiting for you earlier I checked all the venues I could think of. Palaces, churches. If there's a royal wedding tomorrow, they're sure keeping it quiet."

She frowned then shook her head.

"What is it?" Crow asked.

"There's something familiar about that conversation," she said. "I just can't put my finger on it."

"Hell, I can't even think straight any longer." Crow rubbed the back of his neck.

"Hey," Rosenfeld said softly. "Simonin and Delacroix have been murdered. Did it occur to you that your little friend at the cathedral might be next?"

"Yeah, I actually did think about that. Seems death follows me. I told him to be very careful. Said he wasn't worried about it. He's no match for whoever killed his friends."

Rosenfeld's phone vibrated.

"Who's that?" Crow asked.

"My friend, Romain, in Paris."

"You say he was none too impressed with Philippe Babineaux?"

"He said he was mal élevé."

"What's that mean?"

"It means ill-bred, crude."

"And we found out the hard way. What's Romain say?"

She looked down at the text. "'No Otto in our files,' he says. 'Might be an alias. We have lots of straw buyers who love their privacy.' Another dead end." She typed in a few words with her thumbs then put her phone on the bedside table and rested her head on a pillow facing away from him. "I don't know what else we can do."

He got up to leave.

"Crow," she said, looking at nothing in particular in the other direction. "What do you fear?"

Crow smiled and sat back down. "Well, I was scared to death Babineaux was going to kill you tonight."

"I appreciate that, but that's not what I mean. I mean what do you fear long term?"

Crow thought about the question for a moment. "Irrelevancy."

"Irrelevancy?"

"Yeah."

"Explain."

Crow rubbed the stubble on his cheek, looked down, and said

softly, "I fear the time that's coming when I no longer matter. I know it happens to everybody. It's different ages for different people. There comes a time when you're no longer living, you're just existing, because you just don't matter anymore."

Rosenfeld let his answer soak in. "Is that what drives you?"

He thought for a second. "No," he said looking up. "It's what chases me."

Rosenfeld was silent.

"What do *you* fear?" Crow asked.

She closed her eyes slowly then opened them as she formulated her answer. "The future," she said. "This trip has taught me one thing, that I don't get out enough," she chuckled through a tear. "I've spent most of my life with history, living in the past. It's so much easier, so much more convenient. Everything's nice and tidy. I know how it's going to end. There are no surprises. I don't like surprises. I like to be in control. Can I tell you something?"

"Sure," he said.

"You've helped me realize that I haven't really been living my life. I've just been reading about it. I haven't been taking chances. I haven't been putting myself out there. I've just been playing it safe. I know this may sound crazy, but I almost died tonight," she turned to face him, "and I've never felt more alive in my life."

Crow smiled and patted her on the arm. "You've been through enough for one day. Get some sleep."

He pulled a blanket up over her and walked back to his room. He couldn't turn his mind off. He took the tablet and poured back over all the information. He searched again and again for wedding listings on the Internet that fit. Nothing. His eyes began to glaze over. He didn't find anything unusual or even remotely important. He gave up for the night and headed for the bath. He disrobed and slipped into the opulent shower. The appointments at the Hotel Las Arenas Balneario were exquisite. Italian marble was everywhere in the bath. The Matouk Milagro Egyptian cotton towels were a perfect complement to the ornate gold fixtures. Crow let the hot water cascade over his tired body. He began to feel the stress wash away. All of the events since Sunday replayed in his head. He closed his eyes and relaxed.

The opening door of the shower startled him but just for a moment. Stepping inside to join him in all her splendid nakedness was Sidney Rosenfeld. He had never seen anything so exquisite. The water beaded as it hit her shoulders. She placed her slender hand on the back of his head and gently kissed him with her voluptuous coral lips. A feeling of elation flooded over him. He wrapped his arms around her waist and kissed her down her neck. Her wet hair matted to her caramel skin. *Babineaux had been right about one thing,* Crow thought. *She is, indeed, absolutely flawless.*

Chapter Thirty-Seven

Crow dropped his bicycle in the cold gravel drive and pulled the collar of his coat up close around his neck. His dad's black pickup was in the drive. He hadn't seen him in weeks. He vaguely remembered the times when 'Daddy's home' meant an excited child jumping into his father's arms and a surprise gift picked up along his travels in exchange for the long bouts of absence. Those times were long gone. The familiar knot gripped his stomach. Everything depended on his father's mood. Crow hiked the backpack higher on his shoulder, hesitated, then pulled open the screen door.

He rubbed his hands together to warm them then stopped at the sight of the half-empty bottle of whisky on the kitchen counter. He braced himself for the storm.

The words that passed between Crow and his mother had been little more than awkward small talk since "the incident." Nothing was ever verbalized about the subject. She acted as though it never happened, but she was always a lousy actor. The unmentionable episode was like a barge that passed between their two ships, large and looming, but it was never the topic of conversation. He couldn't even be sure she knew he knew. Her silence gave him every indication she did.

"Hi, Dad," Crow said from the doorway of the den.

The warm fireplace crackled in the corner. The large man with the unshaven face sat in his easy chair. He jingled the ice in his glass then took a sip and looked straight ahead. His wife sat on the sofa, her legs close together, her hands fidgeting atop her knees.

Crow gave his father ample time for a response to his greeting. Hearing none, he started in the direction of his bedroom.

"Come here, boy," the low voice growled.

Crow stopped then walked slowly in front of his father's chair.

"Your mother tells me you've been skipping school."

Crow cut his mother an injured expression. She looked away. "Not lately," Crow said.

"Not lately," he repeated with a chuckle. He took another gulp. "You're right," he said to his wife, "he *is* a bad liar." He set his drink down and rose from the easy chair. "You listen to me." He took a drunken step backwards but steadied himself with a hand on the back of the chair. "I work my ass off clear across the state. The last thing I need is you screwing off while I'm gone."

"But I—"

"I don't want to hear the excuses. I want to know why the hell you've been cutting classes."

Crow looked down and wondered if the truth was even worth it. "I don't know."

"You don't know."

His mother said, "He goes down to the river to write."

His old man's head swiveled in the direction of his wife then back again to Crow. He laughed, "To write? Write what?"

Now Crow understood. This was a preemptive strike. A way to discredit him in case he had any notion of sharing her indiscretion with his father. "Just stuff. You wouldn't be interested."

"No, I'm interested," the man said. "What kind of *stuff*?"

"Dad, please."

"What kind of stuff!" His bloodshot eyes were on fire.

Crow's mother winced.

"Short stories, mainly."

"Well, let me see," he said, pointing to the backpack.

"Dad, I'd rather not let anyone—"

"I said let me see," he said through clinched teeth.

Crow reluctantly unzipped his backpack. He reached inside and pulled out the notebook and handed it to his father.

"Let's see what we have here," he said, staggering a few steps around the room thumbing through the notebook. "Is this how you spend your time rather than going to school?"

Crow didn't answer. He was afraid any response might enrage him even more. His father turned a few more pages, unable to focus on the writing.

"Could I have that back, please?" Crow took a step toward him and extended a hand.

"Uh, uh, uh," his father teased, pulling the notebook just out of his reach. "Let me explain something to you," he slurred. "You don't go to class, you don't finish high school. You don't finish high school, you can't get a job. You can't get a job and your ass is stuck under my roof. Well, guess what. Your ass ain't gonna be stuck under my roof."

"I plan on going to college," Crow said.

"To college? To do what?"

"I want to be a writer."

The man laughed a cruel laugh. "A writer? Nobody in this town's ever been a writer. You know what the people in this town are? They're hard workers. They work in the mill or the factory or the loading dock or on the farm. They're the backbone of this country. They're what makes this country great. You know what writers are? They're pussies. They're candy-ass elitists who look down their noses at people. People like me. People like your mother."

Crow took another step and reached for the notebook.

"Ah, ah, ah," his father taunted again, pulling the notebook higher in the air. "You know what I'm gonna do? I'm gonna do you a big favor. I'm gonna give you some advice. Because that's what great fathers do. The last thing you need to be doing is wasting your time with all this pie-in-the-sky shit. Crows are proud people. Crows are working people. This notebook's been nothing but trouble, so I have the solution."

"Don't take my notebook." Crow saw the rage in his father's eyes. He tried to reason with him. "Please don't take my notebook." His eyes filled with tears.

"Ah, you gonna cry now?"

"I promise I won't cut classes anymore," Crow said desperately. "Just let me have my notebook back."

"Oh, I know you won't cut class no more," his father said. "You won't have a reason to." With a flick of his wrist, the notebook spun a couple of revolutions in the air before landing in the middle of the fire. He smiled a delighted smile.

"No!" Crow snapped and lunged at the man with the fury of a wild animal, screaming with all the vitriol and hurt in his soul. His father backhanded him across the face so hard it knocked him off his feet. Before his head even hit the floor, he was out cold. The flames from the notebook rose higher in the fireplace until they consumed it all. There was nothing left of months of work except for smoldering ashes. His mother dropped to her knees beside her unconscious son and shook him.

"Benson," the voice said. "Benson," this time louder.

Crow awoke with a start. His breathing was labored. "What? What day is it?"

"It's Saturday," Sidney said, leaning over him in the bed on one elbow. "I think I may have something."

"What?"

"It just hit me. I know why that First Facers' conversation sounded so familiar."

"Why?"

"One of the men in that cafe Alejandro's friend taped said, 'The apparition of monsters presages the outbreak of war.'"

"Yeah?"

"The full quote is, 'According to Nostradamus the apparition of monsters presages the outbreak of war.' You know who said that?"

"Who?" Crow asked.

"Salvador Dalí."

"Dalí?"

"Yes. Read me the transcript of that conversation between the two First Facers." She opened up Crow's tablet.

Crow grabbed his phone from the bedside table and read from the text, "'Did you finish Don Quixote?'"

Rosenfeld searched for Don Quixote. "Yep. Several, in fact."

"Several what?"

"Several paintings. Dalí painted 'Don Quixote' in 1935 and 'Don Quixote and the Windmills' in 1945. Then he did a series of Don Quixote paintings in 1956 and '57. Go ahead with the next line."

A big smile lit up Crow's face. "'I did finish it. Excellent read,'" Crow continued. "'He was the fallen angel.'"

"Hold a second. Fallen angel." She typed in the search box. "Yep, there it is. 'The Fallen Angel' painted in 1951. Go ahead."

"'Yes, he was. Honey is sweeter than blood.'"

"Hold up. 'Honey is Sweeter than Blood,'" she said as she searched. "Three. In 1926, '27, and '41."

"'Is that so?'" Crow continued reading. "'Yes, my cousin Montserrat told me that.'"

"See, this is the one I really should've caught," she said. "It's what sounded so familiar to me." She typed again. "'My Cousin Montserrat' he started in 1919, finished in 1920."

"'He heard it from a couple near the fortress,'" Crow continued.

"'Couple Near the Fortress.' 1918."

"'Near the fortress? Yes, there is a knight at the tower.'"

"'Knight at the tower,'" Rosenfeld repeated. "1932."

"'A real knight? No, do not be silly. Not a real knight. I think he was called the Knight of Death. Sort of the enigma of Hitler.'"

"Let's see. Several knights of death. 1933, '34, two that year, and 1937. 'The Enigma of Hitler' was 1939."

"And the rest is about that quote from Dalí. OK, let's think." He walked around the room like a caged animal. "If Salvador Dalí is the code this guy was passing along…" He rubbed his chin as he thought. "Look up where Dalí was from?"

"I already know. Figueres, Spain."

"Where did he die?"

"Figueres."

Crow digested the information.

"Oh," she added, "the Dalí Theater and Museum is in Figueres, too."

"How far is that from here?"

Sidney typed. "Just under five hours."

"How many churches in Figueres?"

"Let's see." She typed again. "At least three." She turned the tablet for Crow to see.

"Get your stuff," he said. "I'm gonna hit the bathroom, then we need to head out." He turned as he entered the doorway, "Oh, see if there's any mention of a wedding on the news."

She reached for the remote and turned the television on. The news anchor was reporting the day's news while she crammed her few belongings into her shoulder bag.

"The prime minister insisted he has the situation well in hand," the anchor reported in Spanish. "He has asked for a full report from his minister of the treasury by the end of the month. Here locally, a gruesome murder to report this morning at one of Valencia's most famous landmarks." Sidney stopped. She could hear the running water in the bathroom and Crow brushing his teeth. "A caretaker at the historic Valencia Cathedral was found bludgeoned to death in a living area underneath the sanctuary where he resided." A picture of a small man dressed in a monk's robe appeared on the screen. "Alejandro de la Aiza had worked at Valencia Cathedral for almost 20 years. Police believe Aiza was murdered sometime yesterday afternoon. They have no suspects or motive at this time. Azia was 43 years old."

Sidney clicked the TV off and cut her eyes toward the bathroom. Keeping her eyes glued on the door, she tip-toed over to the chair where Crow had laid his clothes.

Crow splashed some water on his face and wiped it with a hand towel. He emerged from the bath dabbing his face then stopped. "What are you doing?"

"I'm packing my phone," she said, unplugging the charger from the bedside table lamp and stuffing it in her purse. "What are you? A cop?" She slid past him into the bath and stuffed her toiletries into her bag.

"Anything on the news?" he asked.

"No. Nothing. Let's go.

CROW AND SIDNEY hurried through the lobby of the Hotel Las Arenas. Crow had ordered their car be brought around as quickly as was humanly possible.

"Señor!"

Crow heard the voice calling from behind him. He turned to see the desk clerk beckoning him over. He and Sidney backtracked and approached the counter.

"Señor," the clerk said. "You dined with Señor Babineaux yesterday, did you not?"

Crow wiped his suddenly sweaty palms on his pants and swallowed. "That's right."

"I need to ask you something, señor."

Crow tried not to look at Sidney. "Fine. What is it?"

"Señor Babineaux is not in his room."

He let that statement of fact hang in the air.

"We're kind of in a hurry. What does that have to do with me?" Crow asked.

"Yes, of course. I'm sorry, Señor Crow. A gentleman is desperately trying to get in touch with him. Do you know where Señor Babineaux is?"

"No," Crow said defensively and turned to leave.

"But we may see him again," Sidney said.

Crow looked at her with disbelief.

"At least, I hope we will. We'll be glad to pass the message along to him if we do," she added.

"I am afraid he did not leave a name or number."

Sidney approached the counter and pulled a sheet of note paper from the registry. "Here." She handed the clerk the paper. "If he calls back, have him call me."

He looked at the paper. “Very good, Señorita Rosenfeld. Gracias.”

“What the hell was that?” Crow said through clenched teeth as they walked toward the door. “Are you out of your mind?”

“Not at all,” Sidney whispered. “That’s obviously Otto trying to track him down, or someone working for Otto. We need every angle we can get. Maybe he’ll get curious enough to give us a ring.”

“Crow,” someone called from behind them.

Crow assumed the desk clerk was calling him again. He turned around. A chill ran down his spine. Marcus Foster had just passed through the revolving door beyond the front desk from outside on the sea side of the hotel and was moving deliberately in their direction.

“Shit,” Crow muttered.

He grabbed Sidney by the arm.

“Wait!” Foster shouted.

They pushed through the revolving door of the hotel entrance just as their car was pulling up. Crow shoved the valet aside and jumped into the driver’s seat. Even before Sidney had slammed the door on the passenger side, Crow was burning rubber on the black brick pavers. Marcus Foster sprinted to a stop where the car had just been and watched helplessly as its image faded in the distance.

Chapter Thirty-Eight

Sidney looked at the map on the tablet. "Turn right at this next intersection."

"Foster's a hit man," Crow stated matter-of-factly.

"How do you know?" she asked.

"Simple deduction. We know Foster was at Delacroix's place, so we can assume he killed him. We saw him in Avignon and Father Simonin turns up dead. Foster's been on our ass since Washington. You think it was just a coincidence that we ran into him at the National Archives? That he was there to meet Kyle right after we did? That he was sitting on that train next to you? And that every damn body I meet with ends up dead?"

Sidney pulled her phone to her ear.

"Who you calling?" Crow said.

"Churches in Figueres."

No answer. She dialed another. The same.

"Nothing," she said after calling the third church on the list. "All closed on Saturday."

"Dammit," Crow said. He looked at his watch. "I wonder how late he stays up." He looked down at his phone. "Crap. My phone's running on fumes. You got power?"

"Plenty," Sidney said. "How late does *who* stay up?"

"Tom. I may be good for one more favor. Here." He handed his phone to her. "Put this number in your phone in case I run out of juice during the call. And dial it on my phone, would you? Run it through the bluetooth on the car."

She called Tom's number, hit the button on the car's display, and a groggy Thomas Browning answered on the other end.

"What is it, Benson?"

"Thomas. I really need you right now."

"Some Bond villain got you tied to a nuclear device?"

"Come on, Tom."

"I'm going back to sleep."

"Don't hang up! I need one more favor and, I promise you, if you can deliver on this one, you'll get that book you've been asking for."

Tom Browning was silent for a moment. "OK, but not too big of a favor. It's the middle of the night over here."

"I need for you to call in some markers with your connections at the papers. See if there's any chatter about a royal wedding in Figueres, Spain, today. We're heading there on a hunch and I want to be sure."

Tom was sitting on the edge of his bed with a pen in his hand. "How do you spell it?"

"F-I-G-U-E-R-E-S."

Tom wrote it down.

"I need to know which church. Look, Tom, this is probably some wedding they've been trying to keep off the radar."

"OK, give me a few minutes, all right? I'll call some newsrooms. Some of these connections are a tad rusty. I'll see what I can do."

"Thanks, Tom. Sidney's going to text you. Call me back at her number. My phone's dying. Oh, and we're looking for a wedding that starts at or around noon."

"Around noon," Browning wrote. "Gotcha. And I'm getting a book out of this. You promise?"

"I promise." Crow hung up the phone and checked the mirrors like he had been doing about every 30 seconds since they left the hotel. "You really think Otto will call?"

"If the desk clerk gives him my number, he'll call," she said.

"You're serious?"

She finished texting Tom Browning and looked up. "Yeah, I'm serious. Why wouldn't he? He can't find his boy. He wants some answers."

They merged onto the Autopista del Mediterraneo, the Mediterranean Expressway, Spain's equivalent to the Pacific Coast Highway.

"If he calls, I wouldn't know what to say to the son-of-a-bitch," Crow said. "He just tried to kill us."

"Us?" she said. "I'll talk to him if you won't."

"You're a big talker now. Last night? Not so much."

"I know," Sidney said. "I was the one with my mouth duck-taped and the gun to my head, remember? We're running out of time, and if we have to talk to this guy to get some information, then that's what we have to do."

"A guy who just tried to kill us?"

"You keep saying that. What's this 'us' business? He tried to kill *me*. Look, he wants the Unriddled Manuscript. We have to play that angle. We want to know when the next prophecy is. We may be able to make a deal."

"But we don't know where the manuscript is," Crow said.

"He doesn't know that."

THE TWO MUSCULAR bodyguards at the office entrance parted and allowed the nervous man to pass. He carried urgent information. Otto sat at his ornate desk with a phone to his ear. The mountains that rose in the distance behind him were stark and snow-capped, so high that clouds rested between their peaks. They seemed to blur out of focus beyond the two suited men who stood as sentries outside just beyond the bulletproof windows. The man waited. Otto jotted down a number on a piece of paper.

"And she said if I wanted to know where Phillippe Babineaux was I should phone her?" Otto said.

"That is correct," the desk clerk at Hotel Arenas said.

"Very well." Otto hung up the phone.

"Your Excellency," the nervous man said.

"What is it?"

"We have decoded the location of the wedding," the man announced.

"Where?"

"Figueres, Spain."

"And you are sure?"

"We are. Everything fits. But…"

"But what?" Otto asked angrily.

The man handed him a piece of paper across the desk. "This is the guest list."

Otto ripped the paper from his hand and threw his reading glasses atop his nose. He read with an irritated countenance until he came across the name. His irritation turned to shock.

"He is definitely on the list?"

"Yes, Your Excellency. Still no word from Herr Babineaux?"

"He has failed in his mission." Otto rested his elbows on the desk and propped his chin on his interlocked fingers. After pondering the situation for a moment he said, "The American is en route to Figueres as we speak. If he is successful in stopping the prophecy, then everyone at that wedding lives."

"That is correct," the man said.

He nodded his head slowly a few times. "Then he must never make it to Figueres."

"But Your Excellency, the prophecy."

"The prophecies come and the prophecies go," Otto said. "We have an opportunity we have not been afforded in 500 years. We must take advantage of it."

"Yes, Your Excellency. How are we going to stop the American?"

"Leave that to me." Otto dialed a number and leaned back in his seat. "This is Otto. Listen very carefully. The mission has changed."

CROW AND ROSENFELD drove in silence. Crow tried to assimilate all the information he had accumulated over the past few days. What would he say to Otto if he called? He knew he was in way over his head. Otto was working on a much larger scale than anything Crow had ever seen. Otto crushed people like bugs under his feet. Crow had to figure out how to avoid his shoe. He looked over at Rosenfeld then back straight ahead. "I know I've said it before, but I really am sorry for getting you involved in all this. It's more than you bargained for, I'm sure."

Sidney didn't respond. Her phone rang. Crow tensed up.

"It's Tom," she said.

"Already? That was fast." He pressed the bluetooth button on the display. "Tom?"

"Benson, I think I may have something for you. My sources tell me there actually is a royal wedding, of sorts, taking place today somewhere in Spain." Crow and Sidney exchanged smiles. "They know the when, what, and who. They just don't know where."

"Who's getting married?" Crow asked.

"Reginald Wentworth is marrying Lady Grace Rich. Wentworth is the Earl of Stockland. It's a small, private ceremony. They've tried to keep a lid on this, but one of the tabloids got wind of it."

"And they don't know where?" Crow asked.

"Well, that's the thing. Nobody knows."

"But you're sure it's Spain."

"That's what my source tells me."

"How do they know?"

"Well, Wentworth's office moved an expensive painting from the UK into Spain. It flew from London to Barcelona, but they don't know where it went to from there."

"What kind of painting?"

"A Salvador Dalí," Tom Browning said.

Crow let out an excited laugh.

"Does that help?" Tom asked.

"Boy, does it. That's fantastic work," Crow said.

"Apparently the earl and Lady Grace met on vacation last year in Salou on the Mediterranean while the earl was vacationing at a villa owned by the King of Spain. They're both big Dalí fans, he and Lady Grace. The earl is great friends with the king who will be one of a handful in attendance. They tell me the earl's cousin, the prince, will be there. Daniel Mercer, the Chancellor of the Exchequer—an old college buddy of his—will also be there."

"You say they know when?" Crow asked.

"Yes. At noon local time. Wherever local is."

"Damn, Tom," Crow slapped the steering wheel, "you hit the frickin' jackpot! I owe you big time."

"Yeah, you owe me a boo—"

Crow hung up the phone.

"That's it!" he said. "Count on good stock. The Earl of Stockland. An earl is also known as a count in many countries. And Lady Grace Rich. Rich in grace, from the quatrains. He said the wedding's at noon. The quatrain said 'When the clock strikes twelve.' This has to be it. You said there were three churches in Figueres?"

"Yes," Rosenfeld said.

"Run a cross-reference. See if there's a Dalí connection."

Rosenfeld typed into the tablet. A smile formed across her face. Crow looked down at her in anticipation.

"St. Peter's Church in Figueres," she said. "It's where Salvador Dalí was baptized. It's also right next door to the Dalí Museum."

"Damn."

"Hmm," she said.

"What is it?"

"Check this out." She turned the tablet so Crow could see it.

He took a quick look at an interior shot of the church. "What am I looking for?"

"Nostradamus' quatrain says, 'Within the well vestals inundated.' We've been looking for a drinking well, but what if it's a place?"

"A place?"

"Yeah," she said. "The well deck of a boat is the lower deck. The well of the Senate is the lower section of the Senate where the senators speak. Look at this photo."

Crow looked back down at it.

"It steps down into the sanctuary," she pointed out on the photograph. "It's the lowest area in the church. 'Within the well vestals inundated.' Remember what Delacroix said? 'Inundated' means 'overwhelmed.' Within this area of the church the bride and bridesmaids will be overwhelmed."

"Wait a minute," Crow said. "Wait just a damn minute."

"What?"

"Delacroix said Nostradamus' predictions have to do with events of monumental importance, but the importance may not be readily apparent. It's not the bride and bridesmaids."

"The King of Spain will be in that church," Sidney said.

"It's not him."

"The prince?"

"Much more important."

"Who?"

"Daniel Mercer, the Chancellor of the Exchequer of the United Kingdom."

"What's so important about some government bureaucrat from the UK?"

"Mercer's a lot more than just a bureaucrat," Crow said. "The Chancellor of the Exchequer also represents the UK in the World Bank. Daniel Mercer is a very vocal and active member of the board of governors for the World Bank. There's a power struggle going on inside that organization. I saw a news story on that in Montreal. Mercer dies and their annual autumn meeting will be dramatically different. I remember Alejandro told me the goal of the Custos Verbi was 'to take their place as the rightful custodians of Catholicism and, second, to control all of the world's banks.'" He looked over at Sidney then back at the road. "'In place of the bride the daughters slaughtered,' the quatrain says. They're just collateral damage. The event of monumental importance is not the wedding. It's the death of a man whose absence at the autumn meeting will alter control over the largest bank in the world."

"If that's true, then what do we do?"

"What do you mean?" Crow asked.

"Is Mercer good or is he bad?"

Sidney's phone rang again. They both looked at the caller ID. 'Unknown.'

"Shit," Crow said. "It's him."

Chapter Thirty-Nine

The only indication that anything was at all unusual inside St. Peter's Church in the small city of Figueres, Spain, was the sprinkling of plainclothes agents who tried not to be noticed on the plaza that separated the church from the Salvador Dalí Theater and Museum by mere feet. One agent was stationed by the church door, two in staggered positions down the street in front of the church, and three roamed amongst the tourists on the small plaza named for Salvador and his promiscuous bride of nearly fifty years. Gala was ten years his senior and the subject of many of his nude paintings. Fans of the great artist lined up on the plaza to buy tickets to the theater and museum designed by Dalí himself. They had no inkling of what was about to take place just a few feet from where they stood. The officers from both the Spanish Royal Guard and the Royalty and Specialist Protection, or RaSP, of the United Kingdom wanted to keep it that way. The former protected His Majesty The King. The RaSP was charged with protecting not just the Earl of Stockland and his family, but the Chancellor of the Exchequer. Security would increase, as would the size of the security force, the closer they edged toward noon. No need to call attention until it was absolutely necessary.

Inside the church, the woman with the auburn hair scurried about to make sure every flower was meticulously arranged and every candle was perfectly straight. Beatrix Cambridge had seen to it that the ordinarily dark interior had been brightened befitting a royal wedding. Greenery and white roses adorned the altar. The first rows of the Cordavan-stained wooden pews on either side were draped in white linen indicating they were reserved for the family. A floral arbor of more white roses and greenery arched over the aisle creating a stunning entrance for the bride.

Just inside the right side of the front doors of the church sat an easel. Resting atop the easel was the wedding present from Reginald Wentworth to Lady Grace, the special gift that Ms. Cambridge had made sure passed through customs without a hitch. A rare original Dalí oil painting purchased from an auction house in London and shipped for the auspicious occasion. The odd shapes and angles and oversized eyes looked as out of place inside the magnificent church as did Dalí's museum just outside of it.

Beatrix Cambridge checked her watch. The bride and her wedding party would arrive just before the ceremony and both bride and groom would be carried away in a horse-drawn carriage specially loaned for the occasion by His Majesty the King of Spain. Arrangements had been made to transport the family and guests from their hotel to the church. Still so much to do, so many details. She grabbed her notepad and began to go down her checklist.

"DO YOU WANT *me* to talk to him?" Sidney asked.

"No." Crow took a breath. "No, I'll talk to him."

Crow hit the speaker phone again. "Yes."

"Mr. Crow," the baritone voice with the German accent said.

"You would be Otto, I presume."

"You would presume correctly," Otto said.

"You keep trying to reach Babineaux. He won't be calling you back."

"How unfortunate. And what do you want?"

"What do *I* want? What I want, you asshole, is to know why you tried to have us killed."

"I can assure you it was not personal."

"Well, that's a relief," Crow said sarcastically. "It wasn't personal? Are you kidding me? We're going to the police."

Otto laughed a laugh that chilled Crow to the bone. "You are not going to involve the police. If you were, you would have called them instead of leaving your number for me."

"You want the Unriddled Manuscript," Crow said.

"That is my only interest. I am willing to pay handsomely for it."

"Purely from a historical perspective, I'm sure."

"My motivations are none of your affair," Otto said.

"I'm not concerned about the money, so it seems we find ourselves at an impasse."

"I would like to speak to Ms. Rosenfeld."

"She's right here."

She was hesitant to answer. "What do you want?"

"I want to offer my sincere apologies. It was never my intention to hurt you. It is just that Mr. Crow was not being cooperative and things, well, things escalated."

"What do you mean I wasn't being cooperative?" Crow said.

"You were supposed to turn over the Unriddled Manuscript."

"You seem rather confident that I have it."

"If you do not have it, you certainly know where it is."

"What makes you so sure?"

"You got close enough to write down the quatrains," Otto said.

"I didn't write down the quatrains. They were given to me—"

"By some unfortunate man in Montreal. Yes, I heard. You said he was murdered."

"That's right."

"The Montreal police have no such record of a murder."

"Maybe they think it was suicide or an accidental drowning," Crow said.

"Stop with the theatrics, Mr. Crow. They have no record of any death of a man as you described because no such man ever existed. Ms. Rosenfeld, he is lying to us both. He is a sociopath. A very convincing one, I might add, but a sociopath nonetheless."

Crow could see concern in Sidney's eyes. "Sidney, don't listen to him. He's trying to manipulate you."

"*I* am trying to manipulate her?" Otto roared. "I have not made up two murder stories that turned out to be false. I have not lured her halfway around the world on some wild goose chase."

"No, all you did was try to have her killed."

"We were never going to harm her. We were just trying to get the information from you and you were more than willing to let her die. How does she know that *you* are not going to kill her?"

"Me? You're wasting your time, Otto. I have no reason to kill her."

"Perhaps not yet. Maybe you are waiting until you get your hands on the Unriddled Manuscript and you have authenticated it. That *is* why you brought her along, now is it not?"

"Don't listen to him, Sidney. He's trying to get inside your head."

"He knows where the Unriddled Manuscript is, Ms. Rosenfeld. He was willing to let you die to keep it a secret. Once you have authenticated it, he will kill you, too. Just like the others."

"That's a lie and you know it!"

The line went dead.

Crow looked over at Sidney. "You know he was just trying to turn you against me, right?"

Sidney looked out the window. "I don't know *what* I know."

"But, you're not buying Otto's crap, are you?"

"No," she said unconvincingly. She curled up next to the door with her eyes to the sky.

Crow drove on down the Mediterranean Expressway. The view was breathtaking at times with glimpses of sanding beaches one moment, then postcard villages, then rocky shorelines meeting the Mediterranean Sea, but Crow hardly noticed. He let his thoughts overtake him. Who the hell was this Otto character? Was Marcus Foster working for him, too? Maybe Otto's muscle man? Or was he working for someone else, someone competing with Otto?

Crow retraced every step of the journey, every clue, every everything. Despite the sidetracks and miscues, he was still on pace to rendezvous with the prophecy. That much added up. The upcoming wedding in Figueres fit perfectly with Nostradamus' quatrains. Apparently Otto didn't know that much or he would never have taken the time to call. Then why did he? He gained nothing from the conversation. Just a sense of satisfaction for having put doubt in Sidney's mind. A petty gain for someone who was evidently so calculating.

Crow gazed over at Sidney then back at the road. Babineaux may have been a snake, but he was rather astute in his assessment. His words played over and over in Crow's mind. *Your life has been filled with one vagarious relationship after another. Hot and cold. Love and hate. You are a loner because of your persistently unstable self-image. You are reckless. You spend too much. You take unnecessary risks. You go to extremes. Your life is chronically empty hoping the next book or the next purchase or the next adventure or the next girl will somehow fulfill you.*

An hour or more passed and Crow was lost in his thoughts while Sidney dreamed in the seat beside him. Or so he thought. She was acutely aware of Crow's every move. Her mind raced through her options and settled on a course of action. He reached over and nudged her.

"Better wake up." Crow pointed at kilometer marker 47. "Won't be too long before our exit comes up."

Sidney stirred and stretched and pretended to awaken from her nap. At kilometer marker 46.5 was an exit for a small rest area. Not the conventional kind like Crow was accustomed to in the States. It looked more like a pitstop at the track. Crow wished he could take it, but there was no time for rest. He had to get to Figueres and stop that wedding. How? Would anyone listen to him? They would have to. He would have to make them listen.

Just as they were passing the lane that merged back onto the highway from the rest area, out of nowhere, their car was rammed from the side. The loud crash of the impact made them both nearly jump out of their skin. Sidney let out an involuntary scream. Crow caught a glimpse as they spun around. A large black sedan with tinted windows. It struck them on the rear quarter panel of the passenger side and almost turned their car completely around. They slid sideways for a moment. Crow fought the wheel but managed to right the car. The sedan did a 360 then fell quickly in behind them. An arm appeared from the passenger side. Crow hit the gas. A handgun was attached to the arm. A shot was fired. The bullet caught metal on the passenger side. Sidney ducked.

"That's what he was doing!" Crow shouted. "Otto was stalling us on the phone with that lame story about me being a sociopath until his goons could zero in on our cell signal. Damn! I'm such an idiot!"

The gunman fired another shot. This one struck the back driver's side door. Crow zigzagged to evade him. He straddled two right lanes of the three available to him. The black sedan tried to pull alongside in the far left lane. Crow brushed him back with a swerve.

"Switch places with me," Crow insisted.

"Why?" Sidney said.

"Because I'm going to have to operate that Mossberg in the backseat."

"I can handle it," Sidney insisted.

"You ever shot a shotgun before?"

"I told you. I grew up with four older brothers."

Crow shrugged. "OK. Have at it."

Sidney unbuckled and adjusted herself. Her knees were facing toward the rear. Her head was down. The gunman pulled his arm back inside the car. She sprang like a leopard between the two front seats into the back. She laid down on her back and reached beneath the blanket on the floor for the Mossberg 500 All Purpose. She felt for the canvas duffel, reached inside, and grabbed a handful of shells. She inserted five of them into the underside of the shotgun.

"Roll down the back driver's side window!" she shouted.

Crow complied. She pumped the action once.

"How we lookin'?" she yelled over the sound of the wind.

"Just a second." Crow maneuvered the vehicle so the sedan was off to the left and rear of their car. "Get set. Go!"

Sidney popped up facing the rear like a jack-in-the-box. She steadied the gun on her right shoulder and fired. The blast hit the hood on the driver's side. The sedan swerved. The shot made nothing more than a scattered scratch. Crow looked in the rearview mirror.

"Damn. Aim for the windshield this time."

Sidney pumped again. The spent shell smoked on the floor of the car. She fired again. The target was too far away for a concentrated blast. The pellets spread about two feet wide and did no damage to the darkened windshield.

"It's armored!" Crow shouted. "You're wasting your time with that thing."

"Not necessarily!" she yelled back. "I have an idea." She looked over her shoulder at the road in front of them. "OK, when we hit this straightaway, on my count, shift to the right lane and slam on brakes. Got it?"

"Slam on brakes? Why?"

"Just do it!"

Crow shrugged, "Got it."

She pivoted to a normal sitting position on the driver's side rear seat. She locked herself down with the seatbelt. Crow gave her a smile in the rearview mirror.

"You ready?" she asked.

Crow nodded.

Sidney gritted her teeth and tightened her grip on the gun. "Get ready. Go!"

Crow changed lanes and hit the brakes. The black sedan came speeding alongside. Sidney took one shot at point-blank range as it passed them on the left. The blast tore a huge hole in the front passenger-side tire of the car. It lunged to the right in front of them then erratically cut back to the left. Crow hit the gas just as it lurched right again. It barely missed the rear of their car. The black sedan crashed into the concrete retaining wall and came to a smoking stop.

They drove on for a short distance, their hearts still racing. Crow looked in his rearview mirror.

"You wanna climb back up here?" he asked.

Sidney stared out the window. "No, I'm good for now."

Crow frowned and rolled the rear window shut. He looked in the mirror then back at the road again. The dotting of little houses became less frequent. They gave way to wide, brown fields of corn that had been plowed over after harvesting. The severed stalks baked in the summer sun. Crow looked back again to see how she was doing. That's when he saw it in his rearview mirror. The Mossberg. It was pointed directly at the back of his head.

Chapter Forty

The private jet touched down at Girona-Costa Brava Airport. Before the wheels came to a complete stop the door was opening and the steps unfolding on the tarmac. Emerging from the interior into the hot Spanish sun was Marcus Foster. A car waited just a few yards away. He slid his sunglasses on his face and hurried down the steps to meet it. He settled calmly into the back for the 38-minute drive to Figueres.

Sidney Rosenfeld looked out the window as they crossed the Fluvià River, the Mossberg still trained on the back of Crow's head. "Stop the car," she insisted.

Crow looked in the mirror with disbelief. "What the hell's going on?"

"Stop the damn car!"

Crow pulled the rental over to the side of the highway. Sidney hopped out of the back, the shotgun still pointed at Crow. "Pop the trunk."

Crow did as he was commanded. "What are you doing?" He

unbuckled his seatbelt and jumped out of the car. Sidney opened the trunk. The shotgun was draped with her jacket and held close to her body but still trained in Crow's direction. He took a couple of steps toward her.

"Stop right there," she said, holding the shotgun up. "I don't want to kill you, but I will if I have to."

"Will you please tell me what this is all about?"

Sidney retrieved her bag from the trunk and placed it over her shoulder. "That little man at the cathedral."

"Alejandro?"

"He's dead."

Crow put both hands to his head. "Oh, my God!" He turned a full circle in the road then looked back at her. "How do you know?"

"It was on the news this morning. In the hotel. I saw it while you were in the bathroom."

"Why didn't you tell me?"

"He was killed yesterday afternoon, Benson. About the time you visited him."

"Wait a minute, you think I killed him? I swear to you—"

"Dr. Grumbling is killed along with his housekeeper and you miraculously escape when you were the only one they'd have a reason to kill. Nobody seems to know this guy in Montreal is dead but you? Was he your first victim? Delacroix ends up dead."

"We both saw him alive after midnight."

"I don't know where you went after I went to bed."

"Oh, come on, Sidney. I—"

"Father Simonin, the same thing. You leave me in the room while you go visit him and then, amazingly, he turns up dead, too?"

"Sidney, please. Otto's filled your head with—"

"Shut up!" She fired once into the air. Frightened birds in the fields on either side of the road took frantic flight. "You used me."

"Used you? For what?"

"For information. For my expertise. You never would've gotten this far without me."

"Do you realize how crazy that sounds? It doesn't make any sense."

"I didn't trust you from the moment you came into my office. I thought you were a con man, somebody who wanted a sensational story for a new book. I should've trusted my instincts."

Crow took a step toward her. She raised the shotgun. "I swear to God I'll blow your head off."

Crow stopped. "I was willing to take a bullet for you in Salon."

"You weren't going to take a bullet for me! You're one of them!" She wiped a tear from her cheek with the back of her hand. "You pulled me into this. You arranged it so I'd have no choice. My life was in danger, you said. The First Facers were after *me*, you said. I had to run. I had to run with *you*. Babineaux and Otto were right. You were after the Unriddled Manuscript and once you found it, you were going to murder me, just like the others. It all makes sense now. Those men at the Chapel of the Virgin in Salon weren't First Facers like you tried to make me believe. They were Custos Verbi. That would explain why they were in a church. First Facers wouldn't be in a church. The creepy robes, the secret ritual. They were trying to conjure up the same power as Nostradamus. When that man chasing us in Salon saw you, he realized you were one of them. That's why he let us go."

"So I'm CV now? This is bullshit, Sidney, and you know it!" Crow shouted. "Think about it. It was your lead that brought us here to Figueres, not mine."

"Exactly! You used me! Damn, I can't believe I was so gullible.

You couldn't quite put it all together and I was stupid enough to connect the dots for you. What's your mission, Benson? To stop the prophecy, like you've been saying? Then to get me to help you find the manuscript?"

"No, Sidney." His tone turned somber and defeated. "None of this is true."

She started walking backwards down the highway. "Death follows you, Benson. That's what you said, isn't it? Huh? Everyone you meet turns up dead. Isn't that what you said? You also said you don't believe in coincidence." Her laugh was sarcastic. "Yeah, well, neither do I."

She turned and walked away. Crow called after her, but the image of Sidney Rosenfeld with her bag hanging from one shoulder and a shotgun wrapped in her jacket slung across her arms grew smaller and smaller.

He looked at his watch. *Eleven-forty-three.* "Shit." He reluctantly jumped back in the car and entered St. Peter's Church into the car's GPS.

"Proceed to the highlighted route," the automated voice said. Crow hit the accelerator and threw gravel behind him. His tires connected with the pavement. "In one kilometer take exit 4."

The kilometer came quickly. Crow paid the toll and screamed to the first roundabout. He fishtailed the turn then floored the gas pedal. He took the first exit, barely missing a delivery truck that couldn't make up its mind where in the roundabout to go. In another kilometer he took another roundabout, cursed it, and took the third exit. After just another 350 meters he was in another roundabout laying on the horn behind a red trash truck.

"Come on, get out of the way!" he shouted.

The car with the darkened windows stopped at the intersection of

Carrer Sant Pere and Pujada Església. Marcus Foster pulled back the slide of his Beretta and chambered a round then placed the weapon back in its holster under his armpit. He checked the area before exiting the vehicle one block from the Church of St. Peter.

A crowd began to gather up and down the tiny street. The increased presence of security personnel around the church and the magnificent horse-drawn carriage let people know that whoever was about to emerge from that church must be someone important. Foster stealthily weaved among the excited tourists. He surveilled the area from behind his dark glasses. He moved further up the street, closer to the church, noting the plainclothes Spanish Royal Guard surrounding the carriage.

After a ridiculous number of roundabouts, Crow found himself squealing around the corner onto Carrer Canigó in Figueres, Spain, past the iconic eggs atop the Salvador Dalí Theater and Museum. "Your destination is ahead on the right." A block later, he was screeching to a halt and jumping out of his car. The clock on the car's dash read 11:54. He bounded up the eight stone steps two at a time onto the Plaça Gala i Salvador Dalí and rounded the corner. Just abreast of a statue of Jean-Louis Ernest Meissonier, Crow was abruptly clotheslined and taken to the ground. Two security officers secured his arms behind his back. Only then did he see that the church was ringed with security detail, a mixture of the British and Spanish variety. The wedding party inside the church, along with the Spanish king, a British prince, and other assorted family and friends from Spain and England, waited for Lady Grace to walk down the aisle.

"You have to get everyone out of there!" Crow yelled from his prone position.

Tourists crowded around to see what the commotion was all

about. Several members of both countries' security teams pulled their firearms and forced their way through the mob. Crow was fiercely pulled to his feet.

"Everyone out!" Crow shouted. "You have to get everyone out! We only have a few minutes!"

A bulky officer held Crow's arms behind his back. Two men rushed forward from the line of security officers that had surrounded him. One was Spanish, the other British, the heads of their respective teams.

"What the bloody hell is going on?" the RaSP officer named Travis asked.

"The wedding party is in danger," Crow said almost out of breath. "Daniel Mercer. He's the target."

"The target of what?" Officer Lorenzo of the Spanish Royal Guard asked.

"An assassination."

"By whom?" Officer Travis asked.

"I'm not sure," Crow admitted. "I just know of a plot. I don't know who's behind it."

"Who are you with?" Travis asked. "Let me see some identification."

"I'm not law enforcement," Crow said. "I've been given secret inside information that something terrible is happening at noon."

"Where'd you get this information?"

"It's complicated. Look, it's not just Mercer. Lady Grace's daughters, everybody in there. All those people inside are going to die unless you get them out of there."

Officer Lorenzo said, "And we are just supposed to take your word for it?"

"We don't have time to argue about this! It happens at noon."

The officers looked at their watches. Three minutes 'til.

The British officer came closer. "And you want us to disrupt this wedding on some wild theory that you have when you don't even know what's going to happen or who's going to do it?"

Crow was adamant. "I knew Lady Grace's daughters were in there, didn't I?"

"Well, everybody knows she has daughters."

"How many people know she's marrying the Earl of Stockland at noon? I'd never even heard of her or him until this morning. Those people are going to die in about three minutes."

"Two minutes until noon," an officer reminded his boss.

His boss fretted.

"Do you want to take a chance that I'm just some kook?" Crow said.

The two heads of security stared at him for a moment.

"OK, dammit," Crow said, using the only option he had left to play. "There's a bomb in there!"

Lorenzo spoke first. "I am getting my people out." He turned to a subordinate. "Detain this man."

Two armed members of the Spanish Royal Guard took Crow from the two British officers, grabbing him by either arm. Another patted him down for weapons. Travis started to feel the pressure. He motioned for his men to follow him.

"If this is some kind of a joke…" he warned as he and his security detail dashed across the plaza toward the church.

Officer Lorenzo was already inside. He calmly walked up to the bishop who was set to begin the ceremony and whispered in his ear.

"Ladies and gentlemen," the bishop announced to the crowd, "there has been a minor emergency. If you would be so kind as to exit the sanctuary in an orderly fashion, we would appreciate your cooperation."

Murmurs swept across the wedding party. The attendants descended the altar. Distinguished guests politely exited the building. Security detail outside created a perimeter. The bridesmaids and groomsmen all stood on the plaza between the Dalí Museum and the Church of St. Peter. Security officers, guns drawn, stood shoulder-to-shoulder with their backs to their charges. Onlookers gawked from behind the human barricade. The British security team escorted the bride-to-be and her daughters into a waiting armored van that arrived up narrow St. Peter Street. The Chancellor of the Exchequer's team surrounded him and whisked him into a separate van along with the king and his wife. The earl refused the safety of an armored vehicle and paced nervously on the cobblestones demanding answers from his security detail.

Officer Travis watched the second hand of his watch count down. Five, four, three, two, one. Noon.

Chapter Forty-One

Officer Travis looked at his watch. It was twelve noon. Nothing. He marched red-faced up to Crow who was detained by both arms between two Spanish security officers.

"You damn well better have an explanation."

Crow felt the blood rush to his face. "All I know is the daughters of Lady Grace and everyone else but her were supposed to be killed at noon."

"You said Mercer was the target."

"He is. They are. They all are." But he wasn't so sure anymore.

"Everyone except Lady Grace?" Travis asked.

"Yes."

"And how do you know this?"

"It's complicated."

Travis drew a furious breath. "I'm all ears."

Had Crow let his imagination get away from him? After all, everything he had come to believe was based on speculation. Speculation that was largely his own. Was Thomas Browning right? Had he simply found an intriguing story and let his inventiveness fill in the blanks? "Maybe I got here just in time," he offered feebly. "Maybe we thwarted the plot and the danger is over."

The woman with the auburn hair pinned to the back of her

head stormed across the plaza, her steps as wide as the skirt of her suit would allow. By then, Officer Lorenzo had joined his British counterpart seeking questions of his own.

"I demand an explanation," she said to Lorenzo.

Officer Lorenzo looked quizzically at the head of RaSP.

"This is the earl's social secretary," Travis explained. He then turned his attention to her. "Ms. Cambridge, we have a man who claims inside information on a plot against the wedding party. We acted on the side of caution. We're sending bomb dogs back in just to make sure."

"But you had the dogs search for bombs before."

"Yes, and we found nothing, but we have a new threat."

"What kind of threat?" she asked.

He pointed over his shoulder to Benson Crow who was being held by the two security officers. "This man claims to have knowledge of a bomb. As soon as they've cleared the area we will resume."

"That's absurd," she snapped. "No one could possibly have known we were here. That is," she turned to Lorenzo, "unless someone on your end was less than discreet. We went to great lengths to—"

Officer Lorenzo held up a finger and looked at the ground, listening intently to his ear piece. He turned to the two agents holding Crow. "Arrest him."

Travis tilted his head awaiting an answer.

"We just found spent shotgun shells all over the floor of his car," Lorenzo explained to his British colleague, "along with a bag of live ammo."

One of the officers holding Crow started to put cuffs on him. Crow squirmed and looked frantically around. That's when his eyes met Marcus Foster's standing there like any other curious tourist in the crowd.

“That’s him!” Crow cried out, breaking a hand free and pointing. “That’s the killer!” His protest was ignored. He had exhausted his last ounce of credibility.

Both Spanish officers were trying to subdue him when the noise caused them to stop in mid-motion. It started as a low rumble like a train was coming or a jet was taking off in the distance, but the rumble quickly turned to a deafening roar. The ground began to rock. The rectangular red pavers looked like the rising and falling of small swells in the sea. Members of the wedding party screamed and people watching scrambled in panic, thrown to the ground as if God had tossed the earth like shaking the dust from a dirty rug. The terror of the earthquake washed over the crowd. Rotating metal racks at a little shop across from the church on tiny St. Peter Street rolled and tipped and finally tumbled to the floor sending postcards scattering out onto the street. The horse attached to the carriage on loan from the king reared violently sending its handler to the bricks, desperately trying to hold on to the reins.

The security team was not immune. They clung to the fence of the monument to Catalan philosopher Francesc Pujols that stood between the church and the Dalí Museum as if they were on a roller coaster. Glass shelves inside the Surrealist Bookstore next door crashed to the floor and books landed in jumbled piles. A statue of a figure wearing a diver’s helmet on the front of the Dalí Museum lurched clumsily forward. Beatrix Cambridge and everyone else around her, including Benson Crow, were thrown to the ground. She cried out, but the tremor of the earthquake muted her cry and all other sounds. Alarms from nearby buildings tripped. Security vehicles on the plaza banged against one another, their occupants looking wide-eyed out the windows in terror. It seemed an eternity of horror. Then, as quickly as there was chaos, there was calm.

The wedding party groaned and cried and hugged one another. The security detail ran to their charges to make sure they were unharmed. Shaken up, some minor injuries, but there were no casualties. Crow was all but forgotten. Bewildered, he staggered over to the church. The Spanish security chief, satisfied that his people were safe, took off after him. Crow opened the doors of the sanctuary. Just inside the foyer the Dalí painting brought from London lay face-up atop the collapsed easel that had held it. Crow looked up at the magnificent ribbed arches of the Gothic structure. Great chunks of stone had slammed to the floor, one smashing the altar completely. Pieces of it lay strewn in several sections. More large stones had crashed down on many of the pews and left them in splinters. Crow tried to absorb the devastation until he felt a hand on his shoulder.

"Come," Officer Lorenzo said. "We must leave at once. It is not safe."

He escorted Crow back out onto the plaza. By then fire truck and ambulance sirens blared. Frantic voices buzzed in the distance. Crow surveyed the area. Some sections of pavers were warped or split. The bookstore and several shops looked as though they'd been looted. The odd figures that stood atop the Dalí Museum stood fast barely noticing anything was amiss except for the leaning diver. Crow looked about frantically for Marcus Foster. No sign of him.

Security officers once again closed in around Crow. The King of Spain emerged from the front door of the church and walked over to the officers and Crow, half-dazed having just seen the devastation inside for himself.

"Is this the man who warned you?" he asked of Officer Lorenzo.

"Yes, Your Majesty."

He held out his hand to Crow. "I want to thank you for saving us. Had you not come along," he looked back over his shoulder at the church, "we would all have surely perished."

Crow nodded in appreciation.

"What about your people?" Lorenzo asked Officer Travis who was just joining them.

"All accounted for and safe," he answered.

All eyes were again on Benson Crow.

"I have to ask you," the king said, "how did you know?"

Everyone waited with equal curiosity. He didn't know how to answer. He was as astonished as anyone.

"I, uh, I'm not sure, Your Majesty. I just knew."

"We found shotgun shells in his vehicle," Lorenzo said.

"Did you find a weapon?" the king asked.

"No, Your Majesty."

"Then I see no reason to treat this man like a criminal. He just saved our lives." He turned back to Crow. "What is your name?"

"Benson Crow."

"Benson Crow? The author?"

"Yes, Your Majesty."

"How could someone possibly know there would be an earthquake on this day at this exact time in this exact place?"

Crow smiled sheepishly and shrugged.

The king mused for a moment. "Señor Crow," he smiled, "you must be some kind of modern-day Nostradamus."

Chapter Forty-Two

"The latest headlines from BBC News, I'm Catherine Brown. More details on that earthquake measuring 6.8 on the Richter scale that hit the Catalonia region of Spain two days ago near the border with France. The epicenter was near Girona, Spain, three miles outside the town on Figueres. There are still no reports of casualties although dozens were injured. Most of the injuries are not life-threatening. Authorities are now reporting damage to the Church of Saint Peter in Figueres where a British royal wedding was taking place between Reginald Wentworth, the Earl of Stockland, and Lady Grace Rich. It was a private affair with friends and relatives, including the earl's close friend, the King of Spain. Also in attendance were the earl's college roommate, Daniel Mercer, the Chancellor of the Exchequer, and the earl's third cousin, Prince Oliver. Miraculously, the noon wedding was postponed due to a security alert and the entire wedding party was outside the church when the earthquake hit. Pieces of the massive ceiling crashed to the floor. According to authorities, had the wedding party been inside the church all would certainly have been killed. Figueres is the birthplace of Salvador Dalí and both the earl and Lady Grace are huge fans of the artist. The earl presented his bride-to-be with a rare Dalí painting that was on display in the church. It was unharmed in the quake. The wedding went on as planned on the plaza that separates the ancient church from the Dalí Theater and Museum, much to the delight of the lucky tourists who were allowed to view the ceremony. The earl joked that he hoped this didn't mean the marriage was off to a rocky start. This is the second marriage for both. The newly-minted Earl and Countess of Stockland departed for their honeymoon at an undisclosed location. Here in the UK, the Prime Minister says the Middle East conference—"

Crow pulled the earbuds from his ears and draped them over the arm of his first-class seat. The flight attendant asked him if he'd like another drink. He nodded and gazed out the window recalling all that had transpired. The experience was as surreal as a Dalí painting. Barely a week prior, he had never even heard of the First Face of Janus or the Custos Verbi. Now, it was all he could think about when he wasn't thinking about Sidney. And he did that until it ached.

He had tried her cell number again before leaving Spain. Disconnected. And why not? She thought he was a murderous lunatic. Would she believe him now? Now that the prophecy had been thwarted? The first Nostradamus prophecy ever to be short-circuited and he had done it. *They* had done it. Together. He smiled to himself. A powerful clandestine organization like the Custos Verbi had tried for nearly 500 years and failed, and he, an author at a low point in his career, had managed to pull off what everyone told him was impossible. He remembered how so many had urged him to give up, to turn back, to forget about ever defeating the mighty forces of the First Face of Janus. He persevered. He always had. He fed on it. He trudged forward in relentless pursuit and now had the satisfaction of knowing he had saved countless lives. Would the First Face of Janus now turn on him? Somehow he didn't really care. He was exhausted. Tired of running. Tired of deception. The only thing that genuinely concerned him was Sidney Rosenfeld.

Guilt gnawed at his belly that couldn't be suppressed by a stiff drink of bourbon. Or three. She had looked so devastated when she thought he was behind the murders. The ugly story she had concocted in her mind. Could she ever trust him again after believing so deeply that he was capable of such unspeakable horror? Could she ever look at him the same? The same as she did that night in Valencia?

Crow deplaned at Logan International and headed for the taxi stand. He gave the cabbie the address for Rothschild's and stared out the window at the Boston skyline. What would he say to her when he saw her? *If* she would see him. Would she laugh at her wild imagination that turned out to be untrue? He certainly held no grudge. Her reaction was understandable under the circumstances. The pressures of being hunted, not knowing who to trust, coming so close to death only to be pulled from its grip at the last moment. Exhaustion, passion, anger, they all played a part. And if she would simply blush at her silly outburst and put the matter behind them, could they take up where they left off? What if the excitement of the chase was what attracted her to him? Relationships born of adventure often die of boredom. Like finally reaching the end of a good book, as interesting and intriguing as it was the first time around, the last thing one wants to do is read it again. That had been his pattern. Maybe it was his defense mechanism. When the titillation was gone, so was he. There was no way of knowing why. He didn't even understand it himself. How could he let anyone else close enough to try? But he was willing to let Sidney try. If she still wanted to. If she *ever* wanted to.

He dialed her cell number one more time just to make sure now that he was back in the States. Same thing. He heard three annoying tones and a message that the number was no longer in service. What was she going to do when he showed up at her doorstep? Kick him out? Call the police? Would she even emerge from behind the key-carded security to face him, or would she leave him hopelessly longing for another chance to hold her? Hold her as he had in Valencia.

As soon as the cab rounded the corner, he knew something wasn't right. The stone etching of Rothschild's was gone from the facade of the building. Odd. He checked the address. This was it, but it looked different, far more than just the missing lettering.

He paid the cabbie and walked to the front door. Locked. On a Monday? Strange. He cupped his hands to block the sun and put his nose directly against the glass peering inside. There was nothing there. No pilasters. No tapestries hanging on the walls. No walls at all. No marble floor. No security entrance leading to the rear. No receptionist. No receptionist's desk. No colleagues' offices with cluttered tables.

No busy conference room. Nothing but an empty shell all the way to the back of the building.

"It's bizarre, isn't it?"

In the second it took Crow to process the voice, to match it to a face, terror and panic seized him. He paused momentarily then whipped around to see the face he knew belonged to that voice. His mind raced through the possibilities of how he had tracked him there, then it occurred to Crow that he didn't need to track him at all. He merely needed to wait. He knew Crow would eventually come looking for her. He must be quite satisfied with himself, with his powers of deduction.

Until that moment, Crow had all but put him out of his mind, but there he was. Forgetting him had caused his guard to drop. A deadly mistake. He allowed the hunter the opportunity he had patiently waited for: for the hunted to walk willingly into the trap. And this was that moment. Standing just a few feet in front of him was the thing of nightmares. Crow's eyes met the steely gaze of Marcus Foster.

Chapter Forty-Three

The very sight of him terrified Crow. His heart was pounding. He gave a fleeting thought to running but cut his eyes in either direction only to see two bulky suited men with sunglasses standing on either side of him casually looking out at the traffic. It would be futile. They had him penned in.

Marcus Foster reached in his coat pocket. Crow thought he was producing a gun, or worse, a knife. He'd never considered the choice. A quick headshot now seemed infinitely preferable to being stabbed in the gut and left to bleed to death on the streets of Boston. But there was a third option. Instead, Foster pulled out a bifold wallet, opened it up, and handed it to him.

"Officer Marcus Morello," the man said with almost a smile in his voice. "CIA."

Crow took the wallet and examined the identification. He'd seen enough official IDs in his research to spot a phony. This was the genuine article.

"If I can buy you a cup of coffee, I'll explain everything," Morello said.

They sat at a small metal table outside. Morello knew he must have a thousand questions, but he didn't even know where to begin.

"Not to sound too cliché," Crow said, "but how about at the beginning?"

"Well, we were tipped off by the Canadian Security Intelligence Service. They'd been watching the homeless man in Montreal as a suspected First Facer. Their man in Montreal saw him make contact with you in the bathroom, so they picked him up."

"That was Canadian Intelligence?"

"Yeah. They found nothing on him. After a couple of hours of questioning, they had to let him go."

"Well, then who killed him?"

"I'm getting to that," Morello said. "Apparently, he knew they were closing in on him. That's why he chose the moment he did to give you the book, knowing they would grab him and you would see it. It was all part of the plan. As to who killed him? The short answer is nobody."

"What do you mean 'nobody?' I saw them fish him out of the river. On the news."

"That was all staged for your benefit. You were meant to see what they had fabricated as a news story."

"What? You're not serious."

"Yeah, they're pretty thorough."

"They?"

"The First Face of Janus. That phony news story was shot weeks ago. We know that because one of their front companies applied for a permit to shoot a movie scene. We heard your description of it on the phone to your publisher and it matched up with the location they used. They simply fed it to your TV in your hotel room."

"This is crazy," Crow said.

"Yeah, well buckle up. It gets crazier. Then, of course, seeing the report of the man murdered on TV only enticed you more, which led you where they wanted you. Here to Boston and Sidney Rosenfeld."

"But I googled Rothschild's. That's how I found Sidney."

"That's how she found you. They controlled everything you saw on that search engine. Your only logical path was to Rothschild's and Dr. Sidney Rosenfeld, or whatever her name really is."

Crow's heart sank. "Wait a minute, what are you saying?"

Morello gave him a sympathetic look.

"She's a First Facer," Crow said sadly.

"I'm afraid so."

Crow remembered Sidney's words when they first met. *You know, it's dangerous to jump to conclusions. Things aren't always as they appear.* That explained her phone being disconnected.

Officer Morello waited for Crow to absorb the blow. "I'm sorry."

"So, she set me up to witness Dr. Grumbling's murder?"

"There is no Dr. Grumbling."

"What do you mean? I met him. I talked to him. I watched him die."

"That was all staged for your benefit as well. I'm telling you, these people are thorough. Like a major movie production company, only a lot faster. They used an old abandoned house. Brought in their own stuff. Props, costumes, the whole works. Set everything up. Staged their actors. The only thing missing was a director yelling 'action.' Rosenfeld sends you to Grumbling or whatever his name really is. Grumbling gets you all lathered up about the First Facers. You're just curious enough to bite. Then you call Rosenfeld to tell her about Grumbling and that's when I get involved. After Canadian Intelligence found nothing on the old man in Montreal, they figured he'd passed the book along to you. They used the convention center's surveillance cameras to identify you. They wanted to detain you in Montreal, but we asked them not to."

"Why?"

"Because the First Facers wanted you to have the book. We

wanted to see how this thing played out. We got a warrant to tap your cellphone. Unfortunately, that didn't come through until after you left Montreal, but once you called to warn Rosenfeld after the drone attacked Grumbling, we had you on the radar. We dispatched a man in Boston to Rosenfeld's office, but she gave him the slip. Another of our guys put an electronic tag on her car and tailed her to the train station. She headed for the rendezvous with you in Washington and I hopped aboard the train on her stop in New York."

"So you're serious. The whole Grumbling murder was staged?"

"All of it. Grumbling. The housekeeper. The drone. All of it."

"No wonder Tom said the police didn't find anything."

"Yeah, our team investigated the scene with the local sheriff's department. There was nothing left behind. Like the Grinch who stole Christmas. Everything they brought in was taken with them, down to the last detail. They even swept the footprints in the place and replaced the dust like nobody'd set foot in there for years. Scrubbed the tire tracks. Everything. Quite professional."

"And Jean-Claude Delacroix? Faked, too?"

"No, I'm afraid Monsieur Delacroix is very much dead. We heard you set up the meeting with Kyle O'Hara at the National Archives. I approached O'Hara posing as an artifacts dealer with a fake Lincoln signature just so we could plant a bug inside his office. We heard him recommend Delacroix. Naturally, I couldn't book the same flight to Paris. That would be too obvious. I caught the next plane, which was several hours later. The museum was closed when I arrived. I went back the next morning to interview Delacroix about your meeting. By the time I got there, it was too late. Tortured. Throat slit from ear to ear. Not a pleasant sight."

"Who did it?" Crow asked.

"The Custos Verbi."

"Rather unnecessarily gruesome, isn't it?"

"It's meant as a message to the rest of the First Facers. They don't often use it. Only when they feel it's necessary to break up a ring."

"Delacroix was part of a First Facers ring?"

"Well, that's the thing. We didn't have any reason to believe that, but he was helping you, and the CV's reaction told us they knew you were part of the plot to fulfill the prophecy. When Philippe Babineaux entered the scene, we realized they thought you were a First Facer agent."

"And what did you think my part in this whole thing was?"

"Honestly?" Morello said. "We weren't sure at first, but once we saw they staged the Grumbling murder in Virginia, it became clear you were just being used. *How* you were being used was the question."

"I'm assuming Babineaux had Delacroix killed," Crow said.

"Actually, we think a man who goes by the name of Otto made that call."

"Otto," Crow said under his breath.

"You're familiar with him?"

"Talked to him on my way to Figueres. His people tried to kill me before I could get there. He's Custos Verbi?"

Morello nodded. "Oh, yeah. Big league CV. Otto's not his real name, of course. Takes his name from Otto the Great. He was an emperor of the Holy Roman Empire. That Otto fashioned himself as the successor of Charlemagne. Our Otto has been running operations for some time. We have no idea where this guy's operating from or who he really is. Otto's people got your location at the farmhouse after torturing Delacroix. Their plan was to eliminate you. Didn't work out that way."

"They were going to kill me just because I had come into contact with the First Facer ring?"

"Well, because they knew you were either a First Facer yourself or being used by them to fulfill the prophecy. Either way, you're a marked man. You have to be eliminated. That's standard operating procedure. If you're Custos Verbi and you find a First Facer, you kill him. And vice versa."

"But Babineaux was helping me," Crow said. "I wouldn't have ended up at Valencia Cathedral were it not for him."

"OK, that's the interesting part. Apparently Otto had dispatched someone to take care of Father Simonin, then you showed up. At that point their plan changed. My guess is they were going to kill you at the farmhouse and just take the quatrains. Your meeting with Simonin probably indicated to them you were in deeper than just someone being used. They hoped you might lead them to the Unriddled Manuscript."

"Hold on a second. Are you suggesting Simonin was a First Facer?"

"Yes."

"But he was a Catholic priest."

"You still don't understand the gravity of this organization, do you?"

Crow said nothing.

"They've had half a millennium to perfect this. Generations and generations have been born into this organization." Morello shifted and crossed his legs. "You ever heard stories where the Soviets plucked kids out of orphanages to be groomed so they could grow up and infiltrate American society?"

"Yeah," Crow said.

"Rank amateurs compared to these people. There are First Facers inside practically every segment of society on earth. Hiding in plain sight. After you survived the drone attack at the farmhouse, Babineaux was tasked with getting the quatrains from you. Babineaux apparently convinced Otto that you had knowledge of where the Unriddled Manuscript was. They were anxious for you to lead them to it before the next prophecy so they could stop not only that one but any future prophecies."

"And I just volunteered the quatrains to Babineaux."

"And once he saw them he was convinced they were from the Unriddled Manuscript and even more hopeful that you just might lead them to it. But the urgency of the prophecy was closing in on them."

"I was trying to stop the prophecy."

"And you convinced Babineaux of that," Morello said. "They were using you just like the First Facers were using you. You don't understand how much they want to get their hands on that book, but their prime objective is to stop the prophecies. If you were going to stop it for them, all the better."

"If the Custos Verbi is more secular than religious, why worry about the prophecies?"

"Who told you they weren't religious?"

"The little guy at Valencia Cathedral."

"Oh, I see," Morello said, taking a sip from his cup. "Not surprising. Catholics who know about the Custos Verbi, which are few, will deny them, but the CV very much see themselves as Catholics. In fact, they believe they're the *true* Catholics. The Medici family has always been extremely religious. It's an internal power struggle. They feel they're the rightful heirs of the Catholic legacy. Sure, they're brutal and they're rich, but their wealth is a means to an end. It's all about controlling the Church. They want the power that comes with Nostradamus' prophecies. Time was when the lines between the CV and the Church were blurred. Early on, they managed to get a few of their popes elected. The Church has changed over the centuries. Now they forbid membership in secret societies, especially the CV. As far as we know, the Custos Verbi has not been able to penetrate the Vatican since Pope Pius IV in 1565. It's much like these radical Muslim groups. Most peaceful Muslims will tell you ISIS isn't really Muslim, but they are most definitely Muslim. They're just not mainstream Muslim. It's like a parallel society within the Church with a life of its own. You're familiar with the antipopes of Avignon."

"I am now," Crow said.

"Well, it's like that. The Custos Verbi is probably the most powerful religious group in the world that nobody's ever heard of."

"And Babineaux? He didn't strike me as an observant Catholic."

"Babineaux was a hired hand. He was just what he appeared to be: an antiquities expert who specialized in Nostradamus. Otto hired him for his expertise in Nostradamus and the Unriddled Manuscript. They needed somebody who could positively determine that the quatrains you were carrying were from the Unriddled Manuscript. They assumed that if you had access to the Unriddled Manuscript, then you knew where it was. After Babineaux determined you had gotten the quatrains from the Unriddled Manuscript, he tried to pump Rosenfeld for information. When he got nowhere, he resorted to more desperate measures."

"And our guardian angel at the warehouse?" Crow asked. "You?"

Morello gave a slight chuckle. "I'd love to tell you that my suit jacket hides my wings, but it wasn't me."

"Who then?"

"A First Facer would be my guess, protecting one of their assets. I arrived late to that party, just in time to hear the shot. Scared the crap out of me, too. Right above where I was standing. Didn't see anybody come or go except you two."

"You were watching me the entire time?"

"Most of the time," Morello admitted. "Whenever you decided to turn your phone back on. That's how we tracked you."

"Answer me this," Crow said. "If they were content to let me go to Figueres and stop the prophecy, why did Otto send his goons to try and kill me before I got there?"

"Interesting question. This is just speculation, but we're assuming when they figured out where the wedding was, they also figured out who was going to be there."

"Let me guess. It had something to do with Daniel Mercer."

"Very good," Morello said. "Why do you think that is?"

"Because Nostradamus only made predictions of major consequence, and Lady Grace and her daughters aren't a major consequence. No offense to them. Not even the earl or the prince or the King of Spain."

"True. So, what's so important about Mercer?" Morello asked.

"He's a major player in the World Bank, although I'm not real clear on *why* he's so important."

"Well, let me tell you. The Custos Verbi have their man in position to take over as president of the World Bank. This is a fulfillment of a goal dating back to the Medici family to control the world's banks. Daniel Mercer was the only person standing in their way. They were convinced, as you were, that the prophecy was a wedding where everyone but the bride was murdered. Once they realized Mercer was on that wedding list, they had to let him die. In order for him to die, they had to stop you."

"But they didn't, thank God. I stopped the prophecy and everyone lived."

Morello drank his coffee. "Did you?"

"Did I what?"

"Stop the prophecy."

"Of course I did. What are you talking about?"

Morello smiled. "You stopped the prophecy only if you were working from the right quatrain."

Chapter Forty-Four

"What do you mean the *right* quatrain? We had the right quatrain," Crow said.

"Read to me the verses the man in Montreal gave you," Officer Morello said.

"By now, I know it by heart. 'In the century of four / His age is seventy-one / His first face sees / When the clock strikes twelve / Add the note of C twice / And take away the score / Count on good stock / Rich in grace.'"

"You were working under the assumption that it was Century 4, Quatrain 71, as were we, but if you add the note of C twice what do you get?"

"That's the part we could never figure out."

"Well, we couldn't either. We only did after the fact by knowing what event to search for in the quatrains. When we looked for an earthquake instead of a wedding, we found it. Logically, when it says 'add the note of C twice' you would think it was something musical, but what is a C-note?"

Crow sighed and leaned back in his seat. "A one-hundred dollar bill."

"And twice?"

He was exasperated with himself for missing it. "Two hundred."

"You add two hundred you get—"

"Century 6 instead of Century 4," Crow said.

"Take away the score. How much is a score?" Morello asked. "And it's not a musical score."

Crow was stumped again. "Well, it depends on the sport."

"They're not talking about a sport. They're talking about—"

"Twenty years! Damn! Why didn't I see that?"

"That gives you Century 6, Quatrain 51."

"Which says?"

Morello pulled out a piece of paper. "Which says, 'People assembled to see a new spectacle / Princes and Kings amongst many bystanders / Pillars walls to fall: but as by a miracle / The King saved and thirty of the ones present.'"

"The King of Spain and the British prince were there," Crow said.

"The prophecy says the king and thirty of the ones present. Thirty-one total. If you count the bishop and the wedding party, how many do you think were there?"

"Thirty-one," Crow said with an ironic smile in his voice.

"And you were their miracle. You didn't stop the prophecy," Morello said with a smile. "You fulfilled it."

Crow was in shock. He looked off into the distance contemplating the whole elaborate scheme. "I was a patsy," he said softly, remembering Grumbling's words about Oswald.

"Yep," Morello said.

"But, wait a minute," Crow said. "I'm confused. I found the wedding site without the help of the First Facers."

"Or so you thought," Morello said. "You got the clue from Alejandro, the little guy from the cathedral in Valencia."

"Which actually came from the First Facers," Crow remembered.

"Right. And who deciphered it for you?"

His puzzled look turned to dejection. "Sidney," Crow said with disappointment in his voice. "She saw the news story on TV that Alejandro had been killed and she knew he hadn't sent me that message."

"Right. She knew if he didn't send it, the First Facers had to have sent it," Morello said. "She didn't tell you because if you'd seen that news story yourself, you'd put two and two together, figure out he was dead before he sent you the text, and discount the whole thing. So she had to go ahead with the Dalí revelation and—"

"Put the last piece of cheese in the trap," Crow finished. "Damn, I'm so frickin' gullible. They played me."

"Don't feel bad. You sure aren't the first. And you won't be the last."

"But she bolted just before we got to the church. Held me at gunpoint. She thought I'd killed all those people, including Alejandro. She accused me of being Custos Verbi."

Morello laughed. "She put you on the defensive. She made you *think* she thought you were behind the murders so you wouldn't think of anything else. She had to have an exit strategy. She couldn't show up at the church with you. First Facers aren't allowed to meddle directly in the prophecies."

"So she stomps off knowing I would continue on to the church and do exactly what they'd set me up to do."

Morello shrugged his shoulders, smiled, and swallowed the last of his coffee.

"Then she disconnects her phone," Crow continued, "they bug out of the office here—"

"And never leave a trace," Morello said.

"And Babineaux had convinced Otto that the quatrains I was carrying came from the Unriddled Manuscript."

"And they didn't," Morello said.

"How do you know?"

"C-note? That term didn't come about until the 1920s, long after Nostradamus was dead. Had Babineaux been smart enough to figure that out, who knows what would've happened?"

"But you said Father Simonin was a First Facer. I told him I was going to *stop* the prophecy and he still tried to help me. Why would he do that if they're all about fulfilling the prophecy?"

"You say he tried to help you. Tried to help you do what?" Morello raised an eyebrow.

"Tried to help me find Alejandro who got me the clue that took me to Figueres and..." his voice trailed off.

"Now you're gettin' it."

"OK, what about Alejandro?" Crow asked.

"What about him?"

"I suppose he was part of the scheme?"

"Unfortunately for him, he was just a good little Catholic with too much time on his hands and an unhealthy interest in conspiracy theories," Morello said. "Delacroix and Simonin were playing him. Easy to do with Simonin being a priest. They planted the First Facers in his buddy's cafe, fed him the clues, and he fed them to you."

"And the First Facers eliminated him to erase their tracks," Crow said.

"Not the First Facers. The Custos Verbi. Remember, they unraveled the First Facer ring. Little Alejandro was an unwitting link in that chain. Babineaux was the one who pointed you to Valencia Cathedral, remember? The CV killed Alejandro before he could send you the text, so the First Facers picked up the ball and ran with it. They're very good at improvising."

Crow was dejected. "I got him killed."

"You didn't get anybody killed. They were going to kill him

anyway. They thought he was part of Delacroix's ring. They knew whatever he was trying to tell you would only lead them deeper inside the society. They were trying to follow the roach back to the nest. That's what they do. Both sides are masters of manipulation. The Custos Verbi uses people to try and stop the prophecies. The First Facers use people any way they can to make these prophecies come true. I know. We've been tracking the First Facers for a long time."

"How long?"

"Well, since the CIA was the OSS during World War II. That's when the agency first got wind of the First Face of Janus. Orchestrating a world war? I mean, come on. Who would believe such a thing? But it's true. Our intelligence indicated that Hitler's rise was orchestrated. Hell, World War II was orchestrated. That's when we set up a special division dedicated to just this. The Janus Division. We've followed them through the Kennedy assassination, 9/11, the death of Princess Diana, you name it. If we could find the Unriddled Manuscript, then we'd be able to get out in front of them. As it is, all we can do is chase them."

"Speaking of chases, why the hell were you chasing me in Avignon?" Crow asked.

"I was trying to save your ass, and you wouldn't stop. First Delacroix in Salon then Father Simonin in Avignon. We were fine with watching this thing unfold and letting them use you, but you're one of us, an American. We have an obligation to keep you from getting killed if we can. We weren't sure you were in danger after Delacroix was killed, but when they eliminated Simonin, it was obvious they were killing everybody you came into contact with. We put a detail on your boy O'Hara back in D.C. just in case. I found the note in your room with Sánchez Muñoz on it. I knew you were on to something. I was trying to find out what you knew before they got to you. I tried to warn you in Avignon then again in Valencia."

"Why didn't you just call me? You had my number," Crow said.

"You kept cutting your damn phone off for starters. But would you have believed me if I *did* call?"

Crow didn't answer.

"I didn't think so," Morello said. "My only play was to detain you by force. That's what I hoped to do in Figueres, but the security team at the church got to you before I could."

Officer Morello let Crow contemplate the whole ordeal. Crow finally asked, "Did you know that Sidney, or whatever her real name is, was a member from the start?"

"No. In fact, we were like you. We thought she was legit. The whole Rothschild's branch checked out. They had permits in the city files and everything that made it look like it'd been here for years. They pretty much think of everything. It wasn't until we came back here today and saw everything gone that it dawned on us. And looking back on it, I was sitting next to the only known member of the First Face of Janus anyone in my division has ever come into contact with. I could've brought her in if I'd known, but I had no idea. I just assumed she was involved because you involved her."

Crow sat back in his chair in total shock. "This is the most fantastic story I've ever heard. And I lived it!"

"I know what you're thinking," Morello said, holding Crow's eyes with his. "You're thinking what a great book this would make, and it would. I'm just telling you for your own good. Don't do it."

"Why?"

"Do you really have to ask?"

"But people need to know," Crow insisted. "This needs to be exposed."

Morello looked at him for a long moment. "However professional these people are, there's one thing they can't rig. Nostradamus predicted an earthquake about 500 years before it happened. Gives you an idea of why the First Face of Janus is so serious about what they do."

"You believe in all this prophecy stuff?" Crow asked.

"It doesn't matter what I believe. My job is to try and stop them from manipulating the future. All I'm saying is you've seen how they operate. You've seen how they cover every minute detail, how they erase any mention of themselves from the Internet. Let me just put it this way. If you write this book, it'll be the last book you ever write."

Crow thought about all that had transpired over the past week until Morello spoke again. "You had your heart set on writing that book, didn't you?"

"Hmm?" Crow's mind was back in the moment. "Oh, that's not what I was thinking about."

Morello's expression turned sympathetic. "It's the girl, isn't it? She duped you. That's bound to sting."

"Actually, I was thinking about the irony."

"The irony?"

"Yes. I'm the guy who makes up the stories. I'm the guy who creates the characters and the worlds and the plots and the conflicts. *She* did all that." He shook his head. "It was like I was living the story *she* wrote. She had me cast as one of her characters. I understand now why people get caught up in the story." He looked up at Morello. "Her story was so good I couldn't put it down."

Morello smiled and stood up. He pulled a business card from his coat pocket. "If they ever contact you again, you know who to call."

He walked out onto the sidewalk. A black SUV with blacked-out windows was just pulling up. Morello stepped inside and disappeared into the Boston traffic.

Crow reflected on the riddle that had so easily been solved *after* the event had happened, like so many of Nostradamus' predictions. That was his genius. He took a sip of his coffee, reached in his breast pocket, and pulled out the quatrains he'd been carrying since Montreal. He opened the paper like he had so many times before. This time it was different. This time, at the bottom of the page, there was an imprint. Crow looked closer. It was the imprint of coral lips.

The First Face of Janus Pronunciation Guide

Custos Verbi - COO-stos VARE-bee
Jean-Claude Delacroix - Zhahn-Klode Day-la-KWAH
Pierre Simonin - Pee-AIR SEE-mo-nin
Capitaine Legrand - CAP-ee-tin Lee-GROAN
Medici - MED-duh-chee
Carl Jung - Karl Yoong
unus mundus - OO-nuhs MOO-duhs
Wolfgang Pauli - VULF-gong POW-lee
Figueres - Fee-GYER-us